A STEP

PAST

DARKNESS

Also by Vera Kurian

Never Saw Me Coming

A STEP
PAST
DARKNESS

VERA KURIAN

PARK
ROW
BOOKS

PARK
ROW™
BOOKS™

Recycling programs
for this product may
not exist in your area.

ISBN-13: 978-0-7783-1076-1
ISBN-13: 978-0-7783-1052-5 (International Trade Paperback Edition)

A Step Past Darkness

Park Row Books
22 Adelaide St. West, 41st Floor
Toronto, Ontario M5H 4E3, Canada
ParkRowBooks.com
BookClubbish.com

Printed in U.S.A.

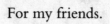

For my friends.

PART ONE: 2015

1

The mountain had existed long before there had been anyone around to name it, pushed up by the inevitable forces that made the Appalachian Range millions of years ago. Hulking, it stood with a peculiar formation at its apex, two peaks like a pair of horns, giving the mountain its eventual name of Devil's Peak. The coal mine inside was abandoned long ago.

On the southern side of Devil's Peak was the town of Wesley Falls, where there were no remnants of the mine except for the overgrown paths crisscrossing up to two entrances, ineffectually boarded up, partially hidden but available to anyone looking hard enough. Down the western side were the steeper paths, far more overgrown with vegetation, leading down to the abandoned town of Evansville. That side of the mountain and beyond grew strange because of the coal fire that had been burning underground for almost a century. The Bureau of Mines had managed to contain the fire to the western side of the mountain so that only Evansville suffered. Only Evansville had bouts of noxious gases, open cracks of brimstone in the roads, residents complaining of hot basements and well water. Over time they left town, leaving behind a ghost.

Unlike its unfortunate neighbor, Wesley Falls had avoided the mine fire and transitioned from a coal-mining town to something not unlike Pennsylvania suburbia. It was the sort of town where one of the billboards outside the Golden Praise megachurch proclaimed, "Wesley Falls: the *BEST* place to raise a family!" and most adults agreed with that assessment. The sort of place where the city council had voted against a bid to allow a McDonalds to open, arguing that it would "lead to the deterioration of the character of Wesley Falls." This had less to do with concerns about childhood obesity or dense traffic than it did a desire to keep the town trapped in amber. The sort of town where the sheriff was the son of the previous sheriff.

Jia Kwon, stepping off a train at the station some miles away from Wesley Falls, looked around the crowded station for that son—the sheriff—now in his thirties, though she had trouble picturing this. *Sheriff Zachary Springsteen* had an air of formality that she couldn't match up with the image of the boy she knew from high school, whom everyone called Blub. He was an inoffensive, nondescript kid who delivered papers via his clackety bike, who then grew to be the generic teen who stood in the back row of yearbook pictures. She had always been friendly with him, but never quite friends, starting from when she had transferred from St. Francis to the Wesley Falls public school system and Blub sat next to her in homeroom.

Was the fact that she had chosen to keep in contact with this not-quite-friend after she moved away from Wesley Falls an accident? No—she knew that now. Blub had been the perfect person to report back town news over the years because he never suspected her interest was anything more than curiosity. Their exchanges over the years had been just enough for him to feel comfortable, or compelled enough, to make the phone call that had brought her here.

Jia paused to put her phone in her purse, pretending she did not notice any stares. No one looked twice at her in Philly, but here she stood out as the only Asian, drawing even more attention to herself because she had dyed her hair a shade of silvery gray with hints of lavender in it. It would only be worse when she got into town, but even as a kid she had been so used to being stared at that she just exaggerated her strangeness, opting for bright clothes rather than trying to blend in.

"Jia?" said an uncertain voice.

She turned her head and instantly recognized Blub, who stood with the gawky awkwardness of someone uncomfortable with his own height. "Blub!" she exclaimed, coming closer. She embraced him, her head only coming up to his midchest. "You've grown two feet!"

He shoved his hands into his pockets, smiling. "Want to ask me if I play basketball?" Their smiles felt hollow, she realized, because of the strangeness of the situation and everything they weren't saying. "I appreciate you taking the time to come out here. I know you're probably busy but…" He led her to his patrol car. "Sorry, you'll have to ride in the back."

"It's no problem," she murmured, surprised to see that he had brought someone along for the ride.

"This is Deputy Sheriff Henry," Blub said, turning the car on. A smaller man whom she did not recognize half turned and nodded at her curtly, though Jia could see him looking at her in the rearview mirror as they pulled away from the station. What on earth had Blub told him?

That once, in one of their email exchanges, when he complained about having to repair his roof, she made a joke about which team to bet on for the Super Bowl, and he did, and she had been right? That she had one too many stock tips that turned out to be good? That she inexplicably sent him a "You okay?" email at 8:16 a.m. on September eleventh, thirty minutes before American Airlines Flight 11 crashed into the North Tower of the World Trade Center? There had been enough incidents as strange as these that when he called her last year asking for help, it felt like something clicking into place. Something that was supposed to happen. Over the years, she had started to feel comfortable with that clicking feeling, rather than being afraid of it. Last winter he had called her saying that Jane Merrick was missing from the old-folks home—she was prone to running—and she was outside in the freezing weather in only a nightgown, and they were worried about her. He did not say why he was asking her, a person who hadn't lived in Wesley Falls for two decades, a person who neither knew nor liked Jane Merrick. She told him to look in the barn on the Dandriges' property without providing an explanation of how she knew. She knew because she saw it. She knew because sometimes she could call up things when she wanted to, though not all the time, but this was still significantly better than when she was a kid and she couldn't control when the visions hit her, or stop them, or even understand them.

And now, in the peak of summer heat, he had called again, saying that there was a missing person, could she help, friends were worried. She did not ask who because she felt something like the deepest note on a double bass vibrating, reverberating through her body. She saw herself walking, her white maxi dress—the one she was wearing right now—catching on brambles as she maneuvered her way down the overgrown path to the ghost town.

She had to go back to Wesley Falls. It was time.

"You all went to school together?" Deputy Sheriff Henry said when they pulled onto the highway.

"Yeah," she said. "We didn't overlap with you, did we?" Henry shook his head. "Blub and I go way back," she said, meeting Blub's eyes in the rearview mirror.

"I'll never get over the fact that people call you Blub," Henry remarked. "How'd you get that name anyway? Were you chubby or something?"

"I don't think there's an origin story," Blub said, looking like he wanted the subject to change.

"I remember!" Jia exclaimed. "It's when you threw up in fourth grade." She leaned forward, pressing against the grate that divided the car, addressing Henry directly. "It was during homeroom. He threw up on his pile of books. I remember because it was clear and ran down the sides like pancake syrup."

Henry laughed and Blub flushed. "Jia, you can't remember that because you weren't there. You were at St. Francis in grade school!"

She stopped laughing abruptly. "I could have sworn I remember that happening!"

"Sometimes when enough people tell you a story, you start to remember it like you were there," Henry mused.

Sometimes, Jia thought. But there were other people who could see things that had happened or would happen, even if they weren't there.

As they drove down the highway and drew closer to Wesley Falls, the mood shifted to an anxious silence. Jia checked her phone for anything work related. She ran a small solar panel company called Green Solutions with her two best friends, both hyper-competent, both probably picking up on Jia's strange tone when she said she had to go back home for a short trip. They probably thought that it had to do with the settling of her mother's estate, and Jia, even though she was uncomfortable with lying, allowed them to believe this. When her mother had died, Jia had come to Wesley Falls to liquidate everything in The Gem Shop and sell the store itself to the least annoying bidder: a fifty-something-year-old former teacher who wanted to open a bakery. A significant part of the decision had been not that her baked items were good—they were—but something about her aggressive combinations of spices had seemed witchy, and, most importantly, she did not attend Golden Praise. Jia's mother, Su-Jin, would have approved.

And now, with Blub turning off the highway, her heart felt torn in different directions. Wesley Falls wasn't home, but it was, because it was where most of her memories of Su-Jin lived. As the car moved it felt as if they traveled through an invisible veil, something that felt uncomfortable in a way she could not put into words anyone else would understand, but was familiar and, she knew, *strange*. *Strange* like how she was *strange*.

But then it came: the feeling that arose every time she had gone home to visit her mother—the feeling that she shouldn't be here. Except this time, it was worse. They had just arrived in Wesley Falls, passing Wiley's Bar, which was on the outskirts of town. It was frequented by truckers stopping for a cheap burger and beer.

"That place is still here?" she murmured.

"They got karaoke now," Blub offered.

"Please kill me," Jia responded, trying to sound light. Blub laughed, then turned onto Throckmartin Lane. The street hadn't changed in twenty years: it still housed Greenbriar Park, which everyone called "The Good Park," and the larger homes where the wealthier families lived. Built before McMansions had hit this part of Pennsylvania, the houses differed in their architecture—some colonial, some farmhouse—but were all similar with their immaculate lawns, American flags, and WESLEY FALLS FOOTBALL signs.

Blub slowed to a stop, making eye contact with her in the rearview mirror. He was waiting for directions.

She gestured for him to turn onto Main Street, that old, curved road with the bottom half of the C drawn out like a jaw that had dropped wide open—it was impossible to drive anywhere in Wesley Falls without driving on Main Street at some point. They passed the police station, then the row of shops. Some of the mom-and-pop stores that lined Main Street had changed, but Wesley Falls still didn't have a Target, a chain grocery store, or a reasonable place to buy clothes. Indeed, the *best* place to raise a family was apparently a place where you had to drive ten miles to the mall to get many of the things people wanted. She gazed at the bakery that used to be The Gem Shop. Spade's Hardware was still there—her mother had had a grudging friendship with the owners. The candy shop had changed ownership but it was still a candy shop. They drove along the north side of town, by the lake and the Neskaseet River—called Chicken River by locals because of its proximity to and usage by the chicken processing plant at the north edge of town.

Wesley Falls and Evansville had both popped up in the 1800s, their economies at first built entirely around the Wesley coal mine, which resided inside Devil's Peak. No matter how many times well-meaning adults attempted to close off the entrance of the mine, which had been abandoned in the 1930s when the coal ran out, high school kids always found their way in. Drawn to the allure of ghost stories, rumors that if you found the right path you could find the mine fire in Evansville, and the inevitable urban legends about the Heart.

Jia pointed and Blub turned onto the unpaved road that crossed the Neskaseet and wound up the side of Devil's Peak to Evansville. From this elevation, she could see the entire tiny, abandoned town. The simple, squared-off eight shape of the town's few roads, the dilapidated strip of larger buildings at the center, then the rectangles of homes, all identical because they had been provided by the mining company.

The road came to an end, trees and shrubbery blocking their passage. Blub put the car in Park, turning to face Jia. "Can't drive farther."

"Then we walk," she said. She led the way, ignoring the looks from both men as she freed herself from prickly branches that caught onto her dress. Blub used his nightstick to whack away a tangle of vegetation, then Jia found a path that led down to the town.

It smelled like sulfur with a hint of cigar. Jia picked her way gingerly down the main road, which was buckled and cracked in places, then turned a corner behind the old church and stopped. There was someone in the road wearing a bright fuchsia shirt. She could only see the top half of the figure's body. The lower part, from the stomach down, was trapped inside the road in what looked like a fresh sinkhole.

Jia knew without looking. Some part of her had known from the moment Blub called her. He needed help finding a missing person, but he hadn't said who. This was the thing that had pulled her back, made her feel an insistent anxiety for the past few months.

Blub and Henry were running to the body, the latter yelling. When Jia finally approached, Blub was trying to get a pulse. She watched the two men huddle over the body, Henry almost making an attempt to pull her from the chasm before Blub stopped him. This could be a crime scene.

Blub sat back on his haunches. The fuchsia T-shirt was soaked with last night's rain. Her blond hair was pulled into a ponytail, tendrils stuck to the sides of her face. That face. Familiar but different. *She's still so pretty*, Jia thought. Her mouth was open and a scratch stood out livid on her pale cheek. Her eyes were closed.

"It's her," Blub stated.

"Maddy Wesley," Henry said, disturbed and awed.

"You knew that Maddy was the missing person? You didn't tell me," Jia said, trying to keep her voice stable.

Blub remained crouched, his elbows on his knees with his hands dangling down. "Didn't think I needed to," he stated, his voice devoid of the warmth it had had while in the car. He didn't look at her as he examined the scene, and it occurred to Jia that he was actually the sheriff. Not Blub, the kid who threw up on his pile of books, but an actual agent of the law.

Jia edged backward, fearful that the road could break under her.

"You know her?" Henry asked.

His gaze made her self-conscious. Jia had never been a good liar. Much of the lying she had done that summer so many years ago had been by omission. She was working on a project. She was hanging out with Padma. These things had been true, but misleading.

"She was in our year," Jia managed. "We all went to high school together."

Blub's eyes went from the body to Jia. "You weren't friends, though, were you?" Maddy ran with the popular crowd, the Golden Praise crowd. Jia had been the opposite of that.

"No," she said finally. "We weren't friends."

2

Jia

The Wesley Falls Inn had vacancy. Jia had never stayed there before, and in her youth had wondered who would vacation in their little town. The rooms were arranged in a square around a courtyard, which featured scattered picnic tables and hummingbird feeders. The innkeeper asked her some invasive questions, which Jia managed to avoid. She needed to think. She needed a car.

The room smelled like stale air-conditioning and had a bed adorned with an obligatory floral duvet. She dropped her purse and collapsed onto the bed, not caring how clean it was. She peered out the window into the courtyard, trying to see if there were any hints of other guests. Would Maddy have booked a room here, or stayed at her parents' house?

The image of Maddy trapped in the road flashed before her eyes, making it hard to breathe. She thought suddenly about the others, about how she hated to think about these things without them. All their decisions back then had been collectively made. She needed Padma's cold logic to talk her out of going into a panic. Kelly's stability. Even Casey's stupid jokes. She unlocked her phone and searched for the nearest car rental place. There was one in Banwood, which would deliver a car to her tomorrow morning.

The man from Enterprise Rent-A-Car knocked on her door at 9 a.m. as promised. *Can't complain about small-town service*, she thought as he handed over the keys. The car was a gray Kia, an ugly but serviceable thing. She pulled down the mirror and observed the circles under her eyes. She was going to show up at the megachurch wearing a day-old dress with her silver hair and, if things were still the same, people would stare. She slapped at her cheeks, reapplied lip gloss.

She drove down Main Street, moving slowly so she could look out the window, although what specifically she was looking for she didn't know. Maddy wouldn't just come to Wesley Falls to visit her parents—she had been estranged from them for years, as far as Jia knew, unless they had reconciled. Maddy didn't seem the type to reconcile. She came here for a reason, and now she was dead. If she was dead, this undoubtedly had something to do with Golden Praise.

After she had moved away from Wesley Falls, she occasionally looked up Golden Praise online. There was no mention of Pastor Jim Preiss and the events of the summer in 1995. Only the same calls to prayer and event listings. Through her college years, the events grew fewer and fewer, and at some point Golden Praise lost its domain name. *Good*, she had thought. The church was dying, unable to afford the twenty dollars a year for GoDaddy. It lost its charismatic leader and now it was dying a slow and well-deserved death.

Over the years, her mother had mentioned harassment from the church less and less frequently. In her occasional contact with Blub, he had never mentioned the church or anything related to it: just small-town stuff, who got married and which stores closed. This convinced her that the past was in the past.

She turned onto the road that led to the Golden Praise complex, the nervous buzzing in her chest getting worse. The complex should have been dilapidated, but as she drew closer, the grass was as lush as it had been during her childhood, and the parking lot had been expanded. At the beginning of the long, U-shaped drive that led up to the main building was a huge jumbotron—a new addition. *Feeling lost?* the sign proclaimed. *Come pray with us!* This followed with an emoji with a halo over it. The sign switched to a new message: *Our Youth Fellowship welcomes all! Sports, camping, overnights, and more!*

Emphasis on the and more, Jia thought. But then the sign

switched again and her heart seemed to stop beating. To the right were dates of services, including special guests. To the left was a high-definition image of a familiar face. Pastor Jim Preiss. Why? Why did they have a picture of him? It had been twenty years. But the sign switched, and she had been too stunned to read all the text that had been on it. She intended to wait to cycle through to the same image again, but then the car behind her beeped. There was a line of cars that she was blocking to get into the parking lot.

She sped up the drive, and then turned in to the parking lot. As she began the trek to the main building where services were held, she observed the families around her. Standard fare for Wesley Falls—even the wardrobes hadn't changed that much.

The pathway from the parking lot was peppered with tables manned by people trying to encourage families to sign up for various things: intramural sports, Bible study. Youth Group. She paused at this table, but hurried away when a woman tried to make eye contact.

When she entered the main building, it was clear it had been renovated since the '90s. The massive stained-glass windows in the foyer cast down colorful light. The multiple sets of double doors leading into the Sanctuary were open, and she could hear the chatter of the thrumming crowd and an organ warming up. She filed into the very last row and attempted to calm her racing heart.

As the service began, she tried to tell herself that nothing she had seen justified a panic attack. Maybe the picture of the pastor had been a memorial. So the church had bounced back since her college days—this didn't necessarily mean anything bad. Who was to say this *wasn't* wholesome, the little girls in dresses, the teenagers in Golden Praise-branded T-shirts? But what was filling her with panic was not the logical side of her brain. It was the part of her that operated on its own rules, its own timeline.

She scanned the fellow churchgoers, looking for anything amiss. But there were just old ladies squinting as they tried to see the main stage, which was too far away to see even with good vision. Others looked to the huge high-definition screens that lined the sides of the building. *How much did those cost?* Jia wondered wearily.

Her stomach gave a lurch—she had failed to notice the new speaker coming onstage. A man in black—black suit, shiny black shoes, black hair. A familiar baritone voice. "It's great to look out here and see so many families," he said, and she could hear the smile in his voice. Jia felt like vomiting. He paced the stage now, gesturing with his hands as he talked. People had their eyes glued to him. Some nodded while others listened with obedient deference.

No.

Jia closed her eyes, counting to ten slowly. But the problem with her vision had never been her actual eyes. It wasn't that she couldn't see things correctly, but that she saw things she wasn't supposed to, and she did this with the whole of her body, not her eyes. The bad feeling that filled her—her stomach, her heart, her intestines—that, too, was a way of seeing.

You are not fifteen anymore, she told herself. *You're an adult and you're not scared of this.* She opened her eyes, feeling better. Yes, she was an adult. She had a mortgage and a college degree and a successful business. She could rent a car and make her own decisions. Not like it was before, when all the forces surrounding her had seemed out of her control.

She turned her head and looked at the high-definition screen. It showed Pastor Jim Preiss walking across the stage as he talked about the meaning of faith. He stopped, making a questioning gesture and more than a few people called out to him. The camera switched: now it was a close-up view of his face.

The world seemed to be spinning, and Jia felt like she was the only one getting dizzy when everyone in that church should have been feeling sick with it. *How?* How was he here? How was no one screaming at the sight of him? How, when they had killed him twenty years ago?

PART TWO: JUNE, 1995

3

Jia

Jia dragged the box from Mineral World to her favorite place in The Gem Shop, where two black velvet couches faced each other, and between them was a table with an ornate display of items. Crystals, dreamcatchers, tarot cards, and other knick-knacks, all with their price tags discreetly placed to not distract from what her mother, Su-Jin, called "the Ambiance." Ambiance included not just the dim lighting, or the gentle bell that rang when you entered, but the smell of rainforest incense, the silk curtains leading to the mysterious back room that not everyone knew about, the delightful notion that the items in the store were constantly moved or replaced with different items. In other words, buy now or you might miss out.

Jia opened the box and began to sort. The deliveries from Mineral World came regularly because the polished semiprecious stones sold well. She tore open some plastic sheeting and plunged her hands into the box, enjoying the feel of the cool, smooth stones, their beautiful assortment of colors. Sometimes when she touched them it seemed as if they were vibrating. She began to sort them in a growing arc surrounding her on the Persian rug. The tiger's eye with its hazel whorls like the planet Jupiter. The rose quartz with its soft pink color, the opaque shards of white cutting through it. Bloodstone with its deep moss hue, freckled throughout with red veins.

Some of the stones they would package together in a set with a velvet bag. Others they would sell singularly in the bins at the

front of the store, each with a hand-written sign beneath extol-
ling the supposed benefits of each. Golden Praise fussed about the
store being Satanic and a "town ill," pointing out that the store
sold Ouija boards, incense sticks, and books about the occult. If
anything, this condemnation was free advertising with the non-
Golden Praise population. This included burnouts, bored but
not particularly religious housewives, and people seeking any
novelty that didn't revolve around football or church.

The bell attached to the door rang, but Jia, knowing it was
her best friend Padma, didn't look up. "Cool," Padma said,
joining Jia on the floor to help sort stones. "What's this one
do?" Padma asked, holding up a honey-colored orb. Her small,
heart-shaped face was framed on one side by the long braid of
her glossy black hair.

"Amber. It helps with healing."

"This one looks like mold."

"Snowflake obsidian. It gives courage and hope." The girls
worked in companionable silence, Jia enjoying the sounds the
stones made clicking against each other.

Jia's mom came through the curtains, already dressed for her
client, and made a gesture to the watch she was wearing. Jia got
up immediately, and Su-Jin nodded a greeting to Padma. Her
mother approved of her friendship with Padma, and Jia suspected
that part of it was because she hoped her good grades would
rub off on her. It also went without saying that the Subramaniams were the only other Asian family in town. In fact, because
Padma's brother Ajay went to a magnet school one town over,
this meant they were the only two Asians at Wesley Falls High.
Jia liked how things didn't have to be explained between them—
they both got stares if they brought "weird" food to school; they
were both discarded socially, either unseen or teased. Often for
Jia it was her piebaldism, the wedge of pure white in her hair
that extended to one eyebrow and exactly four eyelashes where
she had no melanin. But when people called her Skunk this only
made her feel a deep sadness for them. Who were they that they
derived any pleasure from this? How frightened they must be
of the spotlight turning on them!

Jia put on a black robe above her overall shorts, cinching the waist with a red sash. Her mother was wearing a kimono and would sometimes have her daughter arrive midreading to bring tea. Jia knew it was for dramatic appearance as people seemed to think her hair meant something. Jia felt it was all a little sacrilegious, but Su-Jin's perspective was that clients were there for a good time. Jia also understood that her mother enjoyed making fun of them, these small-town people who believed her made-up hoo-ha. If that was what it was.

Jia and Padma hid in the kitchenette behind the reading room to eavesdrop. The reading room was entirely black, with fuzzy damask wallpaper, candle sconces and diagrams of chakras. The table had a velvet tablecloth crisscrossed with blood-red runners, and what would be on top would depend on the client. In this case, Jia had added a stained-glass candle (on sale for twenty dollars), her mother's deck of tarot cards, and a sphere of scolecite, the stone's milky body resting in a brass holder shaped to look like three talons.

Jia put the kettle on for the clairvoyance tea, which was really just oolong mixed with mugwort, and sat next to Padma, who already had her notebook out to take notes. Su-Jin was talking to the client out at the front of the store, then the voices moved closer and into the reading room.

"Please sit! I prepare special tea for you!" Su-Jin exclaimed in her practiced voice. Jia winced and looked at Padma, who was baring her teeth, braces on display. When Su-Jin did readings, she put on an awful dragon lady act, complete with an exaggerated accent that was an amalgamation of every Asian stereotype. It was only one step above "me love you long time," and Jia understood that the fact that people thought it was real amounted to saying something very bad about Wesley Falls. Jia had been born in America, as had her mother, and as had her mother's parents. Her mother spoke perfect English with no accent. Jia only knew a smattering of Korean, and mother and daughter only talked to each other in English. When Su-Jin went to the grocery store on Main Street to poke at the melons and complain about the meat, she had no accent. When she got into the occasional fight at the Town Hall about the store, she had no accent. Did the people who came in for readings simply forget this? Or did they default to thinking that this must be her *real* accent? They never questioned the kimono, which was Japanese, not Korean.

Padma flipped through their composition notebook where she wrote observations down about Su-Jin's readings. Much of what Su-Jin said was vague, "Your family is troubled..." or "Someone misses you deeply..." But other times she said things that were specific and could be verified. The missing keys had been dragged under the couch by the cat. You need to have your liver checked. They had decided that only Padma could write in the notebook, ostensibly because of her neat handwriting in contrast to Jia's chicken scratch, but Jia had only conceded this because Padma was more interested in the project, which she treated with reverence. On the first page in Padma's curly, girlish script was a column of dates beside sums of money. These were lottery winnings. They were all small amounts—fifty dollars here, a hundred dollars there. Su-Jin never won enough to be considered a real lottery winner, but as the numbers marched down the page, it still seemed like she won the lottery a lot. And none of the winnings were from random number drawings: all were Pick Six tickets. She bought them at the gas station, a habit she had picked up when Jia was in fourth grade, shortly after her father had died of a heart attack.

The project had been Padma's idea, as she was perennially interested in anything that her brain couldn't wrap itself around, and Jia went along even though something about it bothered her. The dragon-lady thing was just a business idea her mother had come up with. Oftentimes after the readings, when Jia and her mother would gather on the couch at home for dinner and reruns of *The Golden Girls*, Su-Jin would reenact sillier things clients had said, or how readily they purchased this or that to make their husband or wife more attracted to them.

The notebook bothered Jia because the lottery winnings couldn't be denied. It was not like her mother reading tarot cards, because tarot cards could be bent to fit any situation.

Numbers, however, were *numbers*. Su-Jin telling someone to have their liver checked out only to have that client reappear two weeks later, gushing that they had an obscure disease of the liver, but don't worry it's something you can fix with pills. Not that Su-Jin hadn't also sold the woman some wellness tea to "enhance the path to well-being."

Jia had asked her mother before if there wasn't something to the whole psychic thing, and she had laughed heartily, saying if that were true, why would they be living in this small house, busting their asses at the store every day? She said she made up the things she said to clients, and she won the lottery occasionally because she played it so often. But there had been one Christmas when Su-Jin drank one too many mulled wines and, sitting on the floor by the fireplace with Jia, idly stroking her hair, she had talked about her own mother, who was long dead, and her mother before her, and how they could sometimes see things others couldn't.

Jia didn't think she was special. But Padma's sudden interest in the speckled notebook project began after the bus accident. Back when they went to St. Francis, the entire sixth grade class had a field trip. Jia and Padma had both signed up to go to Philadelphia to see the Liberty Bell and the steps from *Rocky*. They got their permission slips signed and paid for boxed lunches, but early in the morning the day of the trip Jia called Padma, crying, and begged her not to go. Jia had decided not to go, and Padma should not go, either; she could not say why. Padma, ever a person who was logic based, could not accept that as an answer. Jia, near screaming, told her she should not go, that something bad would happen.

They had been fast friends ever since Padma had skipped a year of school and had been added to Jia's class, but the phone call the morning of the field trip had been a pivotal moment in their friendship. Padma was not someone who did things based on feelings. Everything followed the neat rules of science for her. In that moment, so early in the morning that the sun had not yet risen, both girls held their phones to their ears. Jia quieted and could hear Padma breathing on the other end and could practically hear her friend thinking that she did not make sense. That she was being hysterical. But Jia could not explain why neither of them should get on the bus. It was just that she woke up at four in the morning feeling something dark and terrible in the pit of her gut. Something she had never felt before. It wasn't that she could see something bad happening in Philly, but that when she tried to think of Philly, a great blackness seemed to flash and take over her mind's eye. She could not tell Padma this because she could not articulate it and because she would sound crazy. All she could do was beg her not to go, to pretend to be sick; they could even lie together and pretend that one of them had given the other the flu.

And Padma, despite her own penchant for logic, did what her friend asked her, either out of loyalty or faith—Jia never knew which.

The next day word spread quickly even though both girls spent all day in bed, pretending to be sick. The school bus they were supposed to be on had slid on black ice, careened off the road and hit a telephone pole. Several students had concussions, and two had broken collarbones. After she heard, Jia hung up the phone and crawled back into bed. She pulled her comforter over her head, trying to block out the sunlight that streamed into her bedroom. But then she saw a flash of something, Padma with her body contorted in unnatural angles, her eyes blank, blood striping her face. The flash was quick but she screamed and clapped her hands over her eyes.

Jia never told Padma about that flash, and they pointedly never talked about the bus accident again.

Jia made her entrance into the reading room with the tea, attempting to glide gracefully across the floor. She served the tea, bowed, and went back to the kitchenette to have a snack with Padma, who was now excitedly talking about the sophomore capstone project. Each year, graduating sophomores and juniors had capstones, where they worked in groups to complete a project over the summer for college credit. Jia wasn't sure why Padma was so excited—worse than homework it was *sum-*

mer homework. "I wonder what we'll do it on," Padma said. "I hope we can be in the same group!"

"What's the probability?"

"You multiply—"

"I don't want a math lesson! And what's so exciting about it?"

Padma shrugged, picking up a deck of tarot cards that were wrapped in a silk scarf as she avoided looking at her. "I don't know. We could meet new people."

This made Jia sad because she was already Padma's friend—her best friend—but she also understood that one friend wasn't enough. Outside of her mother, Padma was the best person Jia knew and it bothered her that not everyone could see this. But she knew as well as Padma that there was a better place in the world for Padma than here. By midsummer, applications for magnet schools were due. The district that Wesley Falls High was part of had four magnet schools: premed, engineering, art, and foreign languages, and each was based at a high school in a different town. Padma's brother Ajay was a senior in the premed program, and Padma talked endlessly about getting into the engineering one, her parents' expectation that she get in, and the eternal competition between her and her brother. Jia tried to be encouraging whenever Padma talked about it, but there was always the underlying sadness that Padma would leave her behind. Who would she eat lunch with? What other person would want to come to The Gem Shop to sort stones? Padma would sometimes parlay her guilt at leaving her friend behind into encouraging Jia to apply to other magnets, but Jia had neither the interest nor the grades.

"I'll do a reading for you," Jia said, taking the cards from Padma, who immediately brightened. Science or no, Padma had spent many afternoons after school paging through occult books, drawn to unexplained mysteries. She never tired of getting her tarot cards read: she wanted to know about her career, when she would have her first boyfriend, and if she would be more successful than Ajay.

"Ask who will be in my capstone group," Padma suggested.

Jia had Padma shuffle the deck, then select six cards. Padma did this with earnest intensity, making Jia bite her lower lip to keep from smiling. Jia lined up the six cards and leaned forward dramatically to turn them over one by one. "The High Priestess," she whispered, revealing a card of a woman in beautiful blue robes. "Someone who travels between the realms." She turned over another card, this one of a joyous young man carrying a stick with a knapsack attached to it.

"The Fool. Someone on the outset of a journey." The next depicted three people dancing, holding their drinks aloft. "The Three of Cups. A person seeking friendship and collaboration." Padma nodded with grave seriousness, and Jia could practically see her committing these details to memory the same way she did the quadratic equation. She turned over the next card, which featured a man contemplating a long stick that was taller than him with bemusement. "The Page of Wands. Someone who is up for anything. Excited for any opportunity, even if they aren't necessarily ready to face it." The next was a knight, his sword held high as he galloped on a horse. "The Knight of Swords. An intellectual, someone who dives forward to achieve their goals but without thinking about it." Padma frowned when Jia turned over the last card, which featured a man who was upside down, suspended from one foot which was tied to a tree. The look on his face, however, was not tortured. "The Hanged Man. Someone forced to see something from a new perspective."

"Which one am I, do you think?"

Jia considered the cards. Did they mean anything really? Sometimes the person she gave a reading to—usually Padma—walked away feeling like they had gotten good advice, when all she had done was get them to talk about their question. This reading, though, was different because it was just a list of six people. "Maybe…" she trailed off, and both girls jumped when they heard someone pounding on the shop door.

The girls scrambled through the curtains just in time to see Su-Jin unlocking the glass door. On the other side was Sheriff Springsteen. Jia thought the sheriff was scary—he seemed too tall, a human stretched out like a gummy candy. His posture was like a parenthesis. It was hard to believe that Blub, one of their classmates, was his son. Blub was nice and delivered every-one's newspaper on time, riding his bike with cards woven in between the spokes to make a shuffling sound when he pedaled. This was not the first time the sheriff had stopped by.

"Can I help you?" Su-Jin asked with fake politeness.

"How y'all doing tonight?" the sheriff responded.

Jia could practically hear her mother's eyes roll. "We're quite busy. Is there something I can help you with?"

In no hurry, the sheriff stuck his hands in his pockets. Had there been any sun at all, he would have been wearing his mir-rored sunglasses, which Jia thought he did to emulate that char-acter in *Cool Hand Luke*. "We got a complaint about there being a lot of noise here."

"What kind of noise?"

"Like a disturbance."

Su-Jin stepped forward, not intimidated by the sheriff's size, and looked right and left. Spade's Hardware was to the left, and the bookstore was to the right. Su-Jin had made friends with both the Spade family and Mr. Laurent, the old man who owned the bookstore. The three would sometimes coordinate on side-walk sales, and Su-Jin always made them an enormous platter of Christmas cookies. Jia understood that this was not entirely out of the kindness of her heart, but that it was a shrewd move to befriend the two neighbors. "What disturbance?" she asked, confused.

"A lot of racket," the sheriff said flatly.

Su-Jin made a gesture, as if she wanted the sheriff to lean closer, which he did, the parenthesis of his body bending, and she held one hand cupped over one ear, tilting her head to the side as if listening to some far-off noise. The only sound to be heard was from teenagers hanging out in front of the Block-buster a few doors down. "Maybe I get older, I can't hear any-thing!" she near shouted, her voice leaning five percent into the dragon-lady accent.

Padma snorted, then clapped her hands over her face to keep from laughing. No one could throw anything at Su-Jin with-out expecting it to get thrown right back at them. This was not the first time there had been noise complaints about The Gem Shop. There had also been anonymous tips of illegal items being sold—Su-Jin had invited the police in to find a single item that was illegal. The store had been brought up multiple times to the town council and complaints had been filed at the Better Business Bureau. And it was obvious who was behind it.

"Well, we had a complaint," the sheriff said, almost sounding embarrassed. Almost.

"Sometimes complaints are made in error, and some people need to find better hobbies," Su-Jin said and closed the door in the sheriff's face.

"Oh, man!" Padma whispered, awed.

Jia pasted a smile on her face. That the Golden Praise church was targeting their family was obvious to her, and despite her mother's penchant for laughing in the face of threat, Jia worried about their livelihood. It was just the two of them since her father had died. Selling massage oil and books about auras seemed silly, but it paid for groceries.

Jia had never been inside Golden Praise, but had driven by the sprawling complex at the north end of town. There was a billboard out front with a religious message, then a beautiful lawn that led up to the main building. The church was headed by a pastor named Jim Preiss, and while Jia had heard his name many times, she wasn't certain she had ever seen him. He seemed a larger-than-life character in town, and she imagined there must have been a time when she had been at the diner or the post office when he had been there, but she didn't know what he looked like.

She did not think he could be a good man if he led a church that resulted in townspeople making noise complaints against their store when there was no noise. All she knew was that every weekend, thousands from the area would come to Golden Praise for services, and that on Sundays, Main Street was always crowded. On more than one Sunday, someone stood outside their store and shouted at anyone who tried to enter, saying the store was Satanic. She could almost smile at the memory of one boy from school who frequented the store, James Curry, being

accosted by one of these after-church ladies shouting her warning. "Oh, is it?" he yelled as he opened the door. "Great, I'm
looking for some Satanic oven mitts!"

The church mirrored itself over at school. Why oh why did
she know so much about Maddy Wesley and her group even
though she was not friends with them? Why did she know that
Maddy might be getting a car, or that Taylor Anderson had
been asked by three different boys to Homecoming? Was it
standard high school stuff or was it the influence of the church
that made kids as awful as they were sometimes? She hoped it
was not the latter.

Jia did not say any of this, because one rare departure in values
between her and Padma was their differing opinions on Golden
Praise. It was not difficult for Jia to have a negative opinion.
Padma remained conflicted, probably because she stubbornly
did not believe anything unless she saw clear proof. It was also
self-serving because midway through the year, Padma had gotten a job at Golden Praise. Jia tried to push aside what felt like a
betrayal—Padma needed the money. Padma needed to get out of
the house and do activities that weren't dictated by her parents.

Maybe she was wrong. Maybe there was no connection between the church and the people who tried to attack the store.
Maybe the pastor *was* a good man. Everyone, Jia thought, should
be given the benefit of the doubt.

4

Kelly

Kelly Boyle's hand was the first and only to shoot up, eager for the opportunity to leave class with a hall pass. No one else had been paying attention when Mrs. Palmer asked for a volunteer—how could anyone when there was only one week of school left? Mrs. Palmer rapped the stack of permission slips against her desk before handing them to Kelly with a smile to deliver them to the principal.

As she headed down the hallway to Mr. Tedesco's office, she flipped through the permission slips, wondering if there was anyone who wasn't participating. The slips were for the sophomore summer capstones. While she liked the idea of getting college credit, or possibly making new friends, she resented the encroachment on her summertime. Summer was for reading gothic horror novels, for swimming in the lake and drinking cold water straight from the backyard hose. She hoped she would not get grouped with a bunch of goofing-off boys who would leave her to do all the work. Then again, one of the goofing boys could be cute and she did feel it was about time for a boyfriend. Maybe this summer would be different in other ways, too—she had become friends with Maddy Wesley, and Maddy knew everyone in town.

Kelly had gone to St. Francis Catholic School straight from kindergarten through ninth grade, but then the school had abruptly shut down. Her mother blamed the Golden Praise church, which seemed to dominate almost everything in Wesley Falls, but Kelly didn't see why one church would have it out for another.

She was halfway down the hall when she spotted Ashley Miller just leaving the girls' room. "Hi," Kelly said. Ashley said nothing back and just walked away. Had she not heard her? Was it Kelly's imagination, or had she given her a snide look, her lips curling up on one side? No, Ashley was a sweet, benign person. One of Maddy's chief lieutenants in the corps of girls who orbited her uber-popularity. Kelly had sat with that crowd at lunch since Maddy had welcomed her at the beginning of the year, passing some invisible social test that Kelly always felt she had somehow cheated on because she had never been part of the popular crowd before.

Maddy was shockingly pretty, blessed with the sort of easy confidence that only the truly good-looking had. She qualified for All-State choir two years in a row and got straight As. Kelly, on the other hand, thought of herself as a regular girl, a solid B student who likewise occupied nondescript B-level popularity. She was not particularly talented: she played the flute in the school band, but sometimes she lost her place in the sheet music and would pretend to play, miming the motions with her fingers, her mouth forming a silent, breathless O.

I'm imagining things, she told herself. *She was probably blotting her lip gloss.* But still, she felt a ball of anxiety in her stomach. Sometimes she felt she didn't understand the social dynamics of this school as well as she wanted to. There were rules, but no one had ever bothered to hand her a rule book.

When she entered the main office, Kelly could see down the hallway that Mr. Tedesco's door was closed. Mr. Tedesco's secretary, who was actually his older sister, Mary Tedesco, waved her by, saying that he would be free soon. There was no air-conditioning in the school, and she was battling the heat with a stationary fan, which disagreed with her chignon. Kelly sat in a chair outside the principal's office.

Her ears perked when she heard a raised voice from inside the office. Possibly a familiar voice? She tried to appear casual as she turned to look behind her at the frosted glass door, but everything was blurry. Two people were inside, and one had to be the principal behind his desk.

Kelly scooted her chair over an inch, then turned to press her ear to the door.

Something something "this painting?" she heard Mr. Tedesco say. No answer from the other person. "You don't have anything to say about this?" Apparently, the person did not. "What is this a painting of, then?"

"A gun," a voice said. A *familiar* voice. Kelly felt her stomach sink. Instantly, she knew what was going on behind the door.

"I understand that," Mr. Tedesco said impatiently. *He doesn't talk to everyone that way,* Kelly realized. He wouldn't talk to her that way. And he would *never* talk to Maddy Wesley that way. Then again, Maddy would never make a giant, 4' x 5' painting of a revolver, floating inside the strangely cotton-candy pink space of a human intestine. "Is there anything you need to *tell me* about this painting?"

"It's just a painting," said the sullen voice. It was definitely James. It was almost like he wanted to get in trouble sometimes. And Mr. Tedesco was the sort of well-intentioned adult who was too obtuse to know how teenagers actually operated. *Obtuse* was one of the words on Kelly's SAT word-of-the-day calendar. Kelly grew increasingly angry at the disconnect between what Mr. Tedesco was thinking—that James was making some suicidal threat, or perhaps a threat against others—rather than what was glaringly obvious. The painting was about his mother.

"You just like to paint guns?" Mr. Tedesco said. His tone wasn't right. If anyone in any way, shape, or form thought that Kelly wanted to hurt herself, there would be no hint of sarcasm to their tone.

"It's a free country." Stupid James. Why did he say stuff like that when it would only make things worse?

"You know I'm going to have to report this to the relevant authorities," Mr. Tedesco said.

How do you not get this? Kelly screamed internally. James's mother had died of colon cancer when they were twelve. Before then, he had been Jamie, the boy who lived in the trailer that abutted the Boyle property, her best friend since kindergarten. They ran through the woods at the base of Devil's Peak, chewing sassafras, played with the Boyles' dog, and had long, meandering conversations while lying in the grass, fingers sticky with rocket pops. But then his mother grew sick; Jamie became less cheerful and in middle school, he accompanied her to her chemotherapy treatments because his father had skipped town during it all.

She died. The memory of this was so sharp that Kelly's mind involuntarily turned away from it when it tried to surface. Jamie became James, his skeptical nature turning to straight cynicism, his mischievous streak turning to occasional juvenile delinquency. The worst James did was deal pot and make fake IDs, though the reputation that preceded him was far worse. If Mr. Tedesco understood kids, he would understand how unrelentingly *cruel* they could be. Even four years after her death, kids at school sometimes called James "Ass Cancer," and the last time Kelly had seen this it had been in a crowded cafeteria and James had responded by jabbing a metal mechanical pencil down so hard—narrowly missing his intended victim's hand—that the pencil remained embedded in the table.

"I don't fucking care," James said finally. Kelly grimaced. If James enjoyed anything, it was to fan the flames of his own demise.

"Then I'll suspend you for the rest of today if you don't feel like talking, and maybe tomorrow—"

"I won't feel like talking tomorrow, either," James said.

"Fine, you're suspended tomorrow, too," the principal said, now openly angry, which was probably what James wanted.

Kelly pulled away from the door when she heard the scrape of a chair. The principal's door shot open and James burst out. He wore his typical summer gear: black jeans that didn't quite fit his skinny frame, his black Nine Inch Nails T-shirt. His dark hair, which varied in how unruly it was depending on the humidity, hung a few inches past his collarbone. An angry red flush stood out on his skin, camouflaging the acne that resided on his forehead, temples, and cheeks, his blue eyes flashing as he strode past, completely not seeing her.

Agitated, Kelly contemplated what to say. It wasn't right to treat James that way. Sure, he always mouthed off, but why didn't they understand about his mom? *I should say something.* She tried to compose the perfect response. Something that would make an adult understand.

But when she knocked on the doorjamb of Mr. Tedesco's office and he smiled at her so pleasantly, her words seemed to stick together and didn't actually leave her mouth. She handed over the permission slips meekly, and once they had left her hands, it was too late.

It did nothing to assuage her guilt that night when James, who was coming over for dinner and to play America Online, crawled through her window with a black eye. Though James was always free to use the front door, he preferred to climb up the trellis outside her window. "Hey," he said, and neither of them acknowledged the black eye, which was probably from Rick, and was definitely because of his suspension. James lived in the trailer with his aunt and Rick, her boyfriend, whom James called Rick-the-Dick.

"Why are you such a dumbass?" she blurted. She was sitting on the carpet, her back against her bed, watching TV.

"What?" he said, his eyes going wide. She admitted what she had heard, but he changed the topic to making fun of her eavesdropping. He held an empty glass to his ear and said in a falsetto, "Mr. Tedesco, can you repeat what you just said?"

She jabbed him in the side, and he attempted to fend her off with the glass. "Should I get you some ice?" she said. The bruising around his eye seemed a violent color in contrast to the muted freckles on his pale skin.

"Nah, your mom might say something." James picked up the AOL CD-ROM she had brought in from the mail. *20 HOURS FREE!* "You can do this in your room now?"

"The phone line is hooked up. The only thing is that the Harpies kick me off sometimes." The Harpies were her older sisters, Jennifer and Jessica. They were close enough in age that people treated them as twins, although the Boyle girls were evenly spaced out in high school, one senior, one junior, one sophomore. "Let's eat dinner first."

As if on cue, her mother, Emily Boyle, a nurse perennially on time with all meals, called to Kelly's sisters as she headed down the hallway. The Boyles' golden retriever, Milky, nudged the door open with her nose, barreling past Kelly's mother and heading straight for James. Kelly frowned; despite her and her mom doing the bulk of caretaking, Milky favored her dad and James, a harsh display of sexism. Though at least the dog's antics provided enough distraction to hide the black eye as James wrestled with her.

Emily held two plates loaded with food. "Hamburger Helper."

"Thanks," Kelly said, disappointed by the presence of green beans instead of a more palatable vegetable side, like potatoes au gratin. "Is there dessert?" she asked, even though she knew there would be. She had heard that eating more dairy products could stimulate breast growth. She was currently contending with what the Harpies called mosquito bites and would do anything to help the process along.

They ate while watching the news, which was yet again focused on the O.J. Simpson trial that was impossible not to follow. "Do you ever think that the different flavors of Hamburger Helper are just food coloring?" she wondered.

"Don't break my heart, Kelly."

"They taste the same."

"This is the lasagna flavor. It comes with cheese! It's completely different."

"Why didn't you just tell him about the painting?"

A green bean disappeared into James's mouth. James was the only person she could say anything to, but the reverse wasn't true. Sometimes he would get moody and closed off, or would flip things around on her, his cynicism turning aggressive. He gestured to the TV as if she hadn't just asked him a question. O.J. Simpson was attempting to try on the glove that had been found at the murder scene of his ex-wife and the friend she had been killed with. The glove did not fit.

"Shee?" she said, chewing with her mouth open.

"See what?"

"It's too small—it's not his."

"Or it's all crusty with blood so it shrank. Or he's *faking*."

"I don't know if he did it."

"Are you kidding?" James nearly yelled, sitting up straight, rousing the sleepy Milky. "A few weeks ago you were positive that he did!"

"Someone brought a tabloid to school," she said, shoving the last few noodles into her mouth. The remainder of the green beans went to James, who was like a garbage disposal. She knew there often wasn't food at home for him, so she would never complain that between their two meals one serving was always noticeably larger.

It had been Taylor Anderson, one of Maddy's right-hand church girls, who had brought in *The National Enquirer*, complete with photos of the crime scene. Maddy had claimed that it wasn't Christian to look at it, but she also was the one to hold the magazine and control the turning of the pages so they could all see the lurid pictures. One photo of Nicole Brown Simpson's neck had been so bad that the *Enquirer* had superimposed a black box over the wound. "When I saw those photos I just wanted an answer. Like it's better to have *some* answer than not knowing. But then later people on TV were talking about how the police were going after him just because he's Black."

"He beat her up before," James said darkly. "That's all I need to know." He set his empty plate on her bed so Milky, disappointed, couldn't reach it, then picked up the AOL CD. "So how does this work?"

Kelly stacked her plate on top of his and snatched the CD. Hours on the internet were precious. They didn't have computers with internet at school so James had never gone online before. She opened AOL and signed in, turning to watch James's increasingly puzzled face as a series of sounds emitted from her modem—the now familiar and exciting eeeeee-*eeeeeeee-EEEEEEEE-SSSHHHHHHH! Welcome!*

"You can go in places like here," Kelly said as she entered a chat room called "East Coast Party People 4." Usernames and seminonsensical lines marched up the screen.

"What's so great about this?"

"You can also go onto the actual internet." Kelly opened a browser and went to AskJeeves.com. "You can ask any question and he'll find the answer for you."

Where can I get art pencils? she typed. Kelly had always thought a pencil was a pencil, but James had told her that there were a variety of pencils, ranging from one to nine. Sometimes when he didn't have a joint or a clove cigarette stuck behind his ear, he carried a 4B pencil there, his preferred pencil for drawing.

The computer chugged along as it began to download the list of results, but then came a sound effect of a creaky door opening—MaddyWes had logged on. Kelly IM'd her a "Hi," feeling a twinge of nervousness.

"Is that who I think it is?" James asked, wrinkling his nose.

Just then the computer made the sound of a door slamming, the sound effect feeling violent somehow. Maddy had logged off as soon as she saw Kelly's IM.

"Did she just burn you?" James asked, laughing. "What'd you do—take the Lord's name in vain in front of her?"

Kelly contemplated him, the person she trusted more than anyone else. He wasn't laughing at *her*—more like the situation. She *could* ask him what he thought but her friendship with Maddy remained an awkward topic between them. She had assumed, when she switched to WFH, that she and James would be friends at school the same way they were at home or over the summer. But on her first day, their only contact had been walking to school together. As soon as Kelly entered homeroom, Maddy was assigned to be her welcome ambassador. Maddy was cheerful if not a little aggressive. By the end of the day, Kelly was under her spell—she had already been invited to five different social events and peppered with questions by the clique of girls who followed Maddy.

James openly disapproved, saying that Maddy was the absolute worst person at their school, but Kelly didn't think that was fair. James just didn't like her because she was the opposite of a burnout in every way: blonde, fashionably dressed, in honors or advanced classes. Not only was her family connected to the Golden Praise church—apparently they were close with the pastor—but Maddy was a Circle Girl. An elite corps of girls who floated through the halls of school, each wearing a small silver circular pin inset with a gem. Different girls had different gems depending on some inner hierarchy Kelly didn't understand, but she knew that Maddy's was a real diamond. Being a Circle Girl had to do with some combination of popularity in Golden Praise's Youth Fellowship and a purity promise. Maddy was saving herself for marriage, something she would never fail to mention when the topic turned to boys.

"She's just like that sometimes," she said eventually.

James tilted his head back to look at her clock, then scrambled to his feet. "Shit, I'm late. Meeting my hookup." His hookup was not a girlfriend, but a thirty-something-year-old student at the community college who was his source for marijuana. "See ya," he said, scruffing the dog behind her ears before he climbed out the window.

Kelly went into her bathroom to perform her nightly ritual of attacking her skin with St. Ives Apricot Scrub. She tied back her dark, straight hair into a ponytail and her eyes immediately went to the zit, which had somehow formed on her chin within the past few hours. She knew she was blessed to not have real acne like James did, but she was incredulous that over the past year she had *not once* spotted a zit on Maddy's skin. Kelly was tempted to pop the zit, but the Harpies had drilled into her head: you mustn't EVER pop a zit, or you would get BLOOD POISONING and *DIE*!

Freshly scrubbed, she curled up in bed with a crinkly library copy of *The Count of Monte Cristo* but kept reading the same sentence over and over. Was Maddy snubbing her because of what happened at the party last night? Had Kelly run afoul of the Circle Girls for not following their purity edict, *even though she wasn't a Circle Girl*? They couldn't be that strict, could they? And it wasn't as if she had really done anything. *Maddy* had been the one to invite her to Mike Brooks's house, and in the invitation, which arrived in the form of a triangular-folded note, she referenced the fact that they were going to play Seven Minutes in Heaven. Had that been a test? Was she supposed to go into a closet with Scott Wilder and refuse to kiss him?

The party itself was an unpleasant blur. She drank beer—the Circle Girls did not, pointedly adhering to diet soda. The party had consisted mostly of popular athletic boys who made her nervous, all of whom drank, church boys or no. Maddy, stylish as ever, held court from her spot on the rug, her blond hair waved with the expert handling of a curling iron. Her mauve scoop-neck top was technically modest in its cut—as all Circle Girl clothing was—but at some level it was impossible to be modest with breasts like Maddy's. When Kelly ate ice cream or bananas or did push-ups to make her mosquito bites grow, it was to get breasts like Maddy's. Cindy-Crawford-getting-a-Coke-while-boys-ogled-her breasts. Maddy had recently broken up with her boyfriend Brian Roman, a freshman in college, presumably because of "differences in faith" and probably every boy at that party wanted to be locked in a closet with Maddy.

Kelly had assumed that Maddy had her eye on Casey Cooper, who perpetually had a cluster of varsity football guys hovering around him. Casey had always been nice to Kelly—he was one of those guys who was kind despite his extreme popularity—but he intimidated her. Part of it was the sheer adultness of his size—he, too, was finishing his sophomore year but was probably pushing 6'3" and two hundred-something pounds of muscle. Grown men in town fawned over him, the sophomore who led the Wesley Falls Nighthawks to the state championship this year.

There were several rounds of the bottle being spun, couples disappearing into the closet while everyone else hooted and made fun of them. Kelly had gone into the closet with Scott Wilder—who she supposed was cute, but in the dark his mouth latched on to her like an octopus and he kneaded her breasts like they were bread dough. Maddy, she had noticed, had skillfully maneuvered out of ever going into the closet without losing social status.

Surely being groped by Scott wasn't a sin—she hadn't even liked it. But the complexities of romance were more complicated here compared to St. Francis. Part of what bothered her about the purity promise was the way the Circle Girls talked about it constantly. Kelly's mother talked to her frankly about sex. St. Francis had been a religious school, but they still had sex education starting in sixth grade. She had been surprised, upon entering Wesley Falls High, that sex education involved gender-segregated classes, coverage of abstinence as the only viable way to prevent pregnancy and other ills, references to God, and no specifics about biology.

Though what information Kelly had about sex was limited if she did not want to ask her mother questions she would be too eager to answer. She had recently discovered masturbation by accident and was eminently curious about it. She intuitively understood that *that* was closer to what was described in novels than being groped in a closet was, but could not see any conceivable way that the meat sticks attached to oafish boys were somehow going to give her that feeling. Though she did not feel like announcing her thoughts or experiences about sex, she didn't inherently think they were wrong, or that anyone else should have something to say about them, least of all her supposed friends.

Kelly and James typically walked to school together, even if they would part ways and not talk the rest of the day because they shared no classes or social circles. But because of his suspension she walked to school alone the next day, listening to a mixtape he had made her that sounded like industrial machines trying to kill each other.

For the first few periods of school, she didn't have too much overlap with the Circle Girls, though she did notice that none of them came up to her in the hallway between classes. By lunch, she had almost convinced herself that she had been imagining things. She picked up her pizza and headed to her standard table, which was populated with an assortment of athletic boys and Maddy-affiliated girls. Maddy herself was too busy dipping a tiny spoon into her yogurt to notice her. Kelly's heart lifted when Casey saw her and smiled, not pausing in the story he was telling. Everyone laughed when he got to the punchline, but it wasn't that Casey was funny so much as everyone liked him and accepted his insistence of his role as the funny guy. Even if intimidating, Casey was cute. He kept his blond hair shorn short, but the eyelashes that framed his blue eyes were thick and enviable.

The topic of conversation turned to the end-of-the-year party. Kelly listened, quickly realizing that no one was making eye contact with her. Taylor said that Kyle had a nice backyard for a party, but Ashley said it wasn't large enough for more than one grade. "Maybe he could cohost with his neighbors," Kelly suggested.

There was a painful silence. Looks were shooting around. "Did you guys…*hear* something?" Maddy said, her voice suggesting that something *very* funny was happening.

"What, like a *bug* farting or something?" Taylor said, reveling in the nastiness. A couple of the guys chuckled.

Maddy giggled, then made fun of a burnout girl across the cafeteria because she was wearing beat-up Converse sneakers. *Kelly* was also wearing beat-up Converse sneakers. Humiliated, she looked down at her pizza and its congealed cheese, feeling no appetite. When she looked up, Casey caught her eye, his face sympathetic, but she couldn't help but feel a burst of bitterness toward him. Casey could kiss someone at a party, and it would never affect his social standing because he was a boy. It was even rumored that Casey had had sex and with more than one girl.

Kelly got up, trying to hold her head high despite hearing snickers as she walked away. The cafeteria was a sea of faces, and she imagined them all staring at her. There was no table that was entirely empty where she could sit alone in peace. "Kelly!" a familiar voice called. Kelly saw the friendly face of Jia Kwon waving her over, her wrist glittering with power beads bracelets, her streak of stark white hair pinned back with a butterfly clip. She was sitting in her typical spot with Padma Subramaniam, occupying the end of a longer table filled with other students. Jia wore her trademark overalls over a rainbow-striped T-shirt. Padma, in addition to being petite, was also a year younger than all of them because she had skipped a grade. Padma smiled at her, showing her braces, and moved over to make room. Kelly had been friendly with them at St. Francis, close enough that she had considered them friends, but not close enough where they had been to each other's houses. All three girls had switched schools when St. Francis closed, but while Kelly had been sucked into Maddy's orbit, Jia and Padma hadn't.

The girls kindly ignored Kelly's humiliation and continued their conversation about *The X-Files* as if Kelly was a regular at their table. Kelly, picking at her pizza, didn't contribute, still wondering what she had done wrong. "I didn't even do anything," she found herself saying aloud.

"What happened?" Jia finally asked. Kelly didn't have any qualms confiding—Jia never instilled the feeling of apprehension that something could be judged or taken the wrong way the way the Circle Girls did.

"She's like that," Padma said. She unscrewed a round tin, revealing a fragrant soup. "A couple weeks ago she was mad at Taylor and left her at the bus stop. Another time she left off someone's name on a group project and turned it in before the person found out." Kelly, surprised, watched Padma take a delicate sip of her soup. Padma had probably never spoken to Maddy even though they shared a lot of the same classes. Padma was small and often unseen, and as far as she knew, Jia was her only friend.

Kelly leaned forward and whispered to them, relating the events of the party as Jia opened a package of mini donettes for them to share. "Isn't it obvious?" Padma said. "It's not because you kissed a boy. You said Kathy did, too, and she isn't a Circle Girl, either." She gestured to Maddy's table, where indeed Kathy was sitting, laughing at something. You didn't have to be a Circle Girl to be part of the crew, which was why this was confusing. "Maddy likes Scott. She got mad because he kissed you."

"I don't even like him!"

Padma shrugged. "Why would she care if you actually like him?" The bluntness surprised Kelly. But suddenly, it made sense. She had always thought of Padma as someone who was probably smarter than most of her teachers and secretly knew it. She was always in the background, taking in the scene with her huge, dark brown eyes. Just because Padma was not in the game didn't mean she couldn't analyze it. "She wanted a toy and you got it. I saw her a couple weeks ago talking to him by her locker, all like—" Here she wiggled her body in a funny approximation of Maddy's moves. Kelly and Jia laughed.

Both girls walked Kelly to her next class, which was unnecessary but kind. Luckily, none of the Circle Girls were in algebra with her and she could distract herself by dividing polynomials in peace. When class ended, she took her time trudging to her locker, hoping to avoid any nasty comments. She knelt to dump out her schoolbooks and realized that a piece of paper was trapped under her knee. It was worn and had clearly been folded and refolded many times. She stared at the title, "The Ugly List." It started at one hundred and counted down, names added in different handwriting, names erased and crossed out to be replaced with others. People had been passing it around.

It only took her a few moments of scanning the names—all sophomores—to realize that the people with the highest numbers were deemed the most attractive. Maddy was one hundred. Casey was ninety-nine. That top echelon included a number of Circle Girls. Kelly was in the eighties, under some of Maddy's peripheral friends, but above others—it must have been written before Kelly's cardinal sin of being pawed by Scott Wilder.

There were only forty lines on the front of the page and anger started to course through her as she turned the page over, already certain of what she would see. The very bottom of the list was populated by familiar names. "Jia Kwan" someone had written, "Padma Superman," said another's handwriting. Kelly's face grew hot. Neither girl was ugly by any stretch of the imagination. They were just *different*. Jia had beautiful skin, as pure and unblemished as a fresh bar of Dove soap. What *reasonable* human being could call Padma ugly? She had braces, but so did a third of the class. To Kelly, she looked like a human version of a Disney princess, huge eyes dominating her face with its dainty, pointed chin. James was low on the list. He had acne but that didn't make him ugly.

I hate these people, Kelly thought, slamming her locker shut. *Why would anyone want to be friends with them?* At the beginning of the day she had been scared of Maddy's rejection. What the fuck did she care about Maddy's opinion if Maddy and her minions were the sort of people who made lists like this? She was mad at herself, too, mad for being bewitched by the lure of popularity when the two kindest people she had ever met had been sitting in the cafeteria all along, eating by themselves.

She was *done* with Maddy Wesley.

5

Padma

At six in the morning in the Subramaniam house it was peaceful, and Padma could have the internet to herself. Wearing her pajamas, she sat at her desk in front of her computer, swinging her legs and poking at her braces with her tongue as the chat room contents scrolled up the page. Her teeth ached; braces seemed like a lot of suffering for little payoff—her teeth had never been that crooked and no one looked at her anyway.

Suddenly, she heard a familiar clicking sound from her modem, then the loud GOODBYE from AOL. "Ajay!" she yelled, flinging open her bedroom door. "You kicked me off!"

"I need the phone!" he yelled from his room, unapologetic.

She grimaced as she went downstairs. Her father was at the kitchen sink, making chai by pouring milky tea into his mug from a high angle, back and forth, to foam it. Dr. E.M. Subramaniam was the only general practitioner in town, working out of an office near the community college. He bopped his head to music only he could hear as Padma made a toaster strudel. "Have an egg at least," he said.

"I'm fine," she said as Ajay came into the kitchen. As much as Padma wanted to attack him for kicking her off the internet, she was in a delicate position. "I have chess today, so I'll be home late." Her father nodded, and Ajay didn't acknowledge her. He was so smug in his power! Ajay was the only one other than Jia who knew she was not on the chess team, but that this was a lie to cover for the after-school hours she spent working at Golden

Praise. Telling her parents would bring up too many questions: Why did she need a job when she had an allowance? Wouldn't time be better spent actually being on the chess team? She needed to stay in Ajay's favor because he picked her up from work.

The Subramaniams lived on a cul-de-sac just north of the high school. Next to Padma's house were the Parkers, a family with two boys in college. Directly across from the cul-de-sac lived a terrifying football player named Casey Cooper. He was very large and loud and could often be seen playing football in his yard with his even louder brothers. A girl lived in that house, too, a quiet, pretty girl who sometimes read in the grass lying on a towel. Padma sometimes imagined an improbable scenario where she would go over and ask what she was reading.

Padma got dressed, then slipped into the backyard unnoticed, heading for the playhouse. Padma and Ajay stopped using the playhouse years ago. But it was clean and dry and had a small table with two chairs where she liked to read. More importantly, it was an excellent hiding place. She opened a cabinet and reached for her stash. She had been using her paycheck, augmented with her allowance, to buy her own clothes. She did not have the heart to tell her mother that the clothes she picked out for her were hopelessly babyish, hopelessly uncool. Not that Padma had a strong sense of what was or wasn't cool. But as her eyes scanned the hallways of school, she took note of what girls were wearing. The clothes she bought herself were either selected from the dELiA*s catalog or they were secretly purchased from the Banwood mall. Padma changed into wide-leg jeans and a striped top, hurrying out of the playhouse and up the side yard just in time to make the bus.

She did not like the stares, real or imagined, as she boarded the bus, taking the seat directly behind the driver. The bus had unpredictable perils: jocks who suddenly went from ignoring her to wanting to pick on her, mean girls who sometimes pretended they wanted to be friends, only to turn around, laughing to their friends a moment later. Life at high school was a mixture of being invisible when she didn't want to be and being seen when she wanted to be left alone. But she only had to go a couple blocks before the bus hit south of Main Street, where Jia lived. Then the two girls could at least face entering school together.

When they got to school, Padma listened as Jia described a new display she was designing for The Gem Shop, but in the back of her mind she was observing the bustle of students around them. She spotted two girls who were wearing the same jeans from dELiA*s, and she felt sad, knowing that her attempt at dressing cool didn't matter. When she had first transferred schools, she had secretly entertained the idea that maybe she would meet new people and have a high school experience like what she saw on TV. Parties and friendship intrigue. Instead, she went from the boring sameness of St. Francis to the periodic terror of Wesley Falls High.

Why did her parents have to make it so much worse, buying her baby clothes? Why did they have to have accents and ostentatiously drive around loudly playing Indian music? Normal kids did not have every single Saturday blocked off to go to another world. Each Saturday the Subramaniams would drive two hours away to do Indian things. Her parents would see their Indian friends, many of whom they knew from medical school. They would stock up at the Indian grocers, and Padma would be dropped off for Bharatanatyam dancing classes. This was a classical form of Indian dancing from the south of the country, formal and ancient, relying on complicated footwork highlighted by anklets strung with small bells. Padma was conflicted; she liked dance classes. She liked seeing family friends. But she had the sense that she was *away* somehow, doing something that in no way, shape, or form would help her social status, only hurt it.

She sat up in last period when the subject turned to capstones. Projects could be on anything related to history, social science, or civics. Capstone groups would be posted the following week, on the last day of school, and full participation of all members of the group was required with the projects due in August. Padma looked at her capstone handout, listening to the two popular girls on either side of her. "Nobody is even talking to Kelly," the one on her right said.

The other made a *shhh!* noise and made a gesture, which Padma knew was directed at her.

"She can't hear us," the first girl said, and continued to talk about Kelly while Padma listened. When Kelly had been sucked into the popular crowd at the beginning of the year, Padma had been disappointed, but understood. She knew she should be sympathetic to Kelly's sudden loss of social standing, but couldn't help but be a little happy that her lunch table of two was now three. A lot about life at school could depend on something random like that.

Which was why, when it came to the capstone, she had a tentative hope. She had seen that something as small as table assignments led to new friendships. Who you were next to alphabetically could have a serious impact on one's social life. The capstone group would be forced to work together all summer. Maybe they would become friends, and her life would be different.

Hunched over like a turtle with her oversize book bag, she trudged to her locker to unload it before heading to work. The football boys were horsing around, wrestling and yelling in the hallway. The football team had won the state championship this year, something people talked about endlessly. The coach, who was simply called Coach, could pull strings for players who were doing badly in class. The players already goofed off in class and got to miss school for football activities.

Casey Cooper and Mike Brooks laughed as they wrestled and students tried to scoot around their display in the middle of the hallway. Casey, who was wearing a cutoff football jersey, which showed off his disturbingly pronounced abdominal muscles, narrowly avoided plowing into Padma as he slammed Mike into the locker. Padma was relieved when their attention didn't turn to her and they ran down the hall, bellowing.

She opened her locker and was surprised to see a piece of paper stuck into one of the three slits at the top.

The Ugly List, the crumpled sheet of paper said. It was populated by names written in different handwriting, starting at 100 and going down. *Turn it over,* a little voice inside her said. *Turn it over and see.* She didn't, instead crumpling the paper and throwing it away.

Ajay was waiting for her outside in the Honda. They drove

by the football field with its well-manicured grass and turned on Throckmartin Lane.

The Golden Praise complex was on a road, which may or may not have been called Salvation Boulevard. The street sign looked different than all the other street signs in town, so Padma wondered if someone at the church had just made it at a sign store. A massive parking lot was to the right and a long U-shaped drive led up to the main building, which people from the church called Central. Central opened into a massive foyer, which had six sets of double doors leading into the Sanctuary. In the foyer, towering windows looked out onto the immaculate yard, and colorful banners with golden embroidery fluttered downward from the ceiling. To the left of the Sanctuary was a hallway leading to administrative offices. This was where Padma worked.

Ajay dropped her off with a grunt and she headed inside to be greeted by a cheerful girl manning the desk. This girl, whose name was Lila, had a perky blond ponytail and went to the community college. "Padma, great to see you!" she said, clapping her hands as she jumped up to hug her. Padma, who was not a hugger, flushed, but accepted the hug. Everyone at Golden Praise pronounced her name correctly. Despite things she had heard about the church, from Jia and from eavesdropping on burnouts at school, she hadn't seen anything weird other than the amount of money that came into the church.

Padma worked in one of the administrative offices for a woman named Miss Laurie. Her dyed blond hair was always expertly styled, and she only wore dresses or skirts. Her accent was vaguely Southern, and her hand was ostentatiously weighed down by a large wedding ring. "Padma honey, great to see you! I was waiting for you to get on these spreadsheets because I just hate them so much!"

Padma gave the expected little laugh and sat at the computer. Her job was data entry: transferring a confusing paper-and-pen system in a huge ledger to a computer spreadsheet that would automate calculations. Miss Laurie put on a big show about how she wasn't good with numbers, but given that the spreadsheets just did simple math, Padma wondered if the woman wasn't just

shirking her work. The spreadsheets were to keep track of donations, and Padma had color categorized each type of income:
cash donations from people attending services, a few businesses
in town that made yearly or quarterly donations, and a surprising
number of people who paid tithes. When Padma had first started
working here, she hadn't known what a tithe was and had been
too shy to ask Miss Laurie. She searched on the internet, which
said that in some churches people gave ten percent of their income to their church. Ten percent seemed like a lot to Padma.

When she had first set up the spreadsheet for Miss Laurie, she
had thought she made a mistake when she calculated that the
church's total income the previous year had been twelve million dollars. Miss Laurie stopped by to say that yes, that sounded
about right.

Twelve million dollars! How much did Miss Laurie make?
Was the pastor the wealthiest man in Pennsylvania? Or maybe
they gave it away to poor people? But certainly something had
to pay for the huge complex. There was another building with
a basketball and volleyball court and beyond that, not visible
from the road, was the pastor's house. She had heard Miss Laurie talking about how *lovely* it was, and Padma reasoned that
the pastor lived there by himself, because she had never heard
of him having a family. She had never actually seen the pastor,
but had grown increasingly curious because of the way people talked about him. "Pastor Jim saved my life," Lila had once
whispered to Padma. In what way had her life been in danger?
Padma wondered.

Padma was Hindu, but this didn't amount to much other than
special foods on holidays and her mother buying her clothes she
didn't like on Diwali. Ajay had suggested that the only reason
she had gotten her job was because the church wanted to convert their family. Padma had been offended by this, but Ajay
had pointed out that out of the thousands of people who went
to Golden Praise, the one person they had hired to help in the
office was a sophomore with no work experience. Maybe Miss
Laurie was so nice because they wanted to add four more people to their church, and maybe the tithe of a family with two

doctors was tempting. They did ask about her father—how he was doing, if he wanted to stop by their potluck supper. Padma always made excuses, as she had forged her parents' signatures on a document saying she had permission to work even though she was under eighteen.

"Honey, would you run these down to Miss Merrick's office and file them?" Miss Laurie asked, handing her a stack of files. "And let me fix you a plate of food. We got some of that nice chicken."

It would spoil her dinner, but the food at the church was good. Padma went to the largest of the administrative offices, which belonged to Miss Jane Merrick. Padma was unclear what Miss Merrick's specific role was at the church, but had deduced that she was important because Miss Laurie had referenced how close she was to Pastor Jim.

Padma opened the filing cabinet that was part of Miss Merrick's desk and filed the folders. She had trouble closing the drawer, though, and with a shove managed to knock over a glass of water, which spilled onto several papers on the desk. "Shit!" she whispered. Desperate for anything to sop up the mess, she used the cardigan that had been resting on the back of the desk chair. Padma blotted, glancing toward the door and hoping that someone wouldn't appear suddenly. She pressed the cardigan onto some wet papers until the water was absorbed. Then she looked at the paper she had just dried and froze. The Ugly List. Except this one was empty, blank lines marching down the page. What was this doing here?

She edged up the file folder the paper was sitting on and saw that the tab was labeled "May / June 1995." Then she heard the familiar clicking of Miss Laurie's high heels approaching. Padma hid the balled-up cardigan just in time.

"We do have some of that chicken!" Miss Laurie exclaimed from the doorway, holding a plate piled high with fried chicken. "You got to try it cold from the fridge." Padma claimed a drumstick and took a bite. Oh, it *was* good. Cold but perfectly crunchy, salty, and with tender meat. "I don't mean to be unladylike, but you can't help but eat chicken like this with your hands!" Miss

Laurie exclaimed, picking up a piece and sinking her teeth in. They smiled in agreement of how good the chicken was and Padma tried to ignore the nagging feeling. These people were *nice*. They were welcoming to her, gave her nice food, and paid well. But still… Why was that Ugly List here? If it had been filled with names, Padma might have reasoned that some tattletale Circle Girl like Taylor had brought it in to pretend how concerned she was about it. But the names hadn't been filled in.

Miss Laurie made a noise, holding up one well-manicured hand to cover her mouth as she gestured with her head down the hall. "There's the pastor now!"

Padma craned her neck to look. A group of men was moving across the foyer. It was easy to guess which one was the pastor—all the other men were dressed like weekend dads in khakis and polo shirts. The pastor had dark hair and wore all black, from his shoes—shiny even at a distance—to his pants, shirt, and blazer. He did not wear a clerical collar, although Padma supposed that perhaps non-Catholic clergy did not. He looked down at a clipboard, then nodded, looking up for a split second before the men disappeared out the front doors. In that split second, Padma only got a glimpse of his face, which was generically handsome. But what was striking was his posture, how the other men stood at a respectful distance to him, which added to his image—one that projected power. Like the way people wrote about vampires, that there was something supernaturally alluring.

Padma looked at Miss Laurie, who stood frozen, smiling, a slight sheen of oil from the fried chicken on her lips, as she stared at where the pastor had been. The look on her face…what was the word for it?

Enraptured, Padma thought, taking another bite of chicken.

6

Casey

There were certain truths in the Cooper family, most of which went unspoken. One was that Casey did not do chores: in their family of two adults and four children, he was not responsible for washing dishes, laundry, or cleaning. These were all things that were done without him noticing. He could expect, when he got home from his five-mile run, that by the time he showered, breakfast would be ready. Food was important to him because he needed to put weight on, to concentrate on conditioning during the off-season.

Another truth was that after Casey showered in the bathroom he shared with his brothers Steve and GB, he could return to the privacy of his own bedroom. Though he was the youngest brother, the other two shared a bedroom because the family didn't want to interfere with Casey's schedule.

He flopped on his bed. The run had gone well. He was building his endurance in addition to the agility exercises already in regular rotation. He was finishing out his sophomore year but for some students, recruiters came calling early and often. NCAA restrictions meant that right now, only Division II schools could contact him, which they had.

Sundays were supposed to be for the NFL but instead his mother, Irene, dragged the entire family to church. His brothers didn't like church, either, but they probably suppressed their whining because they continued to live at home after graduating high school. Lexie, his younger sister, liked church and was active in the Youth Fellowship, the appeal of which Casey had never understood.

Casey lay on his bed as he read a generic giggly note from Taylor asking about his summer plans. Casey got a lot of notes from girls. They flirted with him, wildly at times, and it got worse after he and his former girlfriend Mina split, but Taylor was one of those Circle Girls and he was never sure what to make of them. Some had strict rules: God this, and Jesus that, no sex before marriage. But there was the issue of raging hormones.

On Saturday nights, a good number of church girls wanted to make out in cars, wanted a hand up their shirt or bra, and would excitedly grind against him. He had slept with some of these girls—some never felt guilty, but others seemed racked with a shame he didn't understand. The more involved a girl was with the Youth Fellowship, the more likely she was to insist that they should not touch each other on their "bathing suit parts."

He had just put some clothes on—the smell of pancakes was starting to permeate the house—when he heard the doorbell ring. His heart sank. It was Coach. And there was only one reason he would be here.

Casey hesitated at the top of the stairs, waiting until he heard his family members greeting Coach. There had been some question about whether or not Casey had failed math, and if he failed that meant summer school again. Coach had said that he would see what he could do about it, but sometimes when you flunked really hard, even Coach couldn't save you.

Everyone was already sitting around the kitchen table by the time Casey slinked into his seat. Coach got up to get cream for the coffee, but then he stood behind Casey rather than sitting back down at the head of the table, which Casey's father had deferred to him. Coach was a large man, a former Penn State linebacker, and as the head of a football program that had just won a state championship and produced a dozen players who went on to play DI or DII football, everyone knew Coach and respected him. Except, apparently, math teachers.

"I hate to pop in on y'all unannounced," he began. Casey's face grew hot as Coach went on to explain that Casey had failed math and that he would need to attend summer school. He looked down at his plate, humiliation pulling his body inward as he felt angry eyes on him. All he had to do was pass his fucking classes and he could play football. It wasn't even real math, it was remedial math. But the problem was that sometimes the numbers swam in front of him. Sometimes he thought he knew what he was doing, and it turned out he was wrong.

Casey glanced up and saw his father staring at him coldly, his anger only kept in check by the presence of Coach. Actually, if Coach hadn't been there, all of them but Lexie would be screaming right now. *You dumb idiot! Why do you screw everything up?* Both his brothers had played football through high school, but neither had attracted interest from high school coaches when they were in junior high. Neither had attracted college scholarships, let alone from DIs or DIIs. Steve sold cars in Banwood and GB worked at the chicken processing plant. They attended all his games, and sometimes his practices, and were quick to mock him about any failing, real or imagined. They watched film of his errors on VHS tapes they recorded from local TV broadcasts. *Hey dumbass, way to drop the ball.*

Casey's thoughts spiraled but this halted when he felt Coach's hand on the back of his neck. "I know you're frustrated. But Casey's one of the hardest working kids I've ever met. He's diligent. He's a *smart* kid—" Neither brother would dare interrupt Coach with a snort, but both were smirking, their eyes lit up with all the jokes about how *smart* he was. He glanced at Lexie, whose big hazel eyes met his sympathetically. Lexie would probably help him with his math, which was even worse, needing the help of your younger sister who didn't get her times tables confused.

Coach, still with his hand on the back of Casey's neck, explained that they would make sure he passed summer school. He would be in touch the whole time to check in on Casey's conditioning, and he would not be a stranger even though it wasn't football season. As Casey observed his father's expression gradually relax, then his mother actually laughing at a joke Coach made as he finally sat down to eat, he realized that the visit had been strategic. Coach had come in person to deliver the news because he understood that the Coopers would not get mad at Casey in his presence.

He had first met Coach in eighth grade. Casey's parents had rejected scholarship offers from private schools. Casey had no say in the matter and didn't mind: the football program was good at Wesley Falls High. By the time Casey had arrived, his reputation had preceded him. He made varsity football as a freshman and a third of the way through his first season, replaced the first-string wide receiver. Casey knew that he was good, but constantly tried to rack and stack and set his expectations appropriately. He could run a forty in 4.4 seconds. This season he had rushed 723 yards and scored six touchdowns. One of these touchdowns included the highly cinematic moment when Casey caught a pass that had been too high with one hand, snaked out of the grasp of a defensive back, then sprinted fifty-two yards to win the state championship for Wesley Falls High. That was the type of thing that attracted recruiters.

The Cooper family, plus Coach, began the long walk through the crowded parking lot to the main building at Golden Praise. Casey hung back so he could walk with Lexie. His brothers were trying to impress Coach with their analysis, but people kept stopping to talk to Coach. He was an Elder in the church— Casey wasn't sure exactly what that entailed, but he knew that it meant that Coach never cursed or missed church.

Lexie with her little legs took quick steps in contrast to his own strides. She had recently cut her auburn hair into what his mother had disapprovingly called a "pageboy," saying it was too boyish. Lexie had cried and locked herself in her room until Casey managed to get in with a bribe of cookies. She was at that awful cusp of puberty. Her little head was so small; he could crush it with his hands. He loved her terribly. Without looking at him, she held out a Werther's Original. He took it, deciding to save it until they got inside: something to occupy his attention for five minutes.

They filed into a row in the Sanctuary, with him and Lexie

at the end. Casey wondered just how many seats the church had, calculating that while it was less than Hersheypark Stadium, where the football championship had been—that had been 15,000 fans—it was still shocking that this many people would show to do something this boring. Sometimes he would pick up one of the Bibles and flip through it, looking for the hot parts. He had only ever found one, something about blowing onto a garden and making the spices flow.

There were only two parts of church he found entertaining. One was the Youth Choir—he didn't like this type of music, but they *were* good. Maddy Wesley had a nice voice, clear and pure as a bell, and she had on more than one occasion made the hair on the back of his neck stand up. Maddy was another Circle Girl he didn't get. She had more than one T-shirt that said JESUS across her boobs but *damn* that girl had a mean streak.

The only other part of church that had the potential to be interesting was when Pastor Jim came out. His speeches often started with a normal tempo, then his talking would get faster and louder, and sometimes people would shout back at him. Sometimes people would run into the aisles, falling to their knees with their hands clasped together; others would hold their hands up in the air, eyes closed. On more than one occasion, Casey had seen someone pass out. He had to admit, that was kind of badass.

Casey started: Pastor was reciting something from memory that was from II Thessalonians, which was the page Casey had randomly flipped to in the Bible. "And then shall the wicked be in revel, whom the Lord shall consecrate them in the spirit of his mouth, and shall envelop them with the brightness of his gaze," Pastor Jim said. Casey frowned. He had his finger over the same verse, and some of the words were different than what Pastor had said.

Casey heard a noise and was surprised to see his sister looking pale. He nudged her, and she shook her head. Maybe she had to throw up. Lexie wouldn't have felt comfortable getting up and walking down the aisle by herself, drawing stares.

Casey put his hand on her shoulder and escorted her out,

heading for the back doors of the Sanctuary, knowing that any stares they drew would likely fall to him rather than her. When they got to the foyer, he figured she would head for the bathroom, but instead she made a beeline for the exit, gasping in the fresh air once they got out. She began to walk, her arms crossed tightly over her chest.

"Lexie! Are you all right?" he asked.

She didn't answer, but didn't object when he walked beside her. He saw that her eyes were shiny, but he knew when not to push her. "We could go to the diner and get a malt?" he suggested. She nodded.

He expected her to warm up by the time they got there, but she seemed anxious when they sat at the long counter with its red leather stools. The guy who worked there, whom everyone called Lunch Dan, always gave Casey free stuff because he loved football. "What do you want?" Casey asked gently.

She shook her head, barely making out, "Not hungry," then looked nervously at the clock on the wall. The diner would be packed after church. Casey got a malt to go, politely exchanging banter with Lunch Dan as he had to if he was getting a free malt. "Let's just go home," Lexie said.

Casey finished the malt by the time they got home—Lexie had refused several offers to have a sip. She marched up to her room, but he dogged her, coming into her bedroom and closing the door just as she flopped onto her bed. "What's going on?" he asked, exasperated. Suddenly, she grabbed the pin she wore on her chest—her Circle Girl pin with its tiny ruby—and chucked it across the room. The violence of this—from his sister, the same girl who rescued nearly dead birds that flew into windows—startled him. "What—"

She began to cry, her body shuddering. He sat next to her on the bed and rubbed her back. "Do you want to tell me what's going on?" he asked. Everything was so heightened for girls when they were that age. He could at least cheer her up, give her some advice.

She stopped sobbing and was now taking deep breaths. "I

don't know," she said miserably, sounding conflicted. He might not have pressed, but she added, "You'll get mad."

"I won't get mad." What on earth would *Lexie* ever do that would make him mad? She was a straight-A student who made her bed every day. Sometimes she even made *his* bed. "You know you can tell me anything."

She wiped her face. "I'll tell you, but only if you promise not to tell anyone or ask a bunch of questions or *do* anything."

"I won't," he said without thinking.

"Promise me." Lexie refused to look at him, staring straight across the bedroom at a poster for *Robin Hood: Prince of Thieves*.

"I promise," he said.

Casey forced himself to remain patient as his sister chewed at her lower lip, knowing that one wrong move could scare her off. "Something happened at Youth Group. I don't want to go back."

What happened? he wanted to yell, but instead willed himself into calmness. "Okay," he said.

She tore at her cuticles. "Someone…did something." Casey felt his heart wrench. "To me," she added. "Someone like… touched…"

"Did someone…" he started to ask with forced calmness. "Did someone touch you in a way that was like…sexual?"

She nodded, her gaze pinned to the floor. He felt a small explosion inside him, a tunnel vision of concentration burning into one single, brutal point. He got up and began pacing the bedroom, stepping on her stuffed elephant. "Who was it?" he asked sharply, his mind already shuffling through the men involved in the Youth Fellowship. There was the guy who organized the volleyball games his sister played in. The kid who played acoustic guitar at church.

He would kill him. He would fucking kill him, whoever he was. Wring his fucking skinny neck. Who does that? Who does that to a fucking fourteen-year-old *kid*? *His* sister. Casey was not a violent person. A lot of football guys *were*. Sometimes a Friday night party ended in a scuffle between players. Casey felt that violence should be contained within the rules of football and had never been tempted to brawl because it was stupid: it risked losing the game.

But this. This was different. "Lexie," he near shouted, now standing still. *"Who the fuck was it?"*

She stared at him, then said quietly, "You promised."

He caught a glance of himself in her mirror. His chest heaving, his face red. "Fuck, Lexie," he said, hinging at the waist, putting his hands on his knees. "How can you force me to make a promise like that?"

"You said you wouldn't tell anyone."

He sat beside her again. She continued to sniff and cry quietly. He gathered her small body to his. "Listen to me," he said, speaking into her hair. "I won't tell. Don't go to Fellowship anymore. We'll make up a lie to Mom—I'll help you." She nodded against his chest. "I'm sorry. It's not your fault. Fuck this person. You're the best kid I know." He squeezed her harder, trying to counteract his own tears. He had failed her. He was her big brother—he was supposed to protect her. Maybe she had dropped hints and he had missed them, too distracted with his own bullshit. "I love you, okay?" She nodded. But what he wanted to say was, *I'll fix this.* But how could he? She would not even tell him what exactly had happened.

They tell you when something bad happens to go tell a trusted adult, a parent, policeman, or priest or whatever. But he could not imagine Lexie telling their mother this—that would *not* go over well. She was obsessed with her precious church and sometimes she said weird things to Lexie just because she was a girl. The Youth Fellowship was a huge part of Lexie's life, and many of the people in it were exactly the sort of people you were supposed to be able to trust. They were the people who were supposed to keep her safe, too. Only they hadn't.

7

James

As soon as he reached the park, James lit up a joint. There were two parks in Wesley Falls: the fancy park where rich people lived on the north side of town, which everyone called the Good Park. The Bad Park was on the south side of town, and at night there were no children, just burnouts, most of whom were in high school, but also a handful of guys who had graduated. Guys like that got jobs at the chicken processing plant or the gas station or didn't work at all.

A cluster of guys was standing around a fire someone had started in one of the barbecue grills, and a couple of them bought some weed. James smoked with them for a bit, discussing the quality of the weed and the stupid but inevitable end-of-year party.

James walked away from the fire in search of Ricky, a junior he had agreed to make a fake ID for. James skirted around a giant plastic spiral slide and then averted his eyes, giving a wide berth to a group of girls sitting in the sand, smoking and laughing. Morgan was with them. She was a junior who had never given him the time of day until a few months ago, when James had sold a couple fake IDs and she had seen them. The tiny lettering had required a magnifying glass, as well as careful study of the font used on Pennsylvania IDs. Morgan suddenly took an interest in him, asking how he made the IDs. He was wary at first—the last thing he wanted was someone to narc on him and have the police raid the shed behind his trailer where he kept all his art stuff.

He had been a little drunk and high that night, and she was acting weird, touching his arm and laughing at everything he said. Morgan was pretty. For burnout girls, fashion was dictated by the goal of setting them apart from the Circle Girl bullshit. While the popular girls were clad in PG-13 attire, burnout girls wore tight shirts, super-ultra low-rise jeans that, when they were sitting in front of you and leaned forward, you could see the mysterious T-shape of their thongs above the top of their jeans.

James was not stupid. He knew that the chances of him getting a girlfriend at Wesley Falls High were nil. Burnout girls went out with older guys. Somewhere in the back of his mind where a tiny pocket of hope lived, he wondered if he got into the art magnet school in Dover, maybe the students there would be more like him, and there'd be a chance of meeting a girl who would like him. Of course, this was not why he wanted to get in. The main reason—when he actually allowed himself to hope—was that the only time he didn't feel self-conscious was when he was lost working on a project.

But Morgan had wanted to drink beer with him, smoke weed and walk through the old abandoned apple orchard beyond the park. Morgan threw apples at him, laughing, and wanted to hear about the magnet school and said it was amazing that he actually wanted to *do* something with his life. They lay side by side in the cool grass and talked about what they would do if they could leave this town. She wanted to do something in fashion. He wanted to get into the Rhode Island School of Design; it was an incredible stretch, but other kids who had gone to the magnet had gotten in.

Morgan kissed him. He had not kissed a girl before. They made out in the park a couple times over a period of weeks. She didn't acknowledge him at school, but he waved this off because their schedules didn't overlap. When he finished her fake ID, she squealed. There was all the praise, and also getting stoned and making out with her again, and in all the fuss, he never asked her to pay for the ID. Then by the following day when she went back to ignoring him, he was too embarrassed to ask for his money. Too embarrassed to admit that he had been duped and stupid enough to think that something good might happen to him.

He found Ricky and waited as he counted out his hundred dollars in crumpled tens and ones. "End-of-year party, man," Ricky said.

"Yeah, I'll go," James said, taking the money, which he recounted. "Where's it at?" Magnet school applications were due in mid-July, which meant he had a month to finish his portfolio. He had been talking about the magnet school since freshman year, mainly with Kelly and Miss Forester, the art teacher at school, because neither would make fun of him for wanting to apply. But whenever he sat down to think about the application, he found himself unable to start putting it together, and now things were down to the wire. The money from the IDs would pay for whatever art supplies he couldn't filch.

"People are saying the mine," said the kid standing next to Ricky. He was a freshman and James didn't know his name.

"The mine?" James asked, confused.

Ricky laughed. "You stoned? That's where the party's going to be."

"Oh," James said, frowning.

All heads turned when a creaking noise cut across the park, followed by laughter. A bunch of guys were attempting to overturn the jungle gym. Girls shrieked and ran out of the way. The guys made another run at it and another creaking noise sounded as they got one side of the jungle gym up in the air. *That's what's wrong with this town*, James thought. That people saw something like this pathetic park that maybe kids actually enjoyed and wanted to destroy it for no good reason. This was why he was not good friends with any of these people. Just because they shared a mutual hatred of the social stratification at school doesn't mean they really had anything in common.

James slung his book bag on, lit a clove cigarette, and walked away from the park without saying goodbye.

Why did they have to have a party in the mine? James was

strangely possessive of the mine, which didn't make any sense—it predated him by a lifetime or two. But he figured that nobody knew the mine as well as he did. When he was little, there were urban legends warning children to stay away from it. Pretty much every kid in Wesley Falls still remembered the rhyme taught to them in kindergarten, allegedly something the miners sang when they worked down there:

Once healthy men with eyes bright
Tunneled down to eternal night
Slaved way for a bit of coal
Came back not quite whole
Lost souls are buried deep
Dig too far, you'll fall asleep

When he got to junior high, the children's stories had been traded in for dares to climb through one of the boarded-up entrances, even if it was just for a few seconds.

There were two entrances to the mine, a larger one north of the footbridge that crossed Chicken River and one much higher up the mountain. In both cases, the entrances had been boarded up multiple times over the years, the old plywood now littered with multicolored graffiti, inside jokes and NIGHTHAWKS RULE! The boards never deterred him—what could be more attractive to a kid like James than an abandoned mine?

The entrance cavern must have been a staging ground for mining operations. The light that passed through spaces between the boards showed ancient, rusty equipment, old carts, and tools. It smelled like rock dust. Getting to the next chamber required passing through an entrance cut into rock wide enough to accommodate a truck, and braced with thick, wooden frames. Just beyond the entrance chamber was something James thought of as a break room because there were ancient lockers mounted to the wall, and he had found an unopened can of beans in them once. He imagined miners stopping here for a rest, drinking coffee and eating sad sandwiches till it was back down the hole for them. Just beyond this chamber, the path dipped down into a smaller room where James had found a dozen or so lanterns.

Most people probably never went farther than those first three chambers, the last of which contained an entrance to the Heart path. Urban legends aside, the greatest danger in those first three chambers was tripping over something and needing a tetanus shot. But past those three chambers, something legitimately dangerous could happen. Everything sloped downward and inward, so that by the time an explorer arrived at the Heart path, the entire environment was different. It smelled like vegetation, and sound was oddly muted, the air somehow thick. If you managed to make it to the Heart, you would suddenly find yourself moving from the constricted space of the dug-out chambers to the massive cavern inside the mountain that had been blown out with explosives and hewn over the years. It was hard to see, even with a flashlight, and shining it upward or across the way was useless because the light would get eaten by darkness. The center of the mine was dominated by this massive hole—the Heart—that seemed to go down forever. Idiots said it went on infinitely, and that if you kept following the spiral path that bordered the Heart, it got progressively hotter and hotter. James knew that this wasn't true, but he had found the temperature inside the mine to be peculiarly mercurial: sometimes hot, sometimes cold.

The path was littered with occasional abandoned machinery. No one had ever thought to install any kind of guardrail to prevent someone from walking or driving straight off the path into the Heart. James had lain on the path before, his head suspended over the gaping hole, and tried to toss a rock down to see if he could hear it land. The problem with this was the strange acoustics of the place—sound was muffled, and sometimes he could hear the rumbling of rock falling in some distant location.

Naturally, such a place was terrifying to any reasonable person afraid of the dark or claustrophobic, and there were always stories of some kid's cousin's brother's friend who went into the mine and never came out, or he did come back, but was weird forever after. In the '50s, some kids had died down there because—so the story went—they had found some old explosives and thought it was a good idea to play with them. When James had been in junior high, a story circulated about how the football team had hazed a freshman by locking him in the mine and wouldn't let him out until he found a hidden jersey. He had gotten lost, and the police and volunteer fire department had been called in to find him, which they did, huddled in some offshoot pathway, terrified, his flashlight dead.

The miners had followed veins wherever they could, and this often led to pathways and offshoots, some of which curved into the rock in snaking loops, and many paths, their purpose unclear, were barely large enough for an adult to move through. Some had dead ends and some looped back to the main pathway, but not necessarily where you thought they would.

James had explored some of these pathways, copying the story of Ariadne in the Minotaur's maze by bringing skeins of yarn to mark where he had been. More than one flashlight and extra batteries were a necessity. And while he had explored substantially more of the mine than anyone he knew, he had still barely scraped the surface despite his curiosity. It was one thing to break his ankle in one of the three main chambers—he imagined he could still crawl out. But if the same thing happened and he was deeper inside, would he keep his bearings about where he was, or get panicked? It sounded like a cliché from every B-movie he had ever seen, but down here, no one could hear you scream.

People who did not respect the mine, James reasoned just as he was getting to Main Street, were exactly the sort to get killed by it.

The diner served food late. Through the large windows, he could see Lunch Dan churning milkshakes at the counter, but he also saw three familiar figures sitting in a booth. Kelly sat morosely in front of a partially eaten hamburger while her two sisters sat opposite her. She must still be mooning over what happened with Maddy.

James came into the diner, saying, "Hey," as he slipped into the booth beside her. The Harpies had nothing snide to say to him, which meant they were in a rare generous mood.

"Kelly is depressed that Maddy Wesley turned out to be a bitch," Jess said.

"No, I'm not," Kelly said sullenly as she played with a French fry.

"Turned out to be?" James asked. "She always was. You just never saw it."

"We're not even in the same grade, and *we* know about her," Jenn said.

"You don't even know the half of it," James said, eating a fry. "One time I opened the door at school the same time she was coming out, and she literally said *Ew* to my face. Like I'm a cockroach."

"Why would you even want to be friends with her?" Jess said.

"She's everything that's wrong with this town," James said.

"Enlighten me, oh wise one," Jenn said, but not unkindly.

"One time," James began, "I think it was seventh grade, all the girls had these slam books. They were these notebooks with a puffy cover that came with stickers. You'd come up with different superlatives for each page and pass it around and people would write names down anonymously. Some of the superlatives were like 'Hottest,' or 'Most Likely to Succeed' or whatever, but a lot of them were mean. 'Biggest Loser' or 'Dumbest.'"

"I remember those!" Jenn said. "They sold them at the bookstore," she said.

"They spread like wildfire. Anyway, of course Maddy had one. She probably *reveled* in that shit. But then it was a huge scandal because someone's book was going around with 'Biggest Bitch' and a bunch of people had written her name. She was ready to kill someone. Then some kid got a girl's book and wrote 'Titty-iest' and wrote her name like fifty times."

Jenn and Jess laughed cruelly—Kelly tried to suppress a smile but then frowned. "You shouldn't make fun of someone's body."

"I mean, why not? If she's a bitch?" James pondered. "Anyway, then she's leading the charge to get slam books banned. She even got the bookstore to stop selling them! But she was the original ringleader!"

"Classic Maddy," Jess said. "Trust me, you're better off without her." Kelly rested her head in her hands, eliciting identical sighs from the Harpies. Jess rolled her eyes and turned to James. "We have to run. Will you tend to our wounded little bird of a sister?" He said he would, and the Harpies left.

"Want to go to Blockbuster?" he asked.

Kelly nodded and got up to leave, then hesitated over her barely touched burger. "Let's get a box for this." Once she had the box in hand and they were a few doors down at Blockbuster, browsing the familiar horror section, she seemed in better spirits. They contemplated *The People Under the Stairs* but instead went with two well-worn favorites, *Arachnophobia* and *Misery*. They went to the candy store next just before it closed to stock up on Twizzlers and caramels.

"Don't you think it's weird that Maddy wanted to be friends with you when you transferred?" James said when they were walking back to her house.

"What do you mean? Because I don't go to church?"

"No. You and Jia and Padma all came here at the same time when your school closed. Don't you think it's weird that basically you got to audition for her little group and they didn't?" There was a silence while Kelly turned this over. "I mean, why? Why did you get to try out and not them? What's different about *you*?"

"You mean because they're Asian?" she said, uncomfortable.

"Do you think it's a coincidence?"

"I guess I hadn't thought of it that way," she said.

Because you don't see things the way I do, he thought. She seemed to be feeling bad at the lack of her ability to pick up on this dynamic, and he didn't want to heap more trash onto the pile. "What does Milky think about all this?" he said as they got to her house.

"As my personal attorney, she has no comments on the matter," Kelly said as the dog greeted her once she opened the door. She microwaved the remains of the burger for James and they settled into her bedroom for a double feature. *Arachnophobia* had just gotten to its final spider confrontation scene—the part that really scared Kelly—when he looked over and saw that she had fallen asleep using Milky's body as a headrest. James finished watching the movie, then set the VCR to rewind it—

Blockbuster charged two extra dollars for not rewinding. He stepped over Kelly to get to her bathroom. When he was washing his hands, he saw that she had stuck Post-it notes to the mirror with different messages on them. YOU ARE GOOD ENOUGH. YOU ARE BEAUTIFUL. One had fallen off, which James replaced with a little smile. YOU ARE SMART.

8

Padma

It was the last day of school, and any reasonable teacher understood that no work would be done. Padma's last class of the year was Honors Geometry. Immediately afterward, she would go to the bulletin boards and see who was in her capstone. The groups were supposed to discuss when to meet for the project, and maybe even what they would do it on. It already sounded like some people intended to blow it off until later in the summer. Padma hoped that would not happen to her group.

Padma's eyes wandered the classroom as the teacher put on some sort of educational video. She wondered if anyone in her class would end up in her group. Almost anyone in an honors class would be a good pull because they would be more likely to actually do the project rather than put it off or turn in something half-assed. Almost anyone.

One of these odd exceptions who appeared in only one honors class was a scary boy named James Curry. Padma didn't understand how he had gotten into an honors class to begin with, but one time when he had been sitting directly behind her in his typical farthest-back row, she glanced at his graded test for as long as she dared before passing it back. He had gotten an A-, strangely getting the hardest question on the test correct while missing two of the softballs at the beginning. He cut class sometimes, but then went all out when assigned a project to design a three-legged chair. The teacher said that the chairs could be scale models—which Padma had done, building a tiny chair out of match sticks, but James had built an actual chair, very much impressing the teacher, which had annoyed Padma. Had he built the chair himself, or had his father helped? His presence in the class seemed disparate from his overall image—he was exactly who her mother was thinking of when she warned Padma to stay away from bad boys. James smoked and talked back to teachers in the hallway. Even today he wore his T-shirt inside out on the order of some teacher because it said something offensive. (She could still read the letters backward—who was Jane and what was she addicted to?) She hoped he would not end up in her capstone.

When the bell rang students scrambled to get out of the classroom. Padma was jostled as she tried to get through the doorway and head to the bulletin boards. When she finally found the sheet of paper with her name on it, she felt a rush of confused emotions.

Kelly Boyle
Casey Cooper
James Curry
Jia Kwon
Padma Subramaniam
Maddison Wesley

She was lucky to be in the same group as Jia and Kelly. But two boys she was scared of for different but valid reasons? And what a terrible situation for Kelly to be put in a group with Maddy when the two were fighting. Padma heard a squeal and someone grabbed her arm—Jia. "We're in the same group!" she cried.

The pair walked outside where a sea of students was sorting itself into groups. They found Kelly, and the three girls claimed a picnic table. "We should get everyone's phone numbers," Kelly said, taking out a notebook. She looked apprehensive but busied herself folding the paper into sixths, then writing her phone number down in each of the different sections before handing it over to Padma, who did the same. Padma paused when she felt a chill in the air—Maddy had joined their table, silently taking the farthest possible seat from Kelly.

"Hi, Maddy," Jia said, ever friendly.

"Hi," Maddy said quietly. She was probably pissed that she wasn't in a group with any of her Circle Girls. But while Maddy was annoying, at least she was a good student.

"Hey, loser," said a voice. James had come to stand behind Kelly, the insult apparently directed at her, but in a friendly way. There was a familiarity between the two of them: Padma thought they weren't exactly friends, but they walked to school together, and he was her next-door neighbor. He nodded to Padma and Jia and ignored Maddy, standing for a moment with his hands in his front jeans pockets, thumbs out, his hips jutted forward, before he decided to withdraw something—a brown cigarette—from his pocket and light it.

Maddy wrinkled her nose. "Do you have to smoke?"

"Do you have to breathe?" James replied mildly. Padma's gaze ping-ponged between the two of them—she had never seen anyone snap back at Maddy, and it was satisfying.

"What should we do our project on?" Jia said, writing her phone number down.

"We should wait for Casey to get here," Maddy said. James rolled his eyes.

"I have an idea," Padma said, but no one seemed to hear her over the loud and very physical arrival of Casey. He was flushed and breathless.

"Hey, guys," he said. "I'm going to football camp at the end of August. So…" He had just arrived and two seconds in was trying to shirk work!

"So we have to finish without your help?" Kelly asked. She said this in a teasing way.

Casey beamed at her. "No, we'll just get it done before I leave!"

"When do you leave?" Maddy asked.

"August fifteenth. It's two weeks."

"Two whole weeks for football?" James said.

Casey held his hands up innocently. "It's not like fun times at sleepaway camp." Really? Padma had never been allowed to go to summer camp and it had always sounded fun. "These things are invite only? Like nationally? College coaches recruit at them. Can't we just get it done before I leave?"

"What should we do it on?" Kelly asked. Kelly slid the paper with the phone numbers across the picnic table toward Maddy without looking at her.

"Padma said she had an idea," James said, much to her surprise. Not just that he had heard her, but that he pronounced her name correctly.

"Um. I thought we could do it on the mine? Like how it started and was a big part of the economy here?" Padma said.

"I don't think that's a good idea," Maddy said immediately. "Maybe—"

"The mine's a great idea," James interrupted. There was something sharklike about the way the corners of his mouth turned up—he thought something was funny. "There's a ton of good stuff at the library about it."

Maddy frowned.

"I like that idea," Kelly chimed in. "We could have cool visuals." There seemed to be a silent conversation between Kelly and James.

"I'm good with whatever," Casey said distractedly as he leaned over to add his number to the sheet. Padma shrank away from his large body, which smelled of boy sweat and athletic gear.

Maddy opened her mouth, but Jia didn't see her because she was looking distractedly out at the crowd of students. "I like that idea. There's a ton of things we could talk about."

"Mine it is!" Kelly proclaimed cheerfully, tearing the sheet with the phone numbers into sixths so they could all have each other's phone numbers. Oh, Padma realized with amusement, there had been a coup! Maddy was used to getting her way. James had simply agreed with Padma's suggestion just to be against Maddy, then Kelly had followed suit. Maddy was probably not used to being overruled, but in this random smattering of people did she hold any power at all? Exactly as Padma had predicted, a summer capstone group could completely change a social dynamic.

Very interesting indeed.

"Actually, the party's in the mine tonight," Casey said.

"What party?" Jia asked.

"Apparently, the whole school is going," James said, sounding annoyed. He flicked away his strange-smelling cigarette still lit, and, miffed, Kelly popped up to ground it out with her sneaker before giving him a stern look. He gave her a wolfish smile—they had had this interaction before.

"End-of-the-year party," Casey said to Jia. Of course Jia had not heard of the party, because no one thought to invite Padma or Jia. "It's in that first big room?" he said, making a bowl-like gesture with his hands. "I'm going to pick up a keg after this. You should come."

"We shouldn't—" Maddy started.

"James knows the mine really well," Kelly said.

"I've been all over it," he said, sticking his hands back into his front pockets. "Why don't you all come, and I can show you around?" He seemed to pick up on the look on Padma's face. "It's kind of scary, but if you're going to go inside, it's probably best to go when there's a bunch of people there. And with a guide who knows it well. I can take you on paths most people don't know about."

"Cool!" Casey exclaimed. James stared at Casey, as if he wasn't sure if Casey was being nice or sarcastic. Padma often had that problem. Jia, she had noticed, didn't because she always erred on the side of assuming the person was being genuine. Padma never knew if this was conscious or not—if Jia was actively choosing to believe in the best of people, or if she just didn't pick up on sarcasm.

"The mine isn't safe," Maddy said, looking pale.

"It's cool, Madds," Casey said, grasping her shoulder. "Everybody will be there."

"If anyone needs weed, I can hook you up," James said. He said this without even lowering his voice. "See ya," he said, and he and Kelly walked off. Casey bounded away when another football player accosted him, and Jia and Padma left the table, leaving Maddy looking confused and crumpled.

Jia and Padma exchanged a knowing glance. Yesterday had been a normal day. But one capstone later, Padma had been invited to her first high school party, witnessed a social coup against the most popular girl in school, agreed to go to an illegal party in an abandoned mine, and been offered drugs.

9

Maddy

Maddy stared at the hefty plate of pasta in front of her. Was her mother doing this on purpose? Her father liked pesto, and her mother planned menus around what her husband liked. She looked mournfully at the space between her mother and father where she could see the kitchen pantry with all the safe foods inside. The cans of soup where she had written the percent of calories from fat in black Sharpie. Quaker oats. Saltines and mustard.

"It's a sin to waste food, Maddison," her mother said. The table was a minefield of bad foods. Spaghetti (bad), swimming in pesto (oil—bad, basil—good, pine nuts—bad, parmesan cheese—bad). Salad (good), dressing (bad). A glass of whole milk—bad. What teenager drank milk?

"I was waiting for it to cool down," Maddy said, her tone careful. A note of sass could lead to an accusation of being, well, *sassy*. She twirled some spaghetti around her fork endlessly. Her father ate quickly—he hadn't said a word since they had said grace, his big hand enveloping hers for less than sixty seconds before she was left to contemplate the table of bad foods. She could have avoided dinner by saying she had something at the Youth Center. If she hadn't stopped at home, she wouldn't have been forced to eat this bad food before the party.

Ugh, the party. They weren't actually going to have a party in the mine, were they? Ever since she was a toddler she had been told never to go into the mine. This was reiterated at church, often with stories about kids who went into the mine to do drugs or have sex only to fall down the Heart and die. Food was an easier anxiety to understand because it was simple: sin was punished, abstinence rewarded. To be holy was to be in control of one's body and all its disgusting desires.

"Maddison," her father said suddenly. She realized that he had been staring at her, his fork poised in midair.

Maddy shoveled down a forkful of pasta, the oil catching at the sides of her mouth. The pesto was good: the sharp basil, fresh from the garden, the velvety oil, cheese—the forbidden pleasure of salty, fatty cheese! She hated it but she loved it—her mother was a good cook. Her parents had some sense that Maddy was "picky" about food. But how, she thought as another bite of pasta went down, how could they accuse her of all these things, demanding that she eat and still chastise her about her unwieldy body? Her mother had never called her fat, but there had been one too many times when Maddy eating something would elicit a comment like, "Make sure to think of your figure."

Maddy's body had become unwieldy after she hit puberty, so much so that her mere existence was somehow a stumbling block for young men and old men and every other type of man. The only way Maddy knew how to tame her body was by being Good. Being Good meant preplanning her food the day before, using measuring cups and scales to be assured of the calorie counts. It was nonfat yogurt, grilled chicken breasts, salads with no dressing, and maybe for a reward a sugar-free nonfat Fudgsicle. Being Good was going for long runs, doing aerobics-with-weights videos from The Firm featuring women with high-cut leotards.

But if she had to eat pesto she would enjoy it, because when would be the next time she would get the smooth taste of olive oil? She could sop up the extra pesto on her plate with Italian bread, do the same for the remains of salad dressing. Because at this point, might as well double down because she could take care of it later.

"I'm meeting up with Taylor and Ashley later," she lied after she had downed half the glass of milk. Her constant parade of activities created a busy schedule, and as long as those activities were directly tied to school or Golden Praise, her parents assumed she was safe—Taylor and Ashley were safe because they were good Christians. And not everyone who went to GP was automatically a good Christian. To be a *real* Christian, Christianity had to permeate your everyday life: it wasn't just weekly church but good, moral activities like LifeGroup or planning fun activities to draw others into the church.

Maddy washed her plate and glass as fast as she could before hurrying to her bedroom and closing the door. When she got like this she felt frantic, her heart beating, her body acting like something else took it over. In her closet, hidden behind a box of choir costumes, was her suitcase of goodies. There were Sour Patch Kids with their painful tartness, their entirely unnecessary coating of sugar. Ho Hos with their chocolaty coating and cream filling that was probably made of something that didn't even remotely resemble cream but who cared because if you were going to go all in, you went to the very bottom of the barrel.

She ended with a Hostess cherry pie, a pie that somehow didn't go bad even though it sat for weeks at the pharmacy before she bought it in secret. She sat for a moment, her stomach uncomfortably distended. She would be Good *tomorrow* and the day after, because today was shot.

Maddy had her own private bathroom attached to her bedroom. Still, she locked the door before she knelt by the toilet. She always made herself look at what she threw up to remind herself of the price she was paying for being out of control. The disgustingly bright green bits of pesto, Sour Patch Kids that were entirely corporeal—not even chewed up. *You are disgusting*, she told herself, sinking down to rest her cheek against the cold tile floor. *You are out of control. You are filled with sin.*

After her body became unwieldy, it wasn't just boys who treated her differently, but men also stared at her, or put their hands at the small of her waist or told her how pretty she was. She did not want this body, and freshman year she decided she needed to lose weight, because what were the jiggling bags of flesh on her chest but sacks of *fat*. You could change your body, said magazines suggesting that she have a gap between her thighs, said Oprah sporting skin-tight jeans as she pulled a red wagon filled with animal fat to represent all she had lost to a screaming audience. This, too, could be you. If you knew how to be Good.

And often Maddy was very Good. It was easiest on a school day because she could take an apple on the way out for breakfast, classes were distracting, and during lunch everyone observed what she was eating so she was likely to make good decisions. Then there were after-school activities. Her body did change, but instead of the weight coming off her chest, hips, or butt, it came off her waist and legs, which, if anything, seemed to exaggerate her curves and make the problem worse. Bad enough that people at church commented, not directly to her face, but through comments directed to her mother. Maybe a boy could wear a tank top, but was it really a good idea for a girl with her figure?

She always felt better once the deed was done, the toilet flushed, and she lay on the tile. She felt closer to God. Her feelings about the sanctity of purging were mixed. On the one hand, she knew that being out of control was a moral failing. On the other, she knew that all men were born in sin, and that God knew what was best for her and had designed her suffering specifically for her on her road to salvation. That regardless of what she did, God still loved her, however disgusting she was, and that the one person who would never judge her was Jesus. Jesus did not think she was unwieldy. Jesus loved her whether she was eating Ho Hos or nonfat sugar-free Dannon strawberry yogurt.

Help me, she prayed. *Tell me what to do.* A tear squeezed out of one eye and then slid over the bridge of her nose before dripping onto the floor. For a moment she felt clean, almost at peace, before she thought to look at her watch. Shoot. Casey was picking her up soon for the party. She scrambled to her feet and then washed her face. Had there been anything in her stomach, it would have churned. Maybe she could talk Casey into not going to the party. He was influential. Two words, and the entire football team would do his bidding. And where the football team went, most would follow.

She jogged to where she had told Casey to pick her up. He had been confused because he knew exactly where she lived. He didn't understand that her parents would not like it if a boy in a minivan picked her up. Something untoward could happen in a *minivan*. It didn't matter that Casey's family also went to Golden Praise because Casey wasn't really a Christian—she never saw him at Golden Praise except for Sunday services, and he drank and had sex. It also didn't matter that he was Wesley Falls's golden football star because Casey was a boy.

The green minivan pulled up blasting Pearl Jam. "Hey, Maddy!" Casey yelled through the open window. The car was filled with football players who thought it was hysterical how the keg they had kept rolling around, too heavy for them to tame. Maddy squished into the backseat, putting on a seat belt that no one else wanted. Some of the boys vied for her attention but she found it hard to focus on them. Boys were always so frustratingly carefree.

How easy it was to be a boy. They ate giant, brick-size Rice Krispies treats in the cafeteria with not one thought of calories. They existed in their bodies with no apparent apology. Women, Miss Laurie had taught her one day in LifeGroup, needed to be the cheerleaders for the men who would be the spiritual leaders of their households. Without thinking, Maddy had asked, "But who would be my cheerleader?" Miss Laurie came over, smiling, and put her hand on Maddy's shoulder, apparently liking the question—good, because sometimes people didn't like Maddy's questions—and waited for the answer to dawn on her, which it did, much to Miss Laurie's delight.

The answer, of course, was Jesus. Jesus would be her cheerleader. But something occurred to Maddy later—last week actually, in the mess of everything that had happened. The answer was a cheat. She was supposed to be the cheerleader for her father and her eventual husband—fine. And Jesus would be *her* cheerleader. But the numbers didn't add up, because Jesus was *everyone's* cheerleader, which meant that the men and boys got more.

Did Casey Cooper need extra cheerleading? He was a dumb, beautiful boy, blessed with uncommon talent and no body fat, and he didn't even go to Bible study, but instead worshipped at the church of football. He would get a scholarship to college without cracking open a textbook. If she believed the rumor mill, he had sex with girls—more than one—within this very same minivan, and he wasn't racked with the same guilt that Maddy had been when she had engaged in heavy petting with her ex-boyfriend Brian. In LifeGroup, they had talked about how boys had uncontrollable urges and how you could not be a stumbling block leading them into sin. Casey seemed different somehow, despite his reputation for being a sex-haver; he seemed less like a boy who would pressure a girl and more like one who would earnestly ask if you wanted to have sex in the same exact tone he would ask "Are you going to eat those fries?"

The minivan headed north on Willow Drive, the closest place to park to walk to the main entrance to the mine. Maddy along with dozens of others climbed out of cars, some bearing bottles borrowed from their parents' liquor cabinets, others with bags of Cool Ranch Doritos, one or two with a boom box freshly loaded with D batteries. Others had opted to walk to the party, their arms bare in the balmy weather.

Maddy and the boys made their way up the path that led to the mine entrance, the boys exaggerating the complication of getting the keg up the mountain. At one point they lost it, having to chase it down the hill before it steamrolled over a freshman. The higher up they got, the more excited they became and the more nervous Maddy became.

The boarded-up entrance to the mine was much larger than Maddy had realized, as large as the two-car garage at her house. It was lit up from the inside by whoever had gotten there first to set up for the party, casting warm yellow light from the spaces in between the slats of wood. The only way inside was through a triangle-shaped hole, the golden light pouring out of it occasionally interrupted by the silhouette of a person climbing inside.

One of the football boys climbed in ahead of her and Maddy followed reluctantly. Once inside, she looked around with wide eyes. She had imagined something sinister, a seedy den with a stained mattress where people did heroin, as Miss Laurie had once described it. The first cavern was perhaps half the size of the gym at school. Camping lanterns were scattered around, and crowds of students clustered into cliques mostly delineated by school year. Many held plastic cups or bottles of beer, and a smaller group closer to a boom box in the corner danced.

Casey stepped through the entrance, then held his hands above his head as if he had just accomplished something. But still, a bunch of people screamed a welcome to him as if he *had* accomplished something.

She looked for a face she knew, feeling unmoored that no one from the Circle was beside her. She latched on to a group where she knew, and reasonably liked, everyone—the benign sort of English class girls and soccer boys who filled out the middle ranks of high school. Someone shoved a Solo cup into her hands before she could say anything. Beer. She contemplated it, realizing that it was extremely unlikely that anyone at this party would care or would report back to her LifeGroup about it. Just then, she looked up and realized that Kelly was standing a few feet away talking to Jia and Padma.

Jia spotted her and waved her over. "Hey!" Maddy tried to shout over a boom box, which had just started to play Mariah Carey's "Fantasy."

"There's our tour guide," Kelly said without looking at her, gesturing toward James approaching the entrance that led to the second chamber. A senior bumped into him, hard enough so that it looked like it was on purpose, then yelled over his shoulder, "Watch where you're going, fag!" James turned, a joint held between his lips, and raised both hands to give double middle fingers, which was moderately impressive because he was holding a bottle of beer in each hand. He seemed to be in a good mood.

Kelly grabbed Padma and Jia by the arms and led them to the second chamber—Maddy followed silently, apprehensive. It was less crowded and blissfully cooler farther into the mine, but the music was louder and more of the kids there were upperclassmen. The ceiling in the second chamber wasn't as high—she didn't think she was claustrophobic, but she imagined a series of successive chambers, each smaller than the last, and the thought made her lungs constrict.

"James!" Kelly yelled when she was just behind him.

"Hey," he said, turning around, the joint wagging. He propelled his two beers into the startled hands of Padma, and his eyes flicked with some amusement at Maddy's Solo cup. "Why don't you gather everyone, and I can show you a couple things before it gets too crazy in here?"

10

Casey

"Hey!" Casey called, putting his arm around Maddy and guiding her in the right direction. "We're getting the grand tour." He had already shotgunned a beer and the alcohol was warming his insides.

Maddy didn't look too pleased to be without her usual clique. Too bad, Casey thought—without feeling that bad for her. "Why does James think he knows the mine well enough to give a tour?" she said.

"I guess he hangs out here?" Casey handed his empty beer to a bewildered freshman. Padma and Jia were just ahead of them, Jia's streak of white hair standing out starkly in the sparse lighting. For a brief moment he wondered if Maddy might know something about what had happened to Lexie. He had never been close with her, but who knew more about church than Ms. Teen Golden Praise herself? But also, he had a feeling that asking her would be putting information into the wrong hands. This thought buzzed in the corner of his mind, not articulated, easily dulled with beer. Sometimes Casey didn't want to think about things because they were too unpleasant, and he could feel one part of him insistently tamping down those things. That one part of him, which was often dominant, wanted things to be easy.

"I think this was the break room," James said, gesturing to a row of rusted lockers that were attached to the stone wall. "There's some cool stuff here." He pointed to a row of shelving that held tools. Padma picked up what looked like a giant pair of tweezers and turned it over with interest, attempting to show it to Jia, who distractedly didn't acknowledge her.

"I don't like it here," Maddy said, under her breath.

"Let me show you the Heart," James yelled ahead of them.

"That's like the hole in the middle of the mine," Casey said, eyeing the crowd in hopes of a fresh beer. He had seen the Heart before, on one of the bonding nights with football guys. When they weren't on a tight schedule, there were always what they called Excursions: nights of adventure. An exploration of the mine, an attempt to break into the chicken processing plant, driving over to Banwood to pick up girls.

The entrance between the second chamber and the third chamber was smaller than the previous entrances and seemed cramped because of a stack of rusty oilcans partially blocking the way through. It was interesting how each chamber carried a completely different mood. Apparently, the burnouts had sectioned off this place as their own. The third chamber was considerably smaller in size and while it was cooler, the air felt strangely thick—an unpleasant thing that Casey knew if he thought about more would make him start to feel light-headed. He had joked around with everyone else on their Excursion, but the place had unsettled him: the thought of the thousands of tons of mountain above him, all crushing down. It was much darker, too, the chamber only lit by two lanterns, one sputtering, and the occasional glowing end of a cigarette or joint. Underneath the skunky scent of marijuana, the place carried a wet, muddy smell he didn't like.

James had stopped in his procession to the Heart, apparently by a guy wearing a beanie who wanted to buy weed. Casey did not smoke weed—he didn't judge people who did, but knew it was not good for his lungs.

"Why don't we—" Maddy started to say.

But then a terrible sound blasted through the chamber. Casey had the crazy notion that a car had crashed into the mine. His ears hurt and the air vibrated as if alive. He looked around, panicked, wondering what had just happened. Maddy clutched his forearm, her nails digging into his skin. He felt like he had cotton in his ears, but beyond that people were screaming, then came a deep rumbling, like boulders falling into each other, crushing. A collapse.

Someone shoved him and he would have fallen if Maddy hadn't jerked him to the side. The chamber was smaller than it had been before, he realized, and darker, dust flying and making it even harder to see. "It's blocked!" a hysterical voice yelled, and this was met by several terrified screams. People shoved, trying to get back through the entrance to the second chamber, but in the dim light, Casey could see that a pile of rocks occupied that space now, the entrance gone. Even now, rocks continued to trickle down the pile. A surge of people was still shoving to get to that entrance even though it was blocked and Casey realized suddenly that not everyone was tall enough to see what he could.

"No, don't go that way—don't push, it's blocked!" he shouted. This did not have the effect he wanted. A few were shoving like panicked animals, knocking people down, the screams contagious. He imagined they could organize something—get the bigger guys to try to move the rocks, but chaos surrounded him: injured people on the ground were being trampled by the people crowding the now-nonexistent entrance, a crush of bodies, but also another vein of traffic pushed toward the other entrance that led to the Heart.

Stunned, he watched a girl get propelled in that direction without seeming to move her own feet, carried along with a current of larger bodies. If they stampeded farther into the mine, he realized, this would be terrible, a group of panicked, half-drunk kids stumbling into the darkness where an endless hole waited to have someone fall into it.

He heard someone calling his name and through the dusty lighting could make out James standing at the north end of the cave. "Get them—I know another way out!" he yelled. Casey saw that he had Kelly with him, her eyes wide with fright. Maddy was right behind him, but where were the other two?

He spotted Padma just before she went down, a larger guy knocking into her, her orange T-shirt disappearing from view as she slipped into the darkness. She was small, smaller even than Lexie, not strong enough to fight against the flow of people crushing toward the Heart. Casey pushed aside a few people just in time to see Padma facedown on the ground, struggling to get up. A cry of surprised horror escaped his lips when he saw someone stepping on Padma's back.

Casey forcefully pushed into the crowd until he could grab Padma by the waistband of her jeans. He clutched her to his side, afraid that someone would knock her loose, and began to head in the direction of James.

"No!" Padma cried weakly over the din of rocks falling and kids screaming. "Where's Jia?"

Casey scanned, attempting to see past the dust in the air and the chaos of many people moving in different directions. It wasn't too hard to spot Jia because unlike everyone else she was standing perfectly still, as if hypnotized. "Jia!" But she didn't seem to hear him. *What is she doing?* he wondered as he pushed toward her, still holding Padma, Maddy in tow. She was staring at the wall with the look of someone completely engrossed in watching TV. Except there was no TV, just the roughly hewn wall of rock. "Come on!" he said, grabbing her shoulder.

For a split second she stared at him with startled eyes, as if awoken from a dream, then the four of them began to push their way across the chaos.

11

James

James felt an urgent jab in his back—Kelly's sign that everyone had been gathered and it was safe for him to lead the way. The cluster of people shoving each other to get out had managed to clog the exit in their panic, which maybe was a good thing as the path beyond was dark, and the Heart had no guardrails. This was exactly why you didn't have a party in the mine.

These people could die and it would be my fault, James thought grimly as he flicked his lighter on and looked at his capstone group. Who of these six, except for himself, would even be this far back in the mine if he hadn't led them here? Luckily, he knew this chamber well: there were two narrow pathways he could take out of here. The one at the south end, where Jia had been standing a moment ago, led directly to the Heart, but the other one, the one he was leading them to now, was safer. It was a climb, a twisting path that led up to a landing that looked down into the Heart—not that you could see anything of its depths.

He knew Kelly was right behind him because she kept a hand on his back—this comforted him as they stumbled through the darkness. They were lined up single file because they had to be: the stone corridor was tight enough that he had to duck in several places and occasionally turn his body sideways to keep moving. He had to block out their sounds—Kelly's fast breathing, Maddy toward the back saying something—someone was hurt; he could hear it in the panicked edge in Casey's voice responding to her—he had to concentrate on the map in his mind.

The flint wheel of the lighter in his right hand grew warm, and he pawed with his left hand against the stone wall, which was cold and wet. The path curved up, not steps so much as jagged juts that had been hacked into the stone. Once he got them up, the path would curve to the right and go to that landing, he was pretty sure. They would be safe there, right? The collapse had been at the entrance to the second chamber. No need to panic now that they were away from that area. Unless the collapse was about to set off another collapse, because he had been in this mine enough times to know that sometimes if you listened closely, you could hear rocks falling in other unknown locations—the place was that big.

He was relieved when the weak sphere of light from his lighter revealed the landing ahead of him. "Hold on to me," he said to Kelly. "Pass it back—there's a ledge with a straight drop, it'd be easy to fall. Stay close to me." The landing was about fifty feet up, overlooking the beginning of the circular path leading down in a spiral, encircling the Heart. As he edged forward, James could still hear the panicked voices of partygoers down below, the sound strangely reverberating through the massive cavern. One moment a girl crying about how she didn't know where she was seemed to come from below them; the next moment a guy saying his ankle was hurt seemed to come from right above. But it wasn't true—it was just the acoustics of the place playing tricks.

James tried to block out the sounds and concentrate. From the landing there was a pathway hugging the side of the cavern, going about a third of the way across, and then there was a choice of three paths. He had taken one several times and it led up in a winding way to the other entrance of the mine, the smaller one, which was a harder climb up from the outside. The correct path was the one on the right...he thought. Or was it the one on the left?

Something grasped at his hand hard—his first instinct was to snatch his hand away. But it was only Maddy, her eyes huge. "Turn your lighter off," she whispered harshly.

Confused, he obeyed. Just then a warbling shriek floated upward, across the cavern. It seemed to go on forever, growing fainter, then louder, then faint again. Someone had fallen. Someone had fallen into the Heart, just as he thought might happen.

But by then his eyes had adjusted better to the darkness, and now he could use what little light there was to see that Maddy had both hands clapped over her mouth. Kelly had a look of confusion and horror written over her face.

James had gotten slightly ahead of everyone else, and they were closer to the ledge, looking down at the main Heart path. He edged closer. He could no longer see the clot of people trying to escape the third cave and make their way into the larger cavern—there was a twist in that path keeping them from view. But there was a light source down there.

Flashlight beams were moving around in the darkness. He could hear voices, but not what they were saying. One beam paused long enough for James to make out a person. Not a high school student, but a big man wearing a shearling coat. The kind a rancher would wear, or maybe the Marlboro Man. James was just thinking that it was odd to be wearing a coat in the summer, but maybe it wasn't, because sometimes it was unexpectedly cold in the mine, and it certainly seemed cold right then. He could have comfortably worn something warmer than a Smashing Pumpkins T-shirt, he was thinking just when he saw something he couldn't comprehend. Down below, a kid appeared from around the bend, probably having found a way out of the third chamber. He rounded the bend in a run that was far too dangerous for where he was. James was thinking *Hey kid you shouldn't be running* when he saw the man in the shearling coat reach out, grab the kid by the front of his shirt, and shove him off the precipice. The kid screamed, his cry an elongated, desperate thing that reverberated, grew more quiet, then louder, and went on for so terribly long that he couldn't help but wonder just how far he would fall until the inevitable would happen, and he would hit the hard rock at the bottom.

There were other men down there in the darkness with the flashlights, other kids coming around the bend. And each time one did, one of the men would move toward him or her, nothing would be said, and he would simply grasp the kid and give them a good shove, sending them tumbling, screaming to their deaths, down into the black depths of the Heart.

PART THREE: AUGUST 2015

12

The Fool

Kelly pressed her hands against the marble countertop and stared at the trickle of water that splashed into the shallow bowl of the sink. It was the type of sink that looked beautiful somewhere else but that she knew would be impractical to clean if she had it at home. Water would splash everywhere and trimmed beard hairs would pepper it. The ambiance of the restaurant Giulia was dark, the bathroom almost too dark to do a reasonable makeup check.

She felt like throwing up. But it wasn't the chicken liver crostini—liver wasn't her favorite—or the heap of fresh pasta that did it.

"I *love* your *dress*," came a chipper voice. A girl had appeared at the sink beside her, splashing her hands with carefree abandon.

Kelly forced a smile. The dress *was* nice—Kelly loved it, too. A burgundy silky thing that showed off her legs, toned from running four half-marathons a year. She had fallen into the habit of long-distance running while listening to audiobooks in college, finding peace in the steady rhythm of her footsteps.

Kelly picked up her clutch purse and resisted the urge to take out her phone and scroll through it in the bathroom, delaying her return. Sometimes she did this when she and Ethan were on the brink of a fight, finding some excuse to delay and think her way out of the problem. Was it really that bad? Was she just being *too emotional*? It was funny how so much of the time spent in a long-distance relationship revolved around perfectly executing what time you did have together. And here she was, idling while their limited time slipped away.

For years, things had been good—she wouldn't deny that. As an academic couple, they understood that the chances of finding two tenure track positions in the same city were nearly impossible. If you found a placement, as Kelly had at Boston College, you could attempt to use the leverage of a job offer into a job for your partner. They had offered Ethan a two-year contract as an Assistant Lecturer in the Math Department. Ethan had been insulted, instead taking a post-doc in Chicago.

Then came a second post-doc, more rounds of applications with no offers. Kelly knew that Ethan was incredibly bright, but as time and distance frayed at her, she wondered exactly how he came off during the grueling campus visits that included not just a job talk but two or three days of structured socializing under watchful eyes. Having seen his practice job talk and how he sometimes got defensive when questioned, she thought about how thin the line was between attractive confidence and arrogance.

Their strain wasn't solely based on career ambitions. She planned for perfection when he visited, romantic time alone, fun activities, some socializing with her friends, as any partner of hers had to fit in with her life. While Kelly's friends were a comfortable horde of Bostonians from different social circles, Ethan's friends were all from school and sometimes had an unfriendly air to them when she visited. She got the sense that they didn't think she was as smart as he was because her Ph.D had been in Early American literature, which wasn't a "real" thing to study.

What had sent her to the bathroom feeling sick had been a playful hypothetical question. She had asked him to imagine a dream scenario where he had to pick between two coveted positions, one at MIT and the other at Berkeley. There was a clear and correct answer: both were top-ranked programs, but only one was in Boston. Ethan, also being playful, said it would be a hard decision but it would have to be Berkeley, then going on to talk on and on about a professor there he liked. *He didn't even think of me in this scenario*, Kelly realized. The fact that she had a tenure track job in Boston had been entirely irrelevant to him. And what if Berkeley did offer him a job—or some other department in Kansas or Podunk, Iowa? Would he expect her to give up all she had worked for because his job was *real* and hers wasn't?

She smoothed her hair and headed back to the dining area. She would pretend nothing was wrong. She would wait and see if he realized what he had said. Anyone looking at them would see a fine couple. Ethan was handsome in a linen button-down, somehow not wrinkled. Anyone would see a man and a woman out on a romantic date, an engagement ring glistening on her finger. He asked what she thought about the chocolate semi-freddo for dessert. She blinked, wanting to scream with her eyes.

Eschewing dessert, they took the subway to her apartment. He had his hand on her knee. A few years ago she would have rested her head on his shoulder. A few years ago she had fewer bumps and scrapes, times when she had wondered about his female friends who were weirdly cool to her.

He wants to have sex, she thought as the underground whirred by through the window. She craved the wisdom of her best friend in Boston, Mimi. Mimi was not a fan of Ethan's and being a blunt person could barely hold this in. *He insisted on the chicken liver*, she imagined herself saying to Mimi. *He wanted the chicken liver even though he knows I don't like liver.*

I'm being unreasonable, she told herself. Why was she upset about liver? And the question about the hypothetical job offer had just been a silly question, not a serious one. *Don't be ridiculous.*

When they got home, he offered to open a bottle of wine but she put a hand over her stomach and said she better not. She slipped off the dress in the bathroom in favor of yoga pants and a tank top. She sat on the closed toilet and opened her text chain with Mimi and thought of what she might say. I've been starting to think, Kelly began typing slowly.

She hesitated, then heard Ethan's phone ring in the living room. "Oh, hey," he said, using the tone of voice he used for his friends. She felt a spritz of irrational anger.

She deleted the text, then mindlessly tapped on the envelope icon and looked at the dozen or so emails that had popped up. Another sale at Ann Taylor. An email about a meeting at the English Department about graduate recruitment. An email from jia.kwon@greensolutions.com.

Kelly's stomach jerked in shock, and as if in response, the email promptly disappeared. "Wait!" she cried. Had she imagined it? She scrolled, but the email was gone. She closed her email app, then reopened it, but the email wasn't there. She hurried out of the bathroom and into her bedroom, where her laptop was sitting on her bed. She went to her Gmail and opened the folder for spam, and there it was. From Jia Kwon. Subject line: Hi, yes it's me, we need to talk.

It couldn't be. It had to be some weird trick. Despite all the years of controlling herself, trying to avoid doing anything that would make it seem like she was looking for one of the Capstone Six online, she could not resist clicking on the spam.

It consisted of one line: It's safe to talk here. This was followed by a hyperlink. It had to be spam. Maybe Jia Kwon was a randomly generated name. Or could it be the FBI baiting her? But beneath the hyperlink was what looked like a real email signature. A little icon with a sparkling green leaf, the name JIA KWON, CEO, a phone number with a Philadelphia area code, and a quote: "Here today—solar tomorrow."

Kelly googled "Green Solutions Philadelphia." There was indeed a website for a Green Solutions based in Philadelphia. It was a company that provided residential solar power panel installation. *That* would *be something Jia would do!* she thought, the hair on the back of her neck standing up. Excited, she paged through the website, looking for any information or pictures of the CEO of Green Solutions, but there weren't any. The Contact Us page led to an online form, rather than a personal email.

Kelly went back to the email and, heart pounding, clicked on the link, half expecting her laptop to emit a squeal of protest, or produce a pop-up saying that she had just been hacked. After a minor delay, she was taken to what looked like a plain website with only a small amount of text on it.

Hi all. This is a private, encrypted message board. It should be safe to talk here. Please see the below—Maddy's funeral is the day after tomorrow. You should come.

I'm already back home and can get rooms or help with any travel plans. We can coordinate here.

Coordinate what? Kelly thought, while at the same time feeling the shock that Maddy was dead. She clicked on one of the two links that followed Jia's message. The first led to an article in the *Banwood Reporter*, the margins of the page filled with ads for local businesses. She skimmed over the article greedily. It detailed that Jeremy and Anne Wesley had been killed in a fatal car crash in Florida. They had been coming back from a mission trip in Central America and had stopped in Florida to take a pleasure cruise for three days. While on the way to the airport, they were killed on impact in a car accident on the highway. The article detailed how, tragically, their daughter Maddison Wesley, their only child, returned home to Wesley Falls, where the family had deep historical roots, and also died in a tragic accident while making arrangements for her parents' funeral.

"What?" Kelly muttered. The last thing she had heard about Maddy had been toward the end of high school. Maddy was attending a strict Christian boarding school, and Kelly's mother had said that she had heard that Maddy was no longer on speaking terms with her parents. This had been after that strange summer, when they had all split apart and as desperate as Kelly had been for news of any of them, she had been too terrified to ask follow-up questions. If Maddy was no longer speaking to her parents, would she have rushed home to make funeral arrangements? Or maybe it wasn't a choice when you were an only child? When Kelly's father had passed away three years ago, the Harpies had called her on a group phone call, and they had all cried and rallied together to help their mom. She had no idea how it went with families who were estranged.

A tragic accident. Something about this didn't seem right. Kelly clicked on the second link Jia had provided, taking her to a Dropbox file of jpgs. The first was a photo of Golden Praise, the building refreshed, and an expensive jumbotron marking its territory.

The next picture was bleary. It looked like an iPhone picture someone had taken while drunk at a party, except instead of a party it was the inside of a packed church service. A few more pictures of the crowds followed: Jia must have taken them surreptitiously.

Kelly felt a shiver of confused panic when she saw the next picture. A man in all black, smiling, addressing the crowd from far away.

No. No, that had to be someone else.

But Jia, as if anticipating her thoughts, had provided more pictures, some closer up. It was him. It was Pastor Jim Preiss. And he hadn't aged a day. If anything, he might have looked a little *younger*.

But how?

All of the emotional weight of the night evaporated—who cared about her theoretical question or the stupid chicken liver. The events of 1995 had never faded away so much as had been tucked into the back corner of her mind. In the movies, old memories were like pictures where time sapped away the saturation of color. But to Kelly, these memories seemed more like a virus—a thing that died down sometimes but occasionally had a vivid outbreak. After what had happened in the mine, they decided that the smartest thing to do was never be seen together. They had each manufactured their separation, each in their own way. Kelly had gone crying to her mother about how she couldn't take going to Wesley Falls High anymore, exploiting her mother's preexisting suspicion of the influence of the church on the public school. She transferred to a private Catholic school before her junior year, riding the bus for a full fifty minutes each way.

The two years before Kelly went to college had been excruciating in many ways. She could not remember a time in her life when James hadn't been there. She filled her afternoons with after-school activities, cross-country running, band, yearbook. There were still times when she was at home that she would catch sight of Padma's family at the diner and miss her friend horribly. She would walk by The Gem Shop and pretend she wasn't looking through the window to steal a glance at Jia. She could still hear people talking in town about how many college football recruiters were after Casey. She dragged a Catholic school friend to a Wesley Falls football game who had probably been puzzled about why she started crying when number 15 scored a touchdown.

When she left for Lehigh University, it was easier to think about it all as some kind of fever dream. Had it even really happened? Something about living within the boundaries of Wesley Falls made everything feel so real when she was there and not when she was gone.

But she couldn't talk herself out of what they saw that night at the mine party: they had all seen three men throwing kids down the Heart to their deaths. As she got older, she had a desire to explain away everything she had thought was supernatural—the pastor, Jia's crystals—but that conflicted with a cold, hard fact: six kids had been murdered that summer.

And the only people on earth she could talk about it with were people she was forbidden to be seen with. In the years after she left, she desperately wanted to know what the other Capstone Six were up to. Occasionally, she would see or hear something that reminded her of one of them. She had been tempted so many times to google their names and find where they were but remained paranoid that somehow someone—the government?—would find out.

The closest she came was innocently going to online white pages and typing in similar names—Cary Cooper and Janet Kwon—hoping that her former friends would end up on the same page. One night in college, while drunk at a friend's house, she saw that they had left their laptop open with their Facebook account signed in. Kelly tried to find them, all five of them, but none of them had Facebook accounts except for Casey. She didn't dare click on his profile, but it said Casey Cooper, Ohio State University, which made her tear up. He had made it to a DI school.

Now, even twenty years later, sometimes when nostalgic talk turned to high school or old friends, she felt a sharp pang when she thought of the friendship that had been denied them. It was strange to be nostalgic for those days because they had also been filled with terror, but even after all these years, the longing she felt for the Capstone Six still lingered.

The hardest to let go of was James. James had always teetered on the precipice: she could easily see him falling into drugs, maybe getting a job at a gas station and perpetually talking about how his life sucked. She could see the cynical, angry part of him self-sabotaging his chances to have the life she thought he deserved. On a better day, she could just as easily imagine him getting into RISD, which had always been his dream. She had looked at RISD's website before, browsing the pictures of art projects and studios, her eyes scanning the pictures of students in hopes of catching a glance of him. Was James an architect somewhere, or in jail?

"Hey," a voice said, making her jump. It was Ethan standing at the doorway to the bedroom. "Are you all right?"

"No," Kelly said, shutting her laptop. She closed her eyes, seeing the double crest of Devil's Peak before opening them and seeing her fiancé, his brow furrowed with concern. "I just got an email. I have to go to Wesley Falls. Right now."

His eyes widened, and as she got up and went to her closet in search of her small suitcase, she realized he probably assumed something had happened to her mother. After Kelly's father had died, Emily Boyle had turned into a snowbird, spending more and more time in Florida while refusing to sell her home in Wesley Falls. Kelly and her sisters had pressured her to leave— Kelly in particular, the town never losing its evil patina for her. But despite Emily's occasional distaste for the town, she associated it and her home with her husband.

"Your mom?" he asked as she pulled the carryon from the closet. His own mother had died from breast cancer while they were in graduate school, and the sudden concern etched in his face softened her. Her death, and Kelly's support throughout, had been a major transition in their relationship from two people who had an intense on and off again relationship to something more serious. He had been there for her when her father died three years ago, buying a same-day flight from Chicago to Boston to be with her. He had held her and helped arrange logistics and made her eat when she had no appetite.

"No, actually." She stopped to put her hands on his arms, feeling empathy for him because he was genuinely concerned, but also because she was about to lie to him. "It's one of my friends from high school. She died in an accident. It's really bizarre. She's our age. Can you believe it?" Kelly turned from him and opened her bureau. What to pack? There would be the funeral but also... well, they would need to deal with Pastor, wouldn't they?

"Are you okay? You look pasty."

"Um," Kelly said, bracing herself against the bureau. Her pulse radiated all through her head as a feeling of claustrophobia filled her. What would await her when she got to Wesley Falls? The black pit of that mine. The huge, wide smiles of Golden Praise. "It's a lot, someone our age just dying in an accident."

"When will you be back?"

She blinked. She had no idea. She didn't even know what she was going home to face, just that Maddy being dead meant that something was very wrong. "Maybe a week?"

"A week?" The implied question was obvious—his visit was supposed to be the remainder of this week.

Kelly shoved a pair of jeans into her bag, then added a pair of hiking shorts. "I'm sorry. I know you came all this way." She turned to him and rubbed his arm again. He looked bewildered but not exactly annoyed. It wasn't like they spent every single second of their time together when they had visits. She still went for long runs and had brunches with her girlfriends. He had a few friends living in Boston whom he sometimes saw without her. He wouldn't be totally alone and was capable of entertaining himself. The notion that he would come with her had luckily not come up—she would have had to fend that off, but he never offered.

13

The Knight of Swords

James put his cell phone down on the counter and bent over, pressing his hands to the stainless-steel and closing his eyes, not allowing the thoughts to swirl just yet. He insisted that the back kitchen of KGBakery always be immaculate. One industrial-size mixer was going with dough for brioche. Beside it were cooling racks, occupied by trays of bite-size lemon ricotta tartelettes. Rows of neatly labeled containers lined the walls, from varieties of chocolate, *Nihonbashi 66%, Tireo 68%*; types of flour, *AP, OO, Heritage—Oklahoma*; to specialty items in clear containers: lavender buds, tiny silver dragées, candied ginger and orange peel. All of these happy, beautiful things seemed wildly out of sync with the conversation he had just had with Jia Kwon.

James took off his black apron and opened one of their refrigerators. He took a clean knife from the block beside the fridge, and cut himself a thin pat of marijuana butter. It melted in his mouth, and he hoped it would calm him. It was derived from an Indica strain called Lucid Pie, one of Duncan's finds from Colombia, which produced an inoffensive, workable butter.

He had to go back to Wesley Falls.

Dazed, James wandered from the kitchen to the café and storefront of KGBakery, which was a high-end bakery selling pastries and sweets featuring marijuana. He and his business partner, a former roommate from RISD, Duncan, had designed the café to distinguish it from the often-sterile-looking dispensaries in Colorado that were their competition. KGB had the look of an old-fashioned apothecary, with small, European-style tables where guests sipped tiny cups of coffee while enjoying pastries that, despite the inclusion of cannabis, "rivaled even the best bakeries in Denver"—at least according to *The Denver Post*. While the front windows displayed fruit tarts glossy with apricot glaze, shiny chocolate bombs, and assorted Viennoiseries, the back part of the shop was dominated by the dispensary.

Duncan was James's closest friend, and knew him in the way that only a friend of over fifteen years could know him. They had first met as freshmen and while James had initially adhered to his general rule of never trusting a white person with dreads, they soon discovered a mutual love of smoking. Over the course of late-night conversations, some not entirely sober, James talked to Duncan about his life—not about everything of course—but about many of the things he was guarded about. The imposter syndrome he had about getting into RISD. His father and his mother and that dark trailer in Wesley Falls. One night James said something bitter about himself and Duncan without even thinking said, "I wish you loved you like I love you." Even now it hurt to think about, the angry, depressed kid he used to be.

James had always thought that there was something dark about his personality—that this was just the way he *was*. Duncan talked him into going to the student counseling center on campus, where despite his initial resistance, he began to see his life in different terms. He was diagnosed with dysthymia—a word James had never heard before, but apparently there was a word for this chronic darkness he felt. He got on antidepressants, continued going to therapy, and had weaned off the pills by the time he graduated. For almost twenty years, it had felt like being in a pit with no understanding that there was a ladder leading out. But sometimes when James thought of that version of himself, the past James, ready to burn down the world, he felt an acute sadness, a sharp tenderness where he wished he could go back and tell his former self that it would be okay, ultimately.

Wesley Falls was tied to that dark pit—strangely, the metaphor James had always used to describe his depression having a literal corollary with the mine.

James approached Duncan at the counter, affecting the posture of someone in a hurry. "Sorry, dude, I just got a phone call. I have to go to Pennsylvania for a funeral. Might be gone a week or so."

Duncan stared at him, then grasped James by the shoulder for a moment and said, "Find your peace, man."

As James walked from the café toward his apartment, he tried to picture Maddy as an adult and found that he couldn't. They hadn't always gotten along, but there had been a fierceness to her that he had grudgingly liked. And when shit had really hit the fan, she had swooped into action with a plan while the rest of them had retreated into a quiet terror.

James opened the door to his apartment and stared at the modern furniture that occupied it. "Hey," said a voice. James jumped, poked from his reverie by the girl leaning on the door frame of his bedroom. She was wearing one of his T-shirts, her hair still rumpled.

Lola, his mind returned helpfully. "You're still here!" he said, more surprised than put out.

"You said I could sleep in," she said coyly. "I was using the WiFi."

"Right," he said amiably, putting his keys on the kitchen counter. "I actually have to head out of town."

"Oh! I'll get out of your hair."

James was conscious of not wanting to seem like an asshole to the girls who flitted in and out of his life. It had been shocking at RISD and after when James discovered that girls liked him. At first, he would get confused, misinterpreting flirting for them making fun of him, but this had to be pointed out time and time again by someone like Duncan. His skin had cleared up, the thin build of his adolescent body turning more into something wiry from his various hobbies: snowboarding, mountain biking, climbing. He wasn't a loser anymore, a depressed burnout who lived in a trailer. Even *The Denver Post* said so. "No hurry," he assured her.

She slid into her sandals and headed out after he said that he would text her "soon." He stared at the closed door after she left.

The lack of intimacy in his sexual relationships didn't bother him because that part of his heart was like a door slammed shut, soldered closed, barbed wire gathered around.

James pawed around his walk-in for his carryon, then got distracted when he remembered the cigar box he had lugged from Wesley Falls to Dover to San Antonio to RISD and beyond. He had not opened it in a long time. But in blocking out everything he hated about Wesley Falls, he was also blocking out the few bright parts he had loved.

He sat cross-legged on the floor and opened the cigar box, laughing at the first item on top, a paper ticket stub from a Nine Inch Nails concert from 1999. Beneath that was a recommendation from Miss Forester, the art teacher at Wesley Falls High, so he could get into the magnet school, which he skimmed, wondering what had happened to her. Under that was a black sketchbook, from which a few Polaroids fell out. He cursed softly as he looked at the first: them goofing off at the lake. Maddy must have taken the picture, because in the next one she appeared making a kissy face, and Casey had been swapped out. *Fuck, we look so young*, he thought.

He paged through the sketchbook, curious to observe his style of drawing back then. There was a colored pencil drawing of the lake, the raft floating in the middle. Then an ink drawing of the orchard, which gave him an unsettled feeling. The orchard was beautiful, probably an inoffensive drawing to anyone else looking at it, but he would never think of the orchard without a shiver.

He froze when he turned the page. It was a sketch of Pastor Jim Preiss, done in charcoal pencil. The passage of time had smeared his face, somehow making his visage more terrifying in its blankness. He turned the page quickly and there were more photos tucked into the book. They were of him and Kelly, Kelly pretending to strangle him while he laughed. He was wearing that stupid beanie he used to love, which was black with flames curling up the sides. He had not looked at a picture of her in so long. In his memory of her, he had apparently misremembered her some, fuzzed up her face, remembering her large, doe-like eyes but forgetting the exact shape of her mouth. In the next picture she was not strangling him but hugging him around the neck, their cheeks pressed together as they both grinned at the camera.

How could it possibly be the case that he had not talked to Kelly in twenty years? As the time passed, what had happened in the mine seemed like a story someone made up as a child, like how everyone in Wesley Falls believed that Blub once flushed a pet alligator down the toilet and then it lived in the sewer. Even as the memories of high school grew less acute and the danger more remote, occasionally his thoughts turned to Kelly, or any of them really, but mostly her.

Once he purchased the next available flight to Scranton, he went back to the message board Jia had created, figuring he would let them know his travel information. He considered how odd it would be to see them all after all this time.

James adjusted his thermostat and fed his sourdough starter, wondering if it would survive in his absence, particularly given that he wasn't sure how long he would be gone. Not sourdough-starter-killing amounts of time, hopefully? He was just turning out the lights, when he realized he had forgotten something. He put down his bag to undo the clasp of the thin plain silver chain he wore around his neck. The chain held a claddagh ring, which made a tiny *tink* sound when he set it down in the bowl in his foyer. He always wore it but couldn't bear the idea of losing it in Wesley Falls, in some godforsaken dark place.

14

The Page of Wands

Casey hesitated, trying to compose himself after he parked his car. He had the terrible misfortune of always wearing his emotions on his face even when he didn't want to. He was only halfway to his front door when Brandon, his nephew, burst out of the house and made a beeline for him, screaming in delight. Casey managed to absorb the impact without dropping the paper drink caddy of the five boba teas he was carrying.

"Uncle Casey, Mom said I could have half before dinner and half after!" Brandon looked up with his face squished against Casey's leg, his brown eyes wide with hope. It was so strange to peer into the faces of his nephews and see so much of Lexie in them.

"Only if Mom says you were good while I was gone," he said, walking with the child still attached to him.

"I was good! You said you would do LEGOS with me later."

"I will," Casey said, wondering when exactly he would do the LEGOS—before or after he figured out his travel itinerary and before or after he explained exactly why he was going there. He left his keys on the table just inside while Brandon ran back to the living room where *Thomas & Friends* was on the TV and LEGOS were strewn about. He did not mind the chaos of his nephews visiting; in fact, he had talked Lexie into buying a house only a five-minute drive from him, and what he imagined—that each house would become both their homes—had come true. He loved spending time with his nephews, sitting on the floor doing projects, wrestling around in the backyard, mediating their squabbles. It was fascinating to see how they formed their own logic of how the world worked.

Lexie was in his kitchen, her hands wrist deep in raw chicken she was massaging. She glanced at him. "You okay?"

"Huh?"

"You look pale."

"Just hungry."

"Dijon chicken okay?"

"Sounds great. Aaron's downstairs?" Lexie nodded, turning back to her chicken, and Casey headed down the basement stairs.

The basement had been renovated to be their podcasting studio, complete with state-of-the-art microphones and Aaron's souped-up computer for editing. Three years into attending Ohio State, a torn meniscus ended Casey's football career. While the loss had been devastating, Casey managed to talk himself into a job in the announcer's booth at Ohio Stadium. He then parlayed this into a popular local radio show centering around OSU football after he graduated and then, at Aaron's urging, became an early adopter of podcasting. The Cooper Files became popular first in the Columbus area because of its focus on all things Buckeyes, but gradually over time it began to cover college football writ large, making it almost fifteen years later a well-known podcast on the topic.

Aaron had his earbuds in and was using his winding-down-a-phone-call voice as Casey set down the taro boba he had gotten for him. Casey's was green tea, no sugar, as he was trying to watch his sugar intake. Like many linebackers, Aaron had shrunk over time; Casey had not.

Aaron got off the phone, took one sip of his boba, and said, "What's wrong?"

"Uh—" Casey was interrupted by the sound of his cell phone, which he had left upstairs on the counter with his keys. Casey hurried to it—it could be Jia calling again, though he was secretly happy to delay a potential interrogation with Aaron. "Oh, hi," he said to the robocall on the other end of the line, which continued to drone on about a political candidate he had never heard of. The joys of living in a swing state.

The problem was that while Casey had never technically lied to Aaron, he had omitted what had happened to them all as teenagers. He didn't think he was *capable* of lying to Aaron even if he wanted to. Aaron, who seemed to know Casey even better than Casey did back in college. The boys had been paired together as roommates their freshman year and did pretty much everything together. Casey was a wide receiver and Aaron an offensive lineman—his literal job was to protect Casey from the D-line so he could get the ball and run with it. They practiced together, worked out together, had many of the same classes together.

Casey found it easy to get along with most people, but it was exceptionally easy with Aaron. He had never known anyone easier to talk to, and unlike a lot of people, Aaron would quietly listen and then sometimes days later would come back with something that indicated that he *really* listened. Aaron invited Casey home for Thanksgiving their first year, and while Casey had never spent a Thanksgiving away from his family, things had been tense in the Cooper household. Leaving Wesley Falls for a DI school was the dream he had worked for years to accomplish, and yet he found his excitement dampened by the strange behavior of his family. Sure, they bragged about him at the diner, or at church, but his parents made occasional comments that he shouldn't "put on airs" about going to college, and his brothers were convinced he would somehow screw up. Even in accomplishing his goal, somehow he had failed.

So he headed to the Kromopawiros' for Thanksgiving and what he found there shocked him. The house was filled with the aroma of delicious foods, the sound of laughter, the open display of affection—it felt full. It felt different. Casey always knew that his family was not like the families he had seen on TV growing up, but he had implicitly assumed that TV families were a fantasy and there weren't any like that.

He found himself irrationally annoyed at Aaron for having such a family, something that Aaron picked up on, asking him back in their dorm room if something had happened. "I think

I thought that being the best at football would make my family be nice to me," Casey had said.

"They should be nice to you regardless," Aaron said. "And you're more than just football."

"But that's when I'm my best," Casey said. He thought about what it felt like the millisecond after scoring a touchdown, when the crowd started to go ballistic, when he could see his teammates closing in on him jubilantly—that was what it was to be loved.

But Aaron stared at him. "Is it?" he asked.

Casey felt his face flush and looked down. Sometimes there was a weird vibe with Aaron. Casey couldn't articulate it. He had felt it over Thanksgiving when he had seen the rapid ease that Aaron had displayed switching from Spanish to English and back, making jokes in either. *Cool*, he had thought. Sometimes he thought a guy was *cool*. Sometimes he met dudes that had a particular essence to them that he thought was *cool*. He often wanted to win over the cool guys. Because who didn't want cool guys to be friends with them?

The boys roomed together again their sophomore year, which was fine except sometimes Aaron got snippy about Casey's frequent female visitors. Casey figured it was jealousy: while Aaron was a good-looking dude, a *cool* dude, he never seemed to be hooking up. It was confusing to Casey at the time, but in retrospect years later it seemed comically obvious. One day they got very drunk and made out, shortly followed by other instances of getting drunk and making out. At some point Aaron said, "Do we have to drink—? We have to be on that bus at 5 a.m." And thus, they embarked on a relationship, at first attempting to keep it a secret when everyone already knew.

Casey sat on the couch, his hand resting on Brandon's hair as they watched TV. He could use the fact that the kids were here to avoid any kind of third degree, couldn't he? The sound of Aaron's footsteps coming up from the basement got closer, then Aaron flopped down next to him.

"This girl I know from high school died," Casey said. "Maddy Wesley. I need to go to Pennsylvania for the funeral—"

"What?" Lexie appeared at the entryway between the kitchen and the living room, drying her hands on a dish towel. "Did you say Maddy Wesley?"

"Like the name of the town?" Aaron asked.

"Yes, Maddy. Her great-great-whatever was the town founder," he explained to Aaron.

"But what *happened*? She's thirty-five, thirty-six," Lexie said.

"Some kind of freak accident. I need to go there for the funeral."

"Of course," Aaron said at the same time as Lexie, surprised, said, "Really?"

Casey stared at a coaster on the coffee table. "I have to. We were friends." He forced himself not to look at Lexie.

"When is it?" Lexie asked. Mark had crawled to her and was attempting to stick his fat little fingers into the top of her sock. She crouched to stroke his head.

"Day after tomorrow."

"I'll move things around," Aaron said immediately.

"I need to go alone," he said abruptly, finally looking at his husband. "I won't subject you to them." Aaron actually *would* go to Casey's hometown to support him, even if it meant running into the Cooper family, whom Casey was no longer on speaking terms with, with the exception of Lexie.

The final straw was a couple years after college when Casey had—stupidly, he realized now—attempted to introduce his family to the idea of Aaron being his boyfriend. This had gone worse than he could have possibly expected, his brothers immediately finding the situation funny, the disgust on his father's face evident, as if he finally had confirmation of what was wrong with Casey all along. He clarified, at his mother's panicked interrogation, that he was not gay, but bisexual and that the person he happened to fall in love with was a man. His mother, pacing furiously, began to cry and talk about mortal sins. Aaron was safely stowed away at the Wesley Falls Inn at the time, so at her insistence of, "Who *is* this person?" Casey had shown her a picture on his cell phone and said he would like for them to meet Aaron. "I do not want a person like that in my house," she had responded. *A person like that* could be interpreted in a variety of different ways, but this occurring directly after her looking at the picture indicated to Casey that Aaron's being brown added another layer of disgust for his parents.

Casey had left Wesley Falls that day and hadn't returned since, driving away with Aaron, who was now his family along with Lexie. His split with the Coopers also precipitated Lexie's estrangement from them, and the siblings grew even closer. The Kromopawiros had adopted them both, subsumed them into their warm, tight-knit group with no hesitation, and Casey finally had the family he had always wanted. Through some of Lexie's old friends, they heard over the years that the estrangement actually drove the Cooper family further into the fold of church.

He felt Aaron's hand on his upper back, rubbing at a spot where he had a knot from lifting. "Do you think you'll run into them? Will they be at the funeral?"

"They're having a service at my mom's church, so I think they'll be there, but it's so big they might not see me."

"Other people will, though," Aaron pointed out. He was right: going from a small football-obsessed town to OSU did mean he was something of a minor celebrity every time he went back.

"I'll just tell them to fuck off," Casey said, rubbing at his face. "I'm—"

"Maddy's funeral is in *Wesley Falls*?" Lexie asked. "When is the last time she was even back there?"

Casey shrugged as if he didn't know. "I'm going to pack." As he walked up the stairs, he could hear Lexie telling Aaron about Maddy. Lexie had never been a fan of hers, forever associating Maddy with the Circle Girls, but of course Casey hadn't told her everything, so her dislike was fair.

Casey began to drop items he thought he should bring onto his bed. He added a giant Maglite flashlight, the kind that took four D batteries. How exactly were they going to find out what happened to Maddy? If the church was going to kill again, what exactly were they prepared to do to stop them? It was so easy to feel helpless as kids, especially when it seemed like there were no adults around they could trust. The shearling men, the men who had thrown those kids down the Heart, seemed huge back then—but now? After Casey had spent three years on the field going head-to-head with the largest football players in the NCAA? Now he could easily clock a church goon with one well-calibrated punch. They were adults now. They wouldn't be threatened as easily.

"You're being weird," Aaron said, now standing in the doorway, making Casey jump.

"Weird?"

"Like there's something you're keeping from me." He had his arms folded across his chest.

Casey made a noncommittal noise, surveying his packing.

"I know you," Aaron said. "Your face looks like the underside of a fish."

"Gee, thanks." He dug the heels of his hands into his eyes and kept them there as he said, "I can't tell you."

"What can't you tell me?"

"You just have to trust me."

"Are you actually going there for a funeral?"

"Sort of."

"Did they *threaten* you or something?"

It took Casey a moment to realize that *they* meant Casey's family, and not the shearling men and assortment of Golden Praise lackeys. "No, it's not like that. It's just…some stuff happened when I was in high school, and I have to go back and help the people it happened with."

"*What?*"

"Lower your voice," he said, making a gesture toward downstairs.

"What happened?"

"I can't say?" he answered, looking sheepishly at Aaron, who was starting to look a mixture of concerned and annoyed.

"Is this some *I Know What You Did Last Summer*-level shit?" Aaron said.

"Sort of?" Casey responded weakly.

"Casey!"

"Come on, you have to trust me."

"Are you in *danger* or something? You have to tell me!"

"I made a promise to these people to keep a secret and you know I don't go back on promises."

"Yeah, but like, marriage vows? What about those?"

"This promise predates the vows."

Aaron gave a snort of exasperated laughter, which sometimes he did when he was frustrated with Casey but not that mad. "You're seriously going to go without giving me an explanation?"

Casey sighed. "When I was in high school a group of my friends saw something we weren't supposed to see. Maddy was one of them, and now she died under mysterious circumstances."

"What did you—"

Casey held up his hands, indicating that he wouldn't answer the question. "We just need to make sure that it actually was an accident and Maddy wasn't murdered."

"Casey! You need to call the police!"

"We will if we need to. I mean, back then we were just *kids*. We didn't know what to do." Aaron opened his mouth, but Casey cut him off. "That's all I can tell you. You just have to trust me."

"Agh!"

"Aaron, please."

"You're not being fair!"

"Do we still have that bear spray from camping?"

"Casey!"

15

The Three of Cups

The call would not be for another half hour. Padma had already arranged the desk in her office: a cup of tea with a lemon wedge, her laptop open with the train schedule from New York to Pennsylvania, a fresh pen. She had climbed up into the attic to retrieve a box of things from her childhood: report cards that she had meticulously saved, the program from eighth grade graduation. At the bottom was the black-and-white-speckled composition notebook with PROJECT written on the cover in purple gel pen.

She sat down in her leather chair, a feeling she couldn't describe coming over her as she opened the notebook. Could someone be nostalgic and scared at the same time? Excited and mournful? The notebook was filled with her girlish handwriting, occasional notations from Jia, their silly observations.

Missing dog LOCATED 5/15/1995! This was a good one!

She brought the notebook to her face and inhaled. The paper had no odor after all these years, but she thought of the incense smell of The Gem Shop, the taste of Swedish Fish shared on the bus. A postcard fell out of the notebook and landed on the desk. There were a few more pressed in between the pages.

Padma had received the first postcard in college on a particularly bad week when she had felt sad. She loved college, and was doing well, but she found herself missing out on the romantic entanglements that her friends seemed to fall into effortlessly. She wasn't unpopular at UPenn, but had spent all four of her years secretly having crushes on boys she didn't really know. Her friends just *existed* and somehow boys found them. She had felt excluded at Wesley Falls High, but not at her magnet school, where she had fit in, but at that time she hadn't really been interested in boys. She'd figured she'd meet someone in college, date them for a while, go backpacking in Europe, get engaged, then get married and have kids. Two kids, specifically.

She remembered pulling the postcard out of her little square cubby in the mailroom of her dorm, flipping over the picture of fall leaves to see the familiar messy handwriting that made up her address. Her breath caught. Her full name, spelled correctly, and her exact dorm address, but no message. It couldn't be…but she knew Jia's handwriting as well as she knew her own.

After that first mysterious postcard, she found herself thinking about Jia a lot, wondering if she had meant to send it with no message, or if she thought that somehow by not writing a message she wasn't violating their promise. But wasn't the promise stupid? The second postcard, this one of a kitten, arrived a few years later, again with no message. Light-years away from Wesley Falls at Cornell when Padma was getting her masters in biomedical engineering, did the promise still matter? It had been years, and no one had ever popped out of the woodwork to demand to know what had happened that summer. Unless… what if they had, but they had only come after James? Maybe they had arrested him, and he was rotting away in a jail somewhere for a mass murder he never committed, or a murder he sort of did? Well, they all did.

A year later she went to Europe for a beautiful trip with a group of friends, including a friend named Tamer who had lately been behaving funny around her. Tamer was Egyptian and had a lilting accent because of constantly moving around as a kid—his parents were diplomats. She was surprised when he revealed that he liked her and thought they should go out. Another postcard arrived on the day of their first date, only she didn't realize it was a date until an hour in and none of their other friends showed up. This postcard had an iris on it. Padma held the postcard to her heart and thought, *You would like him.*

The next postcard didn't come for so long that she started to think Jia had stopped. It arrived seven years later, sitting in the foyer where it had landed after being shoved through the mail slot with the bills and circulars. She and Tamer were coming home from the doctor, having just confirmed what Padma had suspected for the past two years. Pregnancy wasn't going to happen. At least not as easily as she had thought. On the car ride home, she had said, "Obviously, we need to have a longer conversation about adoption but for today, can we just be sad?" Tamer agreed. Tamer was always agreeable.

Padma had scooped up the mail and sat in the living room, flipping through it, thinking about the fact that she was offended both emotionally and *scientifically* about what they had been told: there was "no discernable reason" why she could not get pregnant. As a woman of science, she didn't believe vague notions that "things happen for a reason" but more so "things happened for scientific reasons" and what was she supposed to feel when there was no discernable scientific reason?

She saw the postcard and had a flash of inspiration: she realized why this was happening.

She had killed a man. They had killed him, left his body, and tried to cover it up. This was her punishment. Things like that don't just *go away* into the ether, as she had always hoped they would. She knew there was no way Jia was saying this—Jia would never say anything like that—but she couldn't help having the thought when looking at the postcard.

Since that summer, she had felt as if her mind had split in two, with one part insisting that what she had seen that summer had actually happened. The other part, the logical part, became stronger over time, insisting on facts and details. Eventually, this part won, which became easier as the time and space away from Wesley Falls grew larger. Could she deny her memories? No, but she could deny that her memories were real: she knew from taking Forensic Psychology in college that human memory was fallible. Eyewitnesses to crimes often garbled what they had actually seen, or some constructed memories that hadn't even happened with no malicious intent. And with no other member of the Capstone Six to confirm what had happened, it was easy to tell herself that the world she lived in followed logical rules and it just hadn't happened that way.

Except she knew now that that wasn't true.

Can we talk on the phone? she had written on the message board. No one else had asked that, and she wondered if she was violating some security protocol. But Jia had said yes.

Yes, the circumstances were wild, disturbing, crazy—all that, but she couldn't help the small cry of girlish glee that escaped her lips when her phone rang with an unfamiliar number showing. She brought the phone to her ear, but neither woman said anything. "Is it really you?" she asked finally, surprised by how quickly she choked up.

"It's me," said a voice. Older now, but unmistakably Jia's. "I can't believe we're talking. I—"

"It was you?" Padma asked. "The postcards?"

Now she could hear Jia crying, too. "Yes."

"But how did you even know all my addresses?" Padma asked, something she had wondered for years.

"I'm fucking psychic."

Padma burst into giggles and Jia joined her.

"Well, that and Google. I had to keep tabs on all of you," Jia clarified.

"Google!" Padma had abided their promise of avoiding the other capstone members, and this extended to the internet, however much she had been tempted. Particularly after the first postcard arrived. "What about our pact?"

"Our pact was never updated for the reality of twenty-first-century telecommunications," Jia said.

"Could you see me in some way?"

"Sometimes. Not every time I wanted to. It's like a door, and sometimes it's open and sometimes it's closed."

"You were with me, then," Padma said, wiping tears off her face.

"I was always with you."

"Sorry, this is so weird. What happened? You went back to Wesley Falls because you saw something bad happen to Maddy?"

"No. Remember Blub? Springsteen? He's sheriff now. We stayed friends. I've helped him a couple times, and he called me to find a missing person. Except he never told me the missing person was Maddy." She added the last bit dryly. "But as soon as I got into town, I felt it."

"What?" Padma whispered, glancing toward the door.

"*It*. The way I felt back then. Sick. Then we found her body."

"Do you think she was murdered?"

"I don't think she was murdered. I know she was." Jia stated this so frankly that Padma pulled the phone from her ear and looked at it. Jia back then had always acted as if her abilities were like swimming in the ocean when you couldn't feel the ground. Something that moved her, rather than her moving it.

"And then. You saw *him*?" Padma asked.

"I think it was him…"

"What the hell is going on?"

"I don't know. Maybe we didn't…" Jia trailed off.

"We absolutely did."

"Maybe he can't…?"

Maybe he can't be killed? Padma thought. Gooseflesh rose on her arms. "You think he went after Maddy? God, why was she even there?"

"Her parents died. Sometimes you have to come back."

"You always have to come back," Padma said, sighing.

"So you'll come?"

"I have to. We all do. Jia, if it's a door you can look through, did you ever look back at Wesley Falls? At the church?"

"I need a person I know well to look through. My mom, when she was there."

"She left?"

"She passed away."

"Oh, no. I'm sorry."

"Thank you. Still, last time I was there—when I was settling my mom's things, I didn't feel anything weird. The church was all run-down. I thought—I assumed it was over."

"Apparently not. Are we all coming?"

"Flights are booked. I can get you a hotel room."

"I'm buying a train ticket right now," Padma said, opening a tab on her laptop. "I'll let you know what time it gets in." After they hung up, Padma paid for a train ticket to Scranton.

"Tamer!" she yelled downstairs.

"You need something?" he called back.

"I have to go to Pennsylvania for a week."

16

The High Priestess

Jia took a seat at a small round table. Sweet Sensations was the bakery that had taken over The Gem Shop. According to the store owner, who had been so delighted to see Jia that her coffee cake and latte had been free, it had taken six months to outfit the bakery with an appropriate kitchen, but it had been a good investment because the bakery was doing well. Jia could only smile at the contrast between the gothic ambiance of The Gem Shop and Sweet Sensations's pink gingham and Comic Sans font. Whatever the decor, the coffee cake was delicious.

As she sipped her coffee, she scanned the townspeople heading into or out of shops, hyperconscious every time eyes lingered on her for more than a second. This required no mystic powers; it was a small town and someone checking into the Inn was fodder for idle grocery-store talk. She breathed slowly, trying to relax what felt like a tightly coiled muscle inside her. In her gut, she didn't like being here. Ever since she had found the body, it felt as if a door inside her brain had creaked open a few inches. A door to a room that was dark inside. She could feel something *sinister* that lightly permeated the town. She told herself that she was fine as long as she was in public, that once they were all here, they would have strength in numbers.

Kids were out on Main Street for summer break: girls with their bare, colt-like legs, boisterous boys with questionable haircuts and loud bravado. Did they go to church? She kept looking for Circle Girl pins and was relieved when she didn't find any. The Blockbuster was long gone, replaced by a bike shop, and just then two teenagers exited, a girl with long hair and a tan boy, Latino, Jia guessed, and she realized that she and this boy were the only people of color in sight. There were so few minorities growing up in Wesley Falls that Jia had gotten used to the idea of "everyone" being white when she was a child. When she left for Penn State, which was far more diverse, she joined the Japanese language and cultural club, and, after having to point out that she was a Korean who did not speak Korean but spoke passable Japanese, was occasionally struck by the odd realization that she was in a room full of Asians and not a single white person.

"Ah, just the woman I was looking for!"

Jia looked up, squinting against the morning sun, at the tall figure of Sheriff Blub. He set down a blueberry muffin and sat across from her. "Hi," she said, trying to keep her voice flat. Trying to sound *normal*, as if you had just helped the police locate the body of a girl you definitely weren't friends with, and you and your friends had nothing to do with events surrounding it. That type of voice.

"I always thought your mom's store was cool, but it's nice to have a place to get a decent cup of coffee," he said, tearing off the top of his muffin.

"It's pretty good," Jia said.

"I wanted to thank you," Blub said, looking directly at her. She supposed his eyes were a nice shade of hazel. "I'm not sure how long it would have taken us on our own to find her. There's just hundreds of acres of woods, and we don't have a canine team. So..." He cleared his throat, suddenly awkward. "In terms of payment—?"

Jia shook her head. "No payment."

"I can't expect you to come all this way for free."

"What on earth are you going to write on the receipt?"

He laughed, then sipped his coffee. "I can't help but be curious—do you do this kind of...work for money?"

Jia shook her head. "I haven't, no."

"*Couldn't* you?"

"I'm not sure I'd want to." Blub raised an eyebrow questioningly. "Dead bodies and…whatnot. It doesn't feel good."

"Oh. I guess I didn't think of that. Why wouldn't you play the lottery instead?"

"I can't necessarily call it up on command. Sometimes it's there when I want it to be, but sometimes it isn't. It all terrified me when I was a kid."

"I always knew there was something about you that was different," he mused.

"You don't think it was—?" Here she gestured at her appearance and they both laughed, Blub looking a little embarrassed.

Careful now, she told herself, looking at him. Blub was the sheriff—she didn't know if he could be trusted. His father certainly couldn't be. But he also had twenty years of background information about Wesley Falls that she had missed. If only she could see into him. The only time she had ever seen the past had been that time in Evansville, and that hadn't been on purpose. Sometimes the flashes of the future came on their own. What she could control best was her ability to call up a person, but it had to be a person she knew well. Her mother when she was alive, her best friend in Philly. Once it had been Padma at the doctor's office. Another time it had been Casey in a gym lifting weights—not the most interesting vision, but she had been glad to see him. Now, looking at Blub, she concentrated hard, trying to relax her eyes and open her mind, trying to force something that wasn't there.

After a few moments she realized Blub was staring at her.

"So what happens now? With Maddy?" she asked quickly.

"Medical examiner does his thing. Triple funeral is tomorrow."

Jia frowned. "They're just going to tack on Maddy's funeral with her parents?"

"I guess it was convenient," Blub said, eating the remainder of his muffin.

"But…she wasn't living here. Doesn't she have family or a husband that gets a say? I can't see them wanting to have a funeral in a town she hasn't lived in for two decades."

"No husband, no family other than her parents." His eyes met hers. "It *is* a bit odd, isn't it?"

"Well if *I* died in an accident, I would want all my friends and family to be there."

"Accident?"

Jia widened her eyes. "I thought that's what happened. She was hiking or something, and fell into the sinkhole?"

"Peculiar way to die," he remarked.

What is he saying? "This is coal country. We all know about subsidence."

"I was sure you'd be gone by now," he said.

Why was he changing the subject? "I thought I'd stick around—I have a couple things about my mother's estate to look into," she lied. She concentrated on squishing some of her cake into her plate to pick up stray bits of streusel. "I thought I'd go to the funeral." He raised his eyebrows, but she interrupted him before he could say anything. "It just makes me so sad to think of an entire family gone in a flash."

"No more Wesleys," he said, crumpling up his muffin wrapper. "The Merricks reign supreme."

"Jane Merrick?" she asked.

He shook his head. "Laurie. She's the head of the Board of Directors at Golden Praise. What's weirder is that they're having Maddy's ceremony in that church."

Jia feigned ignorance. "Why's that weird?"

"Don't you remember?"

Jia shrugged. "I didn't go here for high school the last two years, remember?"

"She had some big blowout with her parents and got sent to boarding school—"

"Oh, I heard about *that.*"

Blub shook his head. "It had something to do with the church. My understanding is Maddy became estranged from her family because of it. She never came back here after she graduated high school."

"Not once?"

"Not that I know of. Didn't I see you running around with her?" he asked suddenly.

"Me?" Jia asked. "Do you really think Youth Group wanted to let in the girl who sells Ouija boards?"

He laughed. "Weren't you in her capstone group?"

"Capstone?" she repeated dumbly.

"You know. The summer after sophomore year?"

"Oh, that. Yeah, we did a history project. Maddy was bossy, as you can imagine. I think she was pissed she didn't have any of her minions in her group. Not to speak ill of the dead," she added.

He made a wagging gesture with his head. "She barely spoke two words to me her entire life, and when she did it was to take jabs at me. She probably wasn't easy to be friends with."

"I wouldn't know. I do feel bad, though—I mentioned it to a couple people, I think they might come for the funeral."

"Oh, who?"

"No one really committed, but I think some East Coast locals."

"Huh," he said. *Please stop asking questions*, she prayed. Why all of a sudden did he bring up the capstone? Did he know something?

Blub was at once dangerous with his questions, but also potentially useful because how else were they supposed to get insider information about Maddy's investigation? He stood, picking up his cup and plate. "Maybe I'll see you and whoever else. A real blast from the past."

17

The Hanged Man

It was a five-hour drive from upstate New York to Wesley Falls with one stop at a diner halfway where Maddy had seriously wondered what she was doing. She had not been back to Wesley Falls since winter break of her senior year of high school. For years, she was unwelcome and had no desire to go there anyway. In her parents' eyes, she was irredeemable, which she thought deliciously ironic because the very point of Christianity was that there was no sinner who could not be redeemed.

After that sophomore year summer, when getting out of town seemed like the best possible option, she put together what she thought of as a box of sin containing condoms, marijuana supplied by James, and a hypodermic needle filched from the nurse's office at Golden Praise. It was a laughable collection, like something pamphlets at church would warn about, but it worked. Maddy hid it under her bed, knowing that her mother snooped, and it was off to boarding school her junior year. This was helped by the fact that her parents were embarrassed by her downfall; out of sight and out of mind, her parents could continue to be religious figureheads in town.

As Maddy maneuvered her Honda around town, taking in all the old sights, she realized that going back home didn't raise the specter of wanting to drink like she thought it would, and she felt quietly proud.

New Horizons, the Christian boarding school they had sent her to, had been a great place to develop alcoholism. It was a great place to go on benders with other kids from fucked-up families who didn't know what else to do with them. The sort of place that hired twenty-two-year-olds straight out of Liberty or Bob Jones University to be teachers without any credentials other than a willingness to sign a "faith contract," which included articles on how homosexuality and premarital sex were sins. The sort of place that ground down young women.

Maddy, who had developed a taste for partying by then, barely graduated, and then failed from one job to the next until she got her real estate license, something that she was good at when she could hold it together. It was not, she told herself at the time, that she had a problem. She was young, and going out till three in the morning and getting blackout drunk was normal. That worked till she was twenty-five or so, when the hangovers started hitting harder, and friends started dropping off because apparently, she was a mean drunk. *I'm pretty mean sober*, she remembered thinking as she made a halfhearted attempt to pour her last bottle of wine down the sink.

"You're an angry person," her boyfriend at the time said just before he left her apartment for the last time.

"What did you expect?" she said to the closed door. Of course she was angry. It was all jumbled up in her head. She was angry at herself. At her parents. Her time at New Horizons had only separated her further from Christianity, so much so that even the sight of familiar religious symbols filled her with anger. It was not until much later that she realized what she was going through at the time was a form of mourning: faith had organized the world for her, and when that system collapsed there was nothing to replace it.

She ruminated about what happened at New Horizons and places like Golden Praise with no consequences. "Why don't you do something about it?" one of her friends, or whatever you called someone you drank with a lot, had said, more irritated than supportive.

Maddy had gone home and not entirely soberly written up a manifesto against schools like New Horizons in the form of a long essay. In the morning she found the document on her computer and was surprised that it wasn't half-bad. Maybe if she published it, it would help someone like her. She spent months polishing the draft and submitting it to various websites before it was accepted. It was a proud moment.

Not a month after the publication, Maddy found herself in another situation that she wouldn't have if she had been a little more sober and a lot less reckless. After years of living in upstate New York, she was used to driving in the snow, but had ignored warnings that there was ice on the roads. She was already drunk and the liquor store she liked best was ten miles away.

She did not remember the car hitting the guardrail on the bridge, just the horrible sound it made, then the icy water gathering at her feet. Her car had gone off the bridge and broken through the frozen river. *Oh? This is how I'm going to die?* There seemed to be an eternity of her staring in dumb silence at the shelf of ice visible through her windshield before she scrabbled for her seat belt and the door handle. The shock of freezing water stole her breath, and she wasn't so much swimming as frantically rotating her limbs in a panic. She scrambled to where the shelf of ice ended and attempted to pull herself up, a difficult feat because of her thick down coat—now soaked. This took several attempts; in the process she lost her shoes, and then she lay on the ice, teeth chattering, calling out for help.

But no one was there. What sane person would be driving right now, in the middle of a blizzard when the TV kept telling people to stay home? *There are farms around here*, she told herself. *Head in that direction*. She made her way across the ice, trying to step carefully with her freezing socked feet, the sounds of her own car sinking making her terrified that the ice could crack under her weight and pull her down again.

She climbed up the embankment, realizing that she couldn't feel her fingers, that she couldn't get her hands to move beyond anything like a crab-like grasp. When she got to the top she couldn't tell if her body was shuddering because of the exposure of her wet body to the freezing air or if she was crying at what she saw. Vast expanses of white. Farmland, the vegetation trapped under a foot of snow. She wasn't even sure what direction to walk in because she couldn't see more than a few feet in front of her. She began to shuffle through the snow blindly, falling, getting back up, frantically moving even as it felt as if her very bones were freezing.

Her feet were numb as were her hands—how long before frostbite set in, if it hadn't already? She fell again, this time flat on her face, and this time she could not get up. Maybe she should stay low, curled up like this, protected from the elements. She was tired. She could curl into a ball, and it would preserve her body heat. Suddenly, this seemed like the best idea on earth.

Get up.

She heard this distinctly. A command, but not filled with disdain like she was used to hearing. No, this was a firm yet gentle command.

Get up.

She obeyed, stumbling, fighting her way through the snow. She couldn't feel her body anymore, just the imperative to keep moving. Improbably, she heard the sound of a dog barking. Was it just her imagination? But then a German shepherd burst through the blanket of whiteness, snow peppering his snout. He barked excitedly, jumping out a circle in the snow. "Come here!" she croaked, holding her arms out. The dog, delighted to find a new friend, complied, and Maddy deliriously tried to stick her hands into the dog's mouth for warmth. The dog didn't seem to mind.

"Benny?" called a voice. "Where are you, boy?"

"Help!" Maddy tried to scream, but her voice sounded tiny and ineffective in the sound-muffling snow. She saw a bright orange figure through the whiteness. A man wearing a fluorescent orange coat.

"Oh!" he exclaimed when he saw her. He ran to her and managed to get her to her feet. "I got you, come on. I don't live far from here. We'll get you warmed up." She could barely walk and he half carried her to his farmhouse. The dog ran barking ahead of them, either out of excitement or to alert the man's wife, who said *oh no* and *goodness* several times when she saw Maddy.

"Her car must have run off into the river—she's soaking wet!" the man exclaimed once they got her into the house. It was blissfully warm inside, a cozy abode with the fireplace already going.

"We need to get her to a hospital," the wife said. "I'll put her in the bath but—"

The man was already hurrying to the phone. "I'll call, but I don't know how long it'll take with these roads!"

The bathroom luckily was on the same floor. The woman sat Maddy on the closed toilet—it had one of those plush covers on it—where she shuddered as the woman ran the hot water to fill the bathtub. "We've got to get you out of those clothes and into the tub, honey, okay?" She must have been sixty something, with flushed cheeks and reading glasses: the sort of woman who could make an apple pie from scratch with no recipe.

Piece by piece, they abandoned her heavy, soaked articles of clothing, struggling and giving up when it came to the socks because they were frozen. "Just get in and they'll loosen up," the woman urged, helping her to step into the tub.

The water was blissful and painful. The woman reached into the water a moment later and managed to get her socks off, and Maddy suddenly realized that this was the only time she could recall being naked in front of someone without being self-conscious about her body.

Once she could feel her hands and feet tingling, she managed a thank-you.

"I'm Muriel," the woman said. "I'm going to make you some hot tea!" She ran off before Maddy could say anything. She returned a couple minutes later with a steaming mug of chamomile, urging her to drink up. "Bob called, and it'll be about forty minutes before an EMT can get here."

"I think—I think I'm okay."

Muriel tested the temperature of the water, decided it was too lukewarm, and turned the hot water back on. She bustled over to the cabinet beneath the sink, where Maddy watched her root around. She came up with something spherical and adjusted her reading glasses, contemplating it. It was a bath bomb, and Maddy could see her momentary consideration of throwing it into the tub before realizing this was silly. Maddy broke into giggles, and Muriel joined her, laughing at her own foolishness and probably relief that Maddy was okay enough to laugh.

Twenty minutes later Maddy was dried off, outfitted in an oversize sweatsuit, swaddled in blankets, and placed in front of the fireplace in their living room. She said she was fine, and that maybe they didn't need the EMT, but they said it was probably best she get checked out. Muriel brought her more hot tea and a slice of apple pie with a thick slice of cheddar on top, which Maddy eagerly gobbled up, not once thinking about good foods or bad foods.

Maddy had just about finished the pie when, unbeknownst to her, the EMTs were making their way up Muriel's long, unpaved driveway. She pushed some crust aside with her fork to see that something was printed on her dessert plate with delicate letters. They were familiar words, verses she had seen many times from the book of Matthew, but her eyes lingered at the bottom of the plate, and the words had never hit her quite as hard as they did now:

Blessed are the merciful,
for they will be shown mercy.
Blessed are the pure in heart,
for they will see God.
Blessed are the peacemakers,
for they will be called children of God.

The words struck her in their terrible beauty, and she felt her guts twist with a sob. Muriel had looked at her with curiosity in that exact moment: Was the girl simply overwhelmed by a car accident that had nearly killed her, or had the plate made her upset?

They talked about that moment a lot later.

Maddy's release from the hospital had been humbling. Her blood alcohol level was over the limit and the incident caused her to lose both her license and one and a half toes on each foot.

With her lack of license and expensive DUI charges, she took to riding her bike, and contemplated going to rehab. Rehab was also expensive; the good ones were anyway. AA was cheap and ubiquitous but steeped in God-talk and she wasn't sure she wanted God-talk.

Instead, she put together a basket of goodies and biked her way over to Bob and Muriel's house. Sheepishly, she offered her thanks, and the couple invited her in for supper. They were grandparents and Lutherans. She told them about the DUI, confirming what had been obvious to them because apparently, they could smell the alcohol on her. They accepted this without judgment, remarking that they were glad no one had been seriously hurt. Perhaps there's an automatic intimacy with anyone who has saved your life, or seen you naked, or both, or maybe it was the dessert plate, but they began talking about faith and Maddy's struggle with it. She sat with the dog's head on her lap and told them about her parents' church, the Christian boarding school and her rebellion from it. She was angry at God but longed for his presence and direction.

As troublesome as her relationship with Golden Praise had been, there had always been a part of her faith that had felt separate from that, more private: this had been the part where she felt loved by God and humbled before him, but not in a degrading way like she felt at home. She could not explain how or why, but the closest she felt to God, and the happiest, too, was when she sang in choir.

Bob and Muriel never pressed her, but through what became regular dinners together, Maddy began to see that faith did not have to equal Golden Praise. It did not have to mean a church that told girls they were secondary to boys or that Satan lurked behind every sexual urge. A church could also mean community, singing and soup kitchens, and people like Bob and Muriel, who ran to help someone in need. She would never again be someone whose entire world revolved around church, but she did find community, and she did find sobriety, and it reconnected her to her faith.

She was thinking of one of the Twelve Steps of AA as she

drove her car through Wesley Falls. The one about making amends to people you had hurt through your addiction. She had done this in New York, which she thought of as her home, but not in Wesley Falls. But how many girls had she tortured? How many people had she put down in her own zealous desire to constantly be on top? "For what it's worth," she said to her empty car, "I'm sorry."

The person who had informed her that her parents had been killed in a car accident down in Florida had been—shockingly enough—Blub Springsteen, who was now the sheriff. He had been contacted by the authorities down there who had had trouble finding her parents' next of kin.

She drove on Willow Drive, intending to drive by the lake, forgetting that you could not see the lake from the road. That was what made it feel so private when you were there, she remembered, thinking about all the days she and the other capstone kids had cooled off in the water when they took breaks from their scheming. God—what had happened to them? Kelly was probably married with kids and a white picket fence. Was Casey using his charm at a car dealership somewhere? She had been tempted once at an Apple store, three sheets to the wind, and had attempted to google the easiest of them—Padma. Or at least she had thought so, but Subramaniam was a surprisingly common last name.

She had always imagined that she felt the weight of Golden Praise heavier than the rest of them—even James. Even before Jia's vision, Maddy had understood just how deep the town's roots were entwined with Golden Praise. There was no Wesley Falls without the church forming its foundation. She had been the one who understood that anyone from the church piecing together that the six of them had been together that night meant danger.

After the night they killed Pastor Preiss, Maddy spent several days in terror waiting for someone to figure out what they had done, for the series of panicked phone calls from friends of her parents', bigwigs in the church, for the news to spread like wildfire across town. But nothing was said for several days, and no investigation took place. Maddy pasted a benign expression on her face when her parents told her that Pastor had left to go on a mission trip in Africa. Yes, it was sudden, but there was a famine there, and he felt God calling him. *Why are they lying?* she wondered. Shortly after, her box of sin was discovered and she was shipped off to boarding school. The next time she visited home for Christmas break, a new pastor had been installed, and of course Maddy was expected to attend services, and she was interested to see that the entire dynamic of the church had changed. The new pastor wasn't as good at speaking, nowhere near as dynamic. Each successive time she visited home, Golden Praise seemed dimmer and dimmer, fewer attendees at services, evidence of disrepair becoming apparent.

Maybe it's gone by now, she thought, pausing at the intersection at Throckmartin Lane. She was only a block from her house but wasn't ready to face it. Instead, she drove north, heading to where Golden Praise had been, thinking that the land had likely been sold off by now.

But as she grew closer, she could see the verdant grass and an expensive-looking jumbotron. The image on it, oh no, ha ha, her eyes playing tricks. She laughed aloud but the laugh turned into a croak as she grew closer. The picture of the smiling pastor on the jumbotron was Jim Preiss.

She felt her bowels twist.

Her first instinct was to run, peeling her car away as her heart pounded. *I'm seeing things. This is what happens when you repress your entire childhood.* She told herself that she had been mistaken, that she had imagined it as a distraction from what she needed to be doing, which was going back to her childhood home and revisiting painful memories.

Her hands trembled as she palmed the wheel, turning back toward her childhood home. And there it was: 19 Throckmartin Lane, the longtime home of the descendants of town founder Jeremiah Wesley. The house still looked lived in: the grass well kept, a lawn sign for a politician that Maddy would probably hate if she knew who he was. She pulled up the driveway and turned off her car. *Maybe I do want a drink.*

She rooted through her purse longer than she needed to find the loose Schlage house key she had not used for years. She wasn't sure the key would work. But it did, and when she opened the front door she stood for a moment, breathing in the smell that was familiar: vanilla candles and the vinegar her mother used to clean the floors.

Here was the kitchen, the table where they said grace and ate family meals together. It was never the bustling site of meals like the way it was in movies, with people jovially passing food and making jokes. Every single thing in the kitchen felt steeped in Maddy's eating disorder. The table itself an altar of humiliation. On impulse, she opened the fridge and sure enough all the same items she expected were there: a tub of I Can't Believe It's Not Butter! and CorningWare filled with noodle casserole.

"What are you doing here?" a voice demanded.

Maddy gave a short scream, turning with the full expectation of facing her dead parents, perhaps right along with Pastor Jim Preiss, but receiving an earthlier fright by the sight of three men, two of whom she recognized. Albert Sullivan and his younger brother, Tyson. Two of whom they had taken to calling the shearling men.

"I'm—I'm—" She grew mad at herself for blubbering and found an internal thread of dignity to grab onto before speaking again. "I'm Maddy Wesley."

"I know who you are," Albert sneered. Now that she looked more closely at his face, he had aged in exactly the ways she would have expected: puffy and lined like someone who never bothered to wear sunscreen. "You're not welcome here."

"This is my *parents'* house," she snapped. "I have every right to be here." It was obvious that they expected her to slip in the same power dynamic as before: they were backed by Golden Praise and she was a terrified teenager who only had a driver's permit.

"You don't actually," Albert said. "Your parents made it clear that this house and all their assets would go to the church in the event of their deaths, so please leave."

Maddy gaped. "I didn't come here for the stupid house! I came here because…because…" Because that was what you did when someone died. You came back and you made arrangements and sorted through old belongings.

They were closing in on her. *"Leave,"* Albert said again.

Something's going on, she realized as she darted out the side door, heading for her car. She locked the doors quickly, then pulled away. It was one thing for her to be some wayward child who wasn't welcome back, but this felt like something else. This felt like maybe they specifically didn't want someone rooting around the house.

She drove aimlessly through town, a heavy feeling sitting in her stomach as her eyes scanned the people she drove by. She looked for young girls, slowing down when she saw them, trying to spot Circle Girl pins but she didn't find any. This didn't relax her. There were boys with skateboards at the Bad Park, kids playing basketball at the outdoor court at the high school, toddlers romping in a sprinkler on someone's front lawn. To anyone, this would look like a perfect American town.

Then why did something feel so *off*? The jumbotron, the picture of Preiss, the church goons at her house. None of that felt right. Something was happening. Something that she had thought was over long ago. Those men had made it clear that she wasn't welcome. And when people did that, it was often because they knew that you knew too much. Or that you would ask too many questions.

If you think I'm going to run, you're dead wrong.

PART FOUR: JUNE 1995

18

Kelly

Kelly did not know if James had known about the tiny inlet room in the mine or if he had found it by luck. "Get the door," James said grimly. Kelly assumed he was talking to Casey, who seemed like the only one capable of moving the massive rusty bar to bolt the door shut. But Casey and Maddy were trying to make room on the ground for Padma, who was having an attack of sorts, gasping for breath as she clutched at her chest. The space was pitch-black except for the nervous darting of Maddy's penlight. Kelly joined James, squishing in beside him to push the bolt horizontally into its slot, locking them into safety. Or at least that was the intent.

The past ninety seconds had been a blur of her mind saying *oh shit oh shit oh shit* as they all moved through the darkness. James had grabbed her away from the precipice overlooking the Heart and quickly led them through a confusing series of twists and turns into the darkness. At one point the path they were on grew so narrow that Casey had trouble fitting through.

Once the door was barred, Kelly saw James's lighter flick back on, catching a split second of his pallid face before he waved his arm in an arc, trying to get a view of the chamber they were in. It was about the size of Kelly's living room, except with a much lower ceiling. It was littered with ancient-looking equipment and a pile of rumpled cloth. Kelly caught momentary glances of her classmates through the sweep of light: Jia sitting by herself, knees hugged into her chest, her lips moving silently. Maddy and Casey kneeling on the ground beside Padma, who was on her back, struggling to breathe.

"Does she have asthma?" Maddy whispered. Why she was whispering went unspoken, the same way that James's command to bar the door had been. They were hiding from whatever was going on at the Heart.

"No," Kelly whispered back, coming over. "She's never mentioned it, at least. Jia?" she called, but in the dim light she could barely make out Jia's face.

"I saw someone step on her," Casey said, leaning over Padma. "Listen to me, you have to calm down. Breathe slowly." Padma, her eyes huge with terror, attempted to do so. "You don't have asthma, do you?"

Padma shook her head and managed to say, "My chest… doesn't feel good."

They all huddled around her, not sure of what to do. "I think she just got the wind knocked out of her," Casey said. "Maybe a broken rib. Do you mind if I check?" She nodded, still looking panicked, but breathing slower now in controlled gasps. Casey gingerly reached under her shirt, and he must have pressed in a few places, none of which elicited pain. "I don't think it's a rib. You're going to be fine—it's just a muscle spasm in your diaphragm. Try to breathe slow."

Kelly heard a ripping sound: James had torn off the hem of his T-shirt and was now twisting it. Then she heard another sound, distinct from the rustle of cloth: a shriek, distant, but still piercing in the darkness. "That's four," Maddy said, her tone devoid of emotion.

"What the *fuck* did we just see?" Casey said in an angry whisper.

"One of them was Gordy," James said. He was using his lighter to try to catch the end of a coil of fabric on fire. "And Eddie Hane. I saw their faces."

Gordy was a freshman. Kelly didn't know him because he was a burnout who seemed to skip school more than he attended. She had only seen one of the boy's faces well enough to make out his features, but in that panicked moment hadn't realized that she recognized him.

The fabric caught on fire, producing a taller and more sustained glow than James's lighter. Kelly looked across Padma's body and saw that Jia was still curled up, sobbing into her tucked-in body. Kelly crawled over to her, ignoring the hardness of rock under her knees, and hugged her. "It's okay, we're safe now."

"Are we?" Maddy whispered. "Do you think they saw us?"

"We were above them," Padma managed.

"I thought I saw them look up," James said. Kelly flinched. She thought she had, too, but was hoping she was wrong. Kelly urged Jia to come closer to the circle, to the fire beside Padma's body so they could all see each other. She did not like that there were parts of the small cavern that were so black she couldn't see into them. Jia snapped out of her reverie, crawling toward Padma and taking one of her hands. "I think we're safe here," James whispered. "This cave is off the beaten path."

"We could wait until it's safe and then—" Casey looked at James. "You know the way out from here?"

James nodded. "You can get out the higher entrance from here. No—"

Another scream echoed through the cavern. Padma moaned quietly, then they were all silent, muscles tensed in anticipation.

"We wait an hour," Casey said finally. "Wait till they're gone. You lead us out, and my car's not far from here."

"I told you we shouldn't have come here," Maddy snapped.

"Who were those men?" Kelly asked.

"I recognized one guy," Casey said.

"Why didn't you want us to come here?" Padma asked suddenly, the words clearly directed at Maddy.

There was silence as everyone stared at Maddy. Beyond the door, Kelly could hear the dull sound of rock continuing to fall. Maddy looked at each of them, as if contemplating something. "Didn't you recognize them?" she said. "The guys in the shearling coats—the Sullivan brothers. Albert is a deacon at my church. Tyson runs a landscaping company."

"They do our lawn!" Padma exclaimed, flinching.

"The third guy is Walt something. He lives on a farm on the edge of town and works for Tyson," Maddy said.

"You know all those guys from church?" Jia asked.

"I told you I didn't want to come here, but none of you listened," Maddy said.

James was the only one who could speak what they were all thinking. "Are you saying you knew this was going to happen?" Maddy didn't answer for long enough that suddenly everyone had something to say, their voices getting louder. She held up her hands and shushed them, gesturing wildly at the door. Just then another scream sounded out from beyond. Jia shuddered and Kelly put an arm around her.

Finally, Maddy began to speak. "There's something…going on at Golden Praise. I don't know what it is, but it's bad. People have been talking about something that was supposed to happen, and I thought I heard them talking about the mine. I remember thinking it's weird because they always told us to stay away because it's dangerous."

"Where did you hear this?" Casey asked.

"In the admin building. I was moving some boxes and heard a few adults talking—they didn't know I was there. I think… I think they were planning this."

"*Why?*" Padma managed.

"Like we're supposed to believe anything she says?" James said, the disdain in his voice obvious. "She's one of them."

"Fuck that church," Maddy whispered harshly, startling them all. Kelly had *never* heard Maddy curse. "And the stupid Circle. I hate it all."

"Since when?" James said, not backing down.

Maddy scuffed her sneaker against the ground, reluctant to speak. "Sometimes I'd get in trouble for asking too many questions or being a showoff, but maybe that wasn't a big deal, at least not until two weeks ago." It was now still in the cavern. No screaming. Jia wasn't crying anymore but was staring at Maddy, the irregular light glinting off the shine of tears on her face. The only sound came from the fire. "Two weeks ago Miss Laurie says she wants to see me in one of the back rooms of the Rec

Building on campus." Maddy had picked something up in the darkness, a scrap of metal, and was now using it to dig pointlessly at the stone ground. "I go there and Miss Merrick's there, which isn't too weird, but Dr. Foy is there, too."

"Milky's vet?" Kelly asked, confused.

Maddy nodded without looking at her. "They had a table set up with a sheet on it. Miss Laurie asked me to get undressed. I thought maybe it was to try on a new choir costume or something, but it was wrong that Dr. Foy was there. But she acted like it was normal. So I did." There was a long pause but no one dared break the silence. It was too dark to see Maddy's face with her head bowed, but when she spoke again, Kelly thought she could hear her voice breaking.

"They made me get on the table…and they did an exam. They—they used one of those things." Here she made a peculiar gesture, like a duck opening its bill, and Kelly felt her face flush hot, instantly understanding.

"A speculum?" Padma said, incredulous. "Are you talking about a speculum?" In her bewilderment, she seemed to have forgotten her pain.

Maddy nodded at the same time Casey asked what a speculum was. "It's um…" Kelly started. "Like a tool they use when you go to the gynecologist. To look at your uterus."

"Why is Milky's vet looking at your…whatever?" James asked.

Maddy didn't seem capable of answering but Padma had struggled up to a sitting position, shock written on her face. "Were they doing an exam to see if you're a virgin?" Maddy gave a small nod and Jia gasped.

"What the fuck?" James asked. "Who does that?"

"So what did you do?" Padma asked, her eyes glued to Maddy, who was now jabbing violently at the ground with her piece of metal.

She stopped suddenly, her face twisting into a cruel expression. "What do you think I did? I ran out and slept with the first football player I could find."

There was a long pause. Kelly was too shy to ask what she

was actually thinking, but this had no impact on James's big mouth. "What for?"

Maddy kept talking without looking at any of them. "You know when someone goes to buy a horse and they look at its teeth?"

"I do that with all my horses," James muttered.

Maddy ignored him. "You check its teeth and its heart and its hooves to see if it's good to buy. I felt like that's what they were doing to me. I didn't want to get bought."

19

Padma

The suburban streets of Wesley Falls were quiet and dark as the minivan headed east. Padma, at everyone's insistence, had taken the passenger's seat beside Casey. No one said much after finally leaving the mine, and Padma was sure it was because they were all thinking the same thing: Why did everything look normal? Why were fireflies still blinking and why weren't the streets filled with firetrucks and paramedics and screaming parents? Were kids still at the mine? Did their parents know what had happened to them yet?

Casey had gotten to the T at Willow and Main Street but hesitated. "Do you guys want to go to the diner? It's still open for another hour." There were murmurs of agreement. It was clear they needed to talk more.

Casey pulled into a parking spot, and Padma struggled to undo her seat belt. "Here," Casey said, reaching over to both unclick her seat belt and to open his glove compartment. He had a bottle of Tylenol inside, and he shook out two to give her.

They filed inside and claimed a semicircle-shaped booth. Nothing was out of the ordinary. The TV at the counter, which no one seemed to pay attention to except when there was a game on, was showing an old movie with the sound off. When a waitress came over and asked them what they wanted, they all seemed startled.

"Let's get some, um, milkshakes," Casey said to the waitress. His voice was strangled under the weight of trying to sound normal. "Maybe a couple orders of fries." She left and Kelly played with the container of sugar packets.

Finally, Padma spoke, turning to Maddy to ask what she had been wondering for the past ten minutes. "Do you think what just happened has something to do with the—the exam they gave you?"

Maddy blinked, surprised. "I don't know. I don't know what to think anymore about anything." She lowered her voice.

"But the exam *isn't real*." Padma flushed at having to talk about girl stuff with the boys present. "You can't check to see if a girl's a virgin. You could not have a hymen if you ride horses or use a tampon or something."

"You do both those things," Kelly pointed out.

"Why should we believe anything she says?" James asked. "She's one of them. Her parents are probably friends with those guys."

"They are," Maddy said, sounding confused.

"She's telling the truth," Casey said flatly. Padma, who sat next to him, craned her neck up to look at him, but he was staring stonily at the table. The waitress arrived with plates of fries and two milkshakes. Padma felt suddenly inappropriately hungry. She pulled some fries onto a plate and placed it between her and Jia, who still looked pale. Something about Jia wasn't right. Sure, there was no normal way to act after seeing what they just had, but she knew her friend and normally, when something unusual happened, Jia needed to talk it through exhaustively.

"What do you mean?" Kelly pressed.

Casey fiddled with a straw wrapper, refusing to look up. "Maybe something bigger is going on. I can't go into details... but I don't think Maddy is the only one."

Maddy sat up straight. "What do you mean?"

"I think other girls had the exam, too."

"Who?" James asked, the same time as Kelly said, "Why?"

Casey didn't say anything, but Padma saw his brow furrow with anger.

"Lexie," Maddy said quietly. Shocked, Padma stared at Casey for confirmation.

"I didn't say that!" he said.

"Who's Lexie?" James whispered to Kelly.

"His sister," Kelly said.

"It makes sense," Maddy said, the logic seeming to dawn on her. "Lexie's a Circle Girl."

"But not your level," Kelly said.

"She's the lowest level," Maddy said.

"I don't understand," James interrupted. "Why are they checking if you do this purity pledge and are always running around giving out pamphlets about abstinence?"

Maddy cawed laughter, then continued in a bitter tone. "Are you kidding? They are *constantly* looking at us. *Checking* us. Is that shirt too tight? We heard you went for a drive alone with a boy. Are you right with God?"

"Taylor once told me it was slutty to wear a two-piece bathing suit," Kelly said. "I was wearing a two-piece bathing suit at the time. She just said it to my face, like it wasn't rude."

"The Circle isn't a club," Maddy explained. She eschewed the plate of fries being passed around. "It's your entire life. All my social activities are at Golden Praise. All my friends, my parents' friends. They're on the board, you know. They make it your entire life. It's almost like…you're expected to have their worldview, and if you question it, it's the devil making you do it."

"You know the devil isn't real, right?" James said.

Maddy looked at him doubtfully, as if she wasn't sure if he was making fun of her. She opened her mouth to say something, then hesitated because the waitress was walking by their table. "I don't think it's just those three men that killed those kids. I think the church told them to."

"We don't know if anyone was killed," Padma said. "Maybe they survived? They could have broken legs or something. Maybe we should call 911?"

"They're dead," Jia said abruptly, loudly. She was staring out the window, her dark eyes fixed on some unknown distant point. "All of them."

Kelly met Padma's eyes across the table. *Is she okay?* Padma shook her head.

"It's too far down to the bottom," James said. "There's no way anyone could survive."

"*Is* there a bottom?" Maddy asked.

"Of course there is," he replied disdainfully. "It's a coal mine, not a gateway to hell."

"Are you sure?" Maddy asked.

"Hell isn't real, Maddy. That's just what they tell you at church. I agree with you on one thing, though, that Golden Praise shit is fucked. No offense, but it's totally a cult."

"None taken," Maddy said ruefully.

"It's like they run the entire town. Everything shuts down on Main Street when you have church, as if other people don't exist!" James said.

"My mom doesn't like how the church's involved in assemblies at school," Kelly said. "There shouldn't be church at public school."

"They don't see it that way," Maddy said. "There should be church everywhere."

"They keep coming after my mother," Jia said quietly. She didn't seem entirely snapped out of her reverie. "They don't like The Gem Shop so they always make these fake noise complaints or question our business license."

"Because they think the store's Satanic," Maddy said.

"You guys actually think there's a man with goat legs walking around telling people to buy crystals and incense that smells like BO?" James said.

"We don't sell incense that smells like BO," Jia said defensively, almost sounding like herself. Padma had the odd urge to giggle, and was promptly punished by a wave of pain in her chest.

"Try not to laugh. Or cough," Casey advised her.

"I have a job at the church," Padma said. "They've always been nice to me."

"Because they want you to join. Because of your father." Maddy stated this so casually that Padma was frightened.

"Have they been talking about my family?"

Maddy shrugged and watched Kelly dip a fry into her milkshake. "I've heard some people talking about how nice it would be if your father joined. Because he's a doctor and stuff."

"We're Hindu. We have a religion already."

"Can we stop with the Bible talk?" Casey said. "The only thing I care about is whether or not those guys saw us."

"It was too dark," Kelly said. James cut his eyes at her. She returned his look sheepishly, knowing that what she had said was more likely wishful thinking than anything else.

"I think we should go home and pretend we didn't see anything," Maddy said.

"We have to tell someone," Padma urged. "Our parents?" Jia brightened at this. Padma tried to remember the last time she had asked her parents, *really* asked them for help, not where something was in the kitchen or for a ride to the mall. It had been a while, but she didn't doubt that they would help if she came to them.

"Are you kidding? We *can't*," Maddy said. "My parents are Elders in the church."

"I don't want to think what my dad would do," Casey added.

"Then we call the police," Padma said.

"The police?" Maddy said. "Like Sheriff Springsteen, who comes to every church supper? Or how about the deputy, who's married to Miss Laurie?"

Padma's thoughts swam. All her life, she had been told that if something dangerous happened, call the police. She distinctly remembered in elementary school when 911 was finally rolled out in their town, how every child was taught to memorize the number. How could they see something like this and not do what she had been trained for years to do?

"All the cops in this town are crooked," James said. "They're constantly harassing us." It was clear what he meant by *us*. Burnouts. Kids who hung out at the Bad Park and smoked.

"Aren't you literally a drug dealer?" Maddy asked James.

"What about it?" he asked, deadpan.

"Just go home," Maddy urged them, trying to make eye contact with them all. "Go home and don't say anything, please. Tell people you were somewhere else if they ask."

"But people saw us at the party," Casey said.

"It might not matter," Maddy said. "Everyone is going to be telling lies, just for different reasons."

20

Casey

Casey palmed the wheel of the crowded minivan, glancing at his watch. Ten minutes to get rid of his asshole teammates before meeting everyone at the library. He had received a note in his mailbox this morning, written in girlish handwriting. Padma's, he supposed, because she lived across the cul-de-sac from him. It said simply *1 p.m., the library.*

His teammates were fresh with energy despite the off-season workout they had just endured. Fucking Kyle was always horsing around in the weight room—he never took anything seriously. Allen was fine, but Mike Brooks went to Golden Praise, so Casey carefully listened to everything he said. Not just about what had happened in the mine—because that was the topic of conversation right now—but anything having to do with the church. He was increasingly convinced that what had happened to Maddy was what had happened to Lexie, which was all the more disturbing. Did it happen to all of those Circle Girls?

"Nah, man," Mike said. He sat in one of the back bucket seats, leaning way forward because he wasn't wearing his seat belt. "It was some ghosts and shit. That place is haunted."

"Ghosts aren't real, loser," Allen said. They were talking about one of the kids who was rumored to have died in the mine—Eddie something.

"I'm telling you," Kyle said, "people are saying they were cracked out on drugs and jumped."

"What people?" Allen asked.

"People."

"What for?" Casey asked.

Kyle shrugged. "Fucking fag rage, I don't know."

"People *died*, you piece of shit!" Casey yelled. He glared at Kyle, who cowered in the passenger seat beside him. "They're *dead*. They died a horrible death."

"Dude, why are you being so *sensitive*?" Kyle asked, shooting a bewildered look toward the back of the minivan for support.

"Because people fucking dying is sad! People dying is *wrong*, do you get that, dumbass?" Another bewildered look. No, he didn't get it. People dying wasn't a tragedy because they weren't people like *him*. "All right, get the fuck out of my car. I have shit to do." The players scrambled out, Kyle muttering about how Casey probably had his period.

Casey drove for another few minutes to cool down, then parked behind the library where no one would spot the minivan from the road. Why on earth was the library even open during the summer? Not that he spent that much time there when school was in session. At least it had air-conditioning, the blast of artificial air welcoming him as he stepped inside.

He found the rest of his capstone group settled around a long table in one of the private study rooms, and he didn't pass a single soul on his way there. "Hey," he said, closing the door. "What's everyone heard?"

"There's a list," Maddy said grimly as she pushed a sheet of loose-leaf across the table. Apparently, they had all looked at it before Casey arrived. He scanned over the names, all of which were familiar, but none whom he knew personally.

"They're all burnouts," James said. He had a strange look on his face. "All of them."

"Were they your friends?" Casey asked, not sure how to respond.

"Not exactly," James said. "I just sold Ricky a fake ID. Gordy and Eddie were younger but hung out in the park. Ann used to go out with Ricky. JJ dropped out of high school last year. I think she works at the chicken plant. John is the guy who set off the stink bomb at prom that one time."

"Do you think he had the ID on him?" Kelly said.

"Why do—" James broke off, his eyes widening. "You think people are going to think I'm connected to all this just because he had an ID on him?"

"Everyone knows you make those IDs," Kelly said.

He looked at her as if she had just betrayed him. "There's like fifty kids at school with IDs from me! It doesn't mean anything!" James struck Casey as someone who would rather die than look afraid. He didn't cringe away when guys bullied him, but gave the finger or had some comeback even if it meant he was going to get punched in the face. So it scared Casey that James looked scared.

Kelly continued. "They'll look at the…bodies and ask what happened. Then they'll look through their stuff. And if they find the ID and ask who made it, wouldn't your name come up?"

"Why the fuck are you asking me?" James near shouted.

"I think we should go to the police. They have to uphold the law," Padma said.

Maddy, who was sitting beside her, laughed. "Brian's friend Greg got pulled over three times for drunk driving when he was a senior—guess who never got in trouble. His parents are Elders in the church like mine."

"What's an Elder?" James asked. Casey had heard his parents use the word in reference to Coach being an Elder, but had never given it much thought.

"The Elders lead the church. Most of them come from the families that go back to when Wesley Falls was founded." Her hand went absently to her Circle Girl pin. Casey was surprised she was still wearing it.

"Lexie won't wear her pin," he said. Maddy looked at him, the harsh look on her face softened. "She's too angry."

"I'm angry," Maddy said quietly, staring down at the table.

"Um… Madds, you're about to get angrier," Casey said. She looked up. "Scott's telling everyone you slept with him. Or at least everyone on the team for the past two weeks." Maddy closed her eyes and shook her head.

"Scott, the one who likes you?" Jia asked, looking at Kelly.

"Oh, I see," James said, an edge to his voice. He stared straight at Maddy, who was directly across from him at the long table, each of them at a head. "Scott likes Kelly instead of you, so you decide to be a bitch to her and turn all your little friends against her?"

"He was mean to me after," Maddy said.

"How is that Kelly's fault?" James shot back.

"It's not. I was trying to protect her, to tell her to stay away from him—" Maddy tried.

"You could have just said it, Maddy. You could have just said he's a bad guy," Kelly said.

Padma's head whipped back and forth as if watching a tennis game. Casey felt uncomfortable, as he typically did when there was any kind of social confrontation.

"You and your stupid Circle Girls make everything so fucking miserable," James said. "Like high school doesn't suck enough?"

"I—"

"Some dumbshit likes Kelly instead of you and you freeze her out. Some girl comes in with the wrong shoes and it's *nice shoes* all day. Unless someone's exactly like you, you make everyone feel like shit." Maddy's eyes filled with tears, but James wasn't done. "You think people can't see how you single people out and attack them?" He pointed suddenly—with vehemence—at Padma and Jia. "What'd those two ever do to you? Literally, what have they done other than be the only kids who aren't white?"

Padma, her eyes huge, looked at Jia, then Maddy for response.

James continued even though Kelly put a hand on his arm to stop him. "And we're supposed to feel bad for you because you just found out your precious church sucks? You *did* this." He made a vague gesture, encompassing not just the library, but the entire town. "You made a ladder where you shit on everyone below you for fun."

"You're right," Maddy said, to everyone's surprise. A tear dripped off her face onto the table. Casey felt bad for her, but everything James said was true. "That's exactly what we do." She looked down, thinking. "It *is* like a ladder. They never say it explicitly, but it's under everything they teach us. That there are good people and bad people, and you don't want to be one of the bad people. There's only one way to be."

"A dog doctor touching my sister is not the way to be," Casey said.

"I know, Casey," Maddy said.

"This isn't a good time to fight," Jia said. "Not when we have to figure out what to do about the mine."

"We should go to the police," Padma said. "When you witness a crime, you report it."

"I agree," Jia said. With the look they exchanged, Casey got the sense that they had agreed upon this in private before the meeting.

"We're withholding evidence that they need to solve the crime," Padma said.

"You guys don't get it," Maddy said. *"Every single authority figure in this town* is associated with the church. Sheriff Springsteen. The deputy. The—"

"It can't be *all* of them," Padma said.

"Why don't we vote?" Casey said, wanting the argument to end. "Who votes we go to the police?" Jia and Padma raised their hands along with Casey, while Kelly did so more slowly, cringing as James looked at her with exasperation.

"I'm sorry, but Padma made a good point. They can't be all bad, and we have to tell an adult," Kelly said, more to James than everyone else.

"Well, I vote no," James said.

"Me, too," Maddy said, "but I should get an extra vote." Kelly let out a bitter laugh. "I'm the only one who really understands this town."

"So who should talk to the police?" Padma was already moving on. Casey saw James and Maddy, unlikely allies, look at each other from across the table.

"Who would they trust the most?" Jia asked. The four yes votes discussed this while James and Maddy kept trying to interject about it being a bad idea before they decided on Casey and Kelly. Casey knew that people liked and respected him because of football. Kelly was the innocuous sort of girl who got good grades and would return a lost wallet. Neither would be suspected of concocting a lie. Then they decided that Casey and Kelly should leave right then and head to the police station.

"This is madness," James called at their backs as they left together.

★ ★ ★

But it didn't seem like madness, more like the most consequential thing Casey would ever do. They now knew six people had been killed, and he was an eyewitness. People were going to say, why didn't you come forward sooner, it's been a full twenty-four hours, and he wouldn't have a good answer other than he was scared. Kelly fidgeted in the chair beside him. They had walked into the police station and Casey had said they had information about the mine party. They were put into a small office and told to wait.

"James is mad at me, but I had to vote against him," she whispered. "Because if we don't tell anyone what we saw—"

"I know."

A man came in, Officer David Skeen. He had intelligent, kind eyes and immediately took a notebook out. "My understanding is that you two were at the mine party?"

"Yes, sir. We saw what happened."

"I'm going to take a lot of notes so talk slowly," he said, his pen poised. This made Casey feel better—he was listening. They recounted that they had been at the party, Casey doing most of the talking, with Kelly occasionally chiming in. Skeen interrupted them for a few details—the exact time, who had been there. The collapse had been chaotic—it was hard to say exactly what had happened or why, but then Casey found himself stuttering when he got to the bad part of the story. Should he say that it was James who led them out of the third chamber? Maybe not since he was adamant about not going to the police.

Kelly took over. "We found our way out of the chamber— there was another path to the side. We went around and kind of up and over the Heart."

"Who's we? You two?"

"Me and Casey," she lied glibly, her brown eyes wide and mouth set in a firm line. "We were up on this path that was high, and we could see down to the Heart path. Officer Skeen, we saw what happened to those kids."

He looked up at her, his pen poised on his pad.

She swallowed audibly. "We saw three men throwing them into the Heart."

"Are you sure? It must have been dark."

"They had flashlights, so we could see them," Casey said.

Skeen tapped his pen against his pad, once, twice, three times. Slowly, his gaze went back to them. "Are you *sure* that's what you saw?"

Casey might have been able to convince himself that the way he said it wasn't strange if Kelly hadn't dug one of her fingernails into his thigh. *If I was trying to solve a murder, and someone walked right up to me and told me that they saw it, is that what I would say?* "Well—" he stumbled.

"It can be easy to get confused with so much chaos going on. Were you guys drinking?"

"Um," Kelly said.

"It's okay, I won't arrest you for drinking. I understand kids get together and have a good time. But alcohol mixed with a cave-in must have been pretty disorienting."

"We were drinking," Casey admitted.

Officer Skeen closed his notebook. "You kids have had quite a fright."

Kelly shot Casey a desperate look. One that said, *Maddy was right. We've made a terrible mistake.* Casey took the cue, pulling Kelly up by the elbow. "Well, we've taken up enough of your time. Sorry about all this." They left as quickly as they could, wanting to run, but keeping themselves in check despite a growing uneasiness of what had just happened.

21

Maddy

Maddy hung up her phone, furious. Her cordless phone sat in its receiver, looking perky and sinister. She had her own phone line, which she yanked out of the jack. This was the sixth phone call she'd had about the mine party. First, it was Erika—a fellow member of the choir who was the first person to break the official news. "Some kids *died* at that party!" she had squealed with a mixture of glee and horror. Of course, Erika had not been at the party; Maddy hadn't seen any members of the Youth Fellowship there. She lied easily on the phone, playing dumb. Next came a three-way call with Lisa and Meghan, a pair she occasionally consorted with when she was mad at Taylor and Ashley. Gossip and more gossip, but it was strange that she hadn't received a call from either Taylor or Ashley, her supposed best friends. She couldn't imagine any social situation that they didn't immediately want to dissect like hyenas picking apart a corpse.

Stranger still, and at this point disturbing, was that since the news had broken all over town that six high school students had died in the mine, her parents had not said a single word about it to her. Not a judgmental, "Well, that's what happens when you ignore signs," or a pious request that they pray together. Maddy kept popping downstairs whenever she heard her parents in the living room or kitchen, waiting for them to say something. Even a harsh question would have brought her some relief.

But now everything she believed before was like a sheet of ice—once something hit it hard enough for cracks to appear, any bit of weight on the ice would crack it further. It was hard to deny that she had been questioning things all along about Golden Praise.

Now that the ice was cracked, she could see that it was abnormal that *her* phone was ringing off the hook while her parents' wasn't. In a small town, there was nothing that didn't go without considerable gossip. Like when Mrs. Hobsen had an affair with the gym teacher, or when several families in the church got tricked by an Amway scheme.

Maybe her parents thought the story would scare her, much like their fear that any movie rated PG-13 or higher contained content that would give her nightmares. They did not let her see a Meg Ryan movie called *French Kiss* despite her insistence that the movie was called that because it took place in France. Why, her mother asked suspiciously, did she want to see a movie that took place in France?

Maddy left the house for choir practice on her bike. Normally, she would have parked at the bike racks beside the Rec Building, but poking around Central, which was where she had overheard adults talking about the mine right before the party, might prove more valuable. To the left of the enormous Sanctuary enclosure were all the administrative offices. In this maze of offices was where her medical exam at the hands of Dr. Foy had taken place, right behind Jane Merrick's office. Maddy lingered there as long as she dared, pretending to readjust her sneaker because it was the closest she could come to putting her head against the closed door. Miss Merrick typically had her door closed—and locked—and it didn't sound like there was anyone inside.

Miss Laurie was Jane Merrick's sister, which often surprised people if they didn't know the Merrick family. Along with Maddy's family, the Merricks were one of the founding families, and while Jane was extremely influential in the church, she wasn't actually an Elder. Maddy wondered if this was solely because she wasn't married.

Both of Maddy's parents were part of the circle of Elders who were linked back to the town's founding. Miss Laurie had gotten married in her twenties while Jane Merrick never did and there their two paths diverged. Miss Laurie was viewed as a model for what a young Christian woman should be: she met her husband at junior college, she remained attractive and thin, her hair and nails always done, she kept a beautiful house. This was why she had been chosen to lead the LifeGroup at Golden Praise for young women.

In the past, Maddy had assumed she would become the next Miss Laurie. She and Brian would have stayed together and both attended Penn State, then they would have gotten married and bought their own house in town. Maddy would be thin and wear a big glittering wedding ring and lead the church choir and maybe a LifeGroup of her own.

Where in this equation is a vet looking at my private parts? Maddy wondered as she entered the Rec Building, then the choir room. Everyone was there already, including Taylor and Ashley, but neither made eye contact with her even though they hadn't spoken since the morning of the party. That wasn't a good sign— they couldn't know she had been at the party, could they?

There was barely any time to think about this because Mr. Janger, the choir director, was already starting. He led them in warm-ups and then discussed what the program would be for the next service.

"So Jim, we'll have you do the first solo," Mr. Janger said without looking up from his sheet music. "And Ashley, you'll do the other solo."

Maddy froze. She had never not gotten a solo in a church service, not for as long as she could remember, except for the scant few times when she had lost her voice or wasn't feeling well. Sure, there had been individual *songs* where she hadn't gotten a solo, but the choir sang multiple songs at each service, and she was always featured at some point. Taylor had once made a nasty comment that this was because her parents were Elders, and Maddy had snapped back with the facts: Maddy had also been selected for All-State twice for high school chorus—which had nothing to do with church. And *Ashley* was getting a solo? It wasn't just that Maddy was a better singer, but that Ashley wasn't good at all.

Maddy didn't move, forcing a benign smile, pretending she couldn't see people shooting looks at her. Maybe they gave her the benefit of the doubt and assumed she had a cough or vocal cord exhaustion. She endured the rest of practice and planned to flee the second they were done to avoid any wide-eyed questioning from Taylor. Maddy knew that Taylor's worship of her was a double-edged sword: she would buy the same clothes Maddy had, and do all the same activities, but if she saw cracks in the facade, she derived pleasure in exploiting them. When Maddy started going out with Brian, she had been the first of the Circle Girls to have a boyfriend. This had invited snide comments from Taylor to Ashley about how Maddy was ditching them, that Maddy better be careful, because *you know how boys are—* especially older boys.

But Maddy's plans were foiled when just as practice was wrapping up, Mr. Janger asked her to stay behind. Taylor and Ashley left without even looking at her, and Maddy approached the piano with trepidation. Mr. Janger was one of the few adults at Golden Praise, along with Pastor himself, who never had a negative word to say to her. If anything, Mr. Janger probably praised her more than anyone. She could think of multiple times when after responding to his vocal instruction, he shouted triumphantly, "Yes!" and she would glow with pride and satisfaction and maybe a little love.

"Miss Merrick wanted to see you," Mr. Janger almost mumbled, looking down at his piano where he was making a notation on sheet music. Maddy stared at him for a moment, puzzled as to why he wouldn't look at her, then Jane Merrick appeared at the door. Some of the harshest comments she had ever received about her clothes were passed to her parents from Jane Merrick. Comments Maddy had made during LifeGroup with Miss Laurie that she thought were private were passed to Jane, who then told her mom. It was not a private, sacred space, as a construction paper sign on the wall said at LifeGroup.

But Miss Merrick didn't have her standard smile pasted to her face that she reserved for dealing with Maddy. The sort of smile that said, "I think you are a bad girl but your parents are important so I will at least pretend to withhold my judgment."

Jane Merrick led them down a few twists and turns in the hallway till they got to the Youth Fellowship office where Miss Laurie and Taylor were already waiting. Miss Laurie leaned her butt against her desk in a typical stance, and Taylor stood to the side, a tiny smile on her face. Jane closed the door and went around to sit at the desk. Maddy looked at them all expectantly, but no one said a word.

"Maddison honey, do you have anything to tell us?" Miss Laurie said. She had her head cocked to the side, her voice dripping with that fake, slightly Southern accent.

Do they know about the party? Maddy thought with alarm. "I… About what?"

"Has anything happened recently that we should know about?" Jane asked. Her mouth with its nearly nonexistent lips was pressed into a perfectly flat line.

"No…?"

Miss Laurie stepped forward, her heels making a soft clicking noise against the floor. The shoes made her tower over Maddy, who looked up at her face with its perfectly drawn eyeliner, the blush and lipstick that was methodically applied every single day. Maddy resisted the urge to step backward. Miss Laurie reached out with one manicured nail and pressed it against Maddy's Circle Girl pin. "You know what this pin means, Maddy?"

"Yes."

Miss Laurie wiggled her finger against the pin. "Tell me what it means."

"It means I made a vow to God and myself and my family that I'll wait till marriage. That I'll be pure."

"Wait till marriage for what?"

The blank look in Miss Laurie's eyes was frightening. Maddy flushed. "For sex."

"Did you do that, Maddy?" Jane Merrick asked from behind Miss Laurie.

"Did you keep that sacred promise?" Miss Laurie added.

Maddy stepped back, anger and horror filling her. She resisted the urge to look at Taylor, who in her peripheral vision looked smug. That was why Taylor was here. Taylor had told. But how had she even found out? "Yes," Maddy lied.

"She's lying," Taylor piped up. "She's lying, Miss Laurie!" Maddy allowed herself to look at her erstwhile friend. Taylor's eyes were huge with piety, maybe even shiny from tears. But beneath that mask, Maddy could see secret glee. "I didn't want to believe it, because Maddy's a diamond Circle Girl, and I always looked up to her. But that's why I had to tell you what I heard."

What she had heard. Scott, that idiot Scott. Why had she, in her panic, picked Scott to sleep with? Two weeks before the last day of school and shortly after her veterinary exam, she had been walking home from Wiley's Bar, the one place in town she would occasionally escape to because no one from Golden Praise would ever go there. While it wasn't exactly welcoming there, it was dark, and the bartender would always give her a Shirley Temple and tell her to stay away from the truckers. She had secretly been hoping that there would be a magical man there—someone just stopping by on his way out of town, someone who would never talk to anyone in town. Someone who would be kind to her and have a flirty conversation with her before somehow, magically, they would have sex, because underneath the anger about the virginity exam, she had a panicky intuition that if she had sex, she might gain control of a situation she didn't understand. But there hadn't been any magical man there that night at Wiley's, so she started to walk home.

Scott, driving by in his dad's Honda, had seen her on the sidewalk and asked if she wanted a ride. She got into the car. Scott liked her, she knew. He was cute and nice enough. Did he want to have sex with her? Probably, because according to what she had been taught, boys were perpetually on a tightrope of sexual desire, where anything from pornography to an exposed shoulder could push them toward sin.

How much had she even reasoned through the decision to sleep with Scott that night? Beneath the anger at all the jabs that had been directed at her about her sexuality, that it was out of control and wrong somehow, underneath that was the tangle of confused feelings that was her *actual* sexuality, a thing that had never been given space to breathe. It was within her when she and Brian were going out and they would kiss and a part of her wanted more, wanted his hands on her even though she knew it was wrong and they should stop. It was this part of her that wondered what sex felt like, was it really a big deal, would there be a giant record scratch if it happened?

Scott was only the second person she kissed, so it felt strange but also a little exciting. But it wasn't like it was in the movies where romantic shots of the couple were presented, then fade to black. He had to come up with an excuse for why she should come to his house and to his room, and she had to pretend about the excuse, too, when really the point was getting to his bedroom while his parents were away for the weekend.

She had thought that sex must be really good since it was constantly forbidden—like chocolate cake. What made it good was its density in calories, its unabashed celebration of fat and sugar. But while she had felt desire at times during the evening, it all was weaved in with shame, with anger, with the question of, was it supposed to feel this way? It had hurt almost the entire time.

Afterward she had felt let down. Why was *this* the sin that got all the attention?

Scott had been nice that night, driving her home afterward and saying he wouldn't tell anyone. But after that, he had ignored her at school. It wasn't as if she had been trying to start a relationship with him, but it felt as if maybe he thought she was and was trying to put her off. Or maybe after seeing her naked, he was disgusted by her body. Or maybe all the things Miss Laurie said were true—that boys wanted sex but if they got it they wouldn't respect you.

"People are always going to make up things," Maddy said finally.

"Maddy, this pin is a promise before God," Miss Laurie said, her voice dripping with noxious pity. "A promise to your family and your community. When you bring shame on yourself, you bring shame to the community."

Maddy's eyes filled with tears despite her desperation to show no emotion in front of them. Shame? What about what they did to her? "I didn't do anything wrong." *You did.* That exam was wrong—she knew this deeply in her heart of hearts. It was one thing to argue about what exactly the Bible meant in a specific passage; it was another when something happened that she knew, body and soul, was *wrong* and *bad* and *humiliating.*

Miss Laurie shook her head. "I'm just so disappointed in you. This entire community had such great plans for you. Well, now I just don't know what…" She turned away, as if overcome with emotion.

"My pin means everything to me," Taylor said. When Maddy looked at her through her tears, she saw that Taylor had both her hands over her Circle Girl pin. "I just keep thinking about all the conversations we've ever had. I thought we were in the same place, spiritually. I feel…betrayed." If Maddy could have stabbed Taylor with her eyes, she would have. Then Miss Laurie was touching her, trying to remove the Circle Girl pin from Maddy's shirt.

"You know you're not fit to wear this, sweetie."

"This isn't fair!" Maddy said, batting Miss Laurie's hands away, who seemed startled by her use of force.

"It's plenty fair, Maddy. You know what you did. We're all going to have to talk about this."

We? We who? What did that mean? LifeGroup? A room full of girls judging her, Taylor squirming with pleasure? *Her parents?* Dear God, they were going to tell her parents.

"No!" she shouted, her hands protectively cupping her pin. She ran from the room, not knowing where to go. Was there anywhere in this town where people wouldn't be like them? She stumbled out the back door of the Rec Building, her tears making the sunlight seem unnaturally bright. This was *wrong* and she needed help.

Maddy's eyes went to the one path on Golden Praise's campus that wasn't paved, a simple clay path snaking its way through the grass. The pastor's house was at the end of that path, hidden behind a hill. The house, like the man, was surrounded in mystique, like it was not a regular house where people microwaved soup and watched TV. It was sacred territory—Maddy had never heard of even the uppermost echelons of the church being invited there.

Maddy raced up the pathway without thinking. Pastor had never done anything strange to her, never made her feel bad. He preached words of love, not the crap Miss Laurie and Jane Merrick peddled. He had never humiliated her. He was the head of the entire church—maybe he didn't know what was going on under his own nose. He could do anything—he could overturn the whole thing, sanctify her pin, fire the Merricks, make Taylor go away. She would do anything for him to undo the past few weeks. Maybe he would be enraged if he found out about the exam—exams! Plural! Casey had said she wasn't the only one!

Pastor's house was grander than any house in town, a Victorian with three floors and an ornate carved wooden door—an unlocked door. She ran through a front hallway, then an immaculate kitchen with no hint of food or coffee stains. "Pastor!" she called. "Hello? Please!" She ran through a simple living room, which featured new-looking couches and a table, but no TV.

She circled back to the foyer, standing on the white marble and looking up the curving staircase to the second and third floors. That she had entered the house—screaming—was already a transgression, but somehow going upstairs seemed worse, more of an invasion into his privacy. "Pastor!" she called again.

Maddy thought she heard someone speaking toward the back of the house and raced down the hallway. She made a sharp turn toward the kitchen and nearly ran into the pastor. Though it was a weekday with no service, he still wore his characteristic black, though this time his black pants and blazer were set off with an immaculately white shirt. She had only been this close to Pastor a dozen times—the instances when he had come to her house for dinner, the few times that choir or Fellowship activities were interrupted with a surprise visit from him. She never saw him relaxing at a coffee shop or eating at the diner, and he always seemed to have an entourage surrounding him, people like her parents and Jane Merrick.

He looked at her with surprise, no doubt wondering what she was doing in his house.

Maddy burst into tears—she'd made a mess of everything. Now she was embarrassing herself in front of the pastor. She tried to get ahold of her crying but it only grew worse, making it hard to breathe.

"Oh, no," she heard him say softly. She didn't hear him step forward, but then found herself being taken into his arms as he hugged her. At first, she was stunned, not able to comprehend that this person who had always been behind a velvet rope was touching her, that while running into his house had been a total violation of privacy, he didn't seem to care. But then the hug overtook her. In the simple act of being held, she tried to remember when the last time was that someone had comforted her like this. She hugged her parents, but it always seemed perfunctory. She hugged people at lock-ins and in LifeGroup but what did that even mean if they were rats like Taylor? When had someone ever simply held her and given her comfort while also giving her the space to express her emotions without apology? How strange to know that he was solid, that his chest also moved with breath, that he was an actual human being who lived in this house. His smell also struck her—his clothes were immaculate and had the faint scent of clean laundry, but there was something under that. He smelled like a match that had just been struck.

By then, her sobs had died down but tears were still sliding down her face. Gently, Pastor put his hands on her shoulders and held her back so he could look at her. "My child, what is wrong?"

She wanted to tell him everything, but found herself unable to talk about the exam, the humiliating confrontation with the Merricks, what she had seen happen in the mine, but instead she talked about how they took her solo away, babbling about how she had sinned. She fell silent, realizing that he hadn't responded the typical way adults did when she cried, either moving to comfort her or to dismiss her for being too emotional. He was still holding her gently by the shoulders, staring intently at her. Her gaze flitted across his face, the intimacy of looking directly into his eyes too great for her to bear. Pastor Jim Preiss was generically handsome in a vague sort of way. An expressive mouth, a white smile. Friendly crinkles at the corners of his eyes. But what drew people to him was something greater than that, something that couldn't be captured in a picture, or maybe even with words. He simply commanded attention when he was around.

Even if she didn't want to look into his eyes, she found herself doing so. They were very dark, black even. Like bottomless pools to drown in. Like there was a black hole behind them that had already taken out all the stars. It was as if something invisible came from his eyes and wrapped around her just as his arms had a moment ago, pulling her toward him. *Tell me*, those eyes said. Tell me everything. Bear your heart. Throw yourself off the precipice, and I will take care of all.

Maddy, half in a dream, opened her mouth.

"What!"

"Maddison Wesley, get back here this instant!"

Maddy looked across the kitchen and saw the Merricks. After she had stormed off, they must have figured out where she went and followed. Miss Laurie stalked forward and grabbed her by the arm, her nails digging into Maddy's flesh. "You think you can just barge in here like an animal?" She dragged Maddy toward the sliding glass doors. Miss Laurie paused for a moment—Maddy was shocked at the fury written on the woman's face—and wrenched the Circle Girl pin off Maddy's shirt. It pinged on the tiled floor and Maddy glanced up and at Pastor in shame.

In the years that followed, Maddy often replayed the memory in her head, trying to figure out exactly what emotion she saw on his face, because in the moment, in the panic of everything, she didn't understand it. Miss Laurie was dragging her off and Pastor was standing halfway across the room, a momentary expression passing over his face, but lingering in his dark eyes. The look, she realized much later, hadn't been directed at her as she thought it was at the time, but at the Merricks. There was something complicated going on that she didn't understand, some dynamic, but in that split second, he looked annoyed.

22

James

Kelly edged open the door to her bedroom, peeking her head out, and James watched from across the room. Kelly's bedroom was directly above the kitchen, which made it good for eavesdropping if anyone was down there. They had already gotten interrogated by the Harpies the moment they found out—a full day later, toward the evening—about the party and the "accident." Kelly had played this well, James thought, widening her eyes and playing dumb, giving her sisters the chance to fill her in on everything they knew. It gave him and Kelly a sense of what everyone in town was spreading around. Her parents had no additional information, remarking that it was awful, and they really ought to block off the entrances to the mine for good.

"I think everyone's gone," Kelly said.

"I can't hear anything," James said, getting up. He went over to the TV and turned it on, Milky following him. They had periodically been checking the news, but so far the story hadn't been covered. After lunch Kelly signed on to AOL to see if Maddy or Padma were around. As soon as she did, an IM appeared:

SavageGarden15: have you heard anything?

"It's Padma," Kelly explained to James. He sat behind her on her bed, leaning forward so he could read the conversation between the two girls.

Kellybelly80: Have you heard anything?

SavageGarden15: Just that the victims names are out.

SavageGarden15: My dad said he heard it was a SITUATION when they got down there

Kellybelly80: who got where?

SavageGarden15: when the police or paramedics got to the bottom of the mine. He said it was messy.

Kellybelly80: oh.

Kellybelly80: are you ok?

SavageGarden15: I guess. Are you?

Kellybelly80: James is with me. Jia is with you?

SavageGarden15: yeah she wants to say hi.

SavageGarden15: hi. this is jia

Kellybelly80: hi. R you ok?

There was a long pause.

SavageGarden15: No.

They both stared at the computer, not sure of what to say, but then Padma abruptly disappeared, the computer making a sound effect. "She gets kicked off sometimes when her brother picks up the phone," Kelly explained. "Do you think Jia was acting weird the night of the party?"

James went over to the window and cracked it open. The air-conditioning was on, but it was the only way she would let him smoke. "I don't know her as well as you do...why do you ask?"

"We were all like panicking and running around but she was *zoned out*. She barely talked when we were hiding and then she was kind of scary at the diner, remember?"

James considered this as he blew smoke out the window. Jia had always been a cheerful girl wearing bright colors at school. "I'm not sure how you're supposed to act after seeing something like that... But before," he said, remembering suddenly as he turned to face Kelly. "Right when the collapse happened, I was looking around to see where you all were. She was standing at the far side of the cave, the east side, just staring at the wall."

"Was something there? I couldn't see anything."

James shook his head. "The entrance to the Heart path is north. The blocked off entrance is south. There's two small off-shoots besides those to get out of that chamber. The one I took you out and this other one that's really tight and goes straight to the Heart. I could have sworn that was right where she was standing."

"Jia doesn't strike me as the sort of person who's done a lot of mine exploring," Kelly remarked, stroking Milky's fur.

"Agreed. You think we can sneak out? I'm getting hungry."

They were walking home with a meatball sub from Del Monico's when James noticed a car half a block behind them driving slowly. Shit. A police car. He jabbed Kelly with his elbow. "I think they're following us."

She tried to be subtle about looking behind her but failed. "What do we do?" she whispered.

"Act normal. We're not doing anything wrong."

They did walk faster, though. The car continued to creep along, eventually coming so close that they could see the man inside—Jed Yacobi, a cop James had seen more than a few times down at the Bad Park. He would show up to shoo people away or demand to search their bags. He struck James as the sort of man who as a boy took distinct pleasure in being hall monitor.

"He's *staring* at us," Kelly whispered.

"Just pretend he isn't there."

Only that became impossible when they needed to cross the street. Yacobi promptly cut the car in front of them, blocking their path, and got out of his car. "Mind if I ask you a few questions?" His eyes were on James, not Kelly.

"It's a free country," James said, still moving. Yacobi began to walk beside them. He had a thick blond mustache and was wearing mirrored sunglasses that made him look like a dumbass.

"Heard there was quite a party on Friday," Yacobi said.

James could feel rather than see Kelly become tense. He tried to mentally message her to not give anything away. She wasn't used to goons like this harassing her, but he was. "I wouldn't know about it."

"You weren't there? At the mine?"

"Nah."

"That's funny."

"Why would that be funny?"

"Sure you weren't there?"

"Very sure."

"Because some people thought they saw you there."

"They thought wrong."

"You didn't sell some weed to anybody?"

"Selling marijuana is illegal, sir."

"You think this is funny?"

"I never said it was."

"Maybe you should come down to the station."

"Is he under arrest?" Kelly asked, her tone belligerent. She was making a mistake, though, making direct eye contact with Yacobi. Sure, James had been a pissant to cops more than once, but you couldn't look them in the face while doing it. Kelly had seen one too many episodes of *Law & Order* and thought she knew about the Constitution. "Because you can't harass him."

"No one's talking to you," Yacobi snapped. "You want to

make things easier for yourself, James, and just tell me about Friday night?"

"I was at home."

"You weren't at the party?"

"No, sir."

"That's strange because there were pictures taken at that party, and I saw a real nice one with you in the background."

Could he be lying? Someone might have had a camera, but would they have developed the pictures already? There was the One Hour Foto kiosk in the center of the parking lot at the middle of Main Street, but it was only ever sporadically open. Someone could have had a Polaroid camera, though. "I mean, maybe I was there."

"So you were there?"

"Um. Yes."

"So you admit it?"

"I *said* yes."

"So you admit you lied about being there."

James floundered, not sure how to respond. By now they had reached Kelly's front lawn.

"You know that lying to a police officer is a federal offense?" Yacobi said.

"Why would it be a federal offense rather than a local offense?" Kelly chimed in.

"Kelly Boyle, you have better things to do than hang out with trash like this—"

Kelly opened her mouth, the fury written plainly on her face, but froze when she saw the front door of James's trailer burst open. Rick strode out wearing jeans and a dirty undershirt. Rick-the-Dick hated cops, probably more than James did, because he had been arrested more than once and inherently distrusted a crooked system that had somehow relegated him to a deadbeat lifestyle.

"You wanna explain to me why you're harassing my boy?" Rick shouted. In no time, he had gotten into Yacobi's face. Interesting that when it served Rick's purposes, he would say things like "my boy" when more often it was "that kid of yours" to Lisa, which wasn't fair because Lisa wasn't his mother but his aunt. And it's not as if Lisa seemed to take any ownership of James. He was merely the living accessory that had come with the trailer after his mother died.

"Why don't you tell me? Your *boy* here was at a party where things got violent."

James would guess that Rick had no idea that six kids had died a few days ago—he wasn't the sort to read the news or chat with people in town or really do anything other than be a loser. Rick glanced at James before he unleashed a tirade on the cop, but that glance had been enough. Yes, in any confrontation with the cops, Rick would take the other side based on principle, but that didn't mean there wouldn't be hell to pay once Yacobi was gone and James was back inside the claustrophobic trailer with nowhere to hide.

As the back and forth continued between Rick and Yacobi, it became apparent that perhaps Kelly had been right: they couldn't question him indefinitely and they didn't have enough to force him to the police station. Rick strutted a few steps as Yacobi went back to his car and drove off. Then his eyes turned to James.

"We were just on our way out, Rick," Kelly said suddenly, her voice chirpy. "Jamie's aunt asked us to pick up her prescription for her right away."

This was a lie, but it effectively distracted Rick, who if James had to guess, had just woken up from a nap and had no idea where Lisa was if she wasn't in the trailer. He looked like he wanted to probe more, but he also probably understood that anything that stood in the way between Lisa and a little orange bottle was very bad indeed. His expression changed and James realized that the look Rick was giving Kelly was most definitely a leer. Kelly seemed to want to shrink inside herself, folding her arms across her chest while also not wanting it to look like that was how she was feeling.

Of all the layers of embarrassment associated with his home life, that Kelly could peek into it at times was the worst. It was one thing for James to be in his own bubble, because that was *private*; yes, Rick and Lisa had outrageous fights, sometimes wavering into violence, but as long as no one saw it he could pretend it wasn't happening. But given that Kelly was closer to him than anyone else, sometimes he couldn't hide things from her. Like the fact that Rick was gross enough to be giving her the eye even though he had first met her in her prepubescent days. She wore the same summer uniform that every girl in town wore: jean cutoff shorts and a T-shirt, but Rick was looking at her like she was prancing around in a bikini.

"We'll be back real soon," Kelly said. James could hear the forced lightness in her tone and it stabbed at his heart. She understood that they would not be back *real soon*—they would go somewhere, and he would probably sneak through her window at night so that he could avoid Rick once he found out that they had lied about the prescription.

They began to walk back toward the direction of Main Street. "Do you think it's true? Do you think there are pictures?" Kelly asked.

"I didn't see anyone taking pictures. Wouldn't we remember a flash? I think he was lying."

"Police aren't allowed to lie."

"I think they are."

Kelly absently stepped off the road and onto the sidewalk because a car was driving toward them. The car slowed as it passed them—James couldn't see the person driving, but it seemed deliberate rather than coincidental. Kelly was saying something, but James couldn't pay attention because just for a moment, he could see the person in the car looking directly at him, then the car sped off. "You need to go," he said.

"What!"

"That person was staring at me. Yacobi was acting like I did something wrong." He stopped—they were only half a block from Main Street. "If people are talking about me, we shouldn't be seen together."

"I—"

"No one knows you were with me at the party. Go home

or see if you can find Maddy or something and find out what people are saying. I'll go into town."

She looked frustrated—the look she got on her face when she figured out that he was right. "Here, you take it," she said, shoving the meatball sub into his hands.

He felt a flicker of shame as he took it and began to walk. When he was younger, he got used to eating meals alongside Kelly at her house. But he would never take something from the kitchen if Kelly wasn't eating, too. He was used to Kelly being the one who brought snacks if they were going to spend a summer day at the lake, because her house was constantly stocked with milk, deli meat, Dunkaroos, every variety of fruit. Her mom cut up apples for her. It had occurred to him more than once that sometimes Kelly stopped in her kitchen not because she was hungry but because she thought he was. It was one thing for her to pay for food that they would split—he had gotten used to that, too—but another for her to give him the entire sub.

The plastic bag containing the sub felt heavier as he crossed onto Main Street, which was bustling like usual for a summer Saturday. The diner was crowded and mothers were loading shopping bags into their trunks. One of them looked up, saw him, and shrank back, shoving her shopping cart in a random direction before hurrying into her car. His pulse picked up. Was that a standard Wesley Falls reaction to him or a more exaggerated one? He was used to a certain baseline of staring. Going to Jesus H. Christ High meant that being a guy with long hair meant you were going to get stared at and have random insults thrown in your direction. Never mind the irony that every depiction of said Jesus Christ featured long hair. Wearing all black and listening to bands that had parental advisory labels on them meant that you worshipped the devil. Not playing football and being into art meant that you were a faggot, and living in a trailer and dealing weed meant you were trash.

But if it wasn't his imagination, it seemed like people were staring at him in an alarmed rather than disgusted manner. James realized he was not ten feet away from one of the few refuges in town: The Gem Shop. He darted inside, relieved by the air-conditioning and dim atmosphere: it made the store seem cut off from the rest of the town. There was no one in the shop, or at least there didn't appear to be until Jia's head popped up. She must have been sitting on the carpet by the couch. "James!" she said.

He was glad to see a familiar face that wasn't looking at him suspiciously. He didn't know her very well, but she had only ever been nice to him in passing. The fact that her family ran The Gem Shop immediately accorded them respect in his eyes. James liked the store and had spent almost as much time there as he did the arts and crafts store in town. There were always neat new things to look at: amulets and carved figures and interesting books.

"Is your mom here?" James asked, his meaning clear—is it safe to talk?

Jia shook her head. "She went shopping." She made a gesture for him to come closer and they sat on the couch.

"Everyone's staring at me—what's going on? The police pulled over me and Kelly and were asking all these questions, saying people saw me at the party. Did they come talk to you?"

She shook her head again as she dug through her overalls' pocket for something. It was a smooth silver stone, which she turned over and over in her hands. She was sitting cross-legged, staring down at her hands. "Your bag is dripping," she said.

It was strange, because she said this without looking at his bag, which he realized was dripping oily red sauce. "It's a meatball sub. You want half?"

"Let me get you a plate," she said, popping to her feet. Instead of going to a kitchen, she plucked a black plate off a nearby table. It had constellations painted on it in gold. "But no thanks, I'm a vegetarian."

Vegetarian? What did she eat, then? James unwrapped the sub, obscuring Cassiopeia and Andromeda. "Why are all the dead kids burnouts?" he wondered aloud, looking at the sludge of cheese and sauce and realizing that he didn't feel like eating even though his stomach was empty.

"That's what I was thinking."

"I always knew those holy rollers hate people like me, but not like *that* kind of hate!"

"Maybe it was an accident?"

"They accidentally picked people up and threw them into the mine?" James asked.

"No, an accident that they were all burnouts."

"But if you remember how the collapse happened—"

"I can't. I can't remember any of it!"

James stared at her. "Jia, were you on something that night?"

"On something?"

"Valium? X? Benzos?" She made an exasperated noise, and he couldn't help cracking a smile. "The collapse was at the entrance between the second and third chambers," he said, pointing to the top of the constellation plate to demonstrate. "Only burnouts were in the third chamber, except for us. Well, you guys, anyway. You block off that entrance—" here he positioned the sub on the table to represent the chamber "—the only way out is to go down the main path to the Heart. But people were confused, running every direction—"

"That's not the only way out," Jia interrupted.

He stared at her again. "You're right. There are two other tiny paths out but it's hard to see in the dark and most people don't know them. How did you know about that path? Have you been down there before?"

She played with one of her beaded bracelets. "No. I didn't know until I saw it."

James gestured to the sub. "What I mean is, if you wanted to kill a bunch of burnouts, you could block off that entrance and they'd be trapped like cattle."

"James, that place is a bad place."

"The mine?"

"Yeah."

"A bunch of people got killed there, but that's not really the mine's fault. It's just a creepy place."

"It *is* the mine's fault. It's a bad place. I felt it." He arched an eyebrow at her. "I felt it even before the collapse." She opened her mouth, then closed it.

"What do you mean?" he pressed.

She picked up a heart-shaped crystal from the table. "Nothing," she said after a long pause. "I just wish we hadn't been there that night."

"The way Yacobi was questioning me, it was like he thought I had something to do with it, not like he thought maybe I saw who did it."

Jia flinched. "What if… What if it's because we went to the police? If Kelly and Casey hadn't gone to the police, whoever did this would have assumed there were no witnesses and they could make it look like an accident."

James began to sink into the couch as he realized what she was saying. "But if they were worried about witnesses, they could start to tell a story about who saw what."

"About who saw who," she correctly gently. "If people start talking about this like a murder instead of an accident, they need a scapegoat."

"Baaa," he said, closing his eyes.

23

Jia

Jia's mother, Su-Jin, was no stranger to Town Hall. She attended meetings when they had discussed the cost of resodding the football field at WFH, ordinances related to the size of signs on the stores on Main Street, and once or twice to answer inquiries about The Gem Shop. This time Jia had wanted to come, or rather, she knew that she should.

Jia felt a lump in her throat as she and her mother shuffled into two seats in the middle of the assembly hall. They had gotten there early enough to have their pick, and she imagined that her mother liked sitting in the center to have a full view of everything going on. Sheriff Springsteen stood by the lectern, surveying the townspeople as they pushed for seats, yammering. It was starting to get packed, but Jia didn't see any of her classmates, or that many kids at all. Mostly just parents looking angry. And now that the hall was full—standing room only at the back, with latecomers huffy—it was getting loud with a din of too many conversations. It was still ten minutes before the meeting was due to start.

Jia looked at her mother, whose gaze was moving over the crowd. She had never kept so large a secret from her mother—she had never needed to. Her life had been simple before. But now… It wasn't just what she had seen. It was also what she had *felt*.

Jia did not remember the exact moment of the collapse. She did remember suddenly feeling as if she was not in the same place. She could not hear the screams or the falling rocks; something about the explosion had blocked out her hearing. Was that what it was? Was that why she couldn't hear, or was it that something else was there? Something that slid into her senses as if clicking into place. She could feel something reverberating. Her body wasn't in control of itself. As the crowd attempted to move to either of the two entrances of the chamber—one which did not actually exist anymore—she found herself instead moving to a strange little jut at the side of the cave she hadn't seen before.

It wasn't crowded where she was, but the darkness stretched before her. A cramped path cut into the stone. There was no light beyond, just black-on-black darkness, like velvet waiting for someone to lie on it. Something pulled her toward it, like an invisible fishhook buried into her gut, its gossamer line strong enough to pull her whole body forward, step by tentative step. *Come*, it said. The Heart waited. It terrified Jia, but at the same time, she wanted to move forward. She wanted to see what was there.

What had brought her back was when Jia felt something claw into her shoulder. She shrieked until she looked up and realized that it was Casey. As he dragged her away, she wondered what exactly had she been doing, wandering off like that? What had been that…*thing* that she felt?

Do you feel it, Mom? she wanted to ask. *Do you ever feel this thing?* Her mom noticed her staring at her and gave her a gentle pat on the shoulder.

The sheriff tried to speak into the microphone then realized it was off—Mayor Burbank popped to his feet from the front row and turned it on for him. "Ladies and gentlemen, if you'll settle down, we'd like to get started."

"We'd like to know when *you're* going to get started!" a voice shouted. Everyone's head turned toward the back where a man stood pointing at the sheriff. "When are you going to start making arrests?"

The sheriff held up his hands, trying to tamp down the shouts of agreement. "We called this meeting to update you—"

"*You* didn't call the meeting! *We* asked for the meeting!" a mom yelled from the third row.

"Very active in the PTA," Su-Jin whispered to Jia.

"I know, and thank you for that," the sheriff said, not sounding particularly thankful. "I'm going to update you on what we can." The murmuring died down—parents were angry, but they were hungry for new details. "As you know, a few days ago on Friday a number of students had a party in the old Wesley mine—"

"How did they even get in?" a woman shouted.

The sheriff looked like he was withholding annoyance. "Ma'am, kids will be kids. No matter how much we board it up, they find a way inside."

"We should blow up that mine, is what we should do!" the same man from the back shouted. This was met with applause. Both the sheriff and the mayor, who was standing beside him now, looked tired.

"Let's keep the train on track and talk about what happened on Friday. From what we know, several hundred students attended a party in the mine. The sheer number is making it difficult for us to sort out what happened but we're working on it. At some point there was a minor collapse, during which a handful of kids were injured, no one seriously. Shortly after that, six students fell down the central shaft of the mine." Jia realized it was dead silent: not a single murmur, sniff, or comment. The sheriff read out the names of the six students. Jia looked around to see if the parents of those kids were present—she doubted they were. They were probably at home, horrified by this garish meeting. "We are currently interviewing eyewitnesses and the investigation is active and ongoing."

"What eyewitnesses?" yelled one man—Jia recognized him as an employee at the grocery store.

"Are you saying this is a homicide and not an accident?" someone else chimed in.

"The investigation is active and ongoing," the sheriff repeated. Jia got the impression that he had spent the past week being yelled at by townspeople.

"Do you have any leads?"

"I'm hearing things! I'm hearing it's that kid!"

"When are you going to make an arrest?"

"This town is supposed to be safe!" People were shouting over each other, but this woman, a woman with brightly dyed auburn hair, had also gotten to her feet, pointing an accusing finger at the sheriff. "People like living here because it's a safe place to raise kids! A place where you don't need to lock your doors! It's been like that for over a century!"

"No one has said anything about the families," Su-Jin murmured.

"The kids' families?" said Jia.

She nodded. It was true. There was no talk about how the community could support the affected families—a collection for the funerals or a meal train.

"Ma'am, there is an active and ongoing investigation—" Here the woman made a loud noise of disgust. It was clear that he wasn't going to offer any more details. The mayor made a sympathetic gesture to the sheriff, as if to say "that's enough," and he took over the lectern and began to speak.

But Jia's eyes were instead focused on Springsteen. Once the mayor took the mic, the sheriff took a seat in the front row alongside another man. The man turned to whisper something in his ear and Jia recognized him as the deputy sheriff. He was part of Golden Praise, Jia remembered. Married to that woman Maddy and Padma always talked about, Miss Laurie. On the deputy's other side was a police officer, Yacobi. And to his right, three men. The shearling men. All sitting together. All in a row: the police department allegedly looking for the killers and the three men who did it.

They were all bad. Rotten to the core and sitting together in a row. And now look at what they were doing—trying to calm down a public upset about a mass murder that they had no intent of solving. But why? Why do all this?

Chaotic shouting filled the hall again, but Jia's eyes were drawn toward the side door at the front of the assembly hall. The door opened and a figure strode in. The pastor—it had to be him—moving with no sense of urgency. He sipped from a take-out cup of coffee, handed it to the deputy sheriff without even breaking his stride, and as he approached the lectern, the mayor stepped aside without needing to be told to. When he leaned toward the microphone, he did not say anything but it was as if he had: the clamoring public fell quiet. "Good afternoon. Forgive me, I misspoke, it isn't a good afternoon. Not when we're here to talk about something so grave."

"That's the pastor?" Su-Jin whispered, so loudly that Jia elbowed her. How is it that she had lived in Wesley Falls her entire life and never laid eyes on him? Even if she had never stepped foot inside Golden Praise, it was a small town—why had she never seen him grocery shopping or at the post office? Was he such a figure that he didn't have to do such menial chores?

"Our town has faced a terrible tragedy," he continued. "And it's our natural reaction to panic. But let's not turn against each other. Remember what it is that makes this town great." The platitudes he spoke were less interesting than the man who spoke them, and the way he spoke them. She scanned his face with intense curiosity, glad that his speaking afforded her the opportunity to openly stare. How old was he? Forty-something? Was that young to be the pastor of such a huge church? Just the word *pastor* made Jia think of a man with gray hair. She knew in the Catholic Church that priests had to go to college, then seminary for several years. But maybe it was different in Protestant churches.

As the pastor spoke, his eyes moved over the crowd, as if making eye contact with each person. The crowd that had been foaming at the mouth minutes ago was now completely docile. A young couple diagonally in front of Jia stared at him with rapt attention, the way a mother stared at her baby, the way a dog stared at food.

She realized how her body felt: squirmy, uncomfortable, a heady feeling coming over her. The way she had felt in the mine when she had almost wandered down some dark path almost not of her own free will. She realized that she was now actively resisting the urge to look at the pastor, who was now speaking more passionately.

"We have to have faith in our community. Hope that we can see through the dark times and reach the light."

Look, some part of her demanded. *Look, look, look.* She squeezed her eyes shut. *No.* She felt like a magnet being pulled toward its polarity. It didn't matter how the magnet felt; it simply acted. She opened her eyes, trying to keep the pastor in her peripheral vision rather than looking directly at him. She had a sudden strange feeling that he would know she was looking at him, even though the entire room was staring at him. The pastor smiled, calling on them to have faith in the sheriff's investigation, to have some patience and fortitude. People nodded and smiled.

A thought popped into her head: her mother's strange paranoia about the garbage disposal at home. Jia was not allowed to use it and her mother would frequently warn her not to put her hand down it, as if Jia would ever do such a thing. But more than once, alone at night, Jia had gone to get a glass of water and found herself staring at the flapped eyelids of the disposal and feeling a weird compulsion to do just that. That was like what she had felt when wandering toward that dark path in the mine. What she felt like right now.

The meeting ended. The pastor had somehow mollified the public, telling them to be patient, that progress was being made. "Well, that was useless," Su-Jin huffed. She zipped up her purse, preparing to go, and Jia stood along with her and waited for their turn to file out. People started to trickle out the assembly hall's exits, but others lingered, lining up not to talk to the mayor or the sheriff, but to the pastor. A crowd surrounded him like he was a celebrity. He leaned close to talk to some people, and when one man shook his hand, he closed both hands over it.

The Kwons deferred to an older woman, letting her walk ahead of them, but Jia thought she detected a snide glance thrown in their direction. She was just about to turn to the back of the assembly hall when she looked up, directly at the pastor. He was looking directly at her in a momentary pause in the middle of the conversation he was having with someone. Jia felt a wave of nausea overtake her.

I know what you are.

She heard this distinctly in her head, although no one had spoken.

She clasped her mother's hand suddenly, and was glad that for whatever reason Su-Jin opted to not question what would possess a teenage girl to do something she hadn't done in years. Once they were outside the assembly hall and heading toward Main Street, she let go of her hand, embarrassed. Her mother was saying something, but the words faded away as Jia's attention focused on a police car driving by. One figure drove it, with another person in the back. As the car passed directly in front of them, Jia could make out James in the back, his face pale.

24

Kelly

Kelly dragged her desk chair to her window and perched there for more than two hours, staring out into the darkness toward James's trailer. Word had spread quickly among the capstone group: Jia had spotted James in the back of a police car. They had all been talking for the past two hours, checking with each other to see if they had heard anything more. Had James been arrested? Maddy was grounded indefinitely, her phone calls being monitored, but Padma had talked to her via IM, and Maddy said she hadn't heard anything, either.

Kelly rested her chin on her hands, her hands on the windowsill. There were green-and-yellow fireflies out, blinking occasionally. As children, she and James collected them, and the rarer colors were more valuable. Yellow and green were common, red and blue were the most prized.

They had to let him go. They couldn't arrest him for something he didn't do. That simply couldn't be the way the world worked. Maybe they just brought him in for questioning. Maybe they wanted to scare him. Milky sighed loudly. She rested her head on Kelly's bare feet, a small comfort to the anxiety that Kelly felt.

Time always moved slower when waiting for someone. More than once she thought she saw James, but it was the moonlight reflecting off the trees, or Rick, then Lisa, emerging from the trailer, drinking beers before they went back inside. Did they know where James was? Did they care?

Suddenly, Kelly could see a figure making its way across the grass. She recognized James's gait before she could make out his pale face, his dark hair streaming out behind him as he headed toward the back door of the trailer. Kelly scrambled out of her window, startling Milky. She sped across the yard, the grass wet with dew against her bare feet. "James!" she hissed—he hadn't seen her—just as he opened the back door.

She knew what he was doing. The living room and bedroom where Rick and Lisa slept were at the front of the trailer. When James wanted to sneak in or out, he used the back door.

"Go home," he whispered to her without looking.

She ignored him, following him inside. The TV from the living room was blaring—it was out of sight, so Kelly had no idea if that was where Rick or James's aunt were. She prayed they were sleeping. Kelly did not like to admit it, but being inside the Curry trailer made her uncomfortable. It didn't when James's mother had been around, but then a cozy home for a family of three became two, then one, then three again. It was hard to untangle Kelly's discomfort from her understanding that James didn't like her being inside the trailer. He never said so, but that he was ashamed of where he lived was always an unspoken fact between them.

Beer bottles were strewn everywhere, the kitchen overloaded with dirty dishes, the fridge empty, and every bit of counter space was covered with something. James's room was sparse, significantly neater, but did not seem comfortable in any way. A twin bed with only a sheet on it, no comforter. Milk crates held some books, and his walls were covered with band posters and drawings. She knew that anything of real value would not be kept in his room, but in the shed out back where he kept his art supplies.

She followed him into his room and closed the door. "What happened?" she whispered.

Hurriedly, James dumped out the contents of his book bag, probably not emptied since the last day of school. "They put me in a car. They brought me in for questioning." He wasn't looking at her, and she was struck by the fact that James looked as scared as she'd ever seen him, like how he was at the mine party or the night his mother died. He moved to his closet where he began to indiscriminately shove clothing into his book bag.

"What are you doing?"

"I have to go somewhere."

Where was somewhere? Sometimes he slept at her house if he happened to be over late, but sometimes when things were intolerable, he would disappear for a few days, often missing school. She would look out her window, look for him in between classes, and sometimes he would reappear at the back of the school, smoking and acting like nothing had happened. The last time he had done this had been after Rick had rifled through the shed, probably looking for money or drugs. James was furious and tried to put on a padlock, which provoked Rick even more because as a teenager he didn't "own" anything and how dare he try to claim private space.

But this—this was bad. This wasn't James getting suspended for painting a gun or mouthing off to a teacher. This was the police targeting James, and it was only a matter of time before his so-called guardians found out. It didn't matter if it was contradictory: Rick could hate the police but also be enraged at James for getting in trouble with them.

"Tell me where," Kelly whispered.

James slung the book bag on and headed for the door. "It's fine, I—"

Kelly gave a short scream—Rick was behind the slightly open door. He grabbed James by the shirt and shoved him against the wall. "Where do you think you're going?!"

"Get out of here," James said. Kelly understood this was directed at her, but Rick probably didn't. She edged out of the room, but had no intent of leaving. She knew that it would be worse if she wasn't there.

"You're telling *me* to get out?" Rick was pure fury and even though his back was to Kelly, she could smell the stink of alcohol seeping out of his pores. "I *said* where the fuck you *going*?!" His right hand moved from James's chest and clasped around his neck.

"Get the fuck off me!" James yelled, struggling. He tried to pull Rick's hand off him with both hands.

"I got three people calling me and saying you got arrested, picked up by the police, and half a dozen people killed?"

"What's going on here?" Kelly looked toward the other bedroom and saw Lisa wavering and blinking. Kelly was relieved—maybe the two of them could defuse this. Kelly had not had many conversations with James's aunt—she was friendly while sober, but she had had a few interactions with her that were unsettling. James said they were both addicts, that they were always scrimping to get money because neither could hold down a job and when they did have money, they didn't use it to pay the water bill or buy groceries. Lisa was not like James's mother, the kind, dark-haired woman whom Kelly barely remembered.

"Get back in there!" Rick snapped at Lisa without looking at her.

Stop him, Kelly thought desperately. *I can't do this myself.*

Lisa blinked once, twice, and then went back into the bedroom, closing the door.

Rick let go of James's neck and Kelly felt her muscles relax a little. "Did you get arrested?" he asked.

"No. They were just questioning me." James hitched up his book bag by the straps and took exactly two steps before Rick began screaming.

"DID I SAY YOU COULD MOVE?!"

"Fuck off!" James yelled. *Oh why, James?* Kelly thought. *Why are you so dumb and mouthy at the worst possible times?* "Get—" Rick's fist connected with James's face, making a sickening sound, a sound that reminded Kelly of when her mom tenderized meat with a little mallet. James, knocked to the floor, held his hands over his now-bloody face while he attempted to scramble backward.

"Stop!" Kelly shouted.

"You fucking kill someone, you piece of shit?!" He kicked—Kelly screamed—the kick landing in James's chest. "You think you can talk to me!?" James made a silent gasp—his back had reached the wall and he was able to use it as leverage to try to get to his feet. Rick punched him again, this time blood spattering against the wall, and James fell again.

"STOP!"

"You. Fucking. Kid." Rick was kicking him again, more sickening sounds, and something unfroze in Kelly when she saw him raise his foot in a different way. He was going to stomp. James could die. She could be watching James die right in front of her.

"No!" she screamed, grabbing Rick by the waistband of his jeans and wrenching him backward. Rick had apparently forgotten she was there and turned to look at her, his pupils scarily dilated, and he shoved her. She fell against the door frame of the bathroom, then lost her balance, her butt making violent contact against the tiled floor. Rick turned his attention back to James, still on the ground, dazed and bleeding. Desperately, Kelly searched the bathroom and grabbed the first thing that wasn't bolted down. It was an iron. Strange that an iron would be lying around in a house where no one seemed to wear anything but T-shirts.

Kelly popped to her feet without thinking and used both hands in an upward swing, aiming for Rick's head. The force of impact made her scream and drop the iron, which fell to the floor as heavily as Rick's unconscious body. She looked at James, terror jumping into her throat when she saw the state that he was in. There was blood all over his face—she wasn't sure exactly where it was coming from, and he was making a wheezing sound every time he inhaled. She didn't know how hurt he was but she knew it was bad, and even worse: she had hit Rick with an iron, which meant they had crossed some impossible line in the sand.

She grabbed James by the arm and pulled him to his feet. She dragged him out the back door of the trailer and ran toward her own yard, the floodlight that was supposed to scare away deer guiding her. She was crying, screaming for her mother, the inevitable memories bubbling up because it felt like this had happened before.

They were in seventh grade that year. The two of them had been playing, and James had gone home for dinner. Kelly had just let Milky out and was waiting for her to do her business when she heard a terrible scream. James came running out of the trailer, a look on his face like nothing she had ever seen. He was hysterical, crying, saying that his mother wasn't moving, which confused Kelly and made her start crying, too. Her mother came to the back door, wondering what all the noise was about, and soon she was running across the yard to the trailer, both kids in tow. She didn't let them come inside, but instead told them to go and tell her dad what happened. James tried to resist, wanting to help his mom, but Kelly pulled him by the arm, and they both ran in a panicked confusion back to the Boyle house.

"MOM!" Kelly screamed as she ran through the backyard, James stumbling to keep up. *"MOM!"* Kelly wrenched open the screen door just as she saw her mother appear in the kitchen.

"What—" Then she saw the state that James was in.

Emily Boyle switched from Mom mode into nurse mode. With calm efficiency, she took James and led him to the bathroom closest to the kitchen, telling Kelly to run and get the first-aid kit. Kelly found it under the kitchen sink, and when she got back to the bathroom, her mother had seated James on the closed toilet and was holding a folded washcloth over half his face. "Honey, what happened?"

"Huh?" James said.

"Rick was hitting him," Kelly said, crying more now. "He kept hitting him, I thought he would kill him. He almost stomped on him, I hit him with an iron." Her mother gave Kelly a bewildered glance before asking her to hold the washcloth. "I can't tell where he's bleeding," she muttered. She wet another washcloth and began to wipe his face around the first washcloth, then dared to look under it. "Hon, we gotta get you to a hospital."

"No!" James said, startling them both. "I don't have insurance."

Emily pressed the washcloth against his face, her eyes searching the room as if she was doing math in her head. "Mom, can't you take care of him? And I can call Dr. Subramaniam. He would help. Padma's dad?"

"He needs stitches," Emily whispered. "He could have a concussion."

"He can't afford a concussion. Please?"

"Go call, then, and tell your dad." Kelly ran from the bathroom to the phone in the living room, then realized she didn't have Padma's phone number memorized. But it was on a slip of paper on her desk. She thundered up the stairs, passing her dad, who was curious about all the noise. "Rick attacked James!" she shouted on the way to her bedroom. She snatched the piece of paper with all the capstone phone numbers on it and ran to Jennifer's bedroom, which was the closest phone. She flung the door open without knocking—this elicited protests from the Harpies, who were sitting on the bed, huddled over the very phone she wanted. She ran to the bedside and pressed the button on the receiver, hanging up on whoever they were talking to, and snatched the phone from Jess's hands.

"Hey!"

"What's your problem?"

Her hands trembled as she dialed Padma's number. A man with an accent picked up. "Is this Doctor Subramaniam?"

There was a pause, then, "Yes?"

"This is Kelly Boyle. You might know my mom, Emily Boyle? We have an emergency, and we need a doctor." The twins sat up straight, phone theft forgotten. Kelly tried to speak calmly as she explained, not wanting to sound stupid in front of Padma's father, but found herself unable to keep her voice from wavering. "It's our neighbor. My neighbor James? He's been beaten. Really badly. We can't take him to a hospital. Please. He doesn't have insurance. My mom's a nurse and she can help you."

There was another pause. "What is your address, Kelly?"

When she hung up, her sisters immediately followed her, the trio running down the stairs. Her father stood at the bathroom door, bracing his hands on the door frame. Her father nodded but she couldn't hear what her parents had been saying. He didn't seem to see her as he went to the front hall closet, stooped, and withdrew a wooden baseball bat. "I'll be right back," he said, his jaw set in a grim line of anger.

By now both the Harpies could see into the bathroom and were gaping. "Wait, where are you going?" Jess cried at him.

"I'm just going to poke around," he said, bouncing the baseball bat against his foot as he walked toward the front door.

"Jake," Emily called from inside the bathroom, a warning tone to her voice.

Kelly shoved her sisters out of the way, then went inside the bathroom, closing the door for privacy.

James, still dazed, was holding a clump of gauze to his eyebrow.

"Is it okay if I examine you?" Emily asked. She used the same tone she used when attempting to coax Milky to take medicine. "Let's get your shirt off." With some difficulty—James having to switch hands holding the gauze—the Boyles managed to get his shirt off. Kelly's eyes watered. She had seen him with his shirt off plenty of times—but in the stark fluorescent light of the bathroom, she could see him through her mother's eyes. He was terribly thin, his pale skin marred by stark red marks where Rick had hit him in the chest, on his neck, and also there was a bruise on his shoulder, a sallow shade of yellow indicating that it was old and not from tonight. Kelly saw her mother's lips tighten into a line, then her eyes filled with tears. She put her hands on either side of James's face and said, "Jamie, you are not going back to that house, ever."

James started to cry silently, but looked at the floor to hide this.

Emily did not have a stethoscope, but instead put her head to James's chest and asked him to take a deep breath. This was strangely intimate—Kelly knew at some level that James didn't want her to see him this way, but that her presence was also a comfort. She averted her eyes, but took one of his sticky hands in hers to squeeze.

She left the bathroom when she could hear the commotion of Dr. Subramaniam arriving. The twins had been circling the foyer and, startled by the doorbell, flung open the door to find both the doctor holding his leather bag and Padma standing behind him. Padma's father was short and dressed in a suit, bringing with him the smell of Old Spice. Padma remained in the foyer with the Boyle sisters. Kelly kept the door open because she could see her father starting to make his way back across the front lawn.

"What the hell happened?" Jess asked Kelly.

Kelly recounted the story, leaving out that James had been held for questioning by the police.

"You hit him with an *iron*?" Jenn asked just as their father got to the entryway. Padma's eyes went huge as she saw the baseball bat.

"What did you *do*?" Kelly asked him.

"Just looked around. He's out cold, Kell-bell," he said, then walked to the kitchen hallway where the adults had gathered, Jenn and Jess following. The front door was still open, and Padma looked out into the night.

"Casey's coming. I called him just before we left," Padma said.

Kelly nodded. Padma had probably assumed that James's being hurt had something to do with the mine murders, but it only obliquely did. A few moments later they watched Casey's minivan pull up in front of her house. He ran up the driveway, flushed.

The three went upstairs—the adults had told them all to go away and let the medical professionals do their job. They tried to eavesdrop through the air-conditioning vent in Kelly's bedroom. She retold them what she had witnessed, pausing occasionally when she could hear voices through the vent. She could hear the deep rumble of Dr. Subramaniam's voice, but not James's responses. "Hey," Casey said, gesturing to her window. It was incongruous, but there were the others, Maddy riding her pink ten-speed with Jia perched on the back. Kelly stuck her head out the window and called them over, telling them to climb up the trellis.

"I called Jia before I left," Casey explained.

Maddy was more athletic and made it up the trellis easily. Jia struggled and had to be pulled the final foot by Casey. "I had to sneak out," Maddy said breathlessly.

"Will you get in trouble?" Padma asked.

"How could I possibly be in any more trouble?" Maddy said. "What happened?" Kelly recounted the story, Maddy cringing with every blow.

"Do you think he'll be okay?" Jia asked, her eyes huge.

They all stared at Kelly, whose shirt was covered in blood, who had been the only one of them to actually see James.

They talked in hushed tones and eavesdropped when they could. Through the vent they heard talk of the police—this was the only time they could hear James raise his voice in protest—then came soothing tones from Kelly's father. There were various rumblings, then Kelly's father crossed the yard again, still with the baseball bat, but just when he got to the Currys', they could see the flashing blue-and-red lights of a police car, but not see the actual car—the front of James's trailer was not visible from the angle of Kelly's window. They could hear the static chirps of a police radio, and fifteen minutes later Kelly's dad came back to the house carrying a duffel bag.

Through the Harpies, too shocked by recent events to question how Kelly was suddenly having a sleepover party in her room, they learned that the police had arrested Rick and that Kelly's dad had returned with clothes for James.

It was past eleven o'clock when they heard footsteps coming up the stairs. "It's my mom," Kelly said. She hadn't meant any cause for alarm—neither of her parents would care that friends had come over, but Casey scrambled to get under her bed and Maddy hid behind the door so that when Emily opened it, she couldn't see her. This might have been funny under other circumstances.

Emily took a moment to observe that Jia had been added in addition to Padma, all three girls sitting on Kelly's bed. "I brought you some visitors. Keep an eye on him, will you?"

She stepped aside, revealing James and Milky standing at his side. Just the sight of him made Kelly start to cry again. His face had changed with startling rapidity since Kelly had last seen him:

one eye was swollen nearly shut and the eyebrow above it looked wrong somehow. One of his lips was puffy and split. He looked pale and exhausted but strangely expressionless. Casey crawled out from under the bed, and Maddy was revealed once the door was closed, but James said nothing as he glanced at them.

Jia had started crying silently the second she saw him, and this had a contagion effect on Padma. James pretended he didn't see and, cringing, sat on the bed, baring his teeth as he shifted his body so he could rest his back against the wall. Kelly knew she should be the one to say something to break the tension in the air. Maybe turning the conversation to the mine incident, or saying something about Milky, but before she could think of anything, Jia had crawled across the bed, still crying, and hugged James, tucking her head into his chest. Kelly saw James stiffen, a muscle tense in his jaw. He was humiliated. He did not come up here expecting to see anyone but maybe Kelly, and even that was bad enough. He also didn't like intense displays of emotion. But Jia didn't move, and Padma was solicitously tucking a pillow under his knees for comfort.

Kelly saw James's expression soften a little as he turned his head to say something quietly to Jia as he patted her shoulder reassuringly. Kelly traced James's eyes across the room to where Casey was pacing across her bedroom, restless. Finally, and reluctantly, his gaze fell upon Maddy. He was too tired to have all his walls up: the look he gave her was naked and vulnerable. *What have you got to say about me now?* it said. Maddy bowed her head, and it took Kelly a moment to realize she wasn't taking a moment to gather her words; she was praying. Kelly wasn't sure why, but something about this stabbed at her heart, made everything feel sheared and raw. *We're just kids*, she thought. *How are we supposed to fix this?*

Kelly tried to ask him about what had happened at the police station, but James still seemed dazed, which she found alarming. He could only say the police had picked him up and asked him a bunch of questions. "We can't let him go to sleep," Casey said. "If someone has a concussion, it's bad."

They stayed awake. They put on a VHS of *Evil Dead 2: Dead*

By Dawn because it was James's favorite movie. Kelly stayed at his other side and poked him when he looked sleepy. Maddy and Casey whispered to each other from their positions on the floor. They all dozed except for Kelly—who didn't ever think she could sleep again—and James, whom she wouldn't let sleep.

Once the sun rose, the sound of other Boyles moving around in the house became evident. Casey stood up, stretching, the morning light making his blond hair glow golden. Last night he had looked confused, scared. This morning he looked different. It reminded Kelly of a football party she had been to right before the playoffs. All of the other players were goofing around except for Casey. Instead, he had a focused intensity, a quiet resolve. He looked like that now.

He offered to take Jia and Padma home—Maddy would ride her bike and as far as Kelly knew, James was staying with her. He jangled his car keys in his pocket, looking out the window again. He spoke without looking at them. "We're going to get those shearling fuckers."

PART FIVE: AUGUST 2015

25

Kelly

Kelly walked toward the baggage claim. The occasion was somber—one of the Capstone Six was dead—but she couldn't help the anticipation that buzzed in her chest. She checked her phone again, almost not believing that there was a group text of the five of them. The penultimate text had been from Casey, saying that he was at the car rental place and would retrieve her and James from baggage claim. Then they would get Padma from the train station. James, who had been terse on the encrypted message board—so terse that Kelly wondered if he could actually be coaxed back to Wesley Falls—had simply replied, Got it. See ya.

Kelly paused to text Ethan, Just landed. Will check in tomorrow. She began to wander the claim area, her heart beating embarrassingly loud. James had gotten in an hour before her—he should be here already. James! After twenty years! Her eyes skipped across the crowd, looking for anyone who could be him. Maybe he wasn't here. He *couldn't* be here. But then she realized there was someone in front of her who looked familiar in the way he stuck his hands in the front pockets of his jeans. She came up to him from behind. "James?" she said.

He turned, clearly feeling the surprise that she also felt. A smile was just breaking over his face when her bubble of emotion broke and she threw her arms around him, wanting to hide her face because she knew she was about to lose it. She hugged him tightly, so tightly, not caring that she was crying—

scrunch-faced ugly crying—not after all the times she missed him, worried about where he was, if he had a safe place to stay. She clasped tighter, thinking he might just disappear. With her face pressed into his shoulder, she realized he still smelled the same: like the forest, cedarwood and oak moss and drinking the ice-cold water from the hose behind her house. "I can't believe it's you," she managed.

"It's me," he said. They pulled back, Kelly wiping at her face and laughing, surprised to see that his eyes were shiny, too. James had kept his hands on her shoulders, and they just looked at each other, taking in the similarities and differences. He was an *adult*; she had kept picturing him as a sixteen-year-old. The scar still interrupted his right eyebrow in a small horizontal line. His hair wasn't as long but still fell just to his ears.

"I—"

They were both nearly knocked off their feet by the impact of another body. Kelly felt a powerful arm encircling her. "YOU GUYS!" Casey yelled.

"Casey!" Kelly squirmed from his grasp. Casey was still Casey, perpetually flushed from running somewhere. His neck had the thick look of a football player, and he still exuded the same restless energy. He danced from foot to foot before bearhugging her, picking her up, then she laughed as he did the same to James. He led them to the nearest exit.

"Prepare yourself," he said as they made their way to where he had parked. He stopped and made a grand gesture: his rental was a minivan. "Just like old times!"

Kelly tried to keep smiling as she took shotgun at Casey's insistence. He hadn't realized that they didn't need a minivan anymore—with only five of them, they could fit in a normal car. Maddy should have been in that back row of seats leaning forward intently to say some theory, her blond hair somehow always looking perfect even if it was messy.

Casey started the van and pulled out of the parking spot. "So your, um…flight was good?" They all exchanged a glance, unsure of how to proceed.

"Did you hear anything else about Maddy?" Kelly asked. Casey shook his head.

"I was googling from the airport," James said. "There isn't anything more than that article Jia sent us."

"Do you think—" she began.

"Can we save the sleuthing till we're all together?" Casey said, his voice sad. "I'm just really happy to see you guys." He reached his arm back and attempted to swat at James. "I thought you were dead, man. I thought maybe I was the last of us to ever talk to you." James looked sheepish.

"That would have been me, not you," Kelly corrected. Those last couple weeks of James living at her house after they had killed the pastor remained etched deeply in her memory. What she had wanted was for them to reassure each other, to come to the conclusion that everything would be okay. Instead, James seemed to be in a perpetual state of terror, only leaving the house if forced and constantly smoking pot. He wouldn't talk to her, but on his last night at the Boyles', they slept in the same bed, clutching each other. He did not even say goodbye when he got into her father's car and was driven away. She had cried, and her mother had told her that he was probably upset but not good at expressing it. It had still hurt.

"No," Casey insisted. "This fucker called me."

Aggrieved, Kelly looked at James for confirmation. His eyes said yes, then darted to Casey.

"I'm sitting in my kitchen innocently drinking some milk—"

"As one drinks milk," James interrupted.

"And the phone rings. 'You have a collect call from *Johnny Fuckface*, will you accept the charges?'"

"You knew it was me, right?"

"Who the hell else would Johnny Fuckface be?"

"It was when I was in Dover," James said to Kelly, his tone having a hint of apology. "That was the plan, right? If cops started asking me questions after I moved, I'd take the money you guys saved for me and get out of town."

"That was the plan," Kelly agreed. *But why wouldn't you call me?* Each of them had dropped money in envelopes in the Boyles' mailbox during that two-week period. *This money came from them*, said the unsigned note in Padma's neat handwriting—it was her salary from Golden Praise. Jia had stolen from the till at The Gem Shop. Kelly's had been her savings. Maddy's contribution had been the largest—Kelly had always wondered if she had hocked some jewelry. She had known that at some point when he got to Dover it became unsafe and he left, but she didn't remember how she knew that. "You left me a note," she said, remembering suddenly. A single sheet of loose-leaf paper in a plain envelope. *He left town*, in Casey's handwriting. "You could have included a few more details."

"I was scared," Casey said, slowing to a stop at a red light. He turned to grab James by the chin. "Look at this guy. He looks good! What'd you use? Was it Proactiv?" James started laughing. "Just three simple steps and clear skin can be yours for 19.95," he recited from the old commercial.

"Fuck you, it *was* Proactiv." She had forgotten how the boys played off each other: Casey's bad jokes and James undercutting him. Kelly kept looking from one to the other without really believing they were there. Casey seemed like a suburban dad, someone who hosted huge barbecues and was a regular at PTA meetings. She thought her guess was confirmed when she spied a wedding ring on his hand.

"I thought you were *dead* in a *ditch* somewhere," Casey said, cackling and shaking his head as the minivan began to move again.

"You just can't keep a good guy down," James said gravely.

"Did you just quote *Child's Play* at us?" Kelly shouted. James put his hands on his knees and shook silently from laughter. She had almost forgotten that, that if she made him laugh hard enough, he lost the ability to make sounds. He would laugh silently and not be able to breathe, holding his hands up for mercy.

We're putting on a play, Kelly thought suddenly as the two men kept joking around. Friends reuniting, having a good time. No dark undertone. No one was dead. They were not going back to face something that they couldn't quite name.

Soon they arrived at the train station and Casey began to

circle, looking for Padma. "She says she's waiting by the curb," Kelly said, looking out the window.

"There!" Casey shouted, putting the minivan into Park. His energy was infectious—they all clamored out toward where Padma stood. Adult Padma—Kelly couldn't help labeling her—now had a stylish shaggy haircut and could have easily passed for twenty-something. Casey gave her a bear hug and had tears in his eyes when he pulled away. "You people are making me sentimental."

"You got tall!" Kelly said, hugging Padma.

"A wild five foot four?" Padma said wryly, smiling. James also hugged her, and Padma took the passenger's seat up next to Casey. "Casey, I listen to your podcast!" she blurted before he had even taken the minivan out of Park.

"You know about my podcast?"

"I've been listening to it for years!"

His delight couldn't be contained. "You're into college football?"

Padma turned so she could see them all. "I know we weren't supposed to contact each other, and at first I was scared. I knew you went to Ohio State, but one day I got into my friend's car and I heard *your voice*—" she poked Casey "—and I thought, it couldn't be him, but it was." Things felt surreal as Casey and Padma proceeded to go in deep on college football.

James looked at her and made a *What the hell?* gesture—that same exact gesture she had known for years, the slight arching of his left eyebrow that was so quintessentially *James*—and she laughed, delighted. Casey and Padma kept chattering about football, but as they grew closer to Wesley Falls, Kelly stared intently out the window, looking for the familiar road markers along the way. First, Wiley's run-down bar, then the turn into town. They all fell silent at this point, taking in what had changed and what had stayed the same. It was around dusk and kids were still in the streets bouncing basketballs and walking in groups to unknown destinations.

Wesley Falls was small enough that any one of them could have found the inn without looking it up on their phones. They pulled into a parking spot at the inn and saw Jia waiting right at the door to her room. James was the first to reach Jia, saying "Hey," and pulling her into a hug that looked somber. The burden of all this had fallen more on her than anyone else, Kelly realized. Kelly felt a swell of emotion as Jia and Padma embraced, both crying.

Jia held her hands up. "Obviously, we have a lot of serious things to discuss. But for my sake, can we have dinner to catch up and save the serious stuff for later tonight? I've prepared a bevy of hometown treats," she said, letting them into her room.

She had assembled a smorgasbord from all over town, everything someone who grew up in Wesley Falls would miss, not because it was good so much as because it was familiar. Meatball and eggplant parm sandwiches from Del Monico's, the "classic" salad from the diner that incorporated French fries, shoofly pie, and a few bottles of wine. She had pulled two tables together and arranged pillows so they could sit on the floor.

Kelly sat beside James and they each opened a bottle of wine, one red, one white. After they had poured everyone their preference, Kelly hesitated with a sixth plastic cup in her hand. Even the arrangement of pillows around the table seemed uneven with five.

"Tell me," Casey said, cutting into one of the subs. "All of you, tell me everything."

Padma's trajectory wasn't entirely surprising: UPenn for undergrad, Cornell for a masters in biomedical engineering. "Go back further," Kelly urged. "I always wondered if you liked the magnet school better than our high school."

"Are you kidding? I loved it. It was like I finally found my place. It was the exact opposite of the way things are here. If you were into astronomy and showed up wearing a shirt with planets on it, someone would say, 'Cool, I like planets, too.' And there were more kids of immigrants there."

"More than two?" Jia said, smiling.

"*Way* more than two," Padma said.

"What do you do now?" James asked, pouring more wine.

"I work at a company called Pfizer. My husband and I—

Tamer—we both got jobs there after grad school. We're in New York, right by the border with New Jersey."

"That's not that far from Philly," Jia pointed out.

"We could have been hanging out," Padma said, smiling sadly. "What about you?" she said, patting Kelly's foot.

"I teach up at Boston College. Early American literature." She chatted a little about her life there: the students and small city she loved. That part felt honest, but she felt self-conscious when she talked about Ethan. The whole "I'm engaged and everything is great" felt more than a little hollow after their last interaction. She was eager to have the attention off her. "What about you, Casey? You were the only one to finish at our high school."

"It was weird without Maddy being there," Casey said. "There was all this jockeying for the space she left behind with the Circle Girls. People talked about her," he said, making a disgusted face. "All these ridiculous stories about what she did to get sent to boarding school. She slept with a teacher or stole money from the church to buy drugs. Football was hard those two years—it kind of made me crazy to know that Coach was an Elder but I didn't want to ruin my shot at college because of those assholes so I just kept my head down and worked my ass off."

"Then you went to Ohio State," Kelly filled in, smiling.

"Is that good?" James interrupted, a blank, benign expression on his face.

"Fuck you, it's D1," Casey said, laughing. He explained how he played for three years before an injury took him out, then how he began a podcasting career.

"Do you podcast full-time?" Jia asked.

Casey nodded. "Not at first, but eventually the ad revenue was good enough. I got married. We're working on kids, adoption is a long game."

"Fertility issues?" Padma asked. Her voice was soft; while Padma had always lacked tact, the sympathetic way she asked and the old familiarity between them made it seem forgivable.

"I guess you could say that. I'm married to a man."

There was a pause.

"Very funny," James said, helping himself to more eggplant.

"No, really I am." Casey withdrew his cell phone and showed them his lock screen, which featured a picture of a tan, handsome man holding an iced coffee and smiling at the camera.

Doubtful, Kelly peered at it, her eyebrows raised. Casey sighed, then pulled up another picture, this one featuring Casey and the same man, both in tuxedos, standing in front of a wedding cake, which had a cake topper with two grooms and a bassinet on it. Inside the bassinet was a baby football.

"Wait, what?" Jia said.

"You were the most girl-crazy guy I knew," Kelly said.

"Still am," Casey said, grinning. "It never occurred to me that I could be into guys before I met Aaron. Living in this town is like…" He trailed off, his eyes going to the window. "It's like there was a fog over me when I was here. I couldn't see what was wrong with this place, even with everything that happened with the church, until I left. I couldn't see what was wrong with my family. I couldn't even see inside myself because all I was allowed to think about was football. That was the only thing that felt safe. And you know what? I was right. My family disowned me." Jia made a noise, but Casey shrugged. "They literally picked this devil church instead of their own son. It's 2015, gay marriage is legal, and my parents' religion goes out of their way to say that gays are going to hell."

"Not Lexie?" Padma asked.

"No, she's on my side," Casey said. "So now they don't talk to her, either. She lives in Columbus, too. We're super close. She was going to be our surrogate after she had two kids, but she had post-partum depression after the first one, then she had it even worse after the second, and also other complications, so I said no. She'd still do it for me, but I won't let her. So now we're going through the adoption process."

"My husband and I are, too!" Padma exclaimed. "We should trade notes later."

"Absolutely," Casey said. He refilled their cups of wine and then gestured at James. "What about you, Johnny Fuckface? Raise your hand if you thought James was dead."

"That's not funny!" Jia said, throwing a napkin at him, but everyone else was laughing, even James.

"It's only funny because I'm *not* dead," James said.

"What kind of work do you do?" Casey asked.

"Guess," James said, grinning as he uncrossed his legs, spreading them out before him and leaning back on his hands.

"Architect," Kelly said. "At a boutique firm."

"Graphic designer," Jia said.

"At a video game company," Padma added.

"Come on, guys," Casey said. "You're being nice. I'm gonna say you got busted for selling mushrooms, spent a little time at prison, and now do something weird, like a deep-sea fisherman."

"I own and operate a café that specializes in baked goods made out of marijuana. It's called KGBakery."

"KGB like Russia?" Kelly asked.

"Killer Green Bud," he corrected, smiling at her. "Yes, friends and neighbors, I turned weed dealing into a one hundred percent legitimate profession. And this town said I was a loser who would never go anywhere."

"Oh, man," Casey said, "I love it."

Padma was looking up the café on her phone. "Look at the pastries. I would eat these!"

"Funny you say that!" James said, getting to his feet. He rooted through his baggage until he came out with a dark brown box secured with a deep blue paper cuff. He set it on the table and opened it, revealing a sextet of shiny truffles, gesturing for them to take one. *There will be a spare*, Kelly couldn't help thinking. Maddy would have been the first to pick, taking whatever she thought was prettiest. "These are fleur de sel and burned butter caramel. Ladies, I would maybe only eat half—"

"Wait, what?" Jia said, having clearly put the entire chocolate in her mouth. Padma likewise put a hand over her mouth in a nearly identical expression as Jia.

"This should be a fun evening," Casey said.

"Nah, you'll just sleep well tonight," James said. "I figured we could use it."

"And how do you go from fleeing Dover to *this*?" Casey asked.

"Do you remember how much money you guys saved for me?" James said, taking a nibble of chocolate. "Five hundred and twenty-two dollars. I got on a Greyhound and figured I'd go to LA—the farthest place possible. But then I thought, it's a big city, it's probably expensive. Maybe a small town would be a better place to hide. I would have more money to start my life. I had no clue what rent would be. So every time the bus made a stop I would look around, panicking, trying to make a decision. One morning, even before sunrise, we rolled into the station in San Antonio, and across the street I could see a donut shop with a help wanted sign. I figured, I like donuts and maybe they'll hire me. Which they did, and the family that ran the place, the Morenos, took me under their wing. I must have looked a sight. I think they felt sorry for me, but they helped me get my GED and do a couple courses at the community college while I worked at the shop."

"Did they ever come after you once you left Pennsylvania?" Kelly asked. The *they* here didn't need to be stated. It was the amalgamation of all the people in control of Wesley Falls: the police, the shearling men, the people who had claimed false witness against him.

James shook his head. "Maddy was right—once I was gone, I couldn't be a useful patsy anymore."

"They officially ruled the mine murders an accident caused by the collapse after you left," Jia said. "Which I think was the initial plan."

"How long did you stay in San Antonio?" Padma asked.

"Only a couple years," James said. "I applied to RISD and went there—"

"You got in?!" Kelly exclaimed, grabbing his arm.

"Uh, yeah," he said, flushing. She was the only other one in the room who knew just how much of a dream that had been for him. "I met my business partner there. I've always loved art, but I also liked cooking, so I went to pastry school." Here he brought his hand to his sternum absently, rubbing at the skin under his T-shirt as a shadow crossed his face. "We had the idea for the café, so after I graduated, we got a business loan and cobbled together money from his family and our friends and opened up shop."

"I saw you once," Jia said suddenly.

"In Colorado? You were in Denver?" James asked.

Jia shook her head. "It was a bad day. I think that's why I saw it. You were holding something." Here she made a gesture, cupping her hands as if something lay inside them. "One of those— gosh, what are they called—it's like two hands holding a heart?"

James paled, staring at her. *You couldn't possibly have known that,* that look said. But did he not remember what Jia was? "Clad-dagh," he managed. "A claddagh ring."

"Someone…?" Jia prompted.

"It was my fiancée's. She wore it all the time." Kelly remembered the way James made his body smaller when he reached topics he didn't feel comfortable talking about. "Her name was Dominique. She was French Canadian—we met at pastry school."

"Was?" Kelly asked softly.

"She passed away in 2007. She was visiting family in France and died in a small plane crash."

"Oh, God," Jia said. "I'm so sorry."

"The day I found out, I found her ring. She always wore it, but couldn't find it when she left. She was looking all over but had to leave for her flight." His hand went absently to his throat again. "You saw me? You saw me that day?"

"Is it that hard to believe?" Padma asked gently.

"I don't know—I don't know what to think anymore. As time passed, everything that happened here started to feel like a dream."

"Is it time?" Kelly asked sourly, looking at the empty plates across the table. "Should we get down to business?"

"Jia, what do you know that isn't in the articles you sent us?" Casey asked.

"Only what I've heard from Blub, which isn't much," she said.

"Blub?"

"He's sheriff now."

"Sheriff Blub," James said, trying the words out.

Jia related how Blub had called her to help find a missing person, only that person was dead not missing, and it was Maddy. "All I got out of him was that the medical examiner was going to look at her—at her body—today. He was acting strange."

"Strange how?" Casey asked.

"He asked a lot of questions about back then. About you guys, actually."

"You think he knows something?" Kelly asked. It was hard to imagine Blub in any position of authority. Instead, her mind filled in the blanks by replacing him with the image of his father, who had been intimidating to her sixteen-year-old self.

"I don't know, but if you see him, be careful what you say to him. I want to stay friendly and try to get information about whatever the medical examiner says."

"They must have killed her," Kelly said. "The pastor is back from the dead somehow, and it has to be related to Maddy."

"Hold on a sec," James said, pulling his knees into his chest. "We need to think about this rationally. Is the pastor Jia saw a few days ago really the same person? Maybe it's just someone who looks like him."

"You *saw* the picture," Casey said. "It's him! He's undead or something."

"But the man in those pictures looks younger. That doesn't make any sense," James said, taking out his phone to look. Kelly leaned toward him to look as well.

"How old do you think Pastor was back then?" Jia asked.

"Thirty-five?" Padma said at the same time Casey said "Forty-five," in an absolutely confident tone.

"We can't even remember how old he was back then," James said, taking this as evidence. "Maybe we *thought* we killed him, but we didn't." This was met with stunned silence. Kelly wondered if the pot chocolate was kicking in. Her bones felt more flexible. "It's the only explanation that makes sense."

"A second ago you said you thought it wasn't him, now you think it is?" Casey pointed out.

James shrugged. "Either it isn't him and it just looks like him, or it *is* him and we never actually killed him. But I don't buy that he came back from the dead."

"If we didn't actually kill him, that *would* explain why the church never made up a cover-up story about how he died," Kelly wondered aloud.

"He *died*," Padma insisted. "We all saw him die. I took his pulse."

"No offense," James said, holding up his hands, "but you're not a doctor. We were scared kids. Maybe you were doing it wrong."

"James. His *guts* were coming out of his *body*," Padma said, leaning forward.

"People have survived stranger things!"

"Even if he had survived his actual guts coming out, how long would it have taken for someone to find him and get him help? How does an ambulance get down there?" Padma pressed.

"Then it can't be him!" James said.

"Why are you so sure?" Jia asked.

"Because people don't come back from the dead." He put his phone down on the table. "I've thought about this over the years. About things we thought were supernatural. It seemed like it was back then, because that's what we thought it was, but there has to be a rational explanation for everything that happened."

"The apple orchard?" Kelly said.

"The crystals?" Padma asked. "You don't think Jia is psychic?"

Pained, he looked at Jia. "I... I'm sorry, but no."

"Then how do you think she found Maddy's body?" Padma said.

"Jeez, Padma, I thought you were a scientist!" he said, sheepish.

"I'm enough of a scientist to know that there are things that science doesn't have an explanation for yet. There are wasps that take over the bodies of cockroaches. There are cicadas that wake up every seventeen years—it must have seemed like magic before we had science to understand how. James, she saw you holding that ring."

Kelly felt a violent shiver take over her body. "It doesn't matter if it's supernatural or not," she said. "Regardless of who or what the pastor is, someone killed Maddy."

"The triple funeral is tomorrow," Jia said. "At Golden Praise." Here Casey groaned. "We can get a closer look at him there. And I want to see what they say about her, and her parents, too—that could be a clue."

"I need to see my mom while I'm here," Kelly said. "I'll ask her what I can without her getting suspicious. I'm hoping she'll finally leave this godforsaken place."

Jia handed them their room keys—they had taken over an L-shaped section of the inn—and said they could meet in the morning for coffee in the courtyard. They got their luggage, then headed to their respective rooms. Kelly was at the joint of the L, and James's room was besides hers, the farthest. "You're my neighbor again," she said.

"Just like old times."

She slowed as they had approached her door. The summer cicadas were out in full swing. "Will you come with me to visit my mom? She'd be so happy to see you."

"Your dad...?" he asked. In the darkness, his pupils had dilated.

"Heart attack when I was in grad school."

"God, is this what getting old is?"

"Something like that."

"I'd love to see her."

"It'll make her happy." She pressed her lips together, feeling the urge to cry again.

"Don't get sentimental," he said, turning to head to his room. "Good night, Kelly."

26

James

The next morning James turned the corner on the outside of the inn just in time to see Kelly locking her door. "I didn't think to bring any clothes for a funeral," she said sheepishly.

"I don't know if we need to be respectfully dressed at the megachurch funeral of a woman who was killed by said megachurch," he said.

They walked together to where the rest of the group had gathered around Jia's open door. Jia was on the phone because she couldn't remember if the service was at 11 or 11:15. They had figured if they arrived early and stayed late, they would have more time to explore with plausible deniability. The phone was on speaker, and James was subjected to a full minute of light Christian rock until a chirpy voice came on the line.

"Hello, sorry, I was checking to see what time the Wesley service was?" Jia said.

There was an uncomfortable pause. "You don't know?"

Jia made a face. "I wouldn't call if I knew."

"Did you receive an invitation?"

"I need an invitation to a memorial service?"

"The Wesleys specifically requested a private service for their closest loved ones."

"We're Maddy's loved ones," Casey snapped.

There was another pause—whether it was because of Casey's words or because the woman realized she was on speakerphone, James didn't know. "You're in luck, then. Maddy's service is over at McCallister's Funeral Home. At uh…fifteen minutes from now." Casey made a "what gives" expression as they all looked at each other and Jia hung up.

"At least it's not at Golden Praise," James said as they headed toward the minivan.

"Something about this is weird," Kelly murmured.

"*Everything* about this is weird," James added.

There were plenty of parking spots available at McCallister's. James was the last to leave the minivan, his bones feeling heavy. He had not been inside the place since his mother's service. He didn't remember what it looked like on the inside, just that the overbearing smell of lilies was permanently imprinted on him.

Casey led the way as they entered the funeral home, and James saw the droop in his broad shoulders as he entered. All the seats were empty. Gentle, respectful music played with no one to hear it but them. At the front of the room, somberly lit, was a plain urn. There wasn't even a single bouquet of discount carnations.

They filed into a single row, James repeatedly turning around to see if anyone else was coming. "I was pissed at the idea of her service being with her parents at that place, but this is basically a fuck-you to Maddy," he said.

"Maybe there's a mistake," Kelly said. She went back to talk to the funeral director. James couldn't hear their quiet voices, but Kelly's face continued to fall as he spoke. She came back, her lips pressed together in anger. "This is it. There isn't even going to be a reading or anything. They just cremated her."

"Before the autopsy?" Padma whispered.

"I have no idea," Kelly replied.

"Let's see if anyone shows up," Jia suggested.

They waited twenty minutes, then thirty. They kept glancing back expectantly at the door. Kelly checked on her phone to see what public announcements of the date and time there had been of Maddy's service—there were none. At one point James turned his head to look at Jia and saw people at the back of the funeral home. Two men standing against the back wall.

"Do you recognize them?" James whispered.

Nobody did. "I think they might be from the church," Jia whispered. James agreed.

"Everyone knows everyone's business here," Kelly said. "People probably know we're in town. Maddy doesn't have friends here—so who would show up to this service? Is this—"

"A trap," James finished for her. Casey was the only one with his head still turned in the men's direction. James was about to warn him not to be so obvious when Casey suddenly stood up. Before anyone could stop him, he was striding to the back of the room. This was football Casey. I'm-going-to-plow-you-down Casey. When he was just joking around you could forget how physically intimidating he could be.

"Are you all friends with Maddy?" he asked loudly in a fake friendly tone. The men surveyed him, then the rest of them. They were middle aged, dressed in identical black polo shirts and khakis. *Golden Praise tuxedos*, James remembered suddenly. That was what the burnouts had called that specific outfit back then. "Maybe you knew her from…church?" Casey added. At the sound of his voice the funeral director had reappeared, clearly having no idea what was going on. The men's eyes flicked to him.

"Just checking on the old girl," one of them said.

Casey looked like he was about to clock the guy, but by then Jia was hurrying down the aisle. "I think it's time to get going," she said lightly, smiling at the funeral director and ignoring the two other men.

As they walked out to the parking lot, Jia still clutching Casey's arm, James looked for any cars that hadn't been there before. Now there was a black Toyota Camry. He gestured to it to Kelly. "Goonmobile." Padma opted to drive because Casey was still muttering, *"Old girl?"* to himself.

"Let's go before they come out," Jia warned.

"You think they were checking to see if anyone would show up?" James said.

"Well, if they didn't know we were in town before, they know now."

James and Kelly walked to the Boyle house while everyone else regrouped at the inn, trying to decide their next move.

"No one should die like this," Kelly said. "Maddy probably had friends, people who loved her who would have wanted to say goodbye."

"She was already cremated?" James said. "Do they cremate people that soon, or is that—" James cut himself off when he realized he was just about to refer to Maddy's body as *evidence*. A memory popped into his head: a day when they were all at the lake. He was in the water and happened to look back at the shore where Maddy sat by herself. He had just said something mean to her—a joke with a barb that was maybe too sharp. He did that a lot that summer, because he thought she deserved it, but the barbs grew less over time. On the shore, she caught him looking at her and made a silly face. It was one thing to *trade* barbs with someone—another when they simply accepted it because they thought they deserved it. He didn't like her back then, and it would be strange to call her a friend, but she never once questioned that they would help each other, that what was happening was wrong, and that they had to do something about it. "I didn't always get along with her, but…"

"I always admired her boldness," Kelly said.

"She took whatever shit I threw at her," James said. He turned and checked behind them to see if the Camry was following them.

He had not been in Wesley Falls since he left in 1995. Some of the houses on the walk to the Boyle house were the same, while others had changed their landscaping, or added new siding. They had made this exact walk thousands of times before. Heading home from Main Street in the blistering heat of summer with melting ice cream. Walking gingerly when the roads were too icy for cars but they wanted to see if the diner was open. Kelly with her flute case, him with headphones looped around his neck. "Why is your mom still here if your dad's gone?" he asked.

Kelly sighed. "We've been trying to get her to move. Having a big house doesn't make sense anymore, and she doesn't even like it here. She's just holding on because it's like a piece of my dad."

Her house looked the same, except the door had been painted

green and the front walk had been redone. "Let me do the talking about Maddy," Kelly said as they approached. She rang the doorbell and gleefully shoved him to the side so her mother wouldn't see him.

Emily opened the door, then hugged Kelly. "I brought a surprise," Kelly said.

"What?" James heard Emily said.

"Come on, shy guy," Kelly said, leaning back to address him.

Sheepishly, James stepped out and couldn't help grinning as the shock came over Kelly's mother's face. Genuine shock, then delight, then tears. *"Jamie?"* She hugged him tightly, then shook him by the shoulders. "Look at him! I can't believe it!"

She ushered them to the kitchen for lemonade mixed with seltzer. The kitchen table was the same, but they had replaced the cabinets. James looked reflexively toward the laundry room. Emily caught him and smiled sadly. "Honey, Milky died years ago."

"Oh, right. Dumb of me."

"You came back for Maddy's funeral?" Emily asked, confused. "I thought you parted ways with her. And you—" It didn't need to be said that obviously James would have hated Maddy.

"Mom, of course I went to her funeral. People our age shouldn't be dying!"

"I was in New York when I heard from this one," James said, nudging Kelly. "So I figured I would come."

"Jamie, we really worried about you. I thought everything would be okay once we got you settled in Dover—"

"Once I got out of Pennsylvania it was fine."

"Kelly was worried sick about you. She wouldn't eat for days." James couldn't help glancing at Kelly, catching the flush under her summer tan. She was a professor now, a fancy person, and probably didn't want to be reminded of how silly she had been as a kid.

"I'm still in one piece, see?"

"But where did you *go?*"

James told the abbreviated story, leaving out Dominique because it was too sad, and leaving out the marijuana aspect of his work until Kelly poked him, indicating that her mom would be cool about it. She was both amused and impressed. "I'm glad you've found your way in the world," she said. "I always thought you would."

"Did you?" James asked, chuckling, but she didn't even smile.

"Of course I did. You were a smart boy. And very talented. Once you could get away from Rick, I saw you turning out fine." She made a gesture with her head. "You know it's gone now."

"The trailer?"

"Someone bought the property and the lot beyond it and put up a big house. It's nice. You should take a look. I mean, not that it *wasn't* nice—"

"It was a dump," James said, smiling.

Emily frowned, swirling the ice in her glass. When she looked up, sadness had overtaken her face. "I always thought I could have done a lot better by you."

"Huh?"

"I… I saw things that bothered me, but told myself it wasn't my business until it was too late. We could have done more." To his surprise, she looked like she was about to start crying.

James leaned forward, grabbing her hand. "Mrs. Boyle, your family did so much for me. You gave me a second home. You never looked at me the way other people did."

Now the tears threatened to brim over. "But we could have done more."

"You did more than anyone ever did for me."

"Now *I'm* crying," Kelly said, laughing as she got up to hug her mother. Emily started to laugh, too.

"Why don't I give you two a minute to catch up?" James said, getting up. The volume of emotion in the room was too high for him. That the Boyle family had done a lot for him had always been obvious, but he never imagined that she felt any guilt over what happened to him. What was her alternative— confront Rick and Lisa and ask them to clean up their act? Call Child Protective Services and potentially have him end up in some terrible group home?

The arrangements the Boyles had made for him in Dover

had been fine: he had a place to stay, plenty of food, and responsible adults who didn't resent his very existence. It was the
home of a friend of Emily's from nursing school, a couple with
empty-nest syndrome. On a trial basis, they had agreed to take
James for six months. No doubt Emily had touted that he was
a talented, well-behaved boy and left out all the juvenile delinquency. James had loved the magnet school he attended there,
which made him not want to cut classes, and he worked at the
husband's landscaping business after school. He hadn't minded
the work: he could listen to music while mowing lawns, and
the Weedwacker was fun. He wondered what would have happened if men from the Wesley Falls Sheriff's Department hadn't
showed up to question him yet again, and he hadn't caught that
Greyhound bus.

James headed out the back door to the porch he and Mr. Boyle
had rebuilt his last summer in town. It had held up nicely, and
a vegetable garden had replaced where a flowerbed used to be.
James dug a joint out of the back pocket of his jeans and lit it,
squinting against the summer sun. He inhaled, wandering toward the north side of the yard, where he could see where the
trailer used to be.

It was strange to look at the space that used to hold something
that was no longer there. Both the trailer and shed were gone,
replaced by a lush lawn, and beyond it, a McMansion.

"Can I help you, son?" said a stranger's voice.

James realized there was a man standing just across the property line, holding a pair of pruning shears. Whenever someone
called him "son" he assumed the person to be unsavory in some
way—he was not anyone's "son," and wasn't interested in being
talked down to in the same way he was back then. "Nope. Just
looking. I used to live on this property."

The man frowned. "No, you didn't."

James nearly laughed. "Yes, I did. There used to be a trailer here."

"Oh, wait. You're not the Curry boy, are you?"

"That's me."

"I thought he was in prison."

"You're thinking of Rick. My aunt's boyfriend."

"No, I'm pretty sure it was you."

James took a drag. "You think if I broke out of prison I would come back *here* of all places?" *God, some things never change.* He pinched out the remainder of his joint and headed back inside, where Kelly was washing their glasses. She caught his eye with a look before speaking.

"Mom, have you met the new pastor at Golden Praise?"

"Pastor Dave? I've never met him personally. Why?"

"Just curious. We drove by, and the church was bumping. It was barely scraping by last time I was here."

"The new guy brings in a lot of money," Emily said as she dried dishes. "A real go-getter, from what I've heard."

"Don't you think he kind of looks like the old pastor from when I was a kid?"

"Jim Preiss?" Emily frowned. "I don't know. I only saw him once or twice."

"How has the new guy brought in so much money?" James asked.

Emily shrugged. "Apparently, he's a great speaker? Honestly, I'm not happy about it. It may be the final nail in the coffin for me."

"To move to Florida?"

"Yes. It's starting to be like the way it was when you guys were kids. Every member of the city council is one of them." She hesitated, seeming reluctant to continue until Kelly nudged her with a dish towel. "There's a much bigger Latino population in Banwood than when you guys were little. Mainly folks from El Salvador and Honduras. Some folks are getting worked up about it."

"I think I know what you're about to say," James said, sighing.

"There was a hullabaloo at the chicken plant, because the man who runs it was hiring them, then some locals got upset because they were looking to rent houses nearby, or showing up at services. It's ugly, what people are saying. They won't say it directly, but keep passing ordinances to keep the 'character' of the town."

"You'd think they'd want to pack the seats regardless," James said. "The more donations, the merrier."

Emily laughed bitterly. "If you really believed you were saving souls from eternal damnation, why on earth would you care about the color of people's skin?"

"The woods still smell the same," Kelly observed, pulling her hair into a ponytail. They were walking south on Willow Drive, which was heavily wooded. Through those woods was the lake.

"The woods have a smell?"

"Don't you think? What with your refined palate, can't you smell it?" she teased.

"Do you think the lake's still there?" he asked.

"Where would a lake go?"

"I was just wondering if they left it alone or found some way to ruin it."

The ponytail now up, she wiped sweat off the back of her neck. "Do you remember making thumbprint cookies with my mother that summer?" she asked, glancing over at him.

He remembered cooking with Kelly's mom after he had moved in with the Boyles. "Not specifically?"

"I came down one morning and saw you two, and I was jealous and happy at the same time. Like I wanted her to love you but I also wanted her to myself."

Her honesty struck him. "You never seemed jealous."

"You deserved to be loved," she said, distracted by a tree limb that she had to push out of the way. James was glad for the distraction—her words hit like a dagger because Dominique had said something similar to him more than once. "My dad liked having you around, too."

"I wish I could have seen him again," James said.

"'The sorrow for the dead is the only sorrow from which we refuse to be divorced.'"

"Who said that?" he asked. They had just turned onto Main Street.

"Washington Irving," she said with mock disappointment, turning to look at him as if she expected him to know that.

She's very pretty, he thought stupidly, observing the way sunlight made golden flecks in her brown eyes stand out. He had always known that, but she had been *Kelly*, a person to whom he was so tightly tied that she was part of him. She had seen him at his lowest and highest. That Kelly belonged to a different class of people hadn't been debatable back then. She had a nice house and a nice family. She was kind and pretty enough to be sought after at school. But she never got an attitude about it. She had always remained just Kelly.

He couldn't begrudge her success. It was easy to picture her late at night at a library, paging through old texts about Washington Irving with intense curiosity, doing the optional reading for class. He tried to picture her fiancé but couldn't come up with a face, just a figure in a tweed jacket in front of a whiteboard writing equations. They would have intelligent children and send them to Montessori.

James eyed all the cars in the parking lot of the inn as Kelly knocked on Jia's door. Casey nudged open the door a little, then let them in. "Blub's coming by," Jia said.

"What for?" James asked. He wondered if Blub could conceivably buy that they all came here for Maddy's funeral. Just because Blub had been a bland, benign kid in their childhood, didn't mean he wasn't dangerous now.

"He said he had something to tell me," Jia replied. "Did you find anything out from your mom?"

Kelly relayed what few details they had gathered. "What's our game plan?" Kelly asked, finding a spot to sit in front of the air-conditioner.

"Two things," Jia said. "One, we go to Golden Praise so someone other than me can get a look at the pastor. Maybe we'll see if he remembers us."

"What if he *does*?" Kelly asked.

"Then the fight's out in the open. And he knows we're not afraid of him."

"Aren't we, though?" Kelly replied.

"What's the second thing?" James asked.

"We reconstruct Maddy's day. How does she go from coming into town because her parents died to ending up in a sinkhole in Evansville?"

"I think that's a good idea," Kelly said. "We—"

A knock came at the door. Casey opened it, revealing a man in uniform who immediately looked surprised. It was shocking how tall Blub had gotten—taller than Casey. He didn't look too much like his father, though, excepting the uniform. "Casey Cooper! *James Curry?* I never thought I'd see you fellas again!"

"Come in," Jia said.

As Blub turned to close the door behind him, his eyes went to every new person in the room with curiosity. "Y'all came out for the funeral?" Blub asked.

"Sort of," James said. "I was in New York, and Kelly was going to come. We used to be neighbors."

"I remember," Blub said, looking at him, right into his eyes. The look alone seemed to be a question.

"Maddy and I went to the same church," Casey said.

Blub didn't say anything for an uncomfortably long time, scratching at the stubble on his face as he continued to look around at them. "It's just funny that you're all here. All of you now." James dropped his gaze to the gun that was holstered at Blub's right hip. *Here's the part where he says something like, maybe you should all get going; you're not welcome here.* "I think there's something you all might help me with."

"What's that?" Casey asked.

"You know how this town ain't right?"

Silence.

"What do you mean?" Jia asked.

"It ain't right," he said, looking at Jia. "You can feel it, can't you?"

"Feel…what?"

Blub shook his head. "I've always known. Could never quite put it into words. I always kinda thought so, but it all came to a head that summer. The summer we did the capstones? Six of my classmates died and the reaction to it was *strange.* Yeah, there was a lot of hollerin' and a lot of people looking for someone to string up—" Here he gestured at James, who involuntarily tensed. "There was a lot of talking but it wasn't like anyone was… mourning. What they should have been doing. And that church."

"What about it?" James asked flatly. Whatever this was, he suspected it might be an act.

"I didn't like it," Blub said just as flatly, meeting his eyes. "I don't like the sort of man it turned my daddy into. And when I took over the position, there was this weird expectation from all of them—the people who really run the town—that I'd just slip into his shoes."

"What do you mean *who runs the town*, the mayor?" Kelly asked.

Blub seemed amused and exasperated. "Kelly Boyle, I know you know better than that. I'm talking about Golden Praise. Golden Praise is like the beating heart of cancer in this town."

They were collectively stunned.

Blub addressed Jia, his thumbs hooked into his belt loops. "You know I was planning on leaving? Had a lead for a job out near Pittsburgh. Then this thing with Maddy happens."

"Why would that make you stay?" Jia asked.

"Because that woman was murdered, and the church is covering it up and using my office to do it." Blub spoke this plainly, and James felt dry-mouthed suddenly.

"Why would you say she was murdered?" Padma said. "I thought she fell into a sinkhole and got trapped."

Blub scratched at his stubble. "That's the official story. Problem is there's a rat in the sheriff's office."

"Who?" Padma pressed.

"Me. The second we found her body, I knew something hinky was going on. They called the medical examiner they use out in Banwood, you know, the one who also comes to church every Sunday. So I made arrangements of my own and had another medical examiner come out and do an exam before their crooked one could get their hands on her—it wasn't a full autopsy but was the best I could do without them noticing. Glad I did, because the second after their guy looked at her, they cremated her. I don't even think they tried to track down next of kin, or to see if she had power of attorney somewhere."

"What did the two exams say?" Kelly said.

"That's what I came here to tell you. *Their* exam said that she fell into that sinkhole and broke her neck and that's what she died of. My exam said someone broke her neck *after* she died."

Kelly emitted a noise of dismay, turning her head to look away from Blub. James put an arm around her absently—he knew they were imagining the same thing.

"*My* exam said she died of blunt-force trauma to the back of the head, and that she had been moved after the time of death. We found fragments of some kind of material embedded in her skull. We managed to get some out and I sent it out for testing. That's why you're here, isn't it?" Blub added. "Maddy?"

"I barely knew her," said Padma, still toeing the line.

"Then why *are* you here?" Blub asked, a hint of frustration in his voice. "You can stop playing games. I want to help. I want *your* help. And I already know it has something to do with what happened back then. The capstone group. You did your capstone on the mine, didn't you? I figured you did some research or something and stumbled on something about the mine party."

Jia turned to look at them and they formed a quick circle, communicating with their eyes. The answer was unanimous. They were going to take a risk and trust Blub. "We all were at the mine party," Jia said. "We saw the murders. It was men from the church."

Blub stared down at her, the emotion draining off his face till only a despairing look remained. "And Maddy...when she came here, she was going to spill the beans?"

"We're not sure exactly what happened," Padma said. "That's why we're here."

"I tell you one thing, just based on what I heard about her being back here. That woman wanted to burn down this town."

27

Jia

Padma tucked a tendril of Jia's silver hair up into the scarf that now covered her hair and sighed. "I love your hair. It's a shame to hide it."

"It would attract the wrong kind of attention," Jia said. The plan was to split the group in two: half of them would go to evening service at Golden Praise while the other half would try to retrace Maddy's steps. Casey had objected to setting foot in the place if he didn't have to, so it was decided that he and James would be in the second group. Padma had shown up at Jia's door moments ago with her arms filled with clothes so that they could dress together. It reminded her achingly of their dynamic as children: showing up unannounced but being completely welcome. "Do you think wearing a scarf at church would be rude, like wearing a hat indoors?"

"You know what's rude? Sexually assaulting little girls," Padma said flatly.

Jia sat on the bed beside her. "I knew it was wrong but never thought of what happened to Maddy in those terms back then. There was so much we didn't understand."

"Do you think they're still doing the purity test? They can't be, right?"

Jia turned to look at her friend's dark brown eyes and still saw a hint of teenage Padma in them, a girlish morsel of hope that underlay all the skepticism.

They heard a knock. Jia opened the door to find Kelly, who struck a pose in her new outfit.

"What do you think? Can this pass for suburban mom with three rambunctious boys who need godly direction?" Kelly wore flowing white linen pants and a top with a sunflower on it. She had styled her hair so that the ends curved inward, a throwback to how moms styled their hair back when they were kids.

"It's going to have to," Padma said.

The three women stood in the parking lot, looking down at the expansive front lawn of Golden Praise. There were various tables set up, manned by cheerful devotees, and greeters lined the walkway up to the Central Building. *In a different light*, Jia thought, *this could look wholesome.* The kiddie pool set up for toddlers. The small group of six-year-olds uncoordinatedly playing soccer. And yet, in all likelihood, someone here had snapped Maddy's neck.

They were passing a table festooned with balloons when Kelly made the error of looking for too long. The two people manning the table jumped at their chance. "Would you like to take part in our bone marrow drive?"

"Bone marrow!" Padma exclaimed in bewilderment. Jia surveyed the table and saw clipboards, forms, some snacks, and long cotton swabs.

"One of our beloved members was recently diagnosed with aplastic anemia." The girl who said this couldn't have been more than twenty. She was wearing a white polo shirt with the Golden Praise logo embroidered on it and khaki pants despite the heat. The uniform reminded her of Maddy. She held out a sign-up clipboard that was half-filled with names.

"While it sounds scary, all it takes is a cheek swab to save a life!" she chirped.

Jia opened her mouth and struggled for something to say. She was terrible in these situations: unable to be rude to volunteers on the street asking her to sign petitions.

"We'll catch you on the way out!" Padma said brightly, already moving, her hand clasped around Jia's elbow.

"What's that about?" Kelly whispered.

"So I'm not the only one weirded out at the idea of these people collecting DNA from everyone in town?" Padma said. "It's almost like—"

"Can I help direct you?" a sweet voice interrupted her. They had almost reached Central and one of the greeters was pleasantly standing in their way. Those men at Maddy's funeral, maybe they had spread the word about them being in town—Jia wasn't sure and worried that their plan was about to be stymied.

But Kelly was ready to switch gears. "I would love for someone to show us around," she said, in a drawl that Jia recognized was an approximation of Miss Laurie. "My name's Patricia and these two are my best friends. My husband got a job up over in Banwood—" she gestured northward, flashing her engagement ring "—and we're shopping around for a church. I've got three little ones, and I've heard a lot about y'all's church."

The greeter, who was maybe twenty-five with her shiny hair in a perfect spiral ponytail, clapped her hands. She wore a gold name tag on her chest that identified her as Marla. "I'd love to! Let me give you a tour of the facilities and tell you about our programming." She opened the glass door and ushered them inside. Marla and Kelly walked ahead of them, the latter detailing the ages of her nonexistent children.

Padma nudged Jia and gestured to the stained glass that dominated the massive western wall. "New," she whispered. "That wasn't here when I worked here."

"What do you think it cost?" she murmured. The lobby of Central was filled with people milling around. The greeter opened the doors to the Sanctuary where staff were cleaning up between the rows of seats, and men were doing a sound check.

"Did I hear something about a funeral being here this morning?" Kelly drawled.

Marla put her hand over her chest with a sad shake of her head. "Jeremy and Anne Wesley. Elders in our church and descendants of this town's great founder. It's a massive blow. They were killed by a drunk driver!"

"Oh, my!" Kelly exclaimed.

"It happened down in Florida. I tell you," Marla began as she led them out of the Sanctuary, "it's just safer if people never leave town."

What a strange thing to believe! Jia thought.

Kelly had moved on to ask about youth groups. "I would like my children to be active members of the church. My daughter especially, what with all the pressures kids face these days."

"I thought you said you had three sons?" Marla asked, though not with any particular suspicion.

"Three sons, one daughter," Kelly said seamlessly, then widened her eyes in a flash to Jia when Marla's back was turned.

Marla, as she explained about the various children's groups and Youth Fellowship, was leading them to the back of the building, and, to Jia's disappointment, out the back doors to show them the other buildings.

"I would really like to meet your head pastor," Kelly said.

"He's quite busy, but you should stay for tonight's service."

"He'll definitely be there?"

"Oh, yes. We have several pastors—"

"Yes, but the man leading the church is important to me." Here Kelly leaned forward. "There was a scandal in my last church, which is why we left."

"Oh, no, there's none of that here." Marla continued her tour, showing off the gym, the children's ball pit, and meeting rooms for the Youth Fellowship. "We have an active Youth Fellowship. It's very self-motivated. They're even organizing the bone marrow drive—just about everyone's signed up." She continued talking, and Jia perked up when her spiel turned toward separate programming for boys and girls.

"Girls are under unique pressures these days," Kelly said. "Especially with social media."

"I was in the Youth Fellowship right up until I graduated high school, and let me tell you it was a lifesaver. I made friends for life."

"I want to make sure my daughter—" here Jia could see Kelly struggling for the right words "—keeps faith at the forefront of her mind."

"Rest assured, Patricia, you will find that here. This isn't just a church, it's a community. She'll meet her best friends here. She'll develop her talents. We're also starting up a special program here, just for girls."

Jia's chest tightened. But Kelly only made an inquisitive noise.

"It's called The Circle. A special program within the Youth Fellowship just for girls. I find that making girls see how special they are gives them a strong incentive to stay on the path."

"Did you say it was a new program?" Kelly asked casually.

Marla nodded in the sort of disinterested way that implied she wasn't lying. But facing more pointed questions, Marla only answered in platitudes about how she wished they had had a program like it when she was a younger girl. And that Laurie Waterson was spearheading it—that was Miss Laurie's married name.

They followed Marla from amenity to amenity, hoping that she would let something else incriminating slip, Kelly inserting the occasional comment about how great it would be to meet the pastor.

They stood chitchatting in a narrow hallway, just outside a closed door with the rumble of deep voices inside where Marla said the pastor was in a meeting. Jia felt Padma nudge her, and when she looked at her friend she could read the look in her eyes. *Do you feel anything?* that look said.

It was hard to say what she felt, hard to label anything when a thick anxiety covered everything. The notion that the pastor was behind that door and that she would see him up close, and that it might be the same pastor, made her incapable of hearing exactly what Kelly was asking Marla. Something about the high school.

But then the door opened, and men began to stream out. Mostly men older than them, but then a cluster of three came out surrounding Pastor Dave Lurie. He couldn't be Preiss—he was too young. Now that she saw him up close and with her own eyes and not through a digital screen, she could see that there were no lines on his forehead, no wrinkles at the corners of his eyes. She could see her own error: he *did* look a lot like Jim

Preiss. Or at least she thought he did—she was relying on memories from twenty years ago. It wasn't just his age that made her question her initial assumption, but that she thought she would feel *something* and she didn't. She had been expecting that old, terrible dark pull like falling into a black hole. She reached out with that esoteric part of her mind, like the tentative antennae of a fragile insect, trying to get a reading. But what it came up against was a blank, white, flat wall. There was nothing there.

She had been wrong. She had pulled everyone out of their own lives, brought them back to think about those dark days, all because of a silly mistake.

Dave Lurie was talking to Kelly, saying something about the church services. Other men were streaming out of the conference room into the narrow hallway, and Dave momentarily stood to the side, giving one of the passing men a polite pat on the back as he walked by.

"You seem young to be lead pastor," Kelly said in her affected accent, making Marla flinch.

But Pastor Dave laughed. "Full of sap and very green!" he exclaimed. "But there's the earthly age and your spiritual age! God called me when I was very young."

You don't look old enough to rent a car, Jia thought, irritated, more at herself than him.

He then said he hated to be rude, but that he had to prepare for the service, which of course they were welcome to stay for. He shook Kelly's hand with no expression on his face other than benign friendliness.

There was a shuffle in the crowded hallway—another man exiting the room, and Kelly moving aside so the pastor could shake Padma's hand. Then came Jia's turn and she held out her hand to this young man, feeling entirely foolish. His eyes shifted to Jia's just as their hands touched and that blank white wall disappeared.

The part of her mind that had run up against it seemed to tumble in space, falling downward into blackness that made her stomach sink. It was here—the same feeling she had had before. The yawning blackness that had invited her to disappear into the depths of the Heart. The pastor's hand was dry and cool. He had his index finger straight instead of curved so it pressed against the center of her wrist, the tender little place where someone would take a pulse.

In the small chaos of the crowded hallway, no one saw him lean forward, the tiny look of amusement on his face as he said into her ear, "Nice to see you again."

28

Casey

Casey and James, on foot and sweating, made one final turn and then they were in the center of town. "RIP," James said sadly, looking where The Gem Shop used to be. "Where are kids going to buy Ouija boards?"

"Probably the internet." Casey gestured to the wide windows of the diner ahead of them. "You ready?" They needed some starting point to piece together what happened to Maddy, and the diner was ground zero for town gossip. "Just to warn you," Casey said as they approached the door, "people are going to recognize me, so I'm not sure how low a profile we can keep."

James snorted. "You think you're Obama or something?"

"Football's more popular in these parts than Obama ever was."

He resisted the urge to gloat when, not two seconds after a waitress said she would find a table for them, a voice boomed out: "Is that Casey *Cooper* I see?" It was Lunch Dan, who still worked at the diner. In his loud praise, the slapping of his back, he drew a lot of attention, which made Casey feel uneasy. Lunch Dan followed them over to their table and stood for a few minutes, twisting a rag and asking about Ohio State.

Another man came over to join in on the conversation. He was about Casey's father's age, and he recognized him as one of the men from the football booster club. After they shot the shit for a while, Casey waited for a pause in the conversation to add, "We came for Maddy Wesley's funeral," gesturing to James with his head.

The man turned and looked at James, seeming to see through him rather than at him, then smiled blankly. Casey could not help but wonder if he was one of the fine townspeople who had been calling for James's head on a stick. "It's a shame," the man said, "about the Wesleys. Whole family wiped out in a week." He walked away shaking his head. Just then the waitress came by with two mugs, which she began to fill with coffee. Even though they hadn't asked for coffee, and she just assumed, Casey was grateful.

"Did you happen to see Maddy Wesley before the accident?" James asked her, managing to keep his voice sounding casual as he dumped three creams into his coffee.

"Oh, did I!" she said, and laughed, causing another waitress who was wiping down the lunch counter nearby to laugh, too. They looked at her, puzzled at what could have been funny. "She came in here all right, like a bat out of hell," the woman said in a surly tone of voice. She's old enough, Casey realized, to have known the old Maddy. "She was poking and prodding and causing trouble, which should be a surprise to no one."

"What do you mean?" James asked with an "oh, you can tell me!" smile on his face.

The waitress waved her hand. "You remember what she was like back then—she never changed. I saw her yelling at someone in the parking lot. It broke her parents' hearts when she left the church. That's where she went wrong!"

"Definitely," James said. "Did you hear what she was yelling?"

"Couldn't hear. But I can't think why anyone would have good reason to yell at Burt Randolph! That girl was running her mouth like a banshee the entire day."

"What was she poking around about?" Casey asked.

The waitress leaned forward. "You didn't hear it from me, but I heard the only reason she was in town was to steal everything that wasn't nailed down at the Wesley house."

Immediately after she left, James stopped stirring his coffee and leaned forward to whisper, "Do you know the Randolph guy? Wasn't there a kid a few years younger than us with that name?"

"The Randolphs lived next to the Good Park. They're church people."

"I wonder what he did to piss her off?"

"It could have been anything," Casey said. "Maddy never suffered a fool."

"Also, how is it stealing if she's at her parents' house? Wasn't she the only Wesley left?"

"They probably disinherited her."

"You think?"

"I'd bet you fifty bucks they left everything to the church."

"No," James said, putting his spoon down, shocked. "My family paid a tithe every month. Even when things were tight."

James winced. "I'm not taking that bet, because I think you're right."

The Wesley Falls Town Hall was a small building and the only place to go for official public records. "Can we just go in and ask questions?" Casey wondered as they approached the double wooden doors.

"Yes," James said. "Who owns what house or parcel of land is public information. Unless it's a football fan, let me do the talking. As a purveyor of an only moderately legal product, if there's one thing I know, it's bureaucracy."

The building smelled like old carpet and everyone talked in hushed voices. James, walking slightly ahead of Casey, seemed to know where he was going, and soon they were in the records division. A bored-looking woman with her hair in a tight bun manned the counter.

"I wonder if you could help us," James said, leaning forward on the counter. "We wanted to make an inquiry about the Wesley property."

"It's not for sale, if that's what you're asking."

"Oh," James said, disappointment in his voice. "I thought maybe it would be…"

"Did the deed change ownership?" Casey asked.

The woman nodded as she pulled up a massive binder, then thumbed through it. "I don't think the church will sell. They haven't sold any of the properties left to them."

"Church?" James said with mock dumbness.

The woman looked to her right then her left—the telltale sign of someone about to engage in gossip. "The owners died suddenly in an accident. The daughter came in to inquire about the property—I wasn't working that shift but I heard it was awkward because the house was going to Golden Praise, not her. A few times people have tried to snatch up land when folks die, but the church is never willing to sell when it inherits an estate."

"When you say *church*," Casey began, putting a tone to his voice to suggest that most if not all things confused him, "that means the house goes to what's-his-name? The pastor?"

"Oh, no," she said, closing her binder. "The church is a non-profit corporation."

James turned and looked at him, his lips pressed together to prevent the bitter smile that Casey knew was underneath.

"Is the person who was working when the daughter came by here today?" Casey asked.

"Caleb? No. But I was here the next day when she came back."

"She came back?"

The woman nodded, adjusting her glasses. "The very next day. She said she was trying to find some old family friends to inform them about her parents. Of course that's a bit silly, because who here doesn't know about her parents—"

"Which family friends?" James interrupted, but not rudely.

"Jane Merrick, actually." The woman had dropped her voice to say this, as if there was some tragic quality to that content.

"Oh, right, she used to work for the church," Casey said, as if he had just remembered this fact.

"Do you know where we could find her?"

"I mean, physically..." She saw the blank looks on their faces. "She's at the old folks' home at the edge of town. Alzheimer's. She was close to the Wesleys, you know."

"Do you think anyone can visit Jane Merrick or just people on a list?" James wondered as they exited Town Hall.

"Don't know," Casey said. "But I'm willing to bet that old bat doesn't have many visitors."

"Do you mind if we pop into the art store?" James asked. Casey nodded. "Do you think Jane Merrick just got old and sick, or maybe they did something to her?" he asked as they headed in that direction.

"You can't give someone Alzheimer's. And Maddy always made it sound like she was the pastor's right-hand man. Woman."

"Shit. Convenient that the one person who knows everything doesn't remember it," James muttered.

"What if the girls come back and say the pastor isn't Jim Preiss?"

"Then we figure out who killed Maddy and get out of here."

"And what if it *is* him?"

James glanced at him with amusement. "Then we get out the crystals and potions—I don't know, Case."

They went inside the art store, greeted by a blast of welcomed air-conditioning. Casey had only ever been there a dozen or so times, maybe once or twice for a school project, but more likely because Lexie had wanted something.

As they approached the counter, Casey realized he recognized the clerk. Josh? Jackson? His hair was thinner, but Casey was good at recognizing faces. A pin on his shirt identified him as the manager. Unless Casey was mistaken, he had been behind them a couple years in high school. If James recognized him, he didn't appear to give this away. "Hey, I don't suppose Mr. Desanto is around anymore?"

Josh-or-Jackson blinked. "If Mr. Desanto were alive, he'd be a hundred something."

"I'll take that as a no, then," James said, disappointed. "I used to come here a lot when I was a kid."

"I know. You're James Curry. And Casey Cooper," he said, looking at Casey.

"Josh McCallister," Casey said, the name coming back to him. "I think you were the younger brother of one of my brother's friends?"

"Yeah. How can I help you?"

"Where could I find willow charcoal?" James asked.

"Aisle three," he said, then turned his eyes to Casey as James walked away. "I don't think I've seen you around for years."

"Haven't been around in years."

"You went to Ohio State?"

"Yeah. I still live out in Columbus. Does your brother still hang with mine?"

An awkward expression crossed over Josh's face. "Not so much. They had a falling out."

"My brothers are assholes."

A tentative smile broke out over his face. "I wasn't going to say it, but yeah. I'm glad you got out to Columbus, man. Seems like a cool place. Cooler than here at least," Josh said.

"Places are just amalgamations of people."

"They teach you that shit at college?"

Casey laughed. By then James had returned with willow charcoal, which was not what Casey had imagined but a small box of black sticks. Josh rang him up and James paid with a ten. As he looked down to pull it from his wallet, Casey noticed Josh looking at him for a second too long. "I heard you disappeared."

"Something like that," James said, smiling. "I'm glad this place is still here. This town needs more places like this."

"Yeah, where do the weirdos hang out these days?" Casey asked.

"Still at the Bad Park," Josh said. "Except they turned it into a skate park."

"They *did*?" James asked.

"When I say *they*, I don't mean the town, I mean the kids built it themselves. They watched YouTube videos and got concrete and stuff." Here he rolled his eyes. "Now the town thinks it's a blight upon humanity."

"Stopping the atrocities in Syria and that skate park should be at the top of anyone's list," James said. Josh snorted appreciatively and handed James his change.

"We actually came out for Maddy Wesley's funeral," Casey chanced, hoping that they had built up enough rapport that this wouldn't come across as suspicious.

Josh cringed. "You know I saw her? The day before?"

"You did?" James asked.

"Yeah. I heard she was in town. Then I guess the night before she disappeared, it must have been, I was driving home and I saw her parking her car off the side of the road over on Willow."

She either went to the lake, Casey realized, *or the bunker. But I don't think we left anything there, did we?*

He then realized that James was staring intently at Josh and that the latter looked uncomfortable. "What?" James asked. "Was she upset or something?"

Josh played with a roll of quarters from the cash register. "I must've heard wrong. It doesn't make any sense."

"What?" Casey asked.

"Well, she was by herself but she was yelling, 'I know a fucking reporter at the *New York Times*!' I thought maybe she was on the phone but she wasn't holding anything. Then I thought, maybe she was yelling at *me* because I was the only one there. She seemed…well, kind of unhinged."

"Maybe she had a Bluetooth in?" James suggested.

"Yeah," Josh said, still looking troubled. "Maybe."

They exited the store, James pocketing his charcoals then checking his phone. "Willow Drive?" Casey asked. "You think she went out to the bunker?"

"Either that or the lake." James gestured to Del Monico's with his head. "I don't know about you, but I'd kill for a beer. The girls just texted—we can wait there."

"Second that."

They grabbed seats outside at Del Monico's. When their beers came they were served in the same red plastic cups that looked like glass but weren't. "Who do you think she was yelling at?" Casey wondered.

"Unless she had a radical personality change, I can't imagine her wearing a Bluetooth," James said.

"I wonder if she was being followed and knew it."

"But she said she has a friend at the *New York Times*? If she thought she was being followed, why wouldn't she say something like, 'My husband's got a gun and he's on his way'?"

"Because she had no idea she was about to be killed," Casey

reasoned. "At the diner they said she was running her mouth all over town. Then she threatens whoever by mentioning a newspaper. She was—"

"Making too many noises," James finished.

"Oh, Maddy," Casey said, sipping his beer. If she had been "poking around," she had certainly given the impression that she wasn't going to keep quiet about what she found. "You should have left the second they started pointing fingers at you. I always wondered about that—if we could have gathered up all our money in June and you could have skipped town."

"It's not that easy to leave," James said.

"You literally left with five hundred dollars."

"Only because I had to." James looked out at the parking lot and the people entering and exiting stores. "We all could have left at any point," he said. "When you're a kid, you just think that's the way things are, and you don't have power to change them. You don't know anything outside the box you grew up in, and even if the box sucks, it's scary to think of crawling out of it."

Casey's cell phone pinged: it was Aaron checking in on him. He replied back saying everything was all right. When he looked back up, James was looking at him. "Why didn't you tell us back then? We wouldn't have made fun of you or anything. I mean, maybe Maddy would have said something, but we would have shut it down."

"I didn't know."

"Dude. Come on. How did you not know you're attracted to men? Weren't you looking at guys, or gay porn?"

Casey raised an eyebrow, a smile breaking over his face. "*Gay porn?* Where would I have gotten *gay* porn? You think there was any *gay porn* in the woods?"

James brought a fist to his mouth, laughing silently. It used to be a matter of pride to try to make him laugh like that. When he finally regained his breath, he said, "I was trying to explain to one of my pastry chefs who's younger that back in ye olden times, you couldn't get porn on your computer but you'd have to find a stash out in the woods. He was so confused—*why would it be out there in the woods? What if it rains?*"

"Kids these days don't know the hardships we had to go through. And the brotherhood of dudes who leave porn in the woods for teenagers. Straight porn, mind you. Or at least around here. Maybe there was a seed somewhere inside me that knew," Casey said, "or at least knew a little, but it had to be buried. I'm not the most introspective person. Maybe some part of me knew it wasn't safe. Maybe my dad suspected and that's why he was so hard on me—I always thought it was about football, but maybe it wasn't. I couldn't even see what my family was like until I left. I'm almost glad I didn't fully know back then because it would have made things harder."

"You wouldn't have come out, would you? I got called a faggot constantly because what—? I had long hair?"

"Or because you spend nine dollars on pieces of burnt bark at the art store?"

"Back then I would've stolen it."

"I was so envious of you."

"Me?"

"You stone-cold didn't give a fuck. In a town where everything revolved around fitting in."

"I was just being contrarian. I was probably annoying to be around."

Casey drained the last of his beer. "So before the ladies get here, what's single life like in Denver? Let me live vicariously through you."

"It's fine, I guess," James said, the humor gone from his voice. He struggled for something to say, but just then the minivan pulled up and their friends hopped out.

"Ugh, it's hot, tell us everything," Kelly said, sliding in next to James and downing the last of his beer with relief. Casey watched James looking at Kelly as she did this, a faint smile on his lips, which got wider when she made a faux apologetic face and set the cup down. Back then, the two had always been a pair, the way Padma and Jia had been, and he had seen many instances of silent communication between them, inside jokes, or overly familiar behavior like what she had just done. But until now, he had never seen anything like the look on James's face.

"No, our news first," Padma said. "It *is* the pastor. Jia confirmed."

"I didn't notice anything at first, but then he shook all our hands. When he shook mine, he said, *Nice to see you again*, like it was funny," Jia said.

"It's Jim Preiss?" James asked. "Then why does he look younger than before?"

The women exchanged glances. "It's hard to explain, and that's not his name. Somehow it's him, but younger," Padma added.

They recounted their tour of the church and about the restart of the Circle Girls, then Casey told them what they had found: that the church owned the Wesley property, that Maddy had been overheard threatening to go to the press, and that they needed to make a date with Jane Merrick.

"If she was over on Willow, do you think she went to the lake?" James asked.

But Padma and Kelly immediately became excited. "The time capsule!" Padma shouted.

"She must have gone to dig it up!" Kelly exclaimed, looking at her.

"Time—?" Casey started to say without thinking. But then he remembered. All six of them digging in the woods with their hands. Kelly using a piece of rock. Padma insisting that it had to be buried deep or someone else could find it.

"Shit," James said, remembering. "We buried everything we found out about the mine."

Kelly stood up. "Let's go—we can still get it before sundown."

29

Padma

Padma stooped to pick up a tree branch. It was sturdy, heavier than a wooden baseball bat, though awkwardly long. She tested a swing. "Really?" Casey said from beside her, with a half grin.

"What?" she said. "The thought of Maddy screaming at someone she couldn't even see scares me." Jia was leading the way, claiming she remembered that the time capsule was midway between the bunker and the lake, buried under a tree they had carved something into.

"You don't think...it happened here?" Casey said, looking around.

"I don't know. Wouldn't Jia feel it?" Padma replied.

"It's confusing to me what she can or can't feel. Why can't she just see what happened to Maddy, and we have our answer?"

"I don't think she can pick and choose as much as she'd like to."

Padma jumped at the sound of leaves and broken twigs breaking, clutching her grip around the branch. A squirrel jumped from the bushes to the side of a tree and scurried upward. If someone had been following Maddy, it would have been just like her to get up into their face, not unlike Casey had done at the funeral home. None of them had died that summer—perhaps that had misled her into thinking she was safer than she actually had been.

"I've got your back," Casey said, pausing to pick up a branch that was comically larger than hers. She couldn't help laughing, the fear she had been feeling momentarily lifting.

"You'd be a good dad," she said. "Your kids would never be scared of monsters. I could see you coaching soccer. You'd be the nice coach," she said. "Not the coach who yells, but who takes off his hat when the kids are misbehaving and says, 'I'm disappointed,' and the entire team is devastated."

"You know one of my brothers has two kids, and I never get to see them." Padma made a disgusted noise. "I've never even met them. I only know about them because Lexie has a fake Instagram account. I guess the Cooper clan is worried I'll corrupt them."

Padma kicked a rock. She couldn't imagine not being an aunt to Ajay's children. There were times when she told herself that if adoption didn't work out, she would be content with being an aunt. "Given what you've told me about your brothers, they might seek you out when they get older."

Jia, ahead of them, was starting to look at trees for the carving. "Do you remember what type of tree it was?" Casey asked.

"Birch." Most of the trees were oaks or maples, with only the occasional white birch making an appearance. That must have been why they had picked it, Padma thought. A moment later Casey nudged her, gesturing toward Kelly and James. James was using the low voice he used to imitate someone he thought was stupid, and must have said something funny because Kelly was laughing, shoving him playfully. "What?" Padma asked.

"Come on. *Those two.*"

"They've always been like that." He made an exaggerated skeptical face. "Casey, she's practically married."

"My Spidey sense is never wrong."

She scowled and continued looking for the tree, but kept glancing over at the pair. She disliked it when people saw things before she did. Not to say that Casey was right. But—

"Hey!" Casey said. He had found a gash in a birch tree.

"No," she said. "It was the number six. It should be unambiguous." Casey sighed theatrically. "I will say…" she started with her voice lowered. "I will say the way you talk about Aaron is pointedly different. Like you were excited and your face lit up. She seems more…"

"Reserved. Has she said anything to you about her fiancé?"

"No."

"Because if she tells you and Jia, I need to know."

"You're such a gossip!"

"Men don't gossip!"

"You literally host a show twice a week that is all gossip."

"That's *analysis*."

"You—agh! Look!" Padma exclaimed, pointing at a fat birch tree. It was larger than what she had pictured in her mind's eye, and the carving was lower than she remembered—which perhaps made sense because she had gotten taller. But there it was, the roughly marked 6. She remembered carving with James's Swiss Army Knife, that it was too hard to make curves so it was composed of five straight lines. "We counted six paces out, on the side where the carving is."

James pointed downward. "Is it me, or does that dirt look fresh?"

It did. The soil looked disturbed, and when Padma got down to her knees, she saw it was missing the crust of topsoil that the surrounding ground had. James plopped down to his knees across from her, his hair swinging in front of his face, and she recalled the last time they had been here, hurrying, their grubby little hands digging.

The recently churned soil was softer, and reminded Padma of crumbled chocolate cake. The loamy smell of fresh dirt filled her nose as they dug in silence.

Casey scooped with his big hands entwined, pushing the soil behind him, and they fell into a rhythm of digging. Once the hole was elbow deep, Padma attempted to snake her hands deeper inside, feeling for anything irregular.

"I feel an edge," she said. They crammed around her, uncovering a rectangular shape encased in plastic, then began to dig out around the sides.

"I've got it." Casey's arms disappeared inside the hole and then he wrenched something out in one go, setting it on the ground.

They had wrapped it in garbage bags—four layers. The package was still wrapped, but someone had clearly cut through the tape raggedly. Padma began to pull the bags off, not entirely sure of what would be underneath. She only half remembered what they had put inside. She feared it would be something sentimental and childish—nothing that would prove useful.

Underneath all the garbage bags was a long rectangular box, which had once held a pair of Maddy's knee-high leather riding boots. When Padma pulled off the cover, there was enough inside for everyone to take an item. Padma went for the shiniest: pushed to the corner were six semiprecious stones. One for each of them from Jia's experiment. Padma couldn't remember which stone had been hers.

Kelly leaned forward to pick up a fat envelope, the kind that no longer existed: they were the packets pictures came in from the developer. She sat back and began to flip through them. Padma could see over her shoulder that they were pictures of the six of them from that summer. They had been scared of their friendship being discovered, but had been sentimental enough to take pictures and save them. Mixed in with the silly shots of them hanging out were other pictures: evidence from Evansville.

James picked up a black sketchbook—his, she knew—and flipped through it. "Guys," he said. He held the book open to a drawing. Padma felt a shiver climb up her back. They had been so desperate to find a picture of the pastor back then and 1995 James had produced the next best thing. On the left side of the page was a pencil drawing, a close-up of the pastor's face, and on the right side was a full body-size drawing. The margins of that particular page had only been loosely sketched in but Padma could tell it was the apple orchard. And the perspective of the picture was unusual: as if the viewer was on the ground, looking up at the pastor. "Was this who you saw today?"

"Yes," Kelly said, not sounding surprised.

"Now that I look at him, I remember him. I had another drawing at home, but the face was smeared out," James said.

Casey unfolded a massive piece of thick paper. Padma remembered James on his knees in the bunker drawing on it as Kelly followed him, annotating with what she had discovered from old records. It was a map of the mine. Not something for their capstone project, but something that had taken a considerable amount of time and had proven valuable. The unfortunate thing was that James was the only one who didn't find it confusing to read.

Jia was on her hands and knees, flipping through the old photo album they had taken from the church in Evansville. "Wait," Padma said, staying Jia's hand. A picture had been shoved into the seam of the page, not pasted on to the page as the others had. Padma picked it up—it featured a group of solemn people looking back at the camera, but someone had drawn an arrow on the top right corner. Padma flipped over the picture and gasped. In faint ink at the top right of the picture were the words *Evansville, Penn.1922* but below that, Maddy's handwriting was scrawled in bright blue ink.

This was tucked under another picture—I don't even know if we saw it back then. If you're seeing this and something went wrong assume the worst. This was followed by an unintelligible sentence, clearly written in a hurry, the ink smeared.

"What's the last part?" Padma asked, frustrated.

James took it from her, moving it closer and then farther away from his face. "Ask Jane…hair? No, about. About the… Batch? I can't make out the last word. Body?"

"She knew we would come here," Casey said, sitting back on his heels. "I think she saw the pastor and thought we had a picture of him from back then."

James flipped over the picture, holding it in direct sunlight. "1922," he said. "This is 1922." He held the picture out so they could all see. His hand was shaking but Padma could see why. The picture was of a group of people dressed in what must have been 1922 mining town attire. The girls were young, maybe teenagers, maybe a tad younger—some wore ribbons in their hair, their faces youthful but unsmiling. They wore long skirts and white blouses. A man stood with them and gave Padma an impression of possession. "Tell me that's not the same man," James said, now bringing out the sketchbook with his other hand, holding it open.

James was clearly shaken by this revelation, but to Padma it made sense that the man they just discovered wasn't dead—

despite them having killed him twenty years ago—was walking around in Evansville in 1922 looking more or less exactly the same. It was just another symptom of whatever strange force had taken hold here. James jabbed the picture at Jia. "I mean, is he fucking *immortal* or something? What is this? How can this be?" His eyes were wide, a little wild, like a child. There was something almost funny about James, who wholeheartedly didn't believe in anything supernatural, being confronted with hard evidence of something entirely impossible.

Jia clasped a hand gently around James's wrist, staying the trembling. "James. This is happening whether we believe it or not." Whether she had ever articulated it or not, there had always been something raw and unprocessed about Jia and her emotions back when they were kids. Jia was the girl who, in seventh grade, had excitedly called Padma to come over because she had found an abandoned baby mouse in her yard. She had made a comfortable bed for the thing in a shoebox and was attempting to feed it half and half by dipping a bit of yarn and then letting the mouse suckle on it. The mouse was so young that the skin of its underside was translucent, and Padma could see its organs, including its tiny, furiously beating heart. As Jia fed the mouse, Padma looked at her and realized, *Oh, she doesn't understand that it's going to die.* It would die in her cupped hands, its heart stilled, and Jia would sob, inconsolable for the loss of a creature that had only tasted life for a few days.

But Padma wondered if she had gotten it wrong. Maybe Jia had known the mouse would die from the moment she saw it and still felt it was worth caring for. Maybe to her, their coming back to face whatever this was was inevitable. Maybe what felt raw and unprocessed back then had morphed into a Jia that was more confident, but that Padma understood less.

"What now?" James asked, dropping the photo and closing his eyes, rubbing at them. "We take some magic beans and travel into the astral realm?"

"We see if Jane Merrick's willing to talk to us," Padma said.

PART SIX: JULY 1995

30

Kelly

In the two weeks that followed that awful night when James got stitches, Kelly had an underlying sense of dread that something terrible was going to happen, but in those two weeks, they were still happy.

James was now living with the Boyles, sleeping on the couch most nights, but sometimes falling asleep in Kelly's room if they were hanging out late. Though he had spent many nights at her house, the novelty of him being part of the household filled them both with childish excitement. If the police were still focused on him, something—perhaps his own assault—had caused a respite in his harassment, and his mood was greatly improved. The two whispered on how they could convince her parents to let him stay indefinitely.

Part of their plan was that they were on their best behavior. Not that Kelly ever misbehaved really, but they both did more than their fair share of chores: washing dishes, weeding the yard, helping with groceries. While Kelly had assumed that the Harpies would object to James's presence, they were softened by the violence they had seen that night, probably pleased he was doing their chores, and delighted by the fact that he was indifferent to things like letting them French braid his hair.

After the first week, Kelly's interest in chores waned, but James's did not. He helped with dinner without being asked, popping up to take the dishes despite protests from her parents. He was handy with what Kelly thought of as male things—

anything that involved power tools—and when her father took on the task of repairing the deck, James went with him to the lumber store, and a day later showed him some ideas he had drawn, his ears turning red when Kelly's father adjusted his glasses and considered them.

So far the plan seemed to be working, and Kelly often wondered when the perfect time was to ask how long he could stay, and why not forever. She found her mother in the home office, sitting in the dim room with the lights off as she wrote checks. "Come here, Kell-bell," her mother said. Kelly sat across from her, picking up a paperweight to play with. "Can you tell Jamie to lighten up with the housework?"

"Why?" Kelly asked, feeling a stab of anxiety.

"It doesn't feel right to have this poor boy living in our house doing all the chores that you girls should be doing."

"He just wants to help."

"Kelly, how much of this did you know?" Emily asked, looking up from the checkbook.

"How much of what?" she asked, even though she knew.

"Rick always struck me as…unsavory, but I didn't know. Did you know?"

She considered lying, then decided not to. "Kinda."

"Why didn't you tell me?"

She struggled to answer. She was close to her mom and told her a lot of things, but also withheld some things—but this was different. It hadn't been hers to tell. "He wouldn't have wanted me to."

Emily sighed. "I know how loyal a person you are, but sometimes there are things more important than loyalty. Sometimes you have to risk people getting mad at you to do what's right. And when you see something wrong, you have to say something, even if it's hard."

Kelly's eyes stung as she thought of all the times James had been casual about things Rick did when he shouldn't have been, when he told "funny" stories about "dumb shit" Rick and Lisa did, when sometimes they were disturbing. She thought about when the principal yelled at James for the gun painting, and she meant to confront him but never did. She was cowardly and didn't like to know this about herself.

She looked at her mother and considered telling her everything. She had already told her parents a version of the mine party story: that she had been there with James, she was with him the entire night, but when the accident—this was the word she used—happened, they had nothing to do with it, though the police were harassing him. She considered saying something, but instead what popped out was, "Mom, why can't he stay with us?"

"I don't know, honey."

"It'll just be for two years, then he'll go to college. He won't even be around much, because if he gets into the magnet school, it's an hour bus ride each way. You won't even notice him."

"That's not the point." Emily took off her reading glasses and rubbed the bridge of her nose. "Lisa is still his legal guardian. At any point she can say, 'what is this child doing here?' and take him back. The law will side with her."

"But why? Even after what happened?"

"Rick isn't there anymore." Rick's sentencing was proceeding. He had made a plea deal for his charges, which had to do both with assaulting James and the presence of drugs in the trailer. James had found this funny, and regretted that he didn't have any marijuana of his own stored in the house, which would have made things worse for Rick's sentencing.

"He'll come back," Kelly said darkly. She had little faith in Lisa.

"Right now we're just banking on Lisa's whim. We're trying to figure something out. We're looking for his grandparents, but they weren't close to his mother. We might know some people in Dover who can help out if he gets into that school."

While Kelly did not expect James to work on the capstone, the due date for magnet school applications was in two weeks, and he had offered any number of excuses to not work on it. He was helping with the deck. He wasn't in the mood. He was nauseated or dizzy—these were real effects of the concussion he had received, but he had spent the past two years talking about the magnet school, and now he was self-sabotaging.

Kelly determined that today would be the day that she would convince him to work on it. She went down the hallway and then crept into the living room where James, lying on the couch, didn't hear her.

"Hey, lazy," she said, sitting down promptly on his feet so he could not escape. "If you don't work on your application today, I'm going to murder you."

He laced his hands together behind his head. "You'd have to catch me first."

"I'm faster than you, idiot."

He laughed. "I made muffins. Let's take some to the library. I'll work on it after, I promise." They hadn't been able to all get together for a while because Casey had football things and Maddy was on lockdown. They left early so James could swing by the art store on the way. It might have been her imagination, but Kelly felt as if people were staring at him less than they were before. She liked Mr. Desanto, the old man who owned the store, who was nice to everyone and made donations for art classes at school. James looked at a box of chalk pastels, but then balked at the price, deciding to only buy a container of gesso.

When Mr. Desanto was ringing him up, Kelly's eyes wandered to the back pocket of James's jeans, where he had secreted away an X-Acto knife. Mr. Desanto held up a finger, crouched to look for something, and then presented a different box of pastels, which he opened to show that several were broken. "I could give these to you at a discount," he said. James brightened and they negotiated while Kelly wished to disappear into the floor—negotiating made her uncomfortable. As James was happily counting out his change as he held his bag of items, Kelly looked up at Mr. Desanto and saw him looking at her, smiling. *He knows*, she thought.

"You shouldn't steal things, especially now," she whispered when they were far enough away. James had an extra hop to his step, careless in his attitude when perhaps he should not have been.

"No one's going to arrest me! If they were going to, they would have done it already."

★ ★ ★

Padma had reserved a room for them at the library and popped to her feet when she saw them. Casey was more excited about the muffins. Fair enough—he looked as if he had just run ten miles. "I need to set up my presentation," Kelly said, drawing a few bewildered looks as she wheeled over the overhead projector from the corner.

"They let you out of the house?" Jia asked Maddy. Maddy had relayed to them what had happened with her Circle pin at Golden Praise once it had happened.

Maddy's voice was sour. "Church activities and educational activities are fine. Everyone stares at me."

"What I don't get is why they're trying to pin the murders on James if they could just make up a story about kids getting drunk and falling down the Heart," Casey said.

"They're not trying to pin it on me anymore," James said, his mouth full.

"I think it was some kind of sacrifice," Padma said, her eyes shiny.

"Christians don't do human sacrifices," Casey said doubtfully.

"There's tons of it in the Bible," James said. "I was reading this book from Jia's store about cults—it's probably something like that. The pastor is the leader," James said.

"I'm not sure he's involved," Maddy said slowly. This surprised Kelly so much that she stopped rifling through her transparencies, the sheets of clear plastic that she had carefully drawn on for their meeting.

"He has to be. He's the head of everything," James said.

"He was nice to me just before the Merricks took my pin. I almost felt like he wanted to defend me."

"Almost?"

"Maddy, what if it wasn't the Merricks who ordered that exam, but him?" Kelly said.

"It's the Merricks who make comments to girls about how they're dressed or are acting, not him. For all we know, he could be a victim here, too."

James put his head in his hands and sighed. This elicited some chatter, but the moment Kelly turned the lights off, everyone fell silent. "You have our attention, Mrs. Boyle," Casey said, folding his hands, the picture of the well-behaved student that he most certainly wasn't.

"Unlike any of you," Kelly began, "I've actually been working on our project." Padma started to protest, but Casey shushed her.

Kelly put on the first transparency, projecting a blank outline of the part of Pennsylvania that Wesley Falls was located in. She had drawn topographical lines to indicate elevation in black, then colored over it with blue. "Native Americans have been living in Pennsylvania for more than ten thousand years, including here before this town existed. The main tribe who lived in this area, or at least as far back as we have the maps for, was the Susquehannock," she said. "The blue is where they were living before the Europeans came." She switched the transparency. "Then here's when the Dutch, Swedes, and British settled." She switched to another transparency where the colonial powers were different colors along with the blue. "The Susquehannock were devastated by diseases the Europeans brought, but also warfare. This is where each group lived as the Susquehannock started to be pushed out—" here she switched the transparency again "—and after they were gone. Notice what's the same across time, regardless of who we are talking about."

"The white spot," Padma said, catching it right away.

There was a white spot: a series of wavy topographical lines stacked on top of each other until it grew to two small circles. "Is that Devil's Peak?" Maddy asked.

Kelly nodded. She then layered the transparencies on top of each other, creating a muddle of color except in one place that remained white. "Across a couple centuries one thing stays the same. No one wanted to live on Devil's Peak. Why? When all the colonizing countries are fighting wars with each other for territory and pushing out the Susquehannock to take their land, why did no one want to come near this particular mountain?"

When Kelly looked up at them, Casey seemed uncomfortable. "Maybe just because it's a mountain? No one wants to live there."

"It's land. It's not so steep that it's inhospitable. There are streams and tons of forest to hunt or trap furs in. Timber to cut down. I'm sure other resources, too. People made the conscious decision to stay away from Devil's Peak for some reason," Kelly said.

"The mountain is evil," Jia said.

"Mountains can't be evil. It's just…rock," James said.

"Sorry, dude, I think she's right," Casey said. "That place always gave me the creeps."

"Yeah, abandoned mines are creepy. But places don't have… souls," James replied.

"How do you know?" Padma piped up.

"It's not that it has a soul," Jia said quietly, sinking down into her chair. "It's that it has the opposite of a soul."

"You were acting weird at the party," Casey said. "After the collapse. Totally spaced out."

"The Heart was trying to pull me in," she said.

"*What?*" James exclaimed. Jia went on to explain that after the collapse, she had felt pulled down a dark path, totally without any free will of her own. Similar to when she saw the pastor talk at the town hall, and then him saying, *I know what you are.* Kelly was unable to take her eyes off Jia.

"What do you mean, *I know what you are*? What's that supposed to mean?" James asked.

A long moment passed with Jia and Padma looking at each other. "Jia sees things that other people don't," Padma said. She looked at Jia as if for permission, then began to tell them about a bus accident that they had avoided, about Jia's mom and her lottery tickets.

No one quite knew what to say when she finished talking, but Kelly felt her skin prickle as she wondered, *Maybe it was meant to be us that discovered this. Maybe we were put here for a reason, all six of us.* James looked at Kelly, the look in his eyes clearly saying, *Do you believe this?*

I'm not sure what I believe, she said back.

"Maybe it's supposed to be this way," Maddy said slowly. "Maybe it's not an accident that Jia's the way she is. Maybe the mountain is evil and no one was ever supposed to go inside."

"But someone did," Padma said. "Your family."

"Jeremiah Wesley and his brother Matthew," Maddy said. "They founded the coal mine and Wesley Falls and Evansville." Maddy was looking at her hands, twisting a bracelet she was wearing, uncomfortable. "The Elders killed those kids. We just need to figure out why and stop them."

"But your parents are Elders," Kelly said.

Maddy looked at her, nodding.

Casey sat up straight. "Coach is an Elder."

"I know," Maddy said.

"Coach wouldn't *kill* someone. Are you kidding? You can't possibly—"

"Casey, I've been in this church since I was a baby. There's no way the Elders don't know about it. They probably planned it. I just don't know why."

"Is this how the pastor gets his power?" Jia asked.

Maddy blanched. "What *power*? Have you seen him flying around or something? It's the Elders—"

Kelly held up her hands for silence. "The only thing we all agree on is that the church did this. We need to get inside Golden Praise for more evidence," she said. "Maddy, we could have used you to snoop inside the building if they hadn't turned on you."

"I hope Scott's steak was worth it," James said. He had probably said it to be mean but Maddy barked out a laugh, then Casey started laughing, too.

Maddy rested her forehead on the table, still laughing, and when she picked her head up, Kelly could see tears in her eyes. "No," she said, at last. "But I have an idea. The church is having an open house on Friday. One of us can go—I'll tell you the places where evidence might be."

"Which one of us?" Kelly asked, secretly hoping that it would not be her.

"It can't be you," she said, pointing at James. "You can't step foot inside there."

"I might burst into flames," he added.

"You two are off-limits," she said, using two hands to point to

Casey and Kelly. "Because you went to the police you're com-
promised. They know what you saw, but they don't know *that
we saw it together*. Jia can't go since she's on the pastor's radar. I
obviously can't go. Which leaves…"

It made perfect sense. Padma already had a job there. Everyone turned to Padma, who shrank down into her chair. "Oh,"
she said in a tiny voice.

31

Padma

Padma paced around her room, playing with a lump of dental wax to comfort herself. She paused every few moments to look at her mirror to recheck her outfit. She had chosen it carefully, picking from the many girlish things her mother bought for her, deciding that looking young would help her for once.

Her computer emitted a familiar noise—an IM from Maddy. Never in a million years did she think *Maddy Wesley* would be on her Buddy List but circumstances were beyond strange. Padma figured that she must be pretty lonely to talk to her. They talked about the mine party, but also, two nights ago Padma had asked when she thought she would be ungrounded and Maddy said possibly never. They are making me feel like I am beyond redemption, she had written. My parents think I'm worthless. The words stung Padma. She had occasional conflicts with her parents, but not for a moment did she think they didn't wholeheartedly love her. She struggled with the right thing to say, caught in the odd position of being told something quite personal by someone she didn't know well, and she both wanted to comfort Maddy and wanted Maddy to like her. You know that is just their opinion and they don't know everything, Padma had written. Have 2 go, Maddy had replied, then signed off abruptly. She always IM'd as if her parents were hovering around nearby.

MaddyWes: ready freddy?

SavageGarden15: I am scared

MaddyWes: it will be fine, you can do it

SavageGarden15: says who?

MaddyWes: all five of us think you can

SavageGarden15: why me? maybe Casey can go

MaddyWes: it has to be you.

MaddyWes: youre the smartest person I know. Youll do good

Padma flushed with pleasure. Maddy was her main rival to be valedictorian, so to have her say that was pleasing. She took several deep breaths, and then Ajay was knocking on her door, saying it was time for him to drive her to her loser party.

Remember, she told herself as she got out of the car and Ajay sped away, *you were specifically invited.* The last time she had seen Miss Laurie, she had gushed about how great the open house would be. This was a month ago, when she had been helping with the preparations. But a month ago was before the mine party.

She put her hand protectively over her pink purse and entered one of the sets of double doors that were propped open, decorated with balloons. Inside her purse, she had all her essentials: emergency cash, bobby pins, her keys, maxi pads, and most importantly, a Kodak disposable camera with enough film for thirty pictures. But she knew from having used them before that sometimes they squeezed out a few extra pictures.

The great foyer of Central was crowded with people and small tables set up with snacks. The adults towered over her, which gave her an idea. While Padma thought herself lacking Maddy's social skills or Casey's athleticism, she did have one superpower: invisibility. She had seen it so often at school: teachers didn't see her hand waving, people gossiped or said private things right in front of her. For once, she could use this power to her advantage.

She took a few appetizers: cubes of cheese and a mini egg roll, and moved through the crowd, listening to what people were saying while keeping a distracted look on her face, as if she was looking for someone. The only person who seemed to notice her was one of the regular Golden Praise greeters, who smiled and waved. In one group, someone said something about an arrest, and she lingered for as long as she dared, standing behind them and eating the egg roll.

"I heard pretty soon," one of the adults said. "There's a witness that saw him do it."

But then the subject changed, and Padma had to keep moving. The words in the sentence were wrong. There were *two* witnesses, and *several* perpetrators, as far as the police had been told by Kelly and Casey, so why did they say *a witness*? And why *him* instead of *them*? Padma tried to quiet her nerves as she headed toward the hallway that led down to the administrative offices.

Luckily, the open house really was open, including all parts of the three main church buildings. Maddy had said that the two most important offices—the ones she absolutely had to get inside—were the pastor's office and Miss Merrick's. She already knew where Merrick's office was, and Maddy had drawn her a map that she had committed to memory of where the pastor's was. Maddy said she didn't think the offices would be open during the event; if not, she was supposed to find a way in.

It was a maze of corridors to get to the pastor's office, and along the way she passed a few people, none of whom viewed her with suspicion. Padma held a pamphlet about church activities and put a benign expression on her face. The pastor's office was unfortunately at the end of a hallway, which meant if anyone caught her, it was hard to have an excuse for what she was doing. Still, she undid the buckle on one of her sandals—

she could pretend she had tucked into the hallway to fix it if anyone caught her.

The pastor's office had a plain wooden door with a bold sign that said PASTOR JIM PREISS. Padma put her ear to the door but didn't hear anything but muted silence. Good. Maddy had said it was unlikely he would be in there, as he was expected to be the shining star during such events, mingling with all the potential new church members and important townspeople. She tried the door and it was locked. She examined the keyhole. She had seen this done in movies, but they always made it look so effortless.

She retrieved two bobby pins from her purse and proceeded to bend them. She had just rewatched the movie *Misery*, where a man locked in his bedroom managed to get out by bending a bobby pin and fiddling with it in the keyhole. Padma attempted this, but it didn't seem as if the bobby pin was catching where it needed to. She wiggled around for what felt like an eternity, sweating, terrified that someone would find her. She tried using two bobby pins, but the result was the same.

Sighing, she put the pins away and buckled her sandal. She would try Miss Merrick's office. Padma went down the hallway, heading to where the door to Miss Merrick's office was open. She walked by casually and heard Miss Merrick talking to a man. They were both standing just inside her office, discussing registration forms. As Padma walked by, the man said something in agreement and walked out of the office. Padma paused and turned to see Miss Merrick leaving the office, the door swinging shut behind her. Once it closed, it would automatically lock, which meant there was a limited window. But also, a dangerous one: all it would take was Miss Merrick turning around. Padma crept forward as fast as she dared, staring at Miss Merrick's back. The door was about to click into place. Padma reached it just in time, sticking her fingers into the opening, cringing as the door bounced painfully off her fingers. Miss Merrick didn't hear the muted noise this made.

Padma slipped inside the office and closed the door behind her. How much time did she have? Probably a decent amount because Miss Merrick had just left. She knew that in the front right desk drawer was a small silver key, which opened the filing cabinet in the corner. She had seen Miss Merrick use it before.

She opened the filing cabinet and slid open the long, heavy drawer. Kelly and Maddy had given unhelpful advice the other night on AOL: don't waste a huge amount of time trying to make sense of things, but look for things that looked incriminating. She did not expect to find a file folder entitled *Mine Murders, 1995*. Instead, she found a folder of employee records, which she flipped through rapidly, hoping she would recognize one of the shearling men's names. Nope. In one folder labeled *Tithes* she saw lists of names with numerical figures beside them: how much families gave to the church on a quarterly basis. As she flipped through the folder, she realized these sheets went back a long time—changing from the blue and black ink of now to a typewritten list from the '50s, to incredibly thin sheets of paper encased in plastic protective sheets for what looked like the beginning of the church. She stared the longest at the oldest sheet:

Jeremiah Wesley m. Elizabeth Williams—Edward, Thomas, George, Anna, Martha, Joseph
Michael Sullivan m. Mary Taylor—Cora, Edith

Several other families were listed, and Padma recognized the last names. She didn't understand what she was looking at, but took a picture regardless, and another of the 1950s tithes, and the most recent one toward the front of the folder.

She found a fat folder labeled *Pop*. The first page was entitled *1994*. Padma studied it for a while before she realized that it appeared to be a census of the population and who owned what land. She snapped a few more pictures as she flipped through— this folder, too, went back to the beginning of Wesley Falls. There were documents in a folder called *Mine Assets*, which appeared to be listings of business expenses and the revenue of the mine from the 1800s through to when the mine closed. She found a thick envelope and when she opened it, she discovered similar records for Evansville. *Why would records for another town be here?* she wondered.

Padma tried to stay as steady as possible, knowing that if she moved, the pictures would come out blurry. That was the problem: she would have no idea what they would look like until she had them developed.

Padma saw a folder title that made her freeze. *Ugly List.* She pulled it out and opened it, revealing about a dozen crinkled, folded and unfolded sheets of notebook paper. She stared at the first, confused. Unlike the previous Ugly List she had seen in the office, which had been blank, this was an Ugly List like she had seen in her locker, with different sets of handwriting inserting names and crossing off others. Jokes written in the margins. Someone using a green pen had drawn dots here and there at the end of the list, at the lowest numbers where the burnouts were, and the same green pen made tick marks. The next sheet was a different Ugly List with similar results, and the same green pen.

She began to take pictures rapidly, pushing the camera past the thirty allotted pictures to thirty-three. Hopefully, this would be enough evidence, and they would not need her to come back. She had not worked at Golden Praise since the mine party, begging off her shifts and saying she had family obligations. She tucked the camera back into her purse and began to search Miss Merrick's desk in the off chance she had a key to the pastor's office—alas, she did not, though she was secretly relieved to be off the hook.

She put her ear to the door, not slipping out until it was quiet. She sped down the hallway, having to stop herself from running in her eagerness to leave. She could pass through the crowded foyer, then be out in the semisafety of the front lawn, use the pay phone to call Ajay, and she would be out of there. She had just reached the foyer when she felt an unwelcome gush.

No, not *now.* But maxi pads that needed to be changed needed to be changed *right now* in her experience. She hurried to the nearest bathroom to change her pad, glad that it was empty except for her. She washed her hands, dried them on her shorts as she slipped out of the bathroom, turned, and ran smack into Jane Merrick and the pastor. "Oh!" she shouted.

"This is Padma Subramaniam. She works in the admin offices," Miss Merrick explained to the pastor. Her thin lips were drawn into something that resembled a smile.

"Hello there," the pastor said, leaning down and smiling. "I've heard so much about you."

"Hi," she croaked. She forced her gaze to the starched white of the neck of the pastor's shirt, remembering what Jia told her. *Don't look him in the eyes.*

"Did your family come, too, Padma?" he asked, his voice like a river of molasses.

"Um, no. They had to work."

"That's a shame. I really wanted to meet your parents."

"I'm sure…they'll be around," she lied.

She sensed that he was staring at her. She imagined that he was willing her to look at him, and she tried to keep her eyes fastened to his shirt. But almost of their own will, she found her eyes drifting upward, meeting his gaze. There had been a battle of wills and she had lost. If she didn't imagine it, she thought she saw a flash of satisfaction cross his face. *What were you doing, Padma?* his eyes seemed to say.

But then, blissfully, someone called out to him, and he and Jane Merrick disappeared, but not before he flashed Padma one last smile.

Padma fled the building as fast as she dared, breaking into a run once she was outside, heading for the pay phone. She dialed 1-800 COLLECT then waited for the familiar prompts as she dialed her home number, then waited.

"Caller, at the tone, please state your name."

"Pickmeup!" Padma shouted.

"Please hold while we connect your call."

The phone rang and Ajay picked up as expected. "Hello?"

"You have a collect call from 'Pickmeup!' Do you accept the charges?"

"No," Ajay said, and hung up the phone.

Relieved, Padma hung up the phone, glanced behind her at

Central, then decided to move farther up the drive. How long would it take Ajay to get here? Five minutes? Ten if he was taking his sweet time. Padma hunkered down in the bushes, refusing to feel silly, and watched for the headlights of their family's Honda. Once she saw them, she ran to the car and got inside in a hurry, slamming the door and yelling, "Go!"

"Jeez, what's your problem?" But he drove off.

"Ajay, why do you think Golden Praise is weird?" she asked.

"Don't you?" he asked. "All the people who go there are weird. Like it's a cult or something. Did you want to go home or want me to drop you off somewhere?"

"The diner," she said. Kelly and Maddy were waiting there to debrief. James had wanted to come but Maddy told him not to, that they should try not to be seen together, not as long as people thought James was involved. As soon as she got out of the car, she could see Maddy and Kelly through the glass windows scrambling out of a booth to come meet her.

"I got it," Padma said after they met her at the curb outside.

"What did you see?" Kelly asked breathlessly.

"Later!" Maddy said, gesturing to the One Hour Foto kiosk. "Let's turn the camera in before they close." The three girls dropped off the camera at the kiosk. Padma had always thought the man who worked there was odd, like a human version of a troll. They returned to the diner where Padma and Kelly shared a strawberry milkshake, and she told them the details of her espionage.

"Why would the church have the Ugly List?" Kelly wondered.

"Why were they tallying it?" Padma added.

"It wouldn't surprise me if the list started at Golden Praise," Maddy said, surprising Padma. "They're obsessed with stuff like that. In LifeGroup, we would constantly talk about the social politics of school. Who's in and who's out. Why it was important to never be out."

"They're looking at the population, who is paying tithe and who isn't. Pinning down the social structure of the town," Padma said.

"If you wanted to confirm who's bad in town, you cross reference the lists and, big shocker, it turns out to be a bunch of burnouts. Then they kill six of them," Kelly said.

"My name was low on the list," Padma added quietly. "Are you saying they want to kill me?"

"I don't know," Maddy admitted. "They seem to like your family. And they probably never would have guessed you'd be at the mine party."

"Padma, I think you're pretty," Kelly said suddenly. Padma scowled at her. "I *do*. You're only on the list because people at our school suck."

"There was a lot of paperwork about the beginning of the town, too," Padma said. "Stuff about the founding families."

"They were the first Elders of Golden Praise," Maddy said, then looked at her watch. "Come on, it's almost been an hour."

Sometimes pictures were ready in under an hour, but when they arrived the man said it would be another half hour. They sat on the curb for what felt like a century and tried to pass the time. Kelly said she was having a hard time getting James to do his magnet school application. Padma found this hard to understand. She had already completed her application, but hadn't mailed it in yet because she wanted to sit on the essay for a few days and read it with fresh eyes. "Why would he do that?" she asked.

"Sometimes people are scared of either failing or succeeding so they don't do anything," Kelly said.

This mystified Padma. "I'll get him to do it," she said.

"If you go, Padma, I'll be first in class," Maddy said. A tiny corner of her mouth was turned up in a smile.

"You're welcome," she said graciously.

"Come on," Maddy said. "It's been twenty minutes." She led them back to the kiosk man and forked over the cash for the precious yellow envelope of pictures, and the girls hurried back to the curb to look at their evidence. Maddy sat between them and opened the envelope, pulling out the stack of 3 x 5s. But the first picture was entirely black. As was the second. And the third.

"What?" Kelly muttered. Maddy snatched the negatives from

their compartment in the packet and held them up to the street-light.

"They're all black," she said, crestfallen.

"I… I didn't do anything wrong," Padma said, feeling the urge to cry. "I didn't even load the film." It was a disposable camera—it came preloaded. She knew from observing her father on vacations that popping open the camera and exposing the film would result in black pictures. This was why you had to be careful about loading film and keep the finished roll in a little black canister until it could be developed. But with disposable cameras, everything was tucked away on its own, out of sight.

Padma looked up to see Kelly's head turned and followed her gaze. The man in the kiosk was staring at them intently. Then he picked up a phone. Maddy grabbed her by the arm, and they ran away from Main Street, into the relative safety of people's backyards as they cut across breathlessly.

32

Casey

Casey missed dinner—his workout had run late—but he knew there would be a plate waiting for him when he got home. What he didn't anticipate was the scene he was met with. His family was in a full-on fight, with Lexie at the center of it. Usually if someone was getting in trouble it was Casey, or his brother GB, not quiet, well-behaved Lexie. But her refusal to go to church was apparently unacceptable.

"I'm not going!" Lexie shouted, her face red from crying. GB and Steve were watching from the living room like a pair of hyenas.

"You have to go!" his mother shouted.

"I don't have to do anything!"

"You quit Youth Group, you're staying at home with your nose in a book, what's wrong with you?" his father said. His tone made Casey cringe. *Can't you see? Or can't you at least give her the benefit of the doubt?*

"If she doesn't want to go, she doesn't have to," he said, entering the fray, pointedly standing in front of Lexie.

His father's gaze set on him in anger. "What are you—*her lawyer*? Stay out of this."

"I'm her brother, and I have an opinion," Casey replied.

"He's got opinions!" GB cawed.

"As long as you're under this roof, you will do as I say," his mother said. *"This family goes to church."*

"Then I *won't* live under this roof!" Lexie shouted and ran upstairs, slamming her door behind her.

Everyone's gaze fell to him, but he threw up his hands. "I'm exhausted. I don't want to hear it. She's old enough to decide for herself." He ran up the stairs, hoping they didn't realize that his main freedom—his car keys—were something they could easily take away.

Lexie let him inside her bedroom where, tears streaking across her face, she was shoving clothes into a backpack. "Can you drive me to Kaylie's?"

"Yeah."

Moments later the two Coopers climbed out her window, rather than risking additional wrath trying the front door. It had just started to thunder outside and from the looks of the sky it was about to start pouring. As they strapped into the minivan, Lexie sniffled, and Casey wanted to comfort her but he was too mad. How could they not see behind her sudden outburst? He contemplated telling her that he was looking into what happened, and telling her about Maddy, but decided not to. She had begged him not to tell anyone and he had already broken that promise—plus, maybe Maddy wanted to keep her own exam a secret, too. Lexie would probably stay at Kaylie's a night or two then skulk back home, the flame temporarily subsided until their mother started to worry about her immortal soul come Sunday.

After he dropped her off, he meandered around town. Maddy had said that there was no way that the Elders weren't involved in the mine murders. Coach was an Elder. Casey could not square this. Coach would never hurt anyone. Maybe sometimes he yelled at them or made them run until they puked, but this was to make them better. And while he was a hard man, he was not without kindness. Casey knew that he was Coach's favorite. He was the favorite because he was the best and the most likely to get into a D1 school. Casey reveled in this, he *basked* in it—it was more important than anything else in his life.

As he began to drive in the direction of Coach's house, he thought about the football party they had thrown after winning the state championship. Everyone had been there—all the players, the trainers, the cheerleaders, anyone who was a football fan. They had jokingly invited Coach, knowing that he would never come, but a few hours into the party he had shown up and everyone had screamed and hailed him like he was a god. He even drank a beer with them. He made a brief speech, saying they had been rewarded by the grace of God because of their hard work. Casey had been so happy, very drunk and staring into the bonfire they had built. Just before he left, Coach clapped him on the back and then unexpectedly hugged him. "Nice job, Casey," he had said into his ear.

Casey put the van in Park at the curb by Coach's house. He had been there many times for football events. He had never dropped by uninvited, but he was Coach's favorite. If being an Elder did have something to do with the mine murders, Casey wanted to be sure that Coach wasn't involved. Maybe it wasn't *all* the Elders.

The walk from the van to Coach's front door soaked him, and after he rang the bell and Coach opened it, he flinched when a clap of thunder sounded. "Casey," he said, surprised.

"Can I come in? It's really coming down."

Coach hesitated long enough that Casey started to feel uneasy—he realized now, too late, that Coach had not smiled when he opened the door. Then Coach nodded, standing aside to let him into the foyer. "I'll get you a towel."

When Coach handed him a towel, Casey realized that his clothes were wrinkled and his hair was messy. He had never seen Coach disheveled before. Coach seemed to notice this, then gave a tired smile. "The missus is visiting her parents." There was an awkward pause, which made Casey wonder if they were fighting.

"I, um…" he said, feeling foolish for arriving unannounced. "I just wanted to talk to you about something."

"What's up?" Coach said, taking the armchair across from him.

"You know that party? Where those kids died?" Coach looked back at him silently, but the look on his face wasn't unkind. Casey wondered if he should tell him he had been there. "I was just thinking…it really bothers me."

"What bothers you about it?"

Casey's eyes wandered to the picture frames at either side of Coach's head. One was a framed photograph of him and his wife. The other was a framed piece of embroidery that said, "Blessed are the pure in heart, for they will see God."

"Well, they *died*. It's awful. I can't stop thinking about it. I…" *Please say something. Please say something so I know you didn't have anything to do with it.* "I can't stand the way people talk about it. It's guys on the team, too."

"What are they saying?"

"They talk about it like it's a *joke*. What about…"

He trailed off, realizing that Coach had tilted his head sympathetically. *What a nice boy*, that look said. "Casey, you've got such a big heart and that's an asset, but you shouldn't let it get you distracted. You have to trust the adults with stuff like this and concentrate on your own business. How's your math going?"

Casey did not want to talk about math, but the cursed subject persisted until Coach offered some platitude about faith and hard work, and Casey suddenly came to the realization that he had overstayed his welcome. Casey stood up, saying he was sorry for dropping in unannounced.

He overslept the next morning and snuck down to get food only when he heard that the coast was clear. He made two peanut butter-and-jelly sandwiches and secreted them upstairs. He had allowed his math homework to pile up thinking that Tomorrow Casey would handle it, only the problem was that Tomorrow Casey had become Today Casey because the homework was almost due.

He ate the sandwiches, then tried to concentrate, only to notice a *pink!* sound against his window. There it was again. He went over to look and saw Padma, the pebble she had just tossed missing the glass by a mile. He opened the window and stuck his head out.

"Come on!" she said. "Kelly IM'd me. We're going to meet at the lake in an hour."

"I can't."

"Why not?"

"I have math homework."

She seemed confused. *What?*

"I'm in summer school. My homework is due tomorrow."

"Then get it done and meet us at the lake!"

"I can't. It's going to take me all day." She was bewildered. "I'm not good at math, okay?" he said, annoyed.

"I'll help you. Come to my backyard, where the little house is," she said, and ran off, her braid flying behind her.

Casey had thought that perhaps Padma helping him would mean that she would do his homework for him, but instead this involved the two of them sitting in a giant dollhouse actually doing math. He was embarrassed to have her see the remedial problems he was working on, but she was unfazed and also un-charmed by his attempts to get out of doing work. Her mom even showed up with a snack—onion bhaji—which Padma cru-elly denied him until he completed his worksheets.

They didn't finish within the hour Padma wanted, but ten past, then Casey drove them to Willow Drive so they could walk to the lake. Nobody ever went to Chicken Lake because the runoff from the chicken processing plant went into it and people said you could get all kinds of diseases from even coming near it. Padma crunched through the woods in front of him. "Kelly said there's a safe place to meet here, safer than the library."

He had never been this close to the lake and began to sniff the air, wondering if he could smell the raw chicken. He was surprised when they reached a clearing and he could see a small beach, the twinkle of blue water. Maddy, wearing an oversize men's button-down, was swinging off her backpack. Jia was al-ready in the water.

"You can't swim here! There's raw chicken!" he shouted.

"That's what's wrong about this town," James said, kicking off his Converse. "The chicken plant is east of here. The river runs down the mountain then east. Which means if they dump shit in the water, it goes in the opposite direction."

"Are you *sure*?"

"We've been swimming here for years," James said, gesturing to Kelly, who had stripped down to a blue one-piece. She didn't have much in the way of breasts but she had nice legs. James pulled off his T-shirt revealing his skinny chest—Casey couldn't help but wonder how much weight he could put on him with three solid weeks at the gym and a decent meal plan— and splashed into the water, heading for the wooden raft that bobbed at the center of the lake.

Padma slipped her sandals off and poked doubtfully at the water with one toe. "Are there *things* in the water?"

"Fish," Kelly called, treading water a few yards away. "Some turtles."

"Turtles?" Padma asked doubtfully.

"You're not scared of turtles, are you?" Casey asked, beginning to undress. He tried to hide the fact that he was looking beyond Padma to where Maddy was, her shirt discarded, revealing a highly distracting bright green bikini that her parents most definitely did not approve of.

"I don't have a swimsuit," Padma said.

"Just swim in your clothes, then," he said. "Or do I have to throw you in?"

She shot him a look. They all began to swim for the raft except for Padma, who hesitated, then zoomed toward them with a surprisingly fast dog paddle. Half of them stayed in the water for its coolness, while the other half climbed on top of the raft. Casey, still in the water, rested his arms on the raft. "This is so cool."

"Mainly because no one comes here," James said. "Next time I'll bring a Ziploc bag so we can have snacks. And weed."

"Padma, tell everyone about your reconnaissance trip," Kelly said.

Padma recounted how she had gone inside Golden Praise to take pictures of evidence, only to discover that the pictures didn't come out.

"The kiosk guy overexposed them," Maddy said. "Maybe he goes to Golden Praise."

"Maybe he's just racist?" James suggested.

"I went home that night and wrote down as much as I could

remember, but I wish we had those pictures," Padma said. She described what she found: old records, the Ugly List—which Casey had never heard of—and financial records.

"It seems like they pay a lot of attention to social status," Jia said.

"Between the Ugly List and the population stuff," Maddy began slowly, "it's like they're ranking people."

"Like who's good in town, and who's bad," Padma said. "So they can decide who to kill."

"Are they *done* killing people or will there be more? And *why*?" asked Kelly.

"There was also a bunch of documents about Evansville," Padma said. "Population stuff and about their economy and Matthew Wesley."

"Matthew Wesley was the founder of Evansville," Maddy said. "He was like the mayor of that town while Jeremiah was the leader of Wesley Falls. But I don't know why that would be in the church records."

"One other thing," Padma said. "When I was at the open house, people were gossiping about how there was a witness," Padma said. "They were talking about a single witness seeing who did it and they said *him*." She looked pointedly at James. "I don't think they were talking about Casey and Kelly. What if they made up a witness?"

"So I don't remember everything from the night they brought me in for questioning," James said. "Because—" Here he strangled himself with one hand, sticking his tongue out. No one thought this was funny, but James didn't seem to notice. "But they didn't arrest me. They can't arrest me if there's no evidence."

"Innocent people get arrested all the time," Jia said. "Look at O.J."

There was a pause, then Maddy said, "You think O.J.'s innocent?"

"I don't want people getting suspicious of any of you just because they think I did it," James said. "There's a secret place around here where we can meet so people in town don't see us together. It doesn't have electricity but it stays cool, even in the summer."

As James and Kelly led them to the shore and then on the short walk through the woods, James stopped, waving his arms around theatrically. "Here we are!" James exclaimed. Casey didn't see anything that looked like a secret meeting place, but James reached into the wall of vines that covered a jut of rock, and a heavy sound squealed out. Casey didn't even see the door until James swung it open with Kelly's help. "It's a munitions bunker from World War II," he said, ducking inside. Casey followed, awed. The inside of the bunker was like a concrete igloo. It was dim and significantly cooler than it was out in the sun. There was an old picnic table, a couple of old rugs that someone must have salvaged, a sleeping bag, and a lantern. "If we close the door, no one would even know we're in here because of all the ivy."

Kelly sat at the picnic table, pulling her knees into her chest. Maddy followed suit. "I think I know what we need to do next, based on what you found," Maddy said to Padma.

"What's that, oh wise one?" James said.

"We go to Evansville," Maddy stated, as if this was an obvious fact. "Why would a church *here* have all the records of another town? A Wesley brother founded each town, and one of those towns is now completely destroyed. I think that knowing what happened there could help us here."

33

Maddy

If shame were a location, it would be 19 Throckmartin Lane. The worst of it was not at Golden Praise, the stares Maddy got, the giggles. The multiple instances in LifeGroup where the topic of conversation happened to be premarital sex. A couple of wide-eyed inquiries from girls about why she wasn't wearing her Circle Girl pin. *All of you shits know*, she thought. But she couldn't conceive of a world where she could get out of all her seemingly mandatory Golden Praise activities without some massive blowup with her parents.

But home was far worse. After Maddy had had her Circle pin torn away, she endured several interrogations about what she had done and why. Why had she thrown it all away? Why had she fallen into sin? Her parents had grounded her, taken away her private phone. She felt as if a massive needle was being pressed into her side, and the worse it got, the more she thought about going crazy, screaming, *I thought there was no sin that Jesus could not redeem.*

She was allowed to use the family computer for educational purposes—this included reading preapproved websites. Her parents also allowed her to work on her capstone, having no idea that the capstones were co-ed. The computer had been placed in the living room in an odd position so that they could see what she was up to. Sometimes she *was* working on her capstone or dreaming of California colleges. But she also used the computer to IM Kelly and Padma, turning the sound off to hide the dings and bleeps, and minimizing windows with keyboard dexterity that a parent could never understand. On a couple of occasions, when the weight of the house was too much, she thought about retreating into her closet and indulging in the forbidden things there. Instead, she went downstairs and was surprised to find that Padma was up late on AOL. The girls talked for an hour or so, and Maddy felt better. She wished that that always staved off a binge, but that would not be true. Not all the time.

Her book bag for the planned trip to Evansville looked innocent enough: a notebook, sunscreen, water, but hidden beneath were flashlights and her camera. She wasn't sure what they would find there, but had a sense she would know it when she saw it.

She walked a winding path toward the Good Park, where Casey picked her up in his minivan. Inside, she ducked so that no one passing by could see her through the window—sometimes she jogged with Casey, which she knew would be forbidden, but being spotted in his minivan would be even worse. Padma was already inside, and next they picked up Jia and drove over Willow to park. Kelly and James were waiting on the path that led up to the mine, and then beyond it, to Evansville.

"Has anyone ever gone there before?" Maddy asked.

"I've been a couple times," Casey said. "It sounds interesting in theory, but it's just sort of sad."

"I went once but I was really stoned," James admitted. "Did everyone bring a bandanna?" He wore one knotted around his neck. "It's smoky there."

"I like the idea of a ghost town," Padma said brightly, hooking her thumbs into the straps of her book bag as they began their way up the mountain path. She never would have come here, Maddy realized, if there wasn't a group of people going. And Padma didn't belong to a group. That was partly her fault. Or maybe even mostly, Maddy realized. What reason did any of them have to be nice to her? But as the hour pressed on as they hiked, alternating between joking around and coming up with theories about what was going on, she felt like she was part of a group. There was no false sheen of universal love like at LifeGroup, the ohmigod I *love* you, but there was a feeling of solidarity.

Jia and James were talking about the devil, if he was real, and if he could possibly be the pastor. "I don't think the devil is real," Jia was saying, "but I think evil things are out there because I can feel them."

"Feel them *how*?" James asked.

"In my stomach," Jia said. "But sort of in my head at the same time. The mountain feels evil. The pastor feels like the mountain."

James looked at Jia with interest. "Whatever the pastor is, I don't think he can be the devil. There's no such thing."

"Aren't you some kind of satanist?" Maddy asked. People at school said as much but he sneered at her.

"Because I wore a Megadeth shirt to school once? You know the only people who believe in the devil are *Christians*, right? Every time someone does something bad it's, oh, the devil made me do it, and not just that you're an asshole."

"What do you believe in, if you're not Christian?"

"I don't believe in anything."

"Then how do you know what's wrong or right?"

"I don't read the Bible but I would never do what those people did to you."

"Those were just bad people. It's not religion's fault."

"Isn't it, though? Don't they use it to tell you you're dirty if you have sex or if you're gay or whatever? So we're going to make laws based on things written by old dudes millennia ago and then vote on what goes in the Bible?"

"*What?*" Maddy squawked.

"You know there are books written around the same time that got left out. They're called the Apocrypha. There was this thing called the Council of Nicea, where all these men got to vote on which books would be in the Bible and they left some of them out."

"What? I've never heard this."

"We learned about some council like that in Catholic school," Kelly said. "I forget what it's called."

"There's some weird shit in the Apocrypha," James said, pausing to light a brown cigarette. "Jesus when he was a kid and angels kicking the shit out of each other."

"Why do you know this?"

"We have some books about it at The Gem Shop," Jia said. "That's probably where he got it."

"James only reads things for the sake of getting into arguments with people," Kelly said clearly loud enough that she intended James to hear her. "He'll skim through all the other parts to get to what he wants, which is why he claims to read so fast when really he's not reading."

"There's no devil in Hinduism," Padma piped up. "There's different gods, but no devil."

"Is there a hell?" Maddy asked.

Padma looked at her with her head cocked to one side. "People are what makes hell." It sounded so strange coming from so small a girl, said with such strong conviction. "The bad things we do come back to us."

"Hey," Casey called from up ahead—the discussion of theology had apparently bored him. They had just breasted a steeper part of the path and now had a decent view of what was left of Evansville. The town had been abandoned in the 1930s, and even before then it hadn't been very large. There was what looked like a main street, and a road that looped around what might have been a few stores, a church, and rows of small, identical houses. The main road was littered with graffiti, the paint a starkly bright contrast to the drab buildings. Both local kids and others came from all over Pennsylvania to see the underground coal fire, which had been burning for decades.

Maddy could not see the underground fire, which had been partially contained, but the remnants were obvious. They stepped carefully over the cracks in the road, drawing a wide berth around a fissure that glowed red. The road was pocked and sunken in other places, and Maddy saw smoke hovering above the ground like fog. It smelled awful—she was grateful for the bandanna pulled over her face.

"From what I've read," Kelly said, pointing to the side of the road, "the Bureau of Mines put those vents in to let out noxious gases. But things got so bad here that eventually everyone left town. People's basements were hot and the water smelled."

"Our town might not even be here if they hadn't contained the fire," Padma mused.

"Would that be such a bad thing?" Maddy muttered.

"It's not all bad," Casey said, nudging her with his elbow.

"Name one good thing about our town," she said.

"The football team," he said immediately. There were groans.

"Where do we start?" James wondered.

Kelly gestured down the road, where it was not as smoky. "I think we should start at the church, which doubled as the town meeting place. From what I read, the two pillars of the town were the mine and the church."

Kelly led the way, and eventually the air was clear enough for Maddy to take off her bandanna. She turned to Jia beside her. "Do you... *feel* anything?"

Jia considered this. She had made a tiny braid of her white segment of hair and tucked it behind her ear. "It *smells* bad, but I don't *feel* bad. It feels like...finding an old shoe you've already broken in," Jia said, satisfied that she found the perfect words. Padma caught Maddy's eye with a similarly puzzled look and they smiled.

Kelly led them down a narrow path between two buildings. Casey reached out and touched the slats of wood of the building beside them and then flinched when they emitted a creaking sound. They came around the front where there were double wooden doors leading into the church. It didn't look like a church in the traditional sense—no steeple or stained glass.

One of the ancient wooden doors was slightly ajar. Maddy hesitated, not wanting to show that she was scared. "It's safe," Jia said, pushing the door open. They coughed at the eruption of dust this stirred up. Simple wooden benches took up the front half of the church, and there was no cross or crucifix. There was a desk and a few bookshelves, a little cubby where a few pairs of shoes were. "What exactly are we looking for?" Maddy asked.

"A book called something like *Secrets of Evansville, and How It Relates to Wesley Falls*," James said.

"You guys didn't tell me we'd be reading," Casey whined. "I thought this would be some Indiana Jones shit."

"Then go poke around and be Indiana Jones," Kelly said, stooping to look at the bookcase.

Maddy snapped a few pictures, then found a massive Bible she had to use two hands to carry to where the light was better. "Old towns used to record events in their bibles," she explained. She settled on the floor and felt the delight of discovery when she saw tiny, old-fashioned script marching down the inside cover. James began to root around some boxes and Casey left the church, saying he would check out the old general store that the mine had owned.

It took Maddy a while to make out the old-fashioned curlicue script on the inside cover, but eventually she saw that it recorded the date of the founding of the church, May 14, 1882. It then launched into a list of town families, starting with Matthew Wesley and his wife and kids. Maddy paged through, noting that in addition to births and baptism dates, deaths and their causes were also listed. Some of the people lived to what she supposed was old age back then. Others died much younger, but that was probably common at the time when simple infections could kill and mining was dangerous work.

Paul Black, d. 1899 scarlet fever
Anna Carlson, d. 1901 consumption
Brand child—idiot

Maddy stared at the last entry. How was "idiot" a cause of death? She scanned over the dates. She got to her knees, pulling a notebook out of her book bag and turning to a fresh page. She started by listing years, then scratched that off, listing decades since the founding of the town, making a tick mark every time someone died. People should die in a normal distribution across years, unless there was some specific catastrophe, like a war or pandemic. There were quite a few deaths attributed to flu and the occasional mining accident, but a pattern began to emerge that didn't seem natural. About every forty years, the number of people who died that year spiked, then went back to normal the following year.

That can't be right, she thought. She squinted at the cramped, faded handwriting. She yawned—the heat was making her sleepy—and found her blinks getting longer and longer. It was too quiet: if everyone else had been talking, it would have kept her more alert. When she glanced up, she realized that they all had left with the exception of Jia, who was directly across from her, her back resting against the wall as she looked through another old book. Maddy looked down, blinked what felt like the longest blink, then found herself falling, sinking down into blackness.

It was cold now. How could it be cold in the dead of summer? Also, how did it get so dark out when it had been sunny a moment ago? Maddy felt enclosed, shadows hulking around her. The sulphur smell was gone. *Where am I?* There was a noise coming from somewhere ahead, an unpleasant noise she couldn't see the source of. The sound, though, the heaviness of the place, felt strangely familiar. *I'm in the mine*, she realized. Had she sleepwalked? When had they left Evansville?

Something seemed to flicker and then Jia was standing in front of her, a scared expression on her face. *Jia*, Maddy tried to say, then found her mouth didn't work. It was like trying to speak through water.

Jia turned suddenly and ran through the darkness, toward the direction of the disturbing noises. *Wait!* Maddy called. How could Jia even see where she was going? Maddy's feet didn't seem to touch the ground as she followed. There was no sound of footsteps or the hard feeling of rock beneath her.

There was a flickering light ahead, a confrontation of some kind involving three people. Jia approached without any caution and Maddy was too scared to call out to her, too afraid to alert the three men. But Jia ran straight up to them like a curious child and stared at them. *They can't see us*, Maddy realized.

One of the men held a torch with one hand, and in his other a rope. The rope led back to another man and looped around his neck tightly. He was stumbling because he had a sack over his head, a muffled cry coming from behind the cloth. His long, thick shirt was flecked with something. Blood. His hands were cuffed together with more rope, and that rope led to the hands of a third man. This man was scowling, having more of the burden of dragging along the hooded man, who was clearly resisting.

Who are they? she wondered.

Don't you know? Jia said. Only she hadn't moved her mouth. *Look at their faces.* Maddy inched closer, taking a better look at the man with the torch. His clothes were rough and filthy, and a bandage wrapped around one hand was spotted with blood. His face was sweaty and needed a good washing. But when she looked at his brow, the shape of his eyebrows, and the slope of his nose, he looked familiar. A Wesley?

Jeremiah, Jia said.

What are they doing? Maddy replied.

They had reached an enclosure, and as Jeremiah wedged the torch into a nook to hold it upright, the small light source flickered over what appeared to be a cave. The space felt crowded and heavy somehow—it was before the mountain had been hollowed out. Maddy crept closer to the third man, who was now loosening the bonds on the captive. *Matthew Wesley*, she thought. He was thinner and clearly younger, but had similar features. Jeremiah paced as Matthew forced the third man to sit and then began to pull the sack off his head.

From across the cave, Maddy saw Jia's startled reaction. She was facing the captive, and Matthew was pulling a wad of cloth from his mouth. The man shouted at the Wesleys in French, Maddy was surprised to realize. She had taken French since seventh grade, but she could barely understand what he was saying, only that he was angry. But what had made Jia freeze in her tracks?

Maddy crossed the room and came to Jia's side to see better, and gasped.

It was the pastor.

But how? It couldn't be but it *was*. She knew that face. Yes, the dark hair was longer, and he looked like he hadn't had a bath in months, but it was him. It was unclear to any of them what the Wesleys were doing with him, and his cursing in French seemed more angry than frightened.

The temperature in the air seemed to change. The Wesley brothers had moved across the cave and turned to face the torch rather than their captive. Maddy felt Jia clasp her hand, and though she could see their hands laced together, this was something she felt more with her mind than she did with her skin. Jia was scared. Something was coming. Jia edged closer to the brothers, dragging a confused Maddy with her. When she looked back at the captive, she was mostly looking from behind and could only see a hint of his face as he continued to curse at and taunt the brothers.

But the Wesleys were scared. More scared than even Jia. Maddy felt an uncomfortable feeling, as if a cold spider was slowly making its way up her spine. She looked at the torch just as it flickered, dimmed, and nearly went out. Someone had just come into the room. Jia squeezed her hand tighter, her eyes glued to the wall. Maddy couldn't help but look, or almost look through her peripheral vision because she was so scared.

The Frenchman was sitting still now, silent. "Qui va là?" he said, for the first time sounding frightened. Something electric was in the air, snapping and popping like black electricity. The man began to scream, a shriek of pure terror she had never heard a grown man make, worse than anything she had ever heard in a movie. Jia was screaming, too, somehow, silently, and the Wesley brothers squeezed their eyes shut.

Don't look, Jia was saying. *Don't look, don't look, don't look.*

Then they were tumbling, flipping and roiling with nothing beneath them.

Then there was the soft feel of sawdust beneath Maddy's feet. The familiar smell of horse droppings. They were outside and it was night. Maddy felt that Jia was beside her and both girls looked around, puzzled. Yellow light glowed through the windows of small wooden houses. A man on a horse headed down the street, pulling a cart piled with lumber. Maddy realized that the configuration of the street was familiar: they were in Evansville. Only it wasn't run-down but new and significantly smaller. The general store wasn't there, there were fewer houses, and the road that led northeast to Devil's Peak was a faint path lit with hanging lamps. The woods surrounding them were thicker, untamed as the trees seemed to crowd the tiny town.

She looked at Jia for confirmation. Jia gestured ahead of her. The Wesley brothers, this time cleaner and wearing caps, were talking in hushed voices at the side of the road, the younger brother Matthew holding a lantern with a flickering light inside. "You speak too plainly to him," he said.

"We held up our end," Jeremiah said. He sounded annoyed, and like he had a wad of tobacco stuck under his lip. "That Frenchman didn't come easy." He held up his hand, showing a scar that had healed over—the wound that had been fresh the last time Maddy had seen him. She realized she did not like Jeremiah's face. It was cruel and plain. "We built him not one, but *two* churches with our own damned hands—"

"Wait now, I think we—"

But it was too late. Jeremiah was now striding across the unpaved road and Matthew was forced to follow. They were heading to the church, which was so new that when Maddy crossed the threshold she could smell the pine sap from the wood it was built with. The church looked rudimentary: it had only a few simple benches, and the windows didn't have glass yet, letting in the sound of crickets.

The Wesley brothers shuffled into a small room and quickly donned their hats, holding them apologetically to their chests. Jeremiah had lost some of his bravado and Maddy understood why. She didn't want to go inside the room—neither did Jia—but they had to look, or they would never know. When she came inside, Maddy could see a man in the room sitting alone at a table, his back to them. Unlike the Wesleys, he was finely dressed in a long black coat with a waistcoat underneath. He knew that the brothers were there and something about his posture indicated displeasure. Slowly, he wrapped his fingertips against the wooden table. "You return to me again?" he said, his voice lazy.

Jia seemed as paralyzed as the brothers, but Maddy stepped around them, moving to the side of the table so she could look closer. It was him. The Frenchman. The pastor. His hair was neatly cut, and he was clean-shaven, and certainly looked cleaner than both the Wesley brothers. But...he wasn't the Frenchman. The way he held himself was entirely different. The way he moved as he stood and turned around slowly, arching his neck to the side to elicit a few muted pops.

The brothers stood holding their hats and looking down like two children who had just been chastised. "Well, we were thinking..." Jeremiah began gently.

"You were thinking?" the pastor said quietly as he moved toward the men. They both backed against the wall.

But despite his fear, Jeremiah was determined. "We were thinking... We got you a body like you asked. A good one— he's French but he had good teeth. And we built you a church like you wanted. We built you two if you count...if you count t'other." The pastor was still stepping closer. He was the same height as they were but seemed to tower over them somehow. "One in each town, just as you asked." Jeremiah rotated his hat in his hands. Something about Matthew's face indicated he wanted his brother to shut up. "Well, it seems like we did one thing for you, then another, but you haven't granted us that boon you promised..."

The pastor leaned forward. "Do I appear in a state to be granting *boons*?"

Jeremiah looked at his brother, unclear of how to answer the question.

Pastor continued in a patronizing tone. "I need a *church* because I need a *flock*. I can't do *anything* without a flock."

"People are coming," Matthew mumbled. "More and more people are coming for jobs." He seemed to regret this, as now the pastor's gaze was on him.

"And what is it you wanted again?"

"Just a simple thing, really," Jeremiah said. Braver now—his tone falsely light. "Just for this town to be prosperous."

The pastor clasped his hands together behind his back. "You do realize that that is not a favor for you two, but one for the entire town." Jeremiah looked up, confused. "That is a larger ask. A significant draw on my abilities. This, when I barely have a flock—"

"We'll build you a flock—"

"The *town* needs to give me something. Something of value in order to gain my favor. For the prosperity you ask for."

The brothers were dumbfounded, until Matthew spoke up. "The mine," he said suddenly. "What about half a stake in the mine?" It was clear from the look on his brother's face that this had not been discussed earlier. Matthew almost continued, but then realized that the pastor had gone stock-still.

"You would try to trade gold for gold?" There was quiet fury in his voice.

"It's not gold, it's coal—"

The pastor's face was now inches from Matthew's. *"You think it's money I want?"*

His face was *opening* somehow, not literally but in some other awful way. The patronizing smile was gone. He was angry and all teeth. His *eyes*. They weren't eyes but a squiggling mass of black lines vibrating with energy—raw, hungry, venomous energy. Maddy squeezed her eyes shut, turning away. Jia was screaming, clutching at her, desperate to get away from the hideous face.

They were spinning, tumbling, and then the ground was solid beneath them. The smell of a crackling fire. The Wesley brothers were sitting across from each other at a small table, tin cups in front of them—Maddy guessed they held alcohol. Something strong, judging from the slack look on their faces. "We don't have anything better than the mine to offer," Matthew said. "We had a bad yield for crops the second year in a row. We can't pray on the weather. We can't attract people to work in the mine if we don't have food to eat. Five people are dead already of the fever, and how long will that go on?"

Jeremiah slowly rotated his cup, then sipped, grimacing. "What if... What if he already told us what he wants?" Matthew looked at him blankly. "When we found him, he needed a body," he said. "We got him that fur trapper, and he seemed to like that."

"What are you saying?"

"That Frenchman died. You saw it, too—the light went out of his eyes once he took over. It took a life for him to have a body. Maybe that's what he wants. A life. Lives."

"Jer—"

"He said it's got to be big for the whole town to prosper. Both towns. What price are we willing to pay?"

"What price *are* we willing to pay?" Matthew asked, sounding unsure of his brother.

"Matthew, one more bad yield, one more creditor, and this town is done for. We got people starving. People dying of the fever. We won't last—" A look came over his face. "Those Jensen boys have the fever right now. I don't think they'd last the winter anyway."

It was dawning on Matthew, but Maddy could see some hesitation lingering. Maddy and Jia were thinking the same thing: *Don't do it. You don't have to agree.* "The Davis boy is sickly, too," is what he said instead.

34

Jia

One blink and it was all gone. It was day, the sun shining again. Birds chirped and the first thing that Jia saw that she really registered was Maddy looking disdainfully around her. Evansville again, but this time different. Bright and bustling. Two children, oblivious to their presence, were singing as one shoveled horse manure into a bucket. A woman crossed in front of them with two pails hooked onto a stick balanced across her shoulders.

When the girls walked down the street, they could see that the church now had glass in the windows, that the wood had aged to a darker color. More houses peppered the street. Two women sat at one doorway, shelling peas as they talked, their words indistinct. The general store had been built, modest but still probably exciting in so small a town. A man exited just then, and Jia could hear a tinkle of a bell. His pants and shirt were stained with coal dust, and he carried a brown glass jug in one hand, a lit cigarette in the other.

Look, Maddy said. A blonde woman was walking across the street, carrying a woven basket. She was pretty, her wavy blond hair drawn together at the back of her neck. She was a Wesley, Jia realized. Matthew's child? His child's child—? It was unclear how much time had passed. Her blue eyes sparkled as she waved to a couple approaching her. The movement made something glint off the sun: for a split second Jia could see an old-fashioned key looped onto a thin chain before it disappeared under the woman's blouse again. She was met with friendly chatter as the three, laughing, headed toward the church.

"You're not meeting without me, are you?" came a playful voice.

Jia turned her head and froze. The pastor was striding in their direction. The same but different somehow. Same face, same graceful way of moving. The clothes were of a different era, and his demeanor was different. But it wasn't just that—he wasn't *terrible* as he was the last time they saw him. He looked more like the pastor they knew. He was friendly, patting the man on the back as he made a joke that made them all laugh.

What happened? Maddy asked her.

He put a face on, Jia said, not knowing how else to explain it. While the last time they had seen him he had exuded the energy of a starving but powerful animal, now he seemed restrained. Controlled. Maybe more powerful, but less raw.

More people streamed into the church, chatting as they headed to the back room. The women had various items: baskets and dishes covered with cloth. The men talked loudly as they filled pipes with tobacco. "Elizabeth, don't tell me that's your buttermilk pie!" one woman cooed to the blonde woman. Elizabeth uncovered the pie and everyone made eager noises.

Jia counted: there were twelve—six men, six women, and it was clear that some of the pairings were married to each other. They were all well dressed, their faces healthy and bright. They all had an air of social power to them, but Elizabeth and the man who appeared to be her husband were treated with a subtle deference. Her husband went to close and lock the door as another woman removed a cloth from her basket, revealing a pile of peaches to the pastor. "Those look lovely! Jeremy bring those in?"

She nodded, propelling the basket toward him. "You get first pick."

He scratched at his chin comically, as if making a serious decision, then laid his hands on the peach at the top. He then arched his eyebrow at her and took a second peach. She laughed as he wandered off to the corner, and Elizabeth's husband held up his hands to call them to order.

It was a meeting, Jia realized, not a meal. A prim-looking man had taken out a ledger and the woman beside him had readied herself with a dip pen and inkwell. The prim man began to read out surnames and then the names of people living within each house. A few times someone would interject and the woman would add a name to her new list. "The campers on the west end of town, eight of them, as their house is only half-built."

"What about them?" a woman asked, cutting herself a generous slice of pie.

"We need the men for the mine," Elizabeth's husband said.

"The dredges, then," she said, sliding the pie onto a plate.

The debate continued. Able-bodied men were important for labor, but some able-bodied men proved more troublesome than they were worth. Samuel complained about wages too often, stirring up trouble. Saul took to drinking too often. A child with a birthmark was proposed. Then a woman who couldn't seem to keep a pregnancy.

Jia met Maddy's eyes from across the room. *They're picking who to sacrifice*, Jia said.

She became concerned, tuning out the conversation, as Maddy's furious eyes fell on the pastor. Though this was only a dream, a memory caught in amber, Jia still feared that somehow the pastor's eyes would turn on them. Despite this fear, her heart ached when she saw the look on Maddy's face when she stared at the same face that was Golden Praise's pastor. She had been the last holdout, the last person who thought he might be innocent. The pastor was lounging in a chair in the corner, apart from everyone else, resting one ankle on one knee. His gaze floated across the room as these people—the Elders—debated who should be selected for what they called the Harvest. He did not interject, but only listened, his lips curled into a small smile. *Is this what you want?* he was thinking. *Is this the price you are willing to pay?* Clearly it was. Occasionally, he took a slow bite of his peach. He was feeding, but it wasn't just the peach he was eating.

★ ★ ★

Blackness again. The smell of wet dirt and rock. The only lighting came from a series of hanging lanterns latched to the sides of the mine and the small headlights attached to the helmets of two men, but Jia could make out that they were loading coal into a cart. They seemed to be moving very slowly, but from the way their eyes kept darting to each other, it wasn't because they were tired. They were up to something.

Maddy was ahead of her, farther down the mine tunnel, and turned back to look at her just as one of the men said, "He's gone."

Quickly, the men dropped their tools and began to run farther down the tunnel, the light from their headlamps bouncing. Jia and Maddy ran silently to catch up. They were on their hands and knees now, their fingers rapidly twisting wires together. Once this was done, they scrambled to their feet and went up the tunnel in the opposite direction with Jia and Maddy at their heels.

Once they reached the outdoors they slowed their pace, keeping up casual conversation as they both lit cigarettes. It was dusk and Evansville was bustling. There were more buildings, Jia realized, the general store had gotten larger, and now there was a stable at the north end of town. A man leading a horse by its reins paused to whisper to the two men, "Some are having doubts. They're at Caleb's."

The two miners exchanged a concerned look as they headed for Caleb's house. Jia knew their pace was forced: they wanted to run but had to walk for fear of attracting attention. At the south end of town, the miners entered what must have been Caleb's house from the side. There were people already crowded into the house, many talking over each other, but they quieted once the miners entered. "Is it done?" asked a tall man sitting at a table. The miners nodded. There was a newspaper on his desk, which was dated March 12, 1902, and cost a whopping two cents. These were the last days of Evansville before the fire started.

"I just think we're hurrying into this," said a bald man. Several others seemed annoyed at this, but not everyone. "Let's think some more on it."

"There's no time," Caleb said, standing up. "It's got to be now. Most of the Elders will be there for a week, along with *him*." He held up a flier from his desk and waved it around. With some difficulty, Jia was able to ascertain what it was. An invitation to the grand reopening of the newly renovated church at Wesley Falls. "We won't get another chance to do it and be this safe."

"If we do this, and we do it right, you understand this entire town dies," the bald man said.

"That's the purpose," a woman from the crowd said. "We destroy the mine, we destroy the town."

"They're not all Elders, the people in this town," the bald man said. "There's blacksmiths and children and miners—"

"We're not proposing to kill anyone," Caleb said. "And anyone who's on the right side of God is sitting here in this room." The bald man cast his gaze downward, doubtful, until Caleb softly said, "John, they killed your brother. That man never caught ill, but he falls sick a day after one of *them* pays a visit?" Caleb began to move through the crowd. "Your cousin," he said, pointing to one woman. "Your mother," he said to a man who didn't seem like he needed any reassurance—his hands were already balled into fists. "My son," Caleb said, his voice catching on the last word. "You've trusted me as your foreman for the past ten years. Trust me now. They're never going to stop. It's going to keep happening. They call it accidents or illness. The Harvest. Let this be the last one." People were saying amen, nodding, and a few applauded.

"One might say it isn't enough," someone said. Heads turned. The miner who spoke was sitting, leaning way back in his chair, his legs splayed out before him and his arms crossed stubbornly. The room had gotten quiet. "You're right this town can't prosper without the mine. But even if we take it out, *he'll* still be walking this earth. This goes on in Wesley Falls, too. Five, ten, fifteen a generation, that sit right with you?"

"Jack, what are you proposing?" said a doubtful man next to him.

Jack looked up at Caleb. "There's enough explosives to do more. We can lay them now, wait till they get back—"

Multiple people were talking at once. "I'm not willing to kill anybody!" someone shouted while someone else shushed them.

"They're killing *us*!" Jack shot back.

"I'm scared of him," the bald man said. "At least...at least with our plan he's not here. Whenever we do it, it has to be when he's over at Wesley Falls otherwise he'll—he'll find out."

"This doesn't end unless we kill him," Jack said.

"You're assuming he can be killed," the woman sitting beside him said. Jack looked at her, frowning.

"Let's put it to a vote," Caleb said suddenly. Jack looked at him, exasperated, and the look between them made Jia think that Caleb knew the vote would fail, and Jack knew this as well. Only Jack and one other miner voted for Jack's plan. Jack sighed loudly, but Caleb came to him and put his hands on his shoulders. "My friend. My true and dear friend," he said, shaking him a little until Jack reluctantly smiled. The relationship between these two men had been long and deep. Chatter started to spread around the room, but Caleb held up his hands. "Go about your normal routine tonight. Gather the horses at midnight. Keep the children quiet—give them whiskey and syrup if it helps. Once you're past the town limits, we'll detonate."

"Who stays back to detonate?"

"I do. The detonation'll be deep—they might not even hear it. I'll take Blaze out—he's the fastest of the horses—and meet you where you are. Don't wait for me. Keep moving."

"Stop sleeping," said Jack suddenly.

Jia turned her head and realized that for the first time in this between world someone had noticed her. Jack was staring directly at her. Jia looked around and realized Maddy was gone. "Wake up," Jack said, coming closer to her. His eyes were blue like James's. "Wake up. Jia, wake up. Her eyelids are moving."

Water splashed her, then came a slap. She opened her eyes with a start. James was hovering over her, his face flushed. "You hit me!" Jia exclaimed, confused.

"Guys!" he shouted.

Jia pulled herself to a seated position. Maddy was across the room from her with Kelly and Casey crouched beside her. Padma urged a bottle of Gatorade toward Jia's mouth, but Jia pushed her aside weakly. "I'm going to be sick." The words were barely out of her mouth before she could turn to the side and vomit with shocking force. It was mostly water, and the effort left her on her side, panting, embarrassed. When she looked up, James looked worried, turning to Casey, saying, "She looks too pale."

"What *happened* to you guys?" Kelly said. Maddy crawled across the floor of the church, nudging James out of the way and sat next to Jia, putting her arms around her as Jia began to cry helplessly. She didn't entirely understand why she was crying, she just didn't feel good and she was exhausted and the worried looks on Casey's and James's faces were scaring her.

"Please drink this," James said, propelling the Gatorade toward her again. It was lukewarm and she hated the salty taste of it, but she drank.

"Where were you guys?" Maddy said.

"I was across the street—" Casey began.

"We were at the back of the church—" Kelly said.

"I came back to show you a photo album we found," James said, "and you guys were unconscious. I thought you'd fallen asleep, but I couldn't wake you up. I was shaking you, splashing water on you."

"We thought maybe you breathed in gases or something," Kelly said. Jia handed the Gatorade to Maddy, who took a grateful sip.

"How long were we out?" Maddy asked.

"Half an hour," Casey said. Jia looked at Maddy. Half an hour was a long time to be wondering what to do about two unconscious people. They must have been terrified. "We started to think we'd have to carry you out of here back home, and... and..."

Padma wet a bandanna and cleaned off Jia's face with it. "No really, where were you?" she asked.

"Jia had a vision," Maddy said. "About the past. I came with her, and we saw everything."

"You brought Maddy?" Padma asked. It wasn't accusatory but there was a hint of jealousy in her voice.

"I think…" Jia said. "I think we both needed to be there for it to happen."

Maddy nodded. "Because I'm a Wesley."

"What did you see?" Kelly asked.

Jia and Maddy began to recount what they had seen, starting with the Wesley brothers and the Frenchman in the mine. They must have awoken or freed something, an entity that they bargained with for prosperity. They saw Evansville later as a bustling mining town, at the center of it twelve Elders from important families. They called it the Harvest, selecting a number of people to die each generation for the pastor. They saw what precipitated the end of Evansville. It wasn't an accident, but the deliberate planting of mining explosives to start the fire, perpetrated by a segment of the town who had lost loved ones to the Harvest.

"They set the fire on purpose," Kelly marveled. "Because they knew it would destroy the town. Maybe they even intended for it to spread to Wesley Falls."

"Sounds like they didn't finish the job," James said.

"You sound like Jack," Jia grumbled, getting to her feet.

"Who's Jack?"

Jia offered her hands to Maddy and pulled her to her feet. "Maddy," Jia said. "You now realize he's bad, right? I know he was nice to you that one time, but you have to see now…"

"I know," Maddy said quietly. "We know why they did it now—throwing those kids into the mine. But how are we supposed to stop it from happening again?"

Jia stared at the open church door into the dusty, littered street of the ghost town. She realized they were all looking at her, as if she would know the answer to that question.

35

James

James shoved his hands into his pockets, realizing that in his peripheral vision, a car was slowing down behind him. *Two days ago I thought I was living in a world where asshole cops were the worst thing I might face, and now I have to contend with mountain demons,* he thought. A mountain demon—or whatever the pastor was— and the people who supported him, and James wasn't sure which was worse. Two months ago he had never seen a human being get killed. He had never had the shit beat out of him so hard that he needed stitches. He had never eaten cucumber sandwiches with Maddy Wesley at the lake.

James ground out his cigarette on someone's trash can and dutifully put the butt in the can like a good citizen, using the motion as an excuse to glance behind him. Fuck. It was a cop car. He heard the sound of its door opening and ignored it. "Curry," called a voice. He ignored it and kept walking, but someone grabbed him by his shirt, then shoved him against the car.

"What's your problem?" he shouted. Yacobi twisted his arm behind his back. The car door opened, and James was shoved inside. "What the fuck? I got rights!"

"We can talk about your rights at the station."

James pounded on the cage that divided him from Yacobi. Were they allowed to do this? Did they think he was dumb enough to suddenly confess to something he didn't do?

At the station he was wrenched out of the car and marched across the sheriff's office to a room with a table, same as the last time. Yacobi was joined by Sheriff Springsteen. "Do you have anything you want to tell us?"

"Yeah, fuck your mom."

Yacobi jerked forward as if to hit him but the sheriff stopped him.

"I'll sue you! I'll sue this entire town! Where are my constitutional rights?"

"Do you even know what's in the Constitution?"

"More than you, apparently!"

"This is your last chance. We might be able to cut a deal if you talk."

"I already told you everything. I was at the party. I sold some weed. The collapse happened, and I got out."

"What if I told you we had a witness?"

"A witness to what?"

"What if I told you someone saw you throwing those kids into the Heart?"

"Do I look like I can throw anyone? I can barely do a pull-up."

"All it takes is a little shove," Yacobi said.

"Why would I do that?"

"Do you know Morgan Lotano?"

James froze. "She's a year above me in school."

"You friends with her?"

"Not really."

"People say all you kids hang out at the park."

"She hangs out there. But juniors don't hang out with sophomores."

"She seems like a nice girl."

What the fuck is this? "I guess."

"She said she saw you pushing those kids down the mine shaft."

James felt as if something cold had hit him in the stomach. "She's lying."

"Why would she lie?"

Why would she lie? They must have made her. He did not have a good retort, nor very much steam to fight back as they continued to question him. He responded robotically, already retreating to a quiet place in the back of his mind. Morgan had lied about him. Morgan, a girl he had liked and who had ripped him off for a fake ID. Morgan, the entirety of his sexual experience, and therefore the person he most frequently thought of when he jerked off.

The cops seemed disappointed that he wasn't talking back anymore. He didn't put up a fight when they grabbed his arm again and he was directed to one of the small cells in the sheriff's office. They normally functioned as drunk tanks.

James stood in the cell and leaned his head against two of the bars, only half listening to the men talking about him. They were going somewhere to get someone.

James closed his eyes and listened to the sounds of the cops walking away, then the buzzing of the fluorescent lights. How long before the Boyles would notice he was gone? They had gone to the mall and he had begged off, not wanting Emily to do something embarrassing, like buy him a pair of shorts. What if they decided this was a bridge too far and wouldn't let him live there anymore? He realized that if things were slightly different, he could have been one of the kids who had died in the mine and no one would have cared. They would have said that he was a loser and a drug dealer and a waste, and all of those things would have been true.

James exhaled loudly and the movement of his jaw pushed his head farther past the bars.

His eyes shot open as something occurred to him. He pulled back and examined the space between the bars. This jail cell had been reasonably constructed to hold a man of a normal size. It had not been reasonably constructed to hold a child, or perhaps a particularly skinny teenager. It was easy to work his leg through. The hardest part was squeezing sideways through the chest area where his ribs still hurt. He had a bad feeling that the police were not coming back alone.

James managed to squeeze through the bars and then stood for a moment dumbly stunned by what he had just done. He slipped out the side door of the sheriff's office and walked as fast as he dared, heading southeast. The old apple orchard was just south of the sheriff's office and was not a bad place to hide out until the Boyles returned. The orchard had long since been abandoned, but most of the apple trees were still there in crooked rows, and many still grew apples.

James sat, leaning against a tree trunk. It was almost dusk, and the sun threw a golden light across the trees. These apples weren't like the ones in the grocery store. They were smaller for one, and a mixture of red and green. Tart, and they could be picked before the fall. He did that sometimes, coming with an empty pillowcase to fill. With enough sugar he could make a decent applesauce, which would be good to eat for at least a week or two.

James closed his eyes, welcoming the feel of the sun and hoping it would somehow wash away his troubles. What was going to happen now that there was a witness? Maybe—

James heard a noise, a muted one, like someone stepping in the grass. He opened his eyes and saw a pair of black-clad legs to his left. It was Pastor Jim Preiss. He was biting into an apple, not looking at James, but in the direction of the setting sun. James had seen countless horror movies and had always thought it silly when someone was paralyzed with fear. He had always thought, *I would run for the door.* But he could not move. Every cell in his body was frozen, rebelling. All he could do was stare at the pastor in terror.

"Do you know when they planted these trees?" the pastor said, without looking at James. "It was nearly winter, too late in the season, but there was nothing to be done about that. The children made a thing of it, pushing the seeds down." The pastor took another bite, chewed, then looked directly at James, unsmiling. "We used to crucify men like you upside down." He tossed the apple to the ground, looking back toward Main Street as if bored. "Or weigh them down with rocks on a board. It's a slower death than you'd think." The pastor had moved so that the setting sun blinked out behind him, darkening his face but casting a backlit glow on his clothes. James had a strange feeling as if he were being pulled toward him, even though he knew his body was still sitting on the ground. The pastor turned his head slightly, shadows casting over his eye sockets. There was a blackness there, two swirling, squiggling things that got larger and larger—

A noise escaped James's throat as he scrambled backward and struggled to his feet. He sprinted, regretting every cigarette he had ever smoked as his lungs burned in protest. If that *thing* was behind him—

He ran for the Boyle house, heading for the backyard rather than the front door because it was closer. Kelly and her parents were in the kitchen getting dinner ready and looked up, alarmed, at his appearance. He gave a desperate look to Kelly, and related the only safe part he could tell to all of them. He had been picked up again, questioned, and not exactly arrested. "That's it," Mr. Boyle said, "I'm making a phone call. This is a total violation of civil rights."

James caught Kelly's eye and they went up to her room as soon as they could. James paced the length of the bedroom, frantic, as he retold her what the pastor had said. "What was he doing there? Did they bring him to the sheriff's and when I wasn't there he figured out where I went? *Crucifixion?!*"

Kelly chewed viciously on her lower lip. She began to rifle through her bookcase, eventually pulling out one of her textbooks from Catholic school. "They said one of the apostles asked to be crucified upside down out of respect for Jesus. But I think the Romans just did that sometimes to be extra cruel."

"What did he mean about a board?"

Kelly's face was pale despite her tan. James didn't think he had ever seen her so scared, maybe with the exception of the mine party itself. "They did that during the Salem witch trials. Make you lie on the ground, then put a board on you, and keep adding rocks until you confessed."

"His face! His face fucking opened! It was like a—a—"

"Shh! Calm down. Why don't you smoke some weed?"

Up was down now, because Kelly always got nervous when he wanted to smoke, afraid that her parents would find out. James went over to the window, half expecting to see a dark figure out in the yard. His hands shook so badly that the joint took several tries to light. "Can I sleep in here tonight?" he asked.

"Of course. We'll lock the window and get the dog."

James, his head half out the window, inhaled deeply, feeling the sharp burning in his chest. He was smoking too fast—it would hit him too hard. He needed it, though. What happened to someone's mind when they were absolutely certain that the world was a particular way—that the Easter bunny didn't exist, or that Noah's Ark was just a story—and then they found out that maybe there were things that existed outside those bounds of reality? What then?

36

Jia

In her dream she could see them in the bunker. Kelly and Maddy sitting on a blanket, books in their laps, disagreeing about something, but not in an unpleasant way. Padma and Casey sitting at the picnic table, a math textbook in front of them. Padma was explaining something using an array of Goldfish crackers that Casey kept eating. James was on all fours, drawing on a massive sheet of paper. Jia looked closer and saw that he held a gummy eraser in his right hand, and in his left hand the blue pencil he was drawing with had no eraser on its end, just a gold stamp that said 5H. *5H?* Jia thought. She had always wondered why tests had to be completed with a number two pencil, because she had never seen a pencil with any number other than two.

That thought made her realize she was dreaming. This wasn't like what she had seen with Maddy, and she knew on some level that Maddy's being there had made things feel more organized.

She saw Casey and Maddy jogging, Maddy struggling to keep up. Kelly and James sharing a pink ice cream cone, then offering it to her as they left the candy shop. She saw them all on the lakeshore. Jia, Padma, and Kelly, shrieking with laughter, were trying to pass a football among themselves without Casey intercepting. She glanced out at the water and saw Maddy and James wading, deep in conversation. The expressions on their faces suggested no barbs being exchanged for once. *Good*, she thought, *it's better that they get along, see that they're opposite sides of the same coin.*

Now she was *above*, floating in the sky, looking down on the raft. They were lying on their backs, heads together, bodies splayed out like a sunflower. Each of them had a semiprecious stone above their heads, all in different colors. *Those are from The Gem Shop*, she realized. *But what are we doing?*

No, now it was that other terrible feeling. She saw that velvety blackness; she saw things she didn't want to see. She saw them climbing down like spiders. She pulled valiantly with her mind, struggling against her own body to wake up. *Wake up. WAKE UP.* She did not want to see any more.

Jia gasped as if resurfacing from under water and realized she was staring at the glow-in-the-dark stars she had stuck to the ceiling of her bedroom. It took time to make sense of dreams like these. Jia blinked at the glowing stars and realized something was wrong. Her legs were at a slight decline. That happened when there was extra weight on the end of her bed, like her mom sitting on it. She picked up her head, then froze, her heart jerking in her chest. The pastor was sitting at the end of her bed, looking at her patiently as if he had been sitting there for a long time.

It's a dream. Only a nightmare. Wake up. WAKE UP.

"It's not a dream," he said quietly. In the dim lighting his eyes looked completely black. "You're a special person, Jia Kwon. Do you know that?"

Where's Mom? she thought desperately.

"Don't worry about your mom. She isn't here. There was a fire at your store, and she just got a phone call about it."

What are you doing here?

"You are like me, aren't you?" Pastor said, as if amused. He had his hands folded together in his lap and was now looking around at her possessions with interest. The book on demonology she had taken from The Gem Shop for research. Her deck of tarot cards, wrapped in their silk scarf. Then—to Jia's horrified embarrassment—the box of tampons sitting on her desk. He then looked back at her and leaned forward—Jia tried to move backward and found she couldn't. She squeezed her eyes shut instead. *His eyes. If he does that THING with his face and I see it in real life, I'll go crazy.* He reached out and took her chin with his fingertips, moving her head ever so slightly to the right and left. "The issue is the eyes, though. Those would come out..."

He was between her and the door to the hallway. But the window was another option. The Kwons lived in a ranch-style house. Was she fast enough to get to the window before he got her? The window was open a crack—she liked to keep it open to let in the sound of the crickets and cicadas.

The pastor didn't seem to notice her eyes darting between him and the window. He now had his head thoughtfully cocked to one side. "Jia, do you ever miss your father?" he asked.

Jia bolted, dashing for the window, which she wrenched open. She jumped out headfirst, used her forearms to break her fall, then scrambled to her feet and sprinted. She headed blindly for The Gem Shop. They lived close enough so that soon she saw the fire engine, the figure of her mom standing against the flashing red-and-white lights. She wanted to run to her mother for comfort, but her mother wouldn't understand what had just happened.

Padma and Casey lived close by, two blocks down. It was twelve o'clock at night, but the light was on in Ajay's bedroom, his window open. Jia yelled to get his attention, then asked him to get Padma, and no, she didn't care what time of night it was. Padma appeared moments later in her pajamas, then raced back inside, apparently to call Casey, because they gathered him before taking a hurried walk back toward Main Street while Jia told them what had happened. She was still distressed but was relieved that she was not alone, and that the two of them believed her without needing much explanation.

"I don't understand the thing about your father," Casey said.

"Her father died in fourth grade," Padma said.

"That just makes it even weirder," Casey said. It was unsettling when Casey was not in a jovial mood because that was so rare.

Back on Main Street, it looked as if the fire had been put out. Jia approached her mother and hugged her. "What happened? Why didn't you wake me up?" Jia said.

"What would you have done? Rode the fire engine?" Su-Jin said, pushing hair off Jia's forehead.

"How did it start?" Padma asked. Su-Jin noticed that she was there, then flicked her eyes curiously to Casey.

"Could be electrical. It mainly affected the back, where the kitchen is."

"Maybe it wasn't electrical," Jia said.

Su-Jin sighed. "Maybe not. We have insurance, though."

"They can put everything back?" Jia asked hopefully.

"And then some. This gives us some cash to make renovations. Don't worry about stuff like this—this is grown-up stuff."

It's all grown-up stuff, Jia thought. *It doesn't change; you just get older.* She cast a beleaguered look at Padma and Casey. She was too scared to go back to her own bedroom and begged to sleep at Padma's house. They headed there together, Jia and Padma going through the front door, then letting Casey climb in the window. He had retrieved a wooden baseball bat from his garage. He locked the bedroom door, then sat up against it. "No one's getting in here," he said grimly. She was so grateful to both of them that she almost started crying.

"How did he get into your house anyway?" Casey asked.

"We don't lock our front door," Jia said. Most people in town didn't.

"But *why* did he get into your house?" Padma wondered. She sat cross-legged on her bed. They were all in agreement that the fire at the store hadn't been an accident. Su-Jin needing to attend to it was the perfect opportunity to catch Jia alone.

He said I was special, like him, Jia thought. Who had ever called her special, but her parents? But she had a flicker of an idea, a strange sense just like the one she had gotten in the Town Hall when he had looked at her, that maybe he understood something about her that even she didn't.

PART SEVEN:
JULY 1995

37

Padma

Padma glanced outside the kitchen window, seeing that it was overcast. Her knife cut easily through balls of mozzarella, and the tomatoes were already sliced. They had taken to bringing lunch and snacks with them when they met at the lake or the bunker, which was most days, except when she had dance classes, Casey football, and Maddy various church activities. As she spread pesto on slices of bread, she listened idly as her parents talked in Tamil in the kitchen. She and Ajay couldn't read Tamil but could understand it well.

Her mother said it was funny she didn't get many referred cases from her father. Her mother was a surgical oncologist and worked a half-hour drive away. In contrast, her father was the only general practitioner in Wesley Falls, well-known by everyone in town. He probably had patients who had suspicious lumps or bad blood tests. "I refer plenty of people to you!" her father said with mock offense. "Fortunately for them, most don't pan out, unfortunately for me," her mother joked. This was not something they would say in public, but Padma knew that doctors often had dark senses of humor.

Padma put the sandwiches in her book bag and said she was headed out to work on her capstone. Her parents didn't ask too many questions—they were happy she was going somewhere rather than staying at home and reading, as long as she was home before dark. Her parents knew about the murders—everyone did—and while horrifying, their daughter was not one of the kids who would have ever been at that party! In a dangerous place! Drinking alcohol and doing drugs!

Padma headed to the bunker first—it was closer and there was a chance of rain, which made swimming less likely. The heavy door was ajar, covered by hanging vines but visible now that she knew what to look for, and she struggled to open it before she saw Casey's tanned arm pushing it out for her. "You're late!" he said cheerfully.

James and Jia had wet hair, and everyone was talking about the pastor again. James was describing the pastor's face at the orchard. "When I looked at it, I wanted to die. Like I wanted to exit my skin," he said.

"But he didn't do that to Jia," Maddy said. "Or me."

"When you told me that story about him hugging you, I thought he was going to bite you," Padma said, pulling out the sandwiches, one of which Casey eagerly took.

"But he didn't," Maddy pointed out. "So why does he threaten James but not us?"

"You're girls," Casey said flatly, his mouth full. "I mean, guys aren't getting virginity tests. Maybe he's a creep. He lives alone, he's not married. Pastors are typically married, right?"

"Maddy's part of the church. So maybe he thinks you're already on his team. And based on what he said to Jia, I think he can feel your power," Padma said.

Jia sat on the floor on a beach towel, her knees pulled into her chest, making her look very small. "I don't have any power. I can't control how I see things."

Padma took a sandwich and sat next to Casey on the floor. "My parents said something interesting this morning. My mom's an oncologist, a cancer doctor, and she was saying that she doesn't really get patients from Wesley Falls. I was thinking, what if that isn't a coincidence?" She looked around the bunker—all their eyes were on her.

"Maddy, do I have this right?" James said. "All the founding families have a descendant who's currently an Elder, but there's a couple Elders who aren't from founding families?"

"Yeah," Maddy said. "They're almost always from founding

families. You have to have been in the church for at least three generations to be an Elder, and you have to be married."

James held up a finger and pointed to Maddy with his other hand. "Wesleys. Rich as fuck. Your mom doesn't work and what does your dad even do?"

"Something with real estate," Maddy said.

"Your house is bigger than Padma's and both her parents are doctors," James said. He held up a second finger. "Sullivans. They have a three-car garage and they're always vaguely starting businesses that don't really do anything." Third finger. "Dandridges. Sent both their kids to private college with no scholarships."

"All the founding families are wealthy," Maddy said.

"Right, but that's not it," James said. "Think of the last ten people who died here. Not counting the mine party. Marshall Wake, his truck slipped off the road when it was icy. Not a founding family. That lady who used to work at the candy shop had a heart attack and she was what—fifty? Not a founding family."

"Lily Waterson died two years ago, she's in a founding family," Maddy countered.

"She was a hundred and three," Padma said.

"Can you think of a founding family person who died young?" James asked her. "My mom was thirty-five when she died. Of cancer. Can you think of a single founding family member with cancer?"

Maddy stared at the ground, the wheels spinning in her head. "All of them live long. Like the pastor is protecting them."

"And making them rich," James added. "They keep giving him what he needs, and he gives them a charmed life."

"Well, how do we stop them?" Maddy asked Jia, who shrugged helplessly.

Without a clear answer, they settled into working. They had taken some things from Evansville—the photo album, some books Kelly was convinced would help, and the big Bible Maddy had found, which she was using to draw a family tree of the town's Elders. Kelly had gotten a large piece of thick paper from the art store, and she and James had unrolled it on the floor with the idea of making a map of the inside of the mine. Padma prodded Casey through his math homework, though he got distracted by literally any movement or sound.

"James, what pencil are you using?" Jia said, breaking the silence.

Padma might not have looked up if it hadn't been such an odd question. James, who was on his hands and knees on the floor of the bunker, sat back on his heels and looked at her quizzically. "What do you mean? It's a pencil."

"Why does it say 5H? Why isn't there an eraser?" Jia said. Padma looked at her friend's face and found that it was drawn tight. She had been like that a lot lately, not the open book she normally was to Padma. It made Padma sad and wonder if it was a function of all the bad things that were happening, or the fact that they had formed a group and now she had to share Jia with others.

"It's a drawing pencil. You have a separate eraser. Pencils come from one to nine, and they're either H or B. B is how black it is and H is how hard the lead is."

"But why are you using that one?" Jia asked. Her tone was almost accusatory, and James was bewildered.

"H's are good for detailed work. They don't smear." He gestured to the piece of paper, which he had made a few preliminary marks on. "There's all these paths, it's complicated, so a sharp, detailed line would be good."

Jia seemed unsettled but would not meet anyone's eye.

When Padma looked back at Casey, he had closed his math book and looked at her with wide, innocent eyes. "I'm done with math today."

"Casey, we're almost done. Just ten more."

"Nooooo," he whined, and melted off the table onto the floor. "No more. I'll do capstone stuff, I'll mine coal, please, anything but math. I beg of you!"

"Get up!"

"Make me," he said, smirking up at her.

Padma grabbed one of his arms and attempted to pull him

up, but his weight was like a boulder. Casey laughed; Maddy did, too. Padma planted her feet and leaned fully back, but he couldn't be budged. "I won't take no for an answer!" she shouted. She wanted to laugh, but was also frustrated. If Casey didn't pass math, he couldn't play football in the fall, and she couldn't imagine how depressed he would be if someone took football away. His family would say bad things. He would believe the bad things. Casey, laughing, started to pull her down and Padma, in a moment of inspiration, emitted a sharp yelp, drawing her arm into her body as if hurt.

Casey's humor was instantly gone. "Are you okay? I didn't mean to."

Padma rubbed at her "injured" shoulder. "I think so."

"Okay, okay," he said, then humbly returned to his seat at the picnic table.

By the time it was five it was raining. Casey's math was done and everyone began to pack up their things. He gestured to the open bunker door, where they could see the rain coming down. Kelly and James had already started back, indifferent to the droplets. "You want a ride?" he asked Padma.

"To my dad's office if you don't mind? We're going to that new Chinese restaurant by the mall."

"Sure," he said.

"Jia, they said you could come, too," Padma said, feeling awkward that she couldn't extend the offer to anyone else.

"No, thanks," Jia said, stooping to pick up some books. Padma looked at Casey—he shrugged.

Should she call Jia? she wondered. Or perhaps just come over one day to hash it out? For as long as they had been friends, she had never not felt close to Jia. She had the sense that Jia was frightened, not just of what was happening, but that they had an implicit understanding that she would somehow be the one who would know how to fix it. *Or maybe*, Padma thought, *she doesn't understand that yet.*

Her mood lifted as the minivan pulled up to the building on Bleaker Street, where her father's office was. The dining options in Wesley Falls were limited to the diner and Del Monico's, so any trip out of town for a meal was special. She waved goodbye to Casey and ran through the rain to the main door. Inside the waiting room Ajay was reading one of his stupid fantasy books. Something about sexy cave people. She could hear her parents talking to someone with a deep voice down the hall in her father's office. "It was beautiful!" her mother was saying. "We could see them very well from our backyard!"

She must have been talking about the Fourth of July fireworks. Padma squeezed some water from her braid as she entered the room, then froze. Her dad sat at his desk behind a cup of coffee. In the two chairs opposite him were her mother and the pastor. But it was as if Padma couldn't see anyone else but him as he turned his head and smiled at her. "This is our youngest, Padma," her mother said, putting an arm around her. The arm communicated everything—that she was well behaved, that she had good grades, that she would do well in life.

"Oh, we're well acquainted," the pastor said, switching his smile from Padma to her mother. "Padma helps out in our office sometimes. Our youngest, but most efficient employee!"

Padma could see the split second of surprise on her mother's face, the exchange of glances with her father. Her lie was discovered, but she knew that her parents wouldn't want to face public embarrassment of not knowing where their daughter worked—or used to. "Oh, I'm not surprised at all!" her mother said instead.

They talked more, the pastor saying that they should have come to the church grounds to watch the fireworks. They were welcome, of course, to stop by any time, and Padma could even show them around. Then they started talking about the new Chinese restaurant and that they were headed out there, and *oh no*, it was about to happen, they were about to invite the pastor to come with them, because wouldn't it be rude not to?

"Amma, I'm not feeling well," Padma said. "I thought it was the rain giving me chills, but maybe it's not." She forced her eyes to stay on her mother's as she felt her forehead, then the side of her neck with the back of her hand.

"A summer cold has been going around," her father said. "We can go to the restaurant next week."

Padma was very sad about the lack of Chinese food, and this was so apparent that by the time they were back home, Ajay had agreed to drive out to the restaurant to pick up takeout. The illness even deterred any questions about her lying about working at the church, something she would inevitably have to reckon with. Padma languished in bed, enjoying the room service as Ajay prepared her a plate. She sat up, excited for bean curd in black garlic sauce, fried rice, and an almond cookie, even if it had a strange texture: not quite crisp and not quite chewy.

"Why are you faking?" Ajay asked. His tone was more curious than angry.

"They were going to invite him," she said in a harsh whisper, taking the plate of food.

"I know!" he said.

"I didn't want him around."

"He's weird!"

"I agree. Why do you think so?"

Ajay's brow furrowed. "I don't know." He put his hands on his hips and affected a dumb voice while wearing a huge grin. *"I'm such a nice guy, look at me.* That whole church is weird."

"My friend thinks he's trying to convert our family. That it would look good or something, because everyone knows Dad." Her brother made a face. "Ajay, if you see him around town and he tries to talk to you, just run away." He made his *okay, weirdo* face, but ultimately, he agreed.

38

Maddy

What a perverse pleasure to have her clothes approved of every morning—today a pair of Bermuda shorts and a Golden Praise T-shirt—only to secretly be wearing a bathing suit underneath. An *immodest* bathing suit, a bright green bikini she had specifically chosen because her mother would have hated it. Swimming at Chicken Lake with the capstone group felt innocent and private, tucked away from the rest of town. Despite the danger they were in, it was the first time in a long time where Maddy felt happy.

She, Kelly, and James sat on the raft, which bobbed gently in the tide. Casey had towed a Styrofoam cooler of snacks to the raft earlier because everyone agreed they tasted better here than on the shore. James made his way through a box of Ho Hos with the rapaciousness that only a teenage boy could have. There was no food judgment here. "I can't read the map," Maddy said. "It looks like a ball of spaghetti."

"It's a work in progress," James said, his mouth full.

"Does it make sense to anyone but you?"

"God, woman! How am I supposed to represent something three-dimensional in 2D?"

"You're making a map…?" Maddy's question trailed off but the meaning wasn't lost. James's eyes met hers, then darted to Kelly's then distractedly to his hands. *Why would you make a map,* Maddy thought, *unless you intended to go somewhere?*

"For our project." He shoved an empty Ho Hos wrapper back into the box.

Kelly stood up and held her hands over her head like a ballet dancer. "Rate my dive," she said, then dove into the water.

"What do you think?" James said, digging through the cooler for his baggie of weed. "Nine point five?"

"A nine-six at least," Maddy said agreeably. Things had gradually gotten a tiny bit better with James, but she preferred to have a buffer of at least one other person when he was around.

James twisted a wrapping paper into a joint with practiced dexterity, noticing that she was watching him. "What do you think, Maddy Wesley? Is this why I'm going to hell?"

"I never said you were going to hell."

"But you think so, don't you?" He lit the joint, inhaled, then exhaled smoke not directly at her, but not pointedly away from her. "It's okay. I'm ready to party with devils." She hoped he would stop talking, or enough silence could elapse that she could exit the raft without seeming to admit defeat. "What about her?" James said suddenly, gesturing to Padma with a jerk of his head. She was laughing, attempting to dog paddle away from Casey.

"Her?"

"She's Hindu, right? So you think she's going to hell?"

"I never said that."

"But you think it. You think she deserves to go to hell."

"I never said that!"

"Isn't that what they teach you? That's not what you believe?"

"I don't know what I believe anymore, okay?" she snapped, her voice loud enough to draw attention from some of the others. James made an innocent *yeesh* gesture.

They sat in silence for a few minutes, James smoking, before he gestured toward the water. "Look." It was a duck followed by three ducklings. As they watched the ducks paddle westward, Maddy realized that was the closest she would get to an apology.

She had thought of something—an idea that had come to her but been too scary to seriously consider. She had intended to talk to someone at the lake today, maybe Jia, someone who would give her the encouragement she needed. She did not think that person would be James. "I had an idea," she said. He looked at her. "My father's office. He's always been super strict that I'm not allowed in there."

"So there must be something in there."

"That's the thing. I don't even know what it would be. But he's a Wesley. An Elder. Maybe there's something incriminating in there."

"So how do we get you in? Any idea where he keeps the key?" he wondered.

"It's not locked."

James coughed out smoke. "What do you mean it's not locked? Why haven't you gone in there before?"

"He told me not to," she said. James stared at her, his mouth open, then started to laugh. Maddy started to giggle, too. "I'm scared," she admitted. "They have a church thing at four that I know will take two hours because they said to make my own dinner. But I'm scared they'll come back early."

He rolled his joint between his fingers, thinking, and she realized that her admission was not actually going to lead to him making fun of her. "You need a good cover story in case they catch you."

"There's no legitimate reason for me to be in his office."

"You're…struggling with what you've done. And you think connecting with the Wesley family line would help you get back on the path. You were hoping you could find something there, like an heirloom you could hold on to for strength while praying."

"You really are a delinquent."

He grinned at her. "You realize, now that you've told me, you can't chicken out."

Maddy headed home at 3:45 after changing back into her modest clothes. She rehearsed what she would say if caught, even practiced trying to make her eyes water. It might work. Her parents certainly had a peculiar respect for family history. Her parents barely acknowledged her as they left. She stood at the front window and watched their car drive away, counting to one hundred and twenty before she went into the kitchen, edging toward the closed door to her father's office.

She almost expected the doorknob to burn her hand when she touched it. It turned easily, unlocked. The odor of wood and leather greeted her. She had seen the office before, of course, when her father was inside. But even then, she didn't cross the line where the kitchen tile met the hardwood floor, not even as a child and a toy rolled past.

She stepped inside, holding her breath. One wall was lined with bookshelves, the books interrupted with the occasional framed photo or keepsake. Maddy crept closer and looked at the pictures. It was a mix of family and church photos. Her parents with various other Elders. Elders at a Christmas dinner. She noticed none of the photos featured the pastor. The pictures of her and her parents stung. There they were, a handsome family standing together, smiles on their faces, without any indication of how it actually was in this house. How lonely and empty it often felt.

On the other side of the office were the windows with the shades drawn and her father's desk, computer, and printer. Hanging above the desk was a framed detailed embroidery that Jane Merrick had made, which said "Blessed are the pure in heart, for they will see God."

"Bitch," Maddy whispered under her breath, delighting in the sin. She turned, searching her father's desk, but the surface was immaculate. The middle drawer contained only stationery. The top right drawer had envelopes and postage stamps. The bottom right drawer, the largest, was stuck. Maddy tugged on it, wondering if it was locked, but it gave a little. She gave one hard tug, but her fingers, damp with perspiration, slipped and she jabbed her elbow painfully against the wall. She heard something sliding and turned in time to see the framed embroidery crash to the ground, the glass shattering. Her mouth fell open in horror.

Panicked, she looked through the open doorway, expecting to see her parents there. She crouched down, examining the damage. Maybe she could just clean off all the glass and put it back and they wouldn't notice? No—of course they would! Then they would know she had been in here. Wait. The frame was a plain black one, modest and simple. They had a framed family photo in the hallway upstairs that was identical. She could switch out the frames and take the blame for breaking the frame upstairs.

She sprinted upstairs, snatched the identical frame, and ran back. She turned the broken frame over to begin undoing the clasps. When she pulled off the backing, she expected to see the cloth of the embroidery gathered around some cardboard, but instead she was surprised to see wood. Varnished wood. There was a rectangle embedded within it, like a tiny trap door on a hinge. Maddy dug her fingernail into a little divot at the side and pried the latch open. It was a compartment with something small inside. She shook the frame and something tumbled out into her waiting hand.

It was a key. Three inches long and ornate, hefty and metal. *Old*. Clearly not made for any modern lock.

39

Kelly

Kelly lay on her bed with the map spread out in front of her. It was coming along, but it was harder to find details about the mine the farther down in elevation she went. There were also supposedly records from the Bureau of Mines about their attempts to put out the Evansville fire, but she hadn't been able to locate them. James was sitting at her computer, finally working on his magnet school application. Or at least he was typing while blasting heavy metal into his headphones.

She went downstairs to make cream cheese-and-jelly sandwiches. James had taken off his headphones by the time she got back but was still working. "Where was I on the Ugly List?" he asked without looking at her.

He was staring at the computer screen, its light reflected in his eyes, a seemingly uncaring expression on his face. "I mean..." Kelly hesitated. "All the burnouts were at the bottom."

He bit into a sandwich, not deterred from his reading.

"You know you're not ugly, right?" He was hunt-and-peck typing again, ignoring her. She hugged him half into strangulation around the neck.

"Get off me!" he said, laughing, pretending to cough. She took a sandwich and got back on her bed. "Do you think girls at school think I'm creepy?" he asked suddenly.

"No, they think you're scary."

"Aren't those the same?"

"Creepy is like...someone who makes your skin crawl. Like

Rick, no offense. Scary is when you're worried they might stab you with a pencil."

"I never actually did that."

"Only because you missed."

"Well, I wouldn't hit a girl."

"Just admit that you want people to be scared of you."

"Not girls. They don't like me, though."

"Morgan liked you."

At this he finally turned to face her, chagrined. "The girl who's accusing me of murder?"

"Who knows how they got her to say that. She didn't have to make out with you. Not multiple times."

"She just wanted the ID."

"Maybe she liked you *and* she wanted the ID."

"Then why'd she start ignoring me?"

Kelly shrugged. "Maybe something happened with another boy. Maybe they told her not to hang out with you. I think things will be different somewhere else, like at the magnet school. You'll meet cool people and ditch me."

He turned in his chair to face her. "I won't ditch you."

"You'll meet artsy people who wear black and have tattoos, and you'll forget I even exist."

He frowned, hurt. "Why would you say that?"

"Come on, it's half-true *now*."

"What!"

"I thought when I switched schools, we would be friends."

"We are!"

"Not at school."

"We don't have any classes together."

"Between classes. Or lunch." But she already knew his answer to that: he frequently didn't go to lunch, and if she saw him between classes he might nod at her or only say a word or two.

"When do I go to lunch? What am I supposed to do, say hi when you're sitting with Maddy?"

"That isn't fair. I never picked Maddy over you."

He put his sandwich down. "I didn't want people to like, look at our friendship and make weird comments. All the burnouts would be like, *Oh are you fucking her?*" Here he used the dumb, gruff voice reserved for anyone he thought was an idiot, which was to say, almost everyone.

It was rare for him to be flat-out honest about what he felt. James hated earnestness, or at least it made him uncomfortable. Kelly was on the verge of being teary. "I want you to succeed. Sometimes I think I want it more than you do. I want you to get into the magnet school, and RISD or whatever, but I don't want you to leave me behind." She could not stop the tears. Everything that was happening this summer was too much.

"Hey," he said, getting up and coming to sit next to her. "I'm not going to leave you behind. We'll always be friends."

"Will we?"

"I can't see a future without you in it."

"What if you get in and move to Dover?"

"So what? We can take the bus, or maybe one of us will have a car. And we can visit each other in college."

"You promise?"

"I promise."

In the next hour they operated as they typically did after a fight: silently apologetic, somehow intimate despite the lack of conversation. James fell asleep on her bed reading one of her ElfQuest comics. Kelly got onto the computer and saw an email from Padma.

Jia is being weird. She won't talk to me. What do you think we should do?

We should all talk to her together, Kelly wrote back. She's scared. I would be, too, if that thing was in my bedroom.

Kelly yawned. It was 10:30 and James was dead asleep, her comic book open on his chest. "Move, pig," she said, pushing his body over so she could have some space. She fell asleep reading, and in the morning realized she hadn't washed her face: that certainly wouldn't help her skin.

"Kell?" She heard her mother knocking on the door before she opened it. Emily frowned. "You kids shouldn't be in the same bed."

"He fell asleep," Kelly said, stretching as she got out of bed. "Can we have waffles?"

"If I have the mix."

The Harpies were blissfully not around in the morning that summer, off at their part-time jobs at the mall, where they were saving their money for horseback riding camp in August. Her father made coffee and James heated up some butter and syrup, which for some reason tasted better mixed. "Mom, Padma said something interesting the other day. Her mom's an oncologist, and she said very few people around here get cancer. Who can you think of?"

"Gosh, Marcia Hansley, right?" Emily said, sipping her coffee.

"The snowplow guy."

"Beverly, Jessica's godmother. You barely met her."

"James's mom," Kelly said.

"For God's sake, Emily!" Kelly's father yelled, nearly slamming his mug of coffee down, startling them all. "He's practically a man," he said, gesturing to James, and left the kitchen in a huff. Bewildered, Kelly and James looked at each other.

Emily put down her mug and rubbed her temples. "Mom, what is he talking about?" Kelly prodded.

Silence.

"Mrs. Boyle?" James asked.

"I never wanted to have this conversation with you," she mumbled, half to herself. "I didn't think it was my place."

"Mom."

Emily looked up and directly at James. "Hon, your mother didn't have cancer."

James blinked. "Yes, she did."

"No, she didn't. That's just what she told you. You were a child—I wasn't going to tell you otherwise."

"She had colon cancer. That's what she died of, the treatment didn't work."

"Your mother had addiction issues. She died of an overdose."

"That isn't true," James said, his voice getting louder. "I took care of her. I went with her to the clinic to get treatments."

"You did, but that wasn't chemotherapy. That was a methadone clinic."

"What's methadone?" Kelly asked.

"It's one of the ways they treat addiction to narcotics. You have to go there periodically and get shots because you can't take it at home."

"You're lying," James said. Kelly could see his chest moving, as if he was breathing faster.

"She had access to drugs because she worked in the medical field, and it's not uncommon. She was struggling, and it caused a lot of problems with your father."

"You're lying!" James yelled, standing up. He threw down his fork and stomped out of the house.

Kelly was stunned. How many times this summer could she stand to have her world turned on its head? She could only stare at her mother, the betrayal in her eyes. "Kelly..."

"Don't even talk to me right now!"

She flew out the back door, which James had left wide open. But which direction had he gone? She didn't have to wonder for long, because she heard a crashing sound from the side of the house. She ran across the lawn and saw James heading down Willow, apparently after knocking down a metal trash can. Debris was strewn across the asphalt. James was cursing loudly, fury written plainly across his face.

"James!"

"FUCK THIS TOWN!" he shouted, kicking another garbage can over.

"James, be quiet!"

"I DON'T FUCKING CARE! FUCK THIS!"

"You *can't* make a *scene!*" She jogged after him, speaking in a loud whisper. All it would take was for some nosy neighbor to hear the noise, see James knocking over trash cans and mailboxes, and find an excuse to call the police. "Please stop." She grabbed him by the back of his shirt, but he squirmed away. There was a whole row of trash cans, because the garbage men didn't come till nine. She panicked, paralyzed, but then to her relief she saw a familiar figure ahead on the road. She frequently saw Casey in the morning going on long runs that looped around town. She waved her arms frantically, though this was entirely unnecessary given the racket James was making. Casey ran over to them, taking in the bizarre sight of James's foul-mouthed tirade.

"Hey, buddy, do you want to calm down?" Casey said calmly.

"FUCK OFF!"

What happened next was strange—Kelly had seen football games before and had seen tackles, but what Casey did to James was different; it was in slow motion, physical without being violent. Casey somehow took him down gently, and once in the grass, James turned into a feral cat, struggling against the larger boy for freedom. It was like watching how Milky went from her well-mannered self to a scratching, clawing terror when Kelly tried to trim her nails. But James was no match for Casey. "Calm down," Casey said quietly. "Just calm down."

James struggled, then when he realized it was futile, stopped moving, staring dully into the grass with eyes shiny with tears. He was whispering something Kelly had to lean down to hear. "I hate it. I just hate it."

Casey rested his head on the grass beside James, still catching his breath. "I know," he said. "I know, man."

40

Jia

Padma was never one to hold her tongue but the dynamic of her relationship with Jia had changed, confused by a tangle of six people when previously there had only been two. And it was Padma who pressed her the most with what to do next, and Jia, frustrated, would think *Why are you asking me?* Maddy knew the most about the church. Casey was the strongest. Padma the smartest.

But now Jia had an idea. She did not like the idea because of its implications, but at least it was *something*. She called them all to The Gem Shop, sending word by their method of communication. A phone call to Padma, then Padma would contact Maddy and Kelly on AOL, then tell Casey at his house under the guise of math tutoring. Kelly would tell James and then they would all meet at the store around eleven.

Jia prepared for the day, taking one of the black velvet bags they sold and filling it with an assortment of semiprecious stones from the mixed bin. The selection needed to be large enough for it to be a true test.

Jia gestured for them to sit on the two couches in the center of the store. "I think I know what we need to do next."

"Shoot," Casey said.

"It's a test," Jia said, holding up the velvet bag, which she had cinched shut. "I had a dream about what happens, only I'm not sure if it's the future or not. It wasn't like what I saw with Maddy, where everything seemed to make sense. I saw you two fighting over math," she said, gesturing to Padma and Casey. "I saw James drawing with a number five pencil when I didn't know that number five pencils existed. I saw some other things—" She hesitated. "But I'm not sure if they're right, so I came up with a test."

"What do we have to do?" Kelly asked.

"It happens at the lake around sunset, so that's where we should go." Jia looked down at the bag, feeling its weight under her hands, knowing that her friends were all looking at each other, puzzled.

Casey balanced the Styrofoam cooler on his head as they stepped their way through the woods. He was saying something to Maddy but Jia wasn't listening. They had until sunset. One last lazy afternoon until they would not be able to go back to the way it was before. She wanted to savor it.

Jia sat on the shore and watched her friends in the lake, smiling as she saw them goof off and joke around, ignoring the ball of foreboding that sat in her stomach. Maddy was teaching Padma how to do a herringbone braid in her hair. Casey showed them how to do a proper football tackle. This game moved to the raft, where Casey simply flipped anyone in the water who tried to tackle him. Sunset grew closer. Maddy and Kelly treaded water while talking, but everyone else was on the raft. Jia tied the velvet bag around her neck and swam to the raft. When she got there, James was carefully unwrapping a joint from its protective Ziploc bag. He offered it around—Padma shook her head. Drugs still scared her, though James did not anymore.

"Nah, that stuff isn't good for your body," Casey said.

"Says who?" James scoffed.

"I mean, look at me and look at you."

James broke into laugher, his shoulders shaking. "Cold, man," he said, lighting the joint finally. He had been in such a subdued mood the past few days; it was nice to see him laugh. Maddy and Kelly began to make their way to the raft, and Jia felt a shiver of nervousness in her stomach.

"Guys," Jia said, gesturing to the setting sun. "It's time." By now everyone was curious about the test and how the wet velvet bag would be involved. They arranged themselves in a circle, facing the bag in the center. "In the dream, we were all lying down on the raft on our backs and we each had a stone over our heads. Each a different one," Jia said.

"Why?" Maddy asked. "Is that some kind of ritual?"

"I don't know, but I want to see if my dream is true. Because if it's true, I know what we have to do next."

"But if we do this ritual thing, and we pass your test, it would have only happened because you thought it was going to happen. So it's a self-fulfilling prophecy," James said.

"A self-fulfilling prophecy is still a prophecy," Jia said, undeterred. She emptied the velvet bag in the center of the raft. The stones tumbled out, shiny and beautiful. Forty or so stones, all different colors. What was the probability they would all pick the ones she had dreamt about?

She couldn't fairly take part herself—in her dream she had the hematite—it was her favorite stone. A metallic opaque oval, like liquid mercury that had turned solid. It felt smooth and right in her hand. James selected next, going for the lapis lazuli without much thought. Maddy ran her hands over the stones—Jia felt an internal lurch when she passed over the pink agate, but then she went back to it and selected it, then looked at her as if for an answer. Three out of three. Padma looked at her from across the pile, then slowly reached out, her eyes still on Jia as she waved her hands over the stones. "I can't tell you, Pad. You have to pick." Padma picked the opal, with its strange multi-fluorescence, which had always made Jia think of a universe exploding. Kelly picked the apatite, an earthy greenish blue-colored stone, then looked at her, but Jia kept a poker face. Five out of five. "Just tell me the answer," Casey whispered, and his smile lifted her heart. No matter what happened, they would at least be together.

"He never wants to do his own work," Padma murmured, eliciting an elbow from Casey.

His brow furrowed as he studied the stones. He then reached out abruptly and picked up a moonstone, the small opalescent thing seeming out of place in his big hand. Relief coursed through Jia's body—she had been wrong. The dream hadn't been real. They would figure out another way. They would tell an adult or maybe things would calm down if James left town, maybe they could *all* leave town and just—

"Wait, I changed my mind," Casey said, dropping the moonstone and picking up, ironically enough, a sunstone. It fit him in a strange way, its cheerful orange tone with speckles of gold. Every single pair was what she had seen in her dream. How could she have been right when the probabilities were so small? In some sense she was relieved to be right—it meant that her power did not have to be this wild, untamable thing she had no hope of understanding. But also, she was scared of what was about to happen.

"Did we pass?" Maddy asked.

"Depends on what you mean by pass," Jia said, trying to hide her face as she reached into her shorts and pulled out a sandwich bag with a piece of paper inside. She had written down what she had seen in her dream, each person and their respective stone. Some water had gotten into the bag, she saw as she passed it to Padma, but the words were all still legible.

"You wrote this before we got here?" Padma asked, frowning.

"Yeah. I saw your choices in the dream."

"These are all right," Padma said. She held up the paper for all to see, her face blank with surprise. This was different than the ambiguous things that Jia's mother said that they wrote down in their notebook. This was specific and detailed and not refutable. Jia had even increased the odds by including many other stones that didn't match the six she had seen in her dream.

"What does it mean?" Casey asked.

"After I saw us with the stones, I saw what we did next, so I know what we have to do. I think you know, too."

"What?" Maddy asked.

"We go back to the mine," James said. He said it with finality, as if he had already known somewhere deep down that this was going to happen. He had, after all, been working on a map—their capstone project had no need for such a detailed map.

"It's where he came from," Jia said. "It's where this all started.

It's where we figure out how this ends." There was a long silence. Part of her wanted someone to object. To say that it was too dangerous, or they were too afraid, or maybe there was another option.

James reached out and put the lapis in her hand, meeting her eyes with a grim smile. The others followed suit, and then she held all six, feeling their weight and irregular shapes. *If this goes wrong, it's on my head.* And she knew, at least a little bit, that it would go wrong.

41

Maddy

It didn't matter that the sun would be shining when they went into the mine. The sky was bright blue, and it was shaping out to be a hot day. The sort that was perfect for lounging on the beach of the lake, idly reading or chatting. Maddy tried to make it all fit the photo album of "Summer Fun, 1995" that she created in her head. If only she could edit out all the bad parts, because once they got inside the mine, it would be blacker than night and the sun would only be a memory.

Maddy was the last to arrive at the mine entrance. Everyone else was preparing, lacing up shoes and going through the contents of their book bags. Maddy had worn her best sneakers, and despite the heat, opted for jeans rather than shorts, figuring there was a fair chance for scrapes. James, who never wore shorts except when swimming, was the only other person wearing jeans, in addition to, somewhat comically, a D.A.R.E. T-shirt. He spooled a length of thin rope into a tight coil, then shoved it to the bottom of his bag. A hand-rolled cigarette was stuck into the corner of his mouth and he smoked without touching it. "I mailed my magnet school application this morning," he said. "You know, just in case I die, people can say, oh what a shame, he got in after all."

Maddy gave a snort of laugher and sat on the ground beside him. "Kelly told me her parents figured something out in case you get in?"

James shrugged. "They have some friends in Dover who said

I could live with them on a trial basis." James wanted to be the sort of person who didn't wear his emotions on his face but he did—he was uncomfortable. In that moment Maddy could see the black clothes, the cigarettes, and the amalgamation of tough guys he tried to imitate—James Dean and the like. He did not want to be seen as the kid who tried to get into the magnet school or had to rely on the kindness of strangers. "What are you going to do when school starts?" James asked.

She tried to imagine her junior year with the Circle Girls sashaying down the hall sharp as vipers and her not being one of them. It was one thing to be cast aside during the summer but another in front of the entire school. Who would she have to talk to? Padma would probably be gone, Jia, Casey, and Kelly would be there, but Maddy didn't want the Circle Girls to target them by association. Maybe Casey was untouchable, but the girls weren't.

"Your grades are good. You could've applied to the engineering program or the premed program."

Maddy shook her head. "My parents would never let me go."

"Why not? It's good for college."

"That's not the point. If I'm an hour away they won't be able to watch me."

Jia and Padma approached with grim expressions on their faces. Padma held a heavy-duty flashlight, the kind cops had, and brandished it. "In horror movies, the flashlights always go out."

"That's why I brought these," James said, holding up the baggie of batteries. "Kelly and I went to the mall yesterday. We got these, too," he said, pulling something out from the outside pouch of his bag. There were a few pale, inch-long things in his palm—she would have confused them for worms if they hadn't been perfectly straight. "Mini glow sticks. The last time I was here exploring I brought a few spools of twine to keep track of where I was going."

"Like Ariadne," Padma said.

James nodded. "But if we're going deep, we'd need more twine than we can carry. We can break these and leave them to keep track of where we are," he said. *We could get lost*, Maddy realized. She already knew this; she had already been dreading the thought of stepping back into the damp, eerie mine. The mine was a dark maze of paths, a labyrinth that seemed to want you to get lost.

They watched as James unfolded the map he and Kelly had labored over. "If we stay on the main path, it shouldn't be too hard." Here he drew his finger down in a slow spiral. Maddy found the map distressingly impossible to read. Yes, there was the clear spiral going down, but there was also a tangled web of offshoots, and annotations in James's oddly John Hancockesque handwriting—beautiful but hard to read. "And...this is where we're going, right?" James asked, looking at Jia as he tapped the very bottom of the map.

Jia stared at the map and blinked. "Basically."

They gathered in front of the boarded-off entrance and the boys began to pull off the old wood that had hastily been nailed together after the mine party. There was a brief moment of hesitation—*are we really going in here?* Maddy wondered—and then they climbed inside.

The first chamber, lit by some sunlight, seemed dusty and ancient, not particularly frightening and not unlike the remnants of Evansville. Police tape crisscrossed the entryway to the second chamber, which James pushed aside. It grew dimmer and they stopped to turn their flashlights on. "I forgot," Casey said, gesturing to the blocked entryway to the third chamber. "How are we supposed to get around?"

"There's a path that skips over to the Heart," James said, starting to head in that direction.

Maddy walked to where the pile of rocks cut off the entrance and squatted, pointing. "Remember the party? There were some big oilcans here. Now it's just rocks."

Casey leaned to pick something up off the floor. It was a shard of metal, twisted and charred. He sniffed it. "Smells like gas."

"Do you think those oilcans might have been part of a bomb?" Padma asked.

"I bet you they were," Kelly said.

James stood impatiently by an outcropping of rock. When Maddy got closer, she could see this was an optical illusion, and that the outcropping hid a slim line of pure black—a path into the darkness. She followed directly behind James.

"I don't want to go last!" she could hear Padma cry behind her.

"I'll go last," Casey said. "You better not fart."

"Who could fart at a time like this?" Padma said seriously, making Maddy laugh. It wasn't that funny, but the point of laughing was to keep from getting scared.

Maddy followed James down the cramped path, at one point having to turn sideways and opting to stick the flashlight into the valley of her breasts so she could use both her hands to feel her way across the cool rock. "Here we are." She could hear James's voice, muffled, from in front of her. They exited the cramped tunnel into the massive cavern that contained the Heart. If she imagined the Heart as a clock face, the shearling men had been at about six o'clock. They were standing at half-past eight. The air smelled musty, like an ancient basement, and there was a strange current almost like wind, giving occasional whiffs of something animal-like, then something that smelled like oil.

"Do you think—?" Kelly started, but James quieted her with a finger over his lips. To Maddy's horror, he started edging toward the precipice, using a flashlight in both hands to guide the way. He set them down as he got on his knees, and then leaned over the Heart. Even the thought of this made Maddy dizzy. She was not a fan of heights and in her mind's eye kept seeing James losing his balance, tumbling head over heels down the mine shaft. Padma apparently thought the same, because she gripped the back of his T-shirt with tight fists. James had his head cocked to one side, listening. Maddy held her breath and listened, too. The rumbling of rock was ever present in the background, and she could hear water dripping.

James got back to his feet. "What were you listening for?" she asked.

"Voices, I don't know." He averted his eyes from her then unfolded his map. "It should be easy. Just continue on the Heart path all the way down. Everyone stay close to each other— grabbing distance. Go slow and watch where you're walking.

I've only been down a little way on this path, and I don't know how clear it is, or how stable."

"It had to be stable if trucks and carts were driving on it," Padma reasoned.

"Yeah," James said, sounding like he wanted to believe her.

"It might get harder to breathe the farther down we go," Kelly said. "There could be gases. No smoking," she said to James.

"I'm not an idiot." He hesitated. "But I don't know how good the air will be. If someone smells gas or passes out, we're leaving." Several people nodded in agreement, including Maddy, but she noticed that Jia, looking distractedly into the Heart, did not. What *if* one of them passed out? Maddy wondered. What if it was Casey—someone too big for them to carry? She stopped this terrified line of thinking when she realized it was more important to pay attention to where she was walking. The Heart path was bumpy and pocked in various places, and Padma and Jia had already stumbled within the first ten minutes of hiking. She could feel one of Jia's hands on her back. "Do you think there are bats?" Jia asked.

"They like caves," Maddy reasoned.

"I've never seen anything alive in here," James said from in front of them.

"I would feel better if there were bats," Jia said. This didn't make sense to Maddy at first, but then it did—bats in a cave were normal. Their absence implied that bats didn't want to live here.

"Do you think the Wesleys were evil?" Maddy wondered.

"You definitely have an evil streak," Casey said.

"The original brothers, they didn't have to do any of this. If everyone thought the mountain was evil, they could have stayed away, but they were greedy. When they saw...whatever it is the pastor is, they should have run the other way, but instead they kidnapped some poor man. Jia, am I wrong? I don't remember him asking them to kill anyone. That was their idea."

"I thought so... But maybe that *is* what he wanted?"

"But what sort of person comes up with that? An evil person."

"Madds, I was just kidding. I don't think you're evil," Casey said. "Maybe you're the first Wesley who isn't."

They walked in silence for a while, Maddy trying to keep her mind off the yawning, massive hole to her left. The air was starting to feel thicker, almost like liquid, and had an increasingly unpleasant smell, like rotting vegetation. "Someone talk about something cheerful," she said.

Casey began to tell the story about how the football team won the state championship. It was a story she had heard many times and for the first five minutes of him talking, she felt a frightful disconnect between where they were and his bright voice. Perhaps they should have been talking more quietly or not at all, particularly given the echoes and strange reverberations of sound this place had. But after a few minutes her attitude shifted, and she began to see his excitement as something that stood in defiance to the darkness. They would bring their flashlights and apple wedges in baggies and loud voices, whether the mine liked it or not.

"WHOA!" James shouted suddenly, and they all halted, Kelly's elbow jabbing into Maddy's chest.

"What!" Padma called from behind.

"Uh… We have a problem here." He was shining his flashlight on the ground and warned them to step carefully as they crowded around to look. The path they had been walking on had started with a leisurely width, wide enough for a Jeep to drive on. But the farther the spiral went down, the narrower the path had become—she hadn't noticed because they were walking single file and she had walked as closely to the wall as possible the entire time. But the path had grown narrow to the point where only two could walk comfortably beside each other. Now, where all their flashlight beams were wiggling, she could see that the path had collapsed for a section, too far to jump. Kelly dropped a small rock down the missing section, and though they all listened, they never heard it hit a bottom.

"We need to take another way down," James said, unfolding the map again. He didn't sound happy about it and though Maddy couldn't read the map, she could see why. The normal way down was a straightforward spiral. Taking any alternative way would involve a lot of twists and turns and the potential for the map itself to be wrong. While he and Kelly shone their lights over it, talking quietly, Casey had edged forward, unafraid of the heights, to examine the crumpled section.

"Hey, guys?" he called. James and Kelly looked up. "I can jump this."

"No!" Padma shouted.

"Dude, no offense," James said. "You can't."

"I can," Casey said. "I've made lateral jumps longer than this and I jump vertically on boxes every time I'm at the gym."

"What are you jumping on boxes for?" Maddy wondered, looking at the black space of the broken path. Now was not the time for bravado.

"Plyometrics. Athletes do it. I can definitely make it."

"I think that's a bad idea," James said doubtfully.

"What's the probability of this—" Casey asked, pointing to the path "—compared to the probability of us getting lost?" he said, pointing to the spaghetti-like drawing on the map. "You said yourself the other day that we had less information the farther you go down the mine."

"What if you fall?" Kelly asked.

"We'll use the rope. I'll tie it around my waist and then all of you can hold it." Casey pointed his flashlight at the stone wall beside them. "Look, the wall isn't smooth. There's footholds. Once I get across, I'll be the anchor and whoever's next doesn't have to jump blind, they can hold the rope and put their feet on the wall."

Some debate continued—Padma protesting the loudest, there had to be another way—but Casey was already tying the rope around his waist. "Now or never," he said, cinching the final knot. Kelly and James, deemed the strongest, looped the rope around their waists and gave the remainder to the other three to hold on to. Maddy expected a preamble—a few words or a brief prayer, even a look of concentration from Casey. But he simply looked at the gap as if measuring it with his eyes, and before anyone could say anything he ran three quick steps and launched himself over the chasm, landing with catlike grace. Maddy caught his expression with the beam of her flashlight, triumphant and smug. "Toss me a flashlight. I'll see if there's anything over here I can tie the rope to." Along the way down, they had occasionally passed broken-down and rusted equipment.

Jia attempted to throw one of her flashlights across, but the throw fell short. The flashlight clattered against the stone loudly, then disappeared, and they stood still listening to a seemingly endless stream of thuds and cracking sounds as it went down.

"Never mind," Casey called. "There's nothing over here. I can hold the rope. Just send over someone light but strong."

"I'll go," Kelly said. She seemed unafraid, but perhaps she was making herself act before she had time to be scared. She held on to the rope, now taut from Casey at the other end, and began to place her feet carefully. "I think… I think it's like three steps and I can jump." She moved carefully for the first two steps, her body at nearly a forty-five degree angle from the wall, then she made a wild jump that made Maddy hold her breath. "It's not that bad," she said from the other side. James went next, then Maddy volunteered to go next before fear could paralyze her.

Padma and Jia remained, looking at each other apprehensively. "Can you see? Do we make the jump?" Padma asked.

A strange look crossed Jia's face—she was remembering that the whole reason they were here is that they believed she could see the future. "We don't fall down," Jia said. With sudden determination, she picked up the rope and made her way across. *Did she actually see it?* Maddy wondered. Or was she just reassuring Padma?

Padma hesitated, twice having a false start. "Padma, come on, we'll catch you. Even if you fall, we could easily pull you up," James said. Maddy flinched, realizing that the latter half of his statement likely only served to frighten her more.

"Pad, you know you're over there and we're all over here," Casey said.

"What?" she said anxiously.

"You said you didn't want to be last."

She looked behind her into the blackness, and after apparently frightening herself with something potentially worse than the jump, began to make her way across. Maddy caught her at the other end. "See? It was fine." Padma looked up at her, her dark eyes huge.

As they continued down, the swampy smell grew worse, and the air became thicker and hotter. Maddy felt rivulets of sweat making their way down from her scalp and down the back of her shirt. She regretted her choice of jeans. They resumed their single-file walk, each with one hand on the back of the person in front of them. At one point James cursed loudly—he had walked straight into an aged piece of abandoned equipment, and they all had to make their careful way around it.

"I think we're only twenty minutes from the bottom," James said a few minutes later.

"No," Jia said suddenly. "That's not where we're going."

"It's not?" James asked.

Jia made her way to the front of the line, taking over the first position. "We're supposed to turn here," she said, pointing to an offshoot path, sounding uncertain. It began with an entrance cut into the rock, a shape not unlike a keyhole. Water glistened on the rock as rivulets of water made their way down, but the path itself was too dark to see. Maddy leaned forward and sniffed, smelling iron.

James looked at the map, then at Jia. "Are you sure?" he asked, stooping a little so that they were eye to eye. "If we go that way, I don't know where it goes. It gets really confusing this far down. But if you say you know the way, I believe you." Jia studied his face, then nodded. She took a deep breath and began to lead them past the rocky entrance. James followed, taking a second to snap a glow stick, emitting a muted sound like someone breaking a chicken wing, then placing the stick on the ground.

For ten minutes they walked, their beams of light splashing jaggedly across the rock as Jia made one turn, then another. Maddy tried to keep track—left, left, right, left—but after a while she lost track. Did whatever guided Jia toward their destination also give her the ability to guide them out? Maddy wasn't sure.

"I'm out of glow sticks," James said after a dozen or so turns.

"I shouldn't have used any on the way down," he said regretfully. "We didn't need them on the main path."

"It's fine," Kelly said reassuringly. She tore off a piece of paper from the map, then weighed it down with a rock. "This'll be good enough."

There were a few more turns—Casey cursing loudly when he stubbed his toe—then James and Kelly cried out in surprise. "What? What?" the back of the line called. They crowded forward to see what was so interesting.

Their beams of light now met a solid and improbably bright object. A door stuck out in the darkness, painted a glossy, fire engine-red with a shiny brass doorknob. Maddy never would have thought that a clean, run-of-the-mill door could have frightened her, but its presence in a place where it shouldn't have been chilled her. "What the fuck?" James sputtered. "Why is there a *door* down here?"

"Why is there a door anywhere?" Jia said, reaching out without hesitation to try the knob. Maddy almost screamed—she was sure it would burn Jia's hand—but all that happened was that she discovered that the door was locked.

"I've tried to pick locks before," Padma said. "It's not that easy."

"I'll break it down," Casey said. He tried this more subtly at first, holding the knob with one hand and thrusting his shoulder against the door. When this didn't work, he backed up, ran a few paces, then launched himself at the door. Casey burst through the doorway with the sound of splintering wood and fell to the ground.

No, Maddy realized. Not the ground. The *floor*.

42

Jia

Jia stared, confused, as a slightly dazed Casey got to his feet and began to look around, taking in the same sight they were all seeing and not understanding. They had just journeyed down the center of a century-old mine nearly to its bottom, made their way past ancient equipment and crumbling rock, breathed in its awful ancient odor—and now they were looking down a corridor lit with fluorescent light. The same type of lighting they had at school: plastic paneling covering two long fluorescent tubes. The floor of the long corridor was linoleum, shiny and clean.

"Am I high?" James asked softly. "Did we breathe in gas?"

"If we did, then we're all having the same hallucination," Casey murmured.

"Jia, do you know where this hallway goes?" Maddy asked.

Jia shook her head. In the dream, she had seen the red door, and so she knew how to get there. What was past the door had been too hard to see, and she had only seen a flash of something afterward. "I… I don't know where to go from here." She felt lost and certain of only one thing: something bad was about to happen. But the wheels and ancient gears that had set it into motion were already moving.

"I have an idea," Maddy said, taking the lead. Jia followed close behind. In the mine, they didn't have to worry about the sounds their feet made or their voices being heard, but here, their mere dirty, sweaty presence under those fluorescent lights seemed conspicuous. Fluorescent lights meant *people* and *people* implied danger.

The corridor led to an end, and Maddy paused, then peeked her head around to see if the next hallway was clear. This one had a number of doorways on either side. Casey tried one door and found tools: shovels, awls, and a number of axes, one of which he took and stuck the handle through the straps of his backpack. "Just in case," he whispered.

Jia's gaze caught on something in the ceiling. A string hanging down. She had a similar one in her house. Maddy jumped to grab it, but she was too short. Casey pulled it, activating a panel that angled down, and a wooden staircase unfolded, just like the attic door at Jia's house.

Maddy was already climbing up before anyone could stop her, excitedly muttering to herself, "I think I know." There was a trapdoor at the top. Maddy undid the latch and pushed it upward, half her body disappearing into the space above. "One of you come up here."

Jia went before anyone else could volunteer. Once Jia was halfway up the ladder, she could see that Maddy was standing in what looked like an office. A normal office with a desk and a computer and also fluorescent lights but they were turned off. "Do you see?" Maddy whispered.

Jia did not see. She realized she could hear voices faintly. There was a door to her left, and the voices sounded like they were coming from down the hallway.

Maddy's eyes were glittering with excitement. "I recognize the smell. We're in Central. We're in Golden Praise."

"What?" came a voice from below them—Kelly probably.

"I can hear people," Jia whispered nervously, gesturing for Maddy to come back down the ladder. Maddy hesitated, snatching something from off the desk, then the two girls went down the ladder and replaced the trapdoor. Maddy showed them what she had stolen: a piece of Golden Praise stationery.

"There's a direct path from the mine to Golden Praise," Maddy said.

"I want to keep looking around," James said. They went back

into the hallway and kept trying doors. Down another hallway they found a set of double doors that made Jia feel a wave of nausea. Nothing unimportant was ever behind double doors. James tried the knob, opening the door slowly, then disappeared inside. Then he gave an abrupt cry and Jia heard a loud sound. They pushed forward to see James sitting on the floor, rubbing at his side. "I slipped on something. Something with wheels." It was dark—he reached out blindly to find the offending object. Jia looked around, swinging her flashlight beam across the room. It was dominated by a large oval table surrounded by ancient-looking wooden chairs. Twelve specifically.

"Twelve Elders," Maddy whispered. "This must be where they meet."

"What the hell?" James said. He had found what had made him trip and was now holding it up. Jia squinted and moved closer, directing her flashlight on it. "What *is* it?"

Kelly crouched beside James and took it from him. "It's a toy. A horse." A squat little wooden horse with wheels instead of legs.

"So the Elders get together to play horsey?" James said, flinching as he got to his feet.

"Look," Casey said. He had approached the only other piece of furniture, an ornate cabinet nearly as tall as he was on the far side of the room. *Don't open it*, Jia thought, her throat feeling tight. But the others were gathering around it. Jia had been the last one into this room and now she began to back away without thinking. Casey opened the cabinet with a creaking noise. There was an object inside—*don't open it*—a thing of ancient-looking metal, rounded but thinner on the bottom than it was on the top. At its thickest part were two dark slits like eyes. Jia backed up farther, now standing in the hallway looking in. Beneath the eyes was a small door. Kelly tried it—*No!*—but the door didn't move.

"Wait," Maddy said, pulling a chain she was wearing over her head. On it was a single, old-fashioned-looking key. "Remember, Jia? I saw a Wesley wearing a key like this in our dream." But Jia wasn't huddled around the cabinet the way they were.

She was backing up farther. She had to get away. Everyone, including her, was holding their breath as Maddy turned the key.

Nothing. She jiggled the key, then groaned.

"Maybe you need two," Kelly said, sticking her finger into the other slit.

"We're fucked," James said, disappointed. But Jia was relieved. There was no opening that *thing* without—

"Do I have to save the day again?" Casey said. He pulled something from his book bag. A second key. Jia's stomach lurched. The rest of them stared at him in amazement as he slid the key into the second slot.

"Where did you get that?"

"When Maddy told us about how she found the key, I realized I saw the same embroidered thing in Coach's living room." Casey did not sound happy about it. "I went back there last night while he was out at dinner. Are you ready?" he asked Maddy, who took ahold of the other key.

No!

They both turned their keys and something clicked into place. The little door popped open. Maddy pried it open with her fingertips, revealing a small crystal chalice. It flickered in the light from their flashlights strangely. Maddy reached to pick it up. "Don't!" Jia cried weakly. A wave of revulsion hit her.

"What is it?" someone said.

"There's some kind of goo at the bottom."

It's blood, Jia thought. She had backed all the way across the hall into the small office that faced the Elder room. *It's old blood—*

The office door swung shut. The pastor stood just to the side of it. Jia screamed. "Come now," he said. "Don't be dramatic." Jia heard a scream in the other room—Kelly's. Soon there was pounding at the office door, but it was now locked. Jia started to cry silently, realizing that he was coming closer to her.

"I felt you here, so I came to see for myself," he said mildly, as if they were having a normal conversation. "You're a very curious thing, aren't you?"

Jia looked desperately at the door just as something slammed against it.

"I've been around a long time, and I've never met someone quite like you," he said.

"Please. Please just let me go."

"I'm not going to hurt you," he said.

"Yes, you are."

"Jia, if I wanted to hurt you, I would have done so already," he said, perpetually calm. "We could be friends, you know. We could help each other. What is it in your heart that's aching? Is it your father? Would you like to have him back?"

"My father's dead," she said, crying.

"Death is not a boundary I choose to obey." Now he was too close. He put his hands on her shoulders and Jia felt every muscle in her stomach tighten the way it did when she vomited. His face. It began to open, showing the swirling blackness beneath it. She had a sense that she wasn't supposed to see this, the *real* him, but instead this generic handsome face—the face he stole!—the one that Maddy had seen when he had comforted her.

Then, chaos—something jutted through the surface of the door. The tip of an axe. Wood splintered and Casey burst in, screaming. Everyone was screaming. He launched himself at the pastor with the full force of his body just as James grabbed her, wrenching her toward the door by her arm. "Run!"

43

James

James pulled Jia by the arm and Casey slid into the hallway, where farther down he could see Padma and Kelly at the end of the hallway, gesturing wildly for them to hurry. The group of six sprinted, James taking the lead as they made one turn, then another—luckily the complex of hallways was nowhere near as complicated as the maze of the mine. It wasn't hard to find the red door, and once they were outside it, James moved as quickly as he dared, fumbling for his flashlight. "Go, go, go!" Kelly shouted.

But Jia was the one who led us through this part, James thought, panicked. His eyes were still adjusting to the darkness, but his flashlight beam swung wildly, picking up the tiny pieces of paper he had used to mark the way. As long as they didn't miss one, they would be fine…

A left, then a right, then around a curve that started to go up-hill. Maddy cursed and slammed into him from behind when she tripped, nearly making him lose his balance. "Are we lost?" Casey asked him.

Why did it have to fall to him? Why had he assigned himself as navigator? "No. No, calm down," James muttered. If he was right, just after this steep decline they would be back on the main spiral path. It was so close; if it wasn't his imagination, he could feel the faint, warm, unpleasant breeze that gushed slowly upward from the Heart.

"Go! I think I can hear something!" Kelly called from the back of the line.

James jogged slightly ahead of them, and to his relief, saw the glow stick he had used to mark the turn off the spiral path. They were going to be okay. They would go up the way they had come and deal with this all once they were out. "Everyone put your hand on the person in front of you!" he ordered.

His mind was reeling, still trying to process what they had seen, the nonsensicalness of what was behind that red door, that weird cabinet, the fact that Casey had knocked the pastor on his ass. How fast could they go without tripping, falling, breaking an ankle, accidentally stumbling off the side into the abyss? Some part of his mind was somehow able to harness his frantic anxiety and remain laser-focused on leading them out of the mine. He used two flashlights to skim in front of him, calling out whenever there was anything significant—a divot that could twist an ankle, a puddle of water. He was in a zone, not unlike how he felt when he got completely distracted working on a piece of art. Time slipped away and he was only dimly aware of the voices behind him.

They had only climbed for ten minutes when he heard a scream so shrill that it broke his concentration. His two flashlight beams, in addition to several others, flew to the back of the line. Jia was at the back of the line—how had he let that happen?—but she was not alone. The pastor was there, his skin stark against the blackness that surrounded them. He had grabbed her arm and was pulling her back, back toward the red door. Before James could even think, he could see a figure rushing toward them—Kelly. She knocked into the pastor, using her body to split Jia from him, the brunt of her impact hitting him and not her friend. In one quick, terrifying moment, the pastor simply disappeared off the precipice and into the Heart.

For several seconds the entire group stood still, eyes wide and hearts pounding, not quite comprehending what had just happened. Did he—?

"I didn't—I didn't—" Kelly stammered.

"Do you think he's…" Jia's voice trailed off.

They looked at each other, their two choices clear. They could go down there to see exactly what happened and face whatever consequences there were. Or they could continue back toward the daylight and never fully know what they had done.

"We have to go down there," Maddy whispered. The sound of rock falling somewhere in the distance punctuated her words. James knew in his heart that she was right.

"Maybe…" Kelly started.

"We have to know," James said.

"He could—he could still be alive," Padma managed.

"What if his men are down there?" Kelly said.

"Maybe they don't have power without him," Maddy said.

"Something feels different," Jia said cautiously. Her voice was strange. She stood at the lip of the Heart—too close for James's comfort—with her arms stuck at her sides with a strange stiffness. "We have to go down and see." No one could overrule Jia, even if they wanted to.

They rearranged themselves, James first, then Casey, then Jia. "We're going all the way to the bottom, aren't we?" he said into the darkness, his words meant for Jia.

"Yes, that's where he is," Jia responded.

"Jia, are you all right?" Casey asked.

There was a long pause. "I…think so."

After ten minutes of climbing down the spiral, James stopped to consult the map, holding a flashlight with his mouth to free up his hands. The girls were talking in hushed voices.

"What if we killed him?" Kelly whispered.

"It was an accident," Padma said.

"I don't think anyone could have survived the fall," Maddy said.

"No one *human*," Padma said.

"The spiral path doesn't go all the way down," James said, which meant that they would have to take smaller, less direct paths. The farther down they went, the less reliable the map became. Kelly, who had done the brunt of the work on their capstone project, had unearthed tons of content about the economics of the mine and who had owned what when, but none of those records went into specific details of what the bottom of the mine looked like. He looked at Jia, hoping that maybe she would take over again, but she looked back at him helplessly. "Stay close," he advised, and they continued down, stopping every few minutes to consult the map or to have James rip off another small piece to mark their place.

It got hotter, the air as thick as a sauna, and James felt his T-shirt sticking uncomfortably to his back. *I hope this air is okay.* Somehow the blackness was blacker down here, almost tangible like fur hanging in the air. After a while, the gradient abruptly stopped and the ground, after an initial slope of jagged edges, was strangely smooth.

James waved his flashlight around, quickly noticing something that stood like a tower at the bottom of the Heart. It was jagged and maybe ten feet tall and at first, he stared at it without comprehension until he heard one of the girls gasp. Flashlight beams wobbled around wildly, then settled on a single object.

It was the pastor. What James had thought of as a tower was actually a rusty piece of machinery, ancient and unpleasantly shiny with what might have been water or might have been blood. The pastor was impaled on the jagged metal, a full foot and a half sticking through his chest, his body contorted into an impossible angle.

Jia turned to the side and vomited. James realized that the standard unpleasant smell of the mine was now combined with the coppery smell of blood. "Is he dead?" Maddy asked.

"Are you kidding me?" James replied, gesturing to the body.

"Someone has to check," Casey said, looking at Padma.

"What are you looking at me for?" she squeaked.

"Your parents are doctors!" Casey said, pushing her forward.

Padma had never looked younger to James, her hair damp with sweat with loose strands sticking to the sides of her face. She stepped forward gingerly, as if she expected the pastor to pop up at any moment. Instead, the body remained still, its eyes beady. She reached out, swallowed, and pressed two of her fingers to the side of its neck. First in one place, then a second. James held his breath. "I don't feel anything," she whispered.

"He's dead?" Maddy asked.

"Do you think anyone knows he's down here?" Jia asked.

"We have to get out of here," James said. This was not just factually true—because if they had killed the pastor they were headed for a world of shit—but because he couldn't stand another second of being down here. The oppressively thick air, the heat, the feeling of being enclosed and so far underground. There wasn't time to think of what they had just done—he needed to get out of here, and *now*.

They began the ascent, pausing only to check the map. But the feeling that they were closer to their destination seemed to fade with each step. James imagined them walking forever, twisting into the darkness for hours, the pastor somehow holding them there in a final act of vengeance. The walls seemed to expand and crowd them. He did not want to be in this place. He thought of the shimmering waves of the lake. The lush green grass of Kelly's backyard, Milky squirming on her back. The sound of birds.

He wasn't paying as close attention. He was breathing hard and walking fast. He took a step that landed wrong on the uneven ground and stumbled, hearing a noise before he could see what he had done. It was the sound of a rock he had kicked away. He looked down, already feeling dread, a chill running through him despite the heat.

A white piece of paper stood out in contrast against the rocky floor. It was midway between two paths that branched off. He had knocked over one of their markers. Fuck. Which way was it? James looked from one yawning entrance to another. Back to the scrap of paper. Was it closer to one than the other? He looked helplessly at Jia but she still looked sickly, Casey half carrying her. James brought his hands to the sides of his head and squeezed his eyes shut. Which way? Which way, when they were all counting on him. He had fucked up. He had gotten them lost down here and they would all die.

"Let's just look at the map," Maddy said gently, taking it from him.

"This part's not *on* the fucking map!" James yelled, his voice cracking. They were going to die. They were going to die down here and be stuck with that *thing*. The flashlights would run out. The bottles of water. It would all be his fault.

He felt a hand on his shoulder. He knew it was Kelly without opening his eyes. "Just take a breath," she said quietly. "You don't need the map." Her voice had a dreamy quality to it, as if hypnotizing him. "Picture it in your head. You can see us coming down here. You know the way. And if you're wrong, we can double back to this marker. It's fine to double back." He took a deep breath, and she did the same alongside him. When he opened his eyes, he saw that she stood directly in front of him, her face half-illuminated by someone's flashlight, her eyes directly locked on to his. She was coming from somewhere else, from a place where she had absolute faith in him. That somehow together they would figure a way out.

He swallowed, nodded, and chose one of the paths.

44

Jia

Jia gulped air as the six of them finally climbed out of the main entrance to the mine. Padma, exhausted, tried to sit on a boulder but Casey pulled her up by the back of her shirt. She looked up at him, pained, and he grimaced apologetically. "We need to get out of here," he said. They headed for the bunker without having to discuss it.

Casey wrenched open the bunker door and they went inside. Jia and Padma opened the gallon of water they had left just beside the door. Jia washed her face and scooped water into her mouth, grateful for its coolness. After a while she realized that Padma was lingering by the door.

"I might be sick," Padma explained. Jia looked at her, her heart swelling with ache. Just a few months ago Padma had been a girl who was quietly content to spend her summers in the safe confines of her air-conditioned home reading vampire novels. She had never been invited to a party or faced a trial or tribulation worse than being bullied in school. She had longed for something more, a bit of adventure like in her books, more companionship than one friend, but then there was the problem of getting what you asked for.

"It might make you feel better," Jia said, and led her outside into the unrelenting sunlight. She held Padma's messy braid as her friend threw up mostly water. Then she pulled Padma's hair into a fresh braid, for a moment wanting to pretend that they were just two girls playing in the woods, and that the relief she felt at the pastor's death wasn't overshadowed by the fact that they had killed him. But they had to go back inside.

James threw a few handfuls of water onto his head, then squeezed the sweaty water from his hair. Casey rooted around the back of the bunker where they kept their snacks and returned to the center with half a dozen warm sodas. James waited until they all had one before he spoke up. "Who was the last one out of that hallway?"

"Me?" Jia said, alarmed.

"Do you remember if you closed the door?" He worded the question carefully to make sure it didn't sound like an accusation. None of them had been thinking straight in that moment; they had just been running as fast as they could. But his reasoning quickly dawned on Jia. She hadn't closed the door. It was one thing if the pastor's friends and employees didn't know where he was—he could be anywhere really and there was no reason to assume he would be inside the mine. But it was a different story if he was missing, and they went down into that place and saw that the door was both open and broken. A broken door implied an intruder.

"They'll find the door," Kelly said. "And go into the mine and find him."

"Maybe they won't," Casey said. He paused to drain most of his soda. "Maybe no one goes in there but him."

"The shearling men went inside the mine," Maddy pointed out.

"Okay, so they go in there and look for him," Kelly reasoned. "Would they go all the way down?"

"I don't know," Jia said. They fell silent for a moment.

"Say they find him," James said, his voice hoarse. "Say they find his body. Maybe they would think he fell?"

"There's no way to tell if he fell or was pushed, is there?" Padma said, hope undergirding her voice. "Lots of people would fall in a place like that."

"I threw up down there," Jia said suddenly. Kelly rubbed her arm reassuringly. She couldn't help it—the smell, the beady eyes, the organs spilling out of his body. "Is there DNA in throw up?"

"It's so dark down there, and there's water," Padma mumbled. "Would they even know it's there?"

"I don't think there's DNA in vomit," Kelly said. "I read that somewhere." Jia, looking at her with wide eyes, knew Kelly was lying and knew she was doing it to comfort her. Now they were all agreeing; surely there was no DNA in vomit.

James put his head in his hands, his hair, still stringy with sweat, covering his pale hands. "They're going to arrest me. Say that I did it."

"No one knows we were there," Maddy said. "I think we should all leave right now, each go somewhere else where people can see us so we have an alibi. Separately, I mean. Church people have to see us somewhere else, far away from the mine, and not together."

"If no one knows he's missing, maybe we should go back and fix the door?" Casey wondered.

"*No,*" James said fiercely. "No one goes down there again, got it? Every fucking time we go down there, someone dies."

"I killed him," Kelly said in a tiny voice. Her eyes were full of tears. "I killed him."

"No, you didn't," James said, grabbing her arm.

"You were protecting me," Jia said. "It was self-defense."

"What did he want with you?" Casey asked. "What did he say to you in that room?"

"He—I can't remember it all," Jia said. "He touched me and it was like—his face…"

"Was his face like a hole?" James said.

Both relieved and frightened to be understood, she nodded. "He said I was a curious thing, and that we should be friends. He asked me again about wanting my father back."

"He said he could bring him back from the dead?" Padma asked, confused.

"He didn't say that exactly, but that's what he meant. He said that death wasn't a boundary that he obeyed."

Maddy shivered, pulling her legs into her chest.

"What the fuck?" James muttered.

"I want to go home," Padma said suddenly. Her enormous eyes filled with tears.

"I think that's what you should do," Maddy said.

"Huh?" Casey said. "No one goes anywhere until we have a plan."

"We need to go home," Maddy said, her voice more urgent.

"Can you relax for a second? What the hell was that thing we found?" Casey asked.

"Who cares?" Maddy hissed. "Do you understand how pissed they're going to be if they find out it was us? You *never* listened to me." The last sentence had such a tone of harshness that it got everyone's attention. James turned his weary face toward her, distracted from his own misery. Jia was on edge—she didn't want them to fight, not now. Maddy started to gather up her hair to put it into a ponytail, her fingers picking strands of her damp blond hair in a practiced motion. She was angry—maybe something she had tamped down at times because they had invited her into their circle when everyone else had rejected her.

"I told you we shouldn't do our project on the mine. You didn't listen." She looped an elastic around her ponytail once, twice. "I told you we shouldn't go down there for a party, that it wasn't safe, but you did it anyway." Casey looked down at his hands, guilty. "I told you we shouldn't go to the police, that we shouldn't trust them, but you did anyway." Now Kelly's eyes dropped. "They implicate you," she said, pointing to James, "which I don't think was their initial plan, but whatever. Then you two basically tell them you witnessed them committing a mass murder," she said pointing to Kelly and Casey. "We don't know what they think of Padma, if the Foto kiosk guy told on her or not. They think I'm a whore, but have no real reason to think I would associate with any of you."

"I don't think you're a whore, Maddy," Padma said.

She hadn't intended it to be funny but Maddy's face twisted into a smile. "It seems like the pastor had a weird interest in Jia, but we don't know if he told anyone in the church about it."

"I don't think he did," James said, thinking aloud. "Because the church targets her mom's store. If he…liked her, he wouldn't let the church do that, right?"

"No one's figured out that we were all together the night of the party," Maddy continued. "No one has any idea that we've spent all summer together, trying to figure this out."

"They know we're in a capstone group together," Jia said.

"And literally, are you friends with the last group of people you were forced to work on a class project with?" Maddy retorted. "Here's how most class projects work. One sucker does most of the work—" she gestured to Kelly "—one guy completely does nothing—" here she gestured to Casey, who looked injured "—and everyone goes home with the same grade."

"What do you think we should do?" James asked. It was the first time, Jia realized, that James had ever really asked Maddy's opinion on anything of substance. Not the half-mocking, half-serious way he asked her questions about religion at the lake.

"I say we all get out of here, go our separate ways and make sure people see us acting normal. Casey, go to the gym. Padma, go shopping with your family. Kelly, take your dog to the grocery store."

"They don't allow dogs in the grocery store."

"I know, it will make a scene," Maddy replied. "We each go home and don't talk to each other. I know how the church thinks. It might take them a couple days to find that door. The mine is a maze and for all we know, they might not even have a good map, either. Say they find him, they wonder, what happened? Maybe… Maybe… You know what? I think they would be scared."

"Of us?" Padma said.

Maddy shook her head. "Not of us. Scared that he's dead, because he's not supposed to be. The thing that gives them their power is dead. This could be the end of the line for Golden Praise. Are they going to get thousands of people showing up to services when their star is gone? Isn't it his power that draws people?"

"They'll announce that he died and have a big memorial," Padma posited.

Maddy was already shaking her head. "I don't think they will. I think they'll make up a story instead of admitting he's dead."

"Why would they do that?" Kelly asked.

"Because that's their way. Paper over everything and pretend it's fine rather than admit weakness. If they say he died, people will ask questions, and if they start asking questions about one thing, do they start asking questions about other stuff?"

Jia regretted the soda she had drunk—now the beverage felt sickly sweet.

"This is what we do," Maddy commanded, sitting up straight. "We go home. We do our alibis. Kelly, turn the capstone project in and complain that everyone else slacked off. We play dumb and see how this shakes out. We don't talk the rest of the summer. None of us can be seen together. We can't be friends." Jia and Padma flinched simultaneously.

"Why?" Casey said.

"Because they think guilt by association is a thing. Kelly already gets comments about spending time with James."

"We literally live together," Kelly said. James's brow was furrowed, the calculus already running through his head.

"Honestly, James, if I were you, I would get out of town," Maddy said. He was sitting cross-legged, his head in his hands. "You're the person they'll most likely come after."

"He'll move to Dover when he gets into the magnet school," Kelly said, sounding defensive.

"*If* I get into the magnet school," James said without looking up.

"I don't think Dover's far enough," Maddy said. This got his attention—he looked up. "When do they send out acceptances?" she asked.

"Two weeks," Padma said.

"The police here won't have jurisdiction in Dover," Kelly said.

"If I left, where would I even go?" James said. He sounded so childlike then and it made Jia's heart hurt.

Maddy chewed her lower lip. "Okay. Go to Dover and see if it's okay. But we need a failsafe for you just in case. We can col-

lect some cash if you need to get out of town—there's a Greyhound station in Dover."

"You can have my Golden Praise money," Padma said.

"Everyone get what you can and put it in Kelly's mailbox,"
Casey said. "And if you have to go," he said to James, "find a
way to send us a message."

Maddy was nodding. "Out of sight, out of mind. I wish we
could all get out of town, just to be safe. When we're here, we're
an irritant. And if we're together, we're a conspiracy. I'm getting out of here, too." She said it as if she had just decided this,
but she said it firmly.

"How?" Jia asked.

"My parents are always threatening me with Christian boarding school," Maddy said. "Maybe that would be better. Kelly,
you said your mom said you could go to that other Catholic
school if you didn't like our school."

"Yes, but—"

"Jia, you could apply to one of the magnet schools," Maddy
continued, on a roll.

"It's too late," Jia said.

"People break rules all the time," Maddy said.

"I don't have the grades," Jia said.

"You could do the language school," Padma said. "Japanese.
You can write about how you need to connect with your culture."

"I'm Korean!"

"You think the people reading applications know the difference?" Padma said, an edge to her voice. "Or say one of your
grandparents was Japanese. Most of the kids applying are white.
They probably want someone like you."

"But—"

"Casey's off to football camp soon so that's good," Maddy
continued.

"Madds, I can't leave town after that. Recruitment, and the
team, and—"

"You can stay," she said graciously. "Everyone else who can

leave should. But no calling each other, no IMing. No sneaking off in secret to meet up. This has to blow over."

"But my parents know we're best friends," Padma said, gesturing to Jia. "We spend all summer together every year."

"Then stop," Maddy said flatly. "It's only another month till school starts. Tell them you got into a fight, and they'll forget about it by the time fall rolls around." Jia and Padma looked at each other, pained. How could they do this? How, when they had been best friends for so long?

"But what about all this stuff?" Padma asked, gesturing around the bunker. It was clear what she meant—beyond all the material for the capstone project there was everything else they had accumulated. The historical records from Evansville, the evidence that something was horribly wrong with this town.

"We have to get rid of it," Maddy said. "It's incriminating."

"But it's the only thing that proves that we're not the villains here, the town is," James said. He was holding his arm protectively over his stomach—beneath his shirt, the folded map that had taken him so long to create was tucked into the waist of his jeans.

"What if we need it?" Padma said.

"Need it for *what*?" Maddy pressed.

"He said he doesn't obey death," James said, looking at Jia for confirmation. "Doesn't that mean maybe he could come back? Like a vampire or something?"

"He's dead," Jia replied. "Dead-dead. I can feel it."

"We can bury everything," Padma said. "Like a time capsule. Keep it somewhere close by in case we ever need it again." Maddy seemed skeptical, but everyone else was agreeing. Soon, Padma had located a box and now they were stuffing things inside it, James reluctantly giving up his map; Maddy and Jia taped plastic bags around the box to try to keep it dry.

They left the bunker for the sunny woods, looking for a good place to bury it. Padma wandered around, inspecting various trees. "It needs to be a place we can find again," she said.

"We don't have all day," Maddy warned.

"Here," Padma said, pointing to a birch tree. "Give me your knife, James." Most of the trees were pine and oak, but one birch tree in a clearing close to the bunker stood out. Casey started clearing pine needles off the ground as Padma attempted to carve something into the bark.

They all dropped to their knees and began to dig. Dirt got under their nails, and their fingertips stubbed against roots. "I think it needs to be at least a foot down," James murmured. "If not more."

"Once this is done, we wash the dirt off and we go home," Maddy said, her voice containing a warning. "No talking to each other. Do you promise?"

"But James and I live together," Kelly said, still digging, but looking defiantly across the hole at Maddy.

"Because you're neighbors and your parents are being nice," Maddy said, throwing dirt aside unsympathetically. "People would believe it if you stopped talking. Because no one really understands why you're friends anyway."

Jia stole a glance at Kelly and saw the flush of anger on her face—her desire to defend James. Kelly shot a look at James, one of those private looks they so frequently exchanged. *We're not actually going to do this, right? We'll tell Maddy we will because she's bossy, but we won't really go through with it,* is what it said. Or she *tried* to communicate this to James, but he was digging intently. He wouldn't look back at her and there was a strange blank look on his face.

He was scared. Jia noticed that James was someone who did not talk about the future. He wasn't like Padma, who spoke with so much assurance of getting into college, of what would happen after, being successful and buying a house and having a meaningful life planned out. He never talked about how great it was going to be at the magnet school, or that it would be nice to live somewhere else, because it all felt like a pipe dream. Instead, he imagined awful things, the police coming with handcuffs, people looking at Kelly because of him, them somehow figuring out that she had been the one to push the pastor. It was one thing for his life to be screwed up, but her future had always been visible. College, friends, a job somewhere. Not to be dragged down by him.

Jia tried to push with her mind, tried to see if everything would be okay. That maybe a few months from now, by some miracle, everything would be back to normal, and she could call Padma to hang out. Padma had drawn close to her and put her head on Jia's shoulder. If someone found the pastor's body, there was no way someone could possibly track it to Padma Subramaniam, the most improbable girl, a girl who was often invisible. Casey, Jia thought, was undoubtedly thinking about football, and what would happen to his football career if people found out about this, the whispers and the recruiters that would stop calling.

Maddy was probably the only one thinking about right *now*. Because she was the only one of them capable of thinking about what would be best for them logically. How to maneuver around her parents, and how the church was likely to respond to the pastor's death.

The hole was deep enough. They placed the box inside and covered it with dirt, Padma retrieving pine needles and fallen leaves to cover their work.

"James, do you have any marijuana on you?" Maddy asked, drawing everyone's gaze.

"You want weed *now*?" he asked, confused.

"I need something to get me sent to boarding school."

He rooted through his backpack, then came up with a tiny baggie. "First one's free," he said, his voice breaking on the last word because he was exhausted and close to crying. Maddy looked at his D.A.R.E. T-shirt and started to laugh with something that bordered on madness. James met her eyes and started to laugh, too—how improbable that the summer would end with the two most unlikely of people sharing drugs, and oh yes, this was just after they had killed the most powerful man in town.

Jia laughed, too, because laughter always had a contagious effect on her. It was the last thing they shared together that summer, other than the secret. Maybe they laughed a little too hard, because they thought it might be the last time they would ever see each other.

They were almost right.

PART EIGHT: AUGUST 2015

45

Kelly

Kelly blinked sweat out of her eyes and entered the courtyard of the Wesley Falls Inn carrying two iced coffees and pastries from the former Gem Shop. None of them had had a chance to eat a real dinner. After they had dug up the time capsule, they had decided that they couldn't all go talk to Jane Merrick—it might overwhelm her. Kelly and James offered to go, but after-dinner visiting hours wouldn't start for another hour, so the pair waited while everyone else headed to the library. Padma wanted to look for tax records for the church, and Jia had wondered if they could tabulate the number of deaths per year, the way Maddy had done in Evansville all those years ago.

James was sitting at one of the picnic tables in the courtyard with his laptop, talking on the phone about what sounded like a tax mix-up. He gave her an exasperated smile as she set down the pastries. "No, it's *pass-through* income because it's an S corporation!"

Kelly prepped his coffee—three creams, one sugar—and took her own black before sitting down with a fruit tart. It was dusk and the fireflies were already wandering around the courtyard. James finished his call and rubbed his face with his hands. "Handling finances with a stoner, I highly recommend it." He accepted the coffee gratefully.

"Somehow I never pictured you making itemized deductions," she said.

He tore a cream puff in two. "I actually learned a lot here.

How to price a fake ID. Dealing with supply and demand issues." He glanced at his watch—they had another ten minutes.

Kelly took out her phone. "Can I take a picture of you to send to my sisters? They'd get a kick out of it."

He sighed but relented, and she snapped a selfie of the two of them. When she looked at the picture, she was grinning and he was wearing his sheepish "I hate having my picture taken" smile. She input the picture into the group text chat with her sisters, adding a message that said, Guess who I ran into??? They ate in silence for a few moments and watched the fireflies in a companionable silence. It could almost pass for a normal summer moment.

"Do we have a cover story?" James murmured as they approached the Magnolia Home for Adults.

"I'm her cousin's grandchild," Kelly said.

"And me?"

"My bodyguard, obviously."

The woman at reception didn't ask questions when they said they were here to visit Jane Merrick. Kelly took her time signing the visitor's log while she scanned the other names. There—a few days ago—was Maddy's handwriting, but the name written was Lauren Jones. James apparently noticed it, too, catching her eye.

Jane Merrick's room was at the corner of the building. The bed closer to the door was unoccupied, but a woman was in the bed by the window. Kelly looked down at Jane Merrick and felt a mixture of emotions. The Jane she had seen back then in her childhood had been a prim woman who never had a hair out of place. She had hated her on principle based on the things Maddy had told her. But the woman before them seemed half in another world as she looked at them both.

"Jane," Kelly said, taking the chair closest to her as James remained by the doorway. "Do you remember me?" Maddy, of course, knew Jane well, and Padma had occasion to talk to her, but Kelly never had.

"Yes," Jane said. Surprised, Kelly said nothing as Jane studied her. "You came back."

"Um. Yes, I did."

"You changed your hair."

Does she think I'm Maddy? "I… I dyed it."

Jane nodded approvingly. "No one needs to bleach their hair like a trollop."

"Do you remember what we talked about?" Kelly asked.

"Of course I do," Jane snapped, but then realized Kelly was looking at her expectantly. "You were…you were asking about the house. The house is none of your business."

"The house is going to the church." Jane nodded agreement. "Did we talk about the pastor? Dave Lurie?" Jane seemed to lose interest, looking out the window instead. "Dave Lurie?" Kelly prompted gently.

"What about him?"

"He looks an awful lot like Jim Preiss, doesn't he?" Kelly said.

Jane gave her a withering look. "He's the same man, nitwit."

"How does that happen?" Kelly asked. "The Elders, you do something, don't you?"

Jane looked confused, her eyes darting away. "What time is it? Isn't it time for my walk? You know I don't like visitors right now!" she said, raising her voice. Kelly glanced at James anxiously, who leaned back to look into the hallway.

"How does he come back?" Kelly pressed.

"The things we do for this town!" she near shouted.

"Shh, shh."

"Don't shush me! You can't come in here—"

"Jane, I'm such an idiot, I can't even remember what we talked about when I was here last. Can you help me?"

Jane's agitated face changed instantly. Though Kelly would have imagined it impossible, it softened considerably, and almost became pleasant. "We talked about the baby."

Kelly held her breath. Maddy's note hadn't said "Ask Jane about the body." It had said *baby*. What baby? She sat up straight, looking over at James, who looked back at her blankly. He didn't remember Maddy's note or the toy horse he had tripped over twenty years ago. But Kelly understood: where there were toys, there were children.

"Jane, did you keep the baby down there? In the nineties?"

Jane nodded happily. "Of course."

"In that place under the church?"

"Such a sweet baby. That's where we always kept the little one."

Kelly felt sick. "What was the baby for?" But Jane had lost interest, staring out the window amiably with her hands laced together. "Your sister, the board of directors, did they know about the baby, or just you?"

Jane turned her head, scowling. "Laurie is an Elder."

"Yes, she is. And the president of the board."

"She's an Elder, and I never was."

"Why is that, Jane? You did so much for the church."

It was exactly the right thing to say. Jane was now pulling herself up into a more erect sitting position—she was fired up. "Because Laurie got married and I didn't."

"Gosh, you gave your whole life for the church."

"Day and night, and they cast me aside. Do you know, he never comes to see me."

"The pastor?"

She nodded, then her gaze wandered around the room. "It's almost like he hates us," she murmured.

"Why would he hate you?" Kelly asked gently.

"He acts like we have him on a leash—he has everything in the world he could ever want, and still he acts like that."

"How entitled," Kelly chided.

Jane looked at her with alarm. "You shouldn't trust him."

"Why not?"

"He's sneaky."

"How is he sneaky?"

Jane yawned. "Isn't it bedtime soon? I want my Ovaltine."

"The Ovaltine is coming. What did you mean by *sneaky*?"

But Jane seemingly had lost the thread. She looked at James, noticing him for the first time, then leaned back in bed, rearranging her pink blanket. "We built him that beautiful house, and I even made him a quilt but he never slept there."

"Where did he sleep?" Kelly asked.

"He doesn't," Jane said.

They waited until they were several yards away from the entrance to the nursing home before either of them said anything. "Are you thinking what I'm thinking?" Kelly said. It was dark now, the streetlights glowing yellow in addition to a nearly full moon.

"There was a baby. There was that toy down there."

"But what were they *doing* with the baby?" Kelly said, turning to look at him as they walked.

James sighed theatrically. "This is getting too nineties Satanic Panic for me."

"They brought him back from the dead. Maybe the baby is how they did it."

"What baby, though? If there was a missing baby, wouldn't everyone be talking about it?"

"I don't know. I wouldn't put anything past these people."

They walked toward the library to meet up with the others. "Maybe we should add 'missing baby' to our search in the newspaper archive."

Kelly thought about the toy, that stupid horse toy down in that dark, creepy place. It made her sad, thinking of a baby playing down there, confined by the Elders. Her phone vibrated with a text. She looked at it and saw that it was from one of her sisters in response to the selfie she had sent. omg is that JAMIE? Jenn had texted. Kelly smiled at her sister's surprise but then she realized her mistake. Yes, Kelly had answered, but Kelly realized that she had sent the text to the wrong group chat. She had thought it was the group chat of the three Boyle sisters. But it was actually the group chat with her sisters and Ethan.

She fixated on the picture, taking in her silly grin, James's sheepish one, and wondered why she felt so horrified and was suddenly self-conscious of the fact that James was walking right next to her. She wouldn't have felt this way if she had accidentally sent a picture of her and Padma to Ethan. She could envision Ethan looking at it. The questions that would arise of Kelly being with a strange man he didn't know. He liked to be aware of who her male friends were, and to his fortune most of her male friends were gay or married to her female friends. She imagined—or felt?—silent resentment from him emanating through the phone, the inevitable question, *Did you mean to send me that picture?* And *I thought you were at a funeral, not having a good time?*

"Are you okay?" he asked suddenly.

"Fine. Just my sister being silly." They walked for a block in silence, but to Kelly it felt as if the silence was getting heavier with thoughts she'd been having since she had arrived but hadn't said. As a kid, James had always been someone she could say virtually anything to. Silences had never been uncomfortable, but twenty years had passed.

"Why didn't you ever look for me?" she said finally. The look he gave her was both sad and heavy. "I know we weren't supposed to but after a year or two of nothing happening... It's so easy on the internet. I was on MySpace. Friendster. Facebook. Maybe it's pathetic, but a part of me was setting up those profiles in case you ever looked for me." She dared to glance at him. He was looking down, his hands stuffed into his pockets. "I looked for you." She felt tears stinging behind her eyes. "I could never find you. I was scared you were dead. I worried about you all the time."

"Of course I thought about you," he said quietly. "I thought about you all the time. For that first year, I was terrified that someone would come out of the woodworks and come after me. Even after I got to San Antonio. Every second felt borrowed. Every time something good happened, I waited for the other shoe to fall." He kicked a rock, watching it skitter away. "I was scared of you or your family getting implicated somehow because of me. And after I left... I got into college and put this town behind me. I didn't want to come back here mentally. There was a lot of *badness* associated with this place. A version of me that I'm not too proud of—"

"What's not to be proud of?" Kelly's voice had dropped to a whisper because she was trying not to cry, looking forward and not at him. "I loved you the way you were."

James dipped his head the way he always did when he was uncomfortable. "I was so unhappy. And bitter. Wesley Falls was a place where bad people did bad things to me. That doesn't mean that I don't value you—you and what your family did for me. I guess I thought you would move on and not really think about me."

"Of course not," she said.

"I know. I'm sorry. I—" He broke off, pulling one of his hands into his hair. "I have issues with like, allowing myself to believe that people care about me and it's not a trick." His words surprised her. Not that he had the thoughts, but that he was willing to articulate them—he didn't used to be. "'Because how could the end be happy.'"

"If you're quoting *The Lord of the Rings*, you're forgetting what he says just after," she said. He looked at her, grinning. He had been quoting the part at the end of *The Two Towers* when Frodo is exhausted and the task before him seems insurmountable. Sam's response to Frodo was her favorite part of the trilogy. "'It's only a passing thing, this shadow,'" she said, affecting Sam's accent. "'Even darkness must pass.'"

He laughed. "You're a nerd."

"Put a nerd in black and he's a hipster."

"*Excuse* me?"

"I was looking at your café's website," she said. "You sell locally sourced organic oat milk."

"In my defense, it's good."

They laughed and kept walking while they bantered, with Kelly pushing aside thoughts of the baby and its disturbing implications. He was James but also different somehow, lighter, despite the context of what brought them back together. She said something—a bad pun—and he broke up into silent laughter. Pleased with herself, she found herself smiling and looking at him and all of a sudden it hit her, hard and with the whole of her body: *Oh, I am intensely, wildly attracted to him.*

The thought sent a spiral of panic through her, what it meant and could he somehow tell she had thought it, because there had been so many times in the past where they could practically communicate telepathically.

Luckily, they had just reached the library and the distraction of finding the others. They were tucked away in a study room, Jia and Padma clustered at one computer while Casey was working on another. "Find anything about babies?" James asked as soon as he closed the study room door behind them. Their friends stared at them blankly.

Kelly related all that Jane Merrick had told them: that she must have told Maddy about the baby, too.

"I've been trying to log every death in this town since 1995," Casey said. "I didn't see anything about a baby. If someone had a baby back then and it went missing, everyone would have been talking about it."

"Not if they kept the baby down there the whole time," James said, leaning to look over Padma's shoulder and frowning.

"The whole time? *Underground?* Wouldn't you die of vitamin D deficiency or something?" Casey said.

"And who would have given birth to it? We would have known about that," Padma said.

"Not if they kept the pregnant woman down there, too," James said. Kelly shivered. It was terrible to consider, a woman being kept down there like livestock. "Padma, what am I looking at?"

Padma took off her reading glasses and rubbed her eyes. "The tax records of nonprofits are public. I've been looking them up. I remember how much money I saw back then, which made me wonder about tax evasion."

"How would that work if churches are exempt from paying taxes?" James asked.

Padma held up a finger. "They're exempt from paying *income* taxes, but they have tons of employees, and with employees—"

"Payroll taxes," James realized, his face breaking into a smile as he looked up at Kelly. She averted her eyes, finding it difficult to make eye contact with him.

Padma continued. "I don't know what's going to happen here with the pastor, or if we should even go public with all the weird stuff, but worst comes to worst, bankrupting the church and destroying its reputation could prevent it from ever recovering."

Padma: practical as always, Kelly thought. How would this end, though? How can you kill something that doesn't die? "Maddy thought the Harvest happened every forty years, based on what she found at Evansville. In 1995 there was a Harvest, so we're not due for another one."

"But we killed him," Jia said. "So maybe they sacrificed a baby to bring him back?"

"Does it mean they'll do another Harvest sooner than on schedule?" Casey said. "If—"

The lights suddenly went off. Kelly opened the door and poked her head out. The library was dark and silent, and the woman who had been manning the reference desk was gone.

"That's a bit rude," Casey said. "Just warn us if you're closing."

"They're not closing for twenty more minutes," Jia whispered.

Kelly closed the door to the conference room as quietly as she dared. "Someone could be in here." They remained still, listening.

James went over to one of the windows and edged it up. "They're expecting us to go out the front, come on."

They climbed out, then jogged around the back of the library to the parking lot. There were a few cars parked there, their insides dark. They got into the minivan and Casey maneuvered out of the parking lot. Kelly and Jia were together in the back row, peering out the windows. Two cars were on the road behind them, but one turned onto Main Street. "Are they following us?" Casey called back.

"I can't tell," Jia said. "Just drive around randomly."

The black car remained, then a red car appeared behind it. Casey drove conservatively, making Kelly anxious when he finally had to stop at a red light. She saw that the driver directly behind them was wearing sunglasses, even though it was dark out.

There was a whooping sound abruptly, then the red, white,

and blue lights of a police car as it turned off a side street and sped toward them. "Please pull over," came a voice over the car's PA system. Kelly felt her shoulders relax. It was Blub's voice.

"The long arm of the law," Casey said as he slowly ran the red light and pulled the van over to the shoulder. Blub took his time getting out of his patrol car. The red and black cars rubbernecked until Blub, making his way to Casey, made a saluting gesture to them. *Don't worry*, that gesture said, *I got this.*

"License and registration please," Blub said after Casey had put down the window.

Casey produced both. "The lights went out at the library."

"Could be summer fritz or could be…" Blub said as he pretended to look at the license. Summer fritz was what they called it on the rare occasions when the power would go out in particularly hot months. "I try to keep an eye on you when I can. Would you mind stepping out of the car? You, too, James."

"Are you kidding?" James said.

"I'm trying to keep up appearances here."

Both men got out and turned to face the van, putting their hands on it as Blub gave them a pat down. "Do you think it could have been Miss Laurie?" James asked. "We were just talking to Jane Merrick and she was pissed about Laurie being an Elder now."

"She wasn't a fan of Maddy's," Casey added.

Blub considered this as he continued his search. "Before the Wesleys died there was some friction among the Elders. Ostensibly about the direction of the church, but honestly, these people just love to squabble."

"With all the Wesleys dead, the most important founding family is gone," Kelly said.

Blub had paused with his hands on James's lower back. "Do you have a concealed carry license?"

"Uh, no?" James said sheepishly.

Shocked, Kelly watched as Blub pulled a gun from under the back of James's waistband. It was a black handgun, which Blub looked at curiously. "It's a pellet gun," James explained. "From an old Halloween costume."

Blub considered its weight in his hand. "Wow. Fooled me." He hesitated for a moment, glanced around, then stuck it back under James's waistband. "Do you want me to get you a real one?"

Jia leaned forward, craning her head toward the open window. "Are you saying you think we need one?"

46

Casey

The next morning in the shower, Casey thought about the baby. It didn't add up, at least not in a way that wasn't disturbing. A part of him desperately wanted to believe there was a normal explanation for the toy they had found down there: maybe an Elder had bought a present for their child and it had fallen out of her purse. Maybe one of the Elders enjoyed whittling while they discussed the Harvest.

It filled him with a terrible sadness when there were people like him and Aaron who were desperate to have a child of their own. Hadn't it been enough to sacrifice six teenagers to the pastor? Why did there have to be a child, too? What nagged him the most was the thought that perhaps their killing of the pastor had triggered the need for endangering a child.

He got dressed, thumping the partially functioning window AC unit with the heel of his hand, and headed out to the courtyard where everyone else was gathered at a picnic table.

Padma had a legal pad out and had written BABY?? at the top in bold letters. "Okay," she said, now that everyone was there. "How do we find a baby that went missing back in the nineties?"

"Ask the town gossips," Casey suggested.

"But they can't be *too* churchy," Jia warned, "or they won't tell us."

"Town Hall again?" James said. "Wouldn't there be a birth certificate?"

"For a secret baby they kept in the mine?" Casey countered.

"Before we start coming up with wild supernatural theories, we should just assume the most basic thing," James said. "Maybe some holy roller got pregnant, and it was a big deal so they tried to hide it. There might be a birth certificate."

"Or a birth," Kelly suggested, looking at Padma. "A doctor must have delivered the baby, right?"

Padma noted this on her legal pad. "My dad delivered some babies here in emergencies, but mostly people called their OBGYN. I could ask, though, and he knows all the other area doctors."

"You know who I think would know and might actually tell us? Mrs. Tedesco," Casey said.

"The lady who used to work in the principal's office?" Kelly asked. "That's good. What about what's her name—she was the general manager of the grocery store. Someone would have been buying diapers and formula, right?"

"Judy Coleman," Casey offered.

"So we've got maybe four different leads," Jia said. "We can split up."

"Let me get Tedesco on my own," Casey said, looking on his phone for internet white pages. He prayed she was still alive. "She liked me—she'll talk."

As Casey walked up Mary Tedesco's driveway, which was lined with begonias, he tried to conjure the aura he imagined he must have carried back in high school: well liked, filled with potential, but still a dumb teenage boy. He rang the doorbell, waited, and prepped what to say as he heard shuffling sounds approaching. But Mrs. Tedesco—her trademark chignon still present—recognized him immediately. "Casey Cooper! I heard you were in town!" She pulled him into a hug, making him wonder if she was genuinely nice or was the sort of person who would hug him but then talk about him behind his back.

She ushered him inside for some iced tea and Lorna Doone cookies. They exchanged pleasantries—Casey mentioned being married and she gossiped about the comings and goings of various teachers at the high school.

Casey leaned forward, bowing his head and looking at the floor penitently. "Mrs. Tedesco, there's a specific reason I came here."

"Oh?"

"Back then, there was a lot of pressure on me. You know, college recruiters and state championships and all. People did a lot to protect me. Teachers, Coach."

"God rest that man's soul!"

"Yeah. So… Sometimes I got into trouble and people swept it under the rug." He looked at her for a reaction and saw eagerness in her eyes.

"What on earth are you talking about, honey?"

"So… I got a girl pregnant back then and they 'took care of it,' but I don't really know what that meant. They were worried I'd get trapped into getting married, or something that would screw up my chance of getting into a D1."

"Oh, dear, I could see why they would think that." She leaned forward and patted his hand sympathetically. "That would have been a lot for a boy your age to have handled back then."

He shifted uncomfortably in his chair. "Thing is… I'm not really sure who it was."

"You're…not sure who you got pregnant?"

He affected an embarrassed look as he pointedly twisted his wedding band. "Mrs. Tedesco, I slept with a lot of girls. More than you'd think. They didn't tell me which one it was—they were scared that I would tell my family. They just told me that it happened."

"And the girl…?"

"I don't know if she put it up for adoption or, you know, had an abortion. But if I have a kid out there, I want to do right by them. Thinking back, do you remember seeing anyone who might have been pregnant in a quiet sort of way?"

"Oh, I know," Mrs. Tedesco said casually, wiping cookie crumbs off her shirt as she leaned back. "I saw her before she left town—I can always tell a pregnancy just from looking at the face. Her family sent her off to help with an ailing aunt, or so they said!"

"Who?" he asked.

"Taylor. Taylor Anderson. She's an Elder now, you know."

A short while later they were parked on the street where Taylor's house was. "They developed this land in the early 2000s," Jia said as they piled out of the minivan. The loop of houses was just east of Golden Praise's campus. McMansions lined the street, each with unique attributes that indicated the houses were custom made. They clustered at the mailbox at the end of a long driveway. Taylor's mailbox was in the shape of a swan. The house had a three-car garage, but a Lexus and BMW SUV were parked outside.

"If they took her baby, but Taylor's an Elder, is she a victim or a perpetrator?" Jia asked.

"What do you mean?" Casey asked. "She was always awful."

"She was a pregnant kid. Maybe they coerced her or something," Jia said.

"You always have the kindest interpretation of events," Padma observed.

"Taylor wasn't the brightest person," Kelly said, starting up the driveway. "We might be able to get her to talk."

The doorbell played the first five notes of *La Cucaracha* and soon a man opened the door. The husband, Casey figured—he was about their age and had a milquetoast air to him. Someone who would take the backseat to Taylor.

"Hi," Kelly said brightly. "We're here to see Taylor." But she was pushing her way in already. The husband relented, apparently used to uninvited guests.

"They're in the parlor," he said, walking away and leaving them in the massive foyer. A gaudy crystal chandelier hung down from a high ceiling, and dual staircases curved upward.

Kelly turned to the right and they followed, leading them through a dining room, then down two steps into a sunken living room. The living room was white on white, white couches, poofs on the floor, family photographs framed in white frames. A woman with dark hair sat on one of the couches, her back to them as she was talking to a woman sitting opposite her. The woman fell silent as they approached.

It was Miss Laurie. Twenty years had passed, and she looked practically the same. The same tight skirt but conservative blouse. Blond hair perfectly styled. Ostentatious wedding ring. Was it Botox, Casey wondered, or something about being an Elder? "Well, isn't this special. We have visitors," she cooed.

Still seated, Taylor turned around, her face registering surprise and displeasure, but she quickly covered this up. The face that Casey used to consider "cute if not for her personality" had grown into the sort of woman who looked like she regularly yelled at her tennis instructor. "Oh. We heard you were in town," she said.

"I think you know why," Casey said.

An amused expression took over Taylor's face. She turned back to face Miss Laurie. "Laurie, I heard they came back for Maddy's funeral." God, she still had the same nasty tone she used to use in the cafeteria.

"We did," Casey said.

"They were the only ones there!" Taylor squealed.

Casey stepped closer to the couch and Taylor scrambled off it, standing next to Miss Laurie and trying to affect the same cool posture. But while Laurie looked collected, Taylor just looked silly. "Cut the shit. We know everything." Taylor only stared back. "You killed Maddy, didn't you?"

"Poor Maddy," Laurie said, shaking her head. "An awful accident."

"We know she didn't fall into a sinkhole," James said. "You moved her body."

They both looked at him as if he were a cockroach. Casey noticed that James was keeping his left hand by his hip. "Why on earth would someone do that?" Laurie said.

Jia moved across the room calmly, as if she wasn't on edge like the rest of them, though Casey knew that this couldn't be true. When she flopped into one of the oversize white armchairs he detected something in her, a spark, or at least an act of playfulness. "You couldn't stand to have her back here, could you?" Jia said, directing the question to Miss Laurie.

"Maddy was never one to hold her tongue," Laurie said. "On a good day she was shrill. Always trying to trip me up with her little questions. She showed up here and nothing had changed. Destructive and running her mouth."

"Was she asking about the baby?" Jia asked. Nothing passed over Laurie's face, but Taylor was confused.

"Maddy wouldn't have known about the baby."

"Taylor, shut up," Laurie said.

"We knew about the baby twenty years ago," Casey lied. "Because we knew about the virginity exams. All the Circle Girls got them, didn't they?"

"Yes," Taylor said, smirking. She folded her arms across her chest. "I knew Maddy would find out and be bitter about it. That's why she came back here, isn't it?"

"It was," Kelly said, likely having no idea what Taylor was talking about.

"It was supposed to be *her* baby until she screwed up. And then I was the one who was selected. The only one pure enough who could save this town."

"So that's how you became an Elder?" Jia said, gesturing around at the house.

Taylor put her finger on her nose and said, "Bingo! Things are different now. I'm moving the church to a more modern era."

"Collecting DNA," Kelly said.

Taylor shrugged. "Always good to know who has the best stock."

"Taylor, it doesn't have to be like this," Casey said. The sympathy in his voice was real. He looked at her and thought not of the woman living in this ostentatious house, but of the young girl who had always been in Maddy's shadow. Not as pretty, not as talented, not as popular. She had desperately wanted to be picked, only she had been picked for something awful. "Did they take your baby and kill it? Doesn't some part of you think it's wrong?"

A look came over Laurie's face, like a snake that had just swallowed a nice, fat egg. Jia must have seen it, too, her cool expression cracking. Casey had said something wrong, but they didn't know what it was.

"We would love to have you stay," Miss Laurie breathed. "But we're out of refreshments. John?" she called. "Could you come out here?"

Two men entered from what looked like a study room. Casey recognized one of the men, though he couldn't remember his name.

"Would you two be a dear and escort our friends out of here?"

They stepped forward, but Casey's voice stopped them in their tracks. "I know you," he said, pointing to one of them. "You were there." *Albert Sullivan.* One of the shearling men.

"Where?"

"At the mine party. In 1995. We all were. We saw you."

"You saw me what?"

"We saw you throwing half a dozen kids down the mine shaft," Jia said.

The man snorted. "Prove it." The men approached. "I think you've overstayed your welcome to our town."

"Take one more step and I will fucking flatten you," Casey said. They paused.

But Laurie stepped toward him, unafraid, her high heels making a clicking sound on the floor. She knew, or at least assumed, that Casey would not flatten *her.* "Let me give you a piece of advice, Casey. I run this town now. What I say goes. I'm being *nice* right now, but I don't have to be *nice.* Maddy wasn't *nice* and look where she ended up." She looked at the church goons and jerked her head toward Casey and his friends.

"You might want to rethink that." Casey, along with everyone else, turned to see James aiming his pellet gun directly at Laurie. Everyone froze.

"You always were trash," Laurie said.

"Trash with a gun. Back the fuck up." All four of them did, their eyes glued to the weapon. Casey prayed they could not tell it was fake, comforted slightly by the fact that Blub had been fooled by it. James gestured to Jia and she stood up, moving closer to the group. "A word of advice? A lot of people know where we are right now. Maybe we have cameras set up at the inn. Maybe we're recording this right now. Don't mistake the petty thing you're running here with omnipotence."

They began to back out of the living room, back toward the foyer, James remaining last with Jia beside him. Casey wanted to run for the door, but knew they had to seem unafraid. He had almost reached it when he heard Jia say, "And tell him I want to talk."

47

Kelly

"What the fuck was that?" James said the second they were safely inside the minivan.

"Was what?" Jia said.

"'Tell him I want to talk?'" he repeated. "Now we're having Reverend googly eyes over for tea?"

Jia turned from her position in the passenger seat to look back at James, who was in the last row of seats with Kelly. "I mean, why not? Isn't that why we're here?"

"I thought we were here to kill him," James said. "Kill him for good so this shit stops. Then arrest whoever killed Maddy."

Jia blinked. "We're not going to get all the answers with violence."

"We just did," he said, waving the gun. "They basically told us they had Maddy killed."

"But not how or what they're planning next," Padma said.

James leaned back in his seat, rubbing his face with his hands and muttering, "In the library with a candlestick." He looked at Kelly—*Do you believe this?* that look said—and she gave a weak shrug. She was embarrassed and confused about the intense sentiment she had felt about him earlier.

"Did you recognize him?" Casey said. "That guy was one of the shearling men."

"Albert Sullivan," Jia supplied without looking back.

"This can't be enough evidence for Blub to arrest someone, can it?" Padma wondered.

Casey pulled into a parking spot at the inn. They got out, Kelly stretching as Jia unlocked her room door. "Oh, no," she groaned. Alarmed, Kelly peered past her, but only saw a darkened room. Abnormally dark: the alarm clock had no glowing numbers and the AC wasn't making its insistent racket. "Summer fritz!"

Instinctively, Kelly's head turned toward the closest buildings to the inn to see if their lights were off as well. At least half the block didn't have lights.

"Are you kidding? It's nine hundred degrees," Casey said.

"Let's just go to the lake and cool off," James suggested. "By the time we get back the power will be back on."

Twenty minutes later they were walking to the lake with towels borrowed from the inn. The moon had risen, casting a blue-white light over Wesley Falls, making it look oddly picturesque.

"I said something wrong about the baby," Casey said. "Did you see Laurie smirk?"

"Were you thinking Taylor wanted to have the baby and they took it from her to bring back the pastor somehow?" James asked Casey.

"Yeah, what were you thinking?" Casey said.

"I was thinking she had it on purpose for them to sacrifice," James replied.

"Jeez, man!"

"What!" he said, throwing his arms up. "These people are really bad!"

Padma and Casey began a back-and-forth about this, but James held his arm up in Kelly's direction, telling her to hold back. They were already the last two in the group. "Do you think what Jia said was weird?" he whispered when they were separated far enough.

"About wanting to talk to him? I don't know."

"I mean, don't we make decisions as a group?"

"Yeah, but… Jia knows more."

"If she knows things we don't, she should tell us. I don't want to talk to that *thing*. I thought we should just, you know—" He made a gesture here that she couldn't interpret.

"What?"

"Like you'd shove him down the mine shaft again."

She elbowed him violently and he laughed without sound, looking at her. Did he look a second longer than what was natural? No, no, he didn't. They walked in silence for a moment, Kelly too distracted to listen to what the rest of the group was saying. Silence with James had previously always felt comfortable, but now she was afraid that somehow that spark of attraction she felt would introduce an awkwardness.

James procured a joint from his pocket and lit it. Kelly made a "give it here" gesture and he looked at her with shock before emitting a puff of smoke.

"Are you kidding me? I spent my entire teen years trying to get you on the weed wagon and *now* you're down?" He handed it over.

"I had my wild days in college. You still like an old-fashioned joint? No vape pens?" She took a hit and handed it back as he wrinkled his nose.

"Neither me or Duncan would be caught dead with one of those." They walked in silence for a while, passing the joint back and forth until Kelly stopped at three hits. She felt languid, and the stars seemed to glitter more brightly. She was happy being near him.

"Have you ever been to Newton?" James asked suddenly.

"Newton outside Boston? Once, why?"

"My old man is there." James said this far too casually.

Kelly could not help but stop in her tracks. "You *found* him?"

He nodded, a thoughtful expression on his face—not the expression she expected. It was rare for him to acknowledge his father—or at least, this was true for the James of yore—and when he did it was with a sharp anger, a wound that hadn't healed. "Once Google became a thing, it wasn't that hard. He got remarried. He has a whole new family now, two other kids."

"James! You have siblings!"

"Half siblings."

"Have you talked to him?"

"I've thought about it a million times over the years. That

I'd confront him, and what I'd say. Or I'd show up and be like, look at me, I've made something of myself. But then I didn't."

"Why not?"

"Because it's not just about me. I'd like answers, but there are kids involved. Well, not kids, they're in their late teens. Two girls. I don't want to show up and be a destructive force. He had his reasons for doing what he did, and he should have to answer for it, but those girls don't."

Kelly clutched her towel and considered this for the remainder of the walk, even though their conversation turned to other things. High school James would not have said that. Wouldn't have given two shits about these teenage girls. Maybe he would have even hated them.

Kelly joined Padma and Jia as they undressed at the shore, yelping as they dipped into the cool water. It was a delicious relief from the hot, muggy air. She backstroked to the center of the lake, looking up at the moon and the stars. There was something magical about the lake. It was the only beautiful place in town because it was solely theirs, perpetually natural and innocent. No one could touch them here.

Kelly found that her eyes were too often drawn across the water to James's shoulders, pale and lithe. In various groupings of conversations, she slipped away from him a couple times, noticing that he seemed confused at her avoidance. She swam away to involve herself in Padma and Casey's conversation about adoption, leaving James with Jia. When it became clear she did not have much to add to the conversation, she decided to swim on her own to the raft.

She climbed onto the raft, lying on her back. When she craned her head up, she could see Jia treading water, James talking to Padma and Casey, the latter laughing. She closed her eyes for a while, then heard splashing—when she looked up she couldn't see James—he might have been under water, but she could see Padma and Jia on the shore drying off, Casey wobbling out of the water. They waved—they were heading back.

Kelly lay back down, her pulse in her ears. They were alone together, but that wasn't her fault. She hadn't known the others were going to leave. She closed her eyes, heard movement in the water, then the shifting of weight as James pulled himself up onto the raft. "Hey," he said, but she didn't answer.

James lay down beside her, staring up at the sky. She turned onto her side and rested her head on his shoulder. They had touched each other like this countless times when they were younger, but she knew it was different now. Part of her knew she had put herself in this situation—that she "found herself" in a situation where she was alone with him. But these things did not happen to you: you made them happen, however much you wanted to place yourself as a victim of circumstance. She had wanted Jia, Padma, and Casey to go home.

She just wanted to lie here, listening to the lapping water, watching how its movement threw up flecks of moonlight. She was not capable of morally reasoning at the moment. She only knew that there was a pull toward him, that it was probably, technically speaking, resistible, but that she did not want to resist. She thought about that harsh line in the sand, about what would happen if she lifted her head to look at him for too long, and they would end up kissing. Did he want to kiss her? When they looked at each other for too long and the buzzing seemed palpable, it seemed so, but still a fear dwelled in her that he did not, that he would remain the one who rejected her, who loved her a little less.

"What if it was just like this?" he said suddenly, his voice vibrating against her ear.

"What?" she asked.

"What if the town was just like this? Like this lake. The only place that never went wrong."

She felt foolish that she thought he was talking about her, the emotion so strong that combined with a breeze, chilled her into a shiver.

"Cold? We can go back."

"No, it's fine," she said. She did not want to go back. He moved his arm, the one that was beside her head, and put it around her, pulling her closer. Eventually, it was she who suggested that they go back.

Their walk back to the inn was silent. It felt heavy and anticipatory, spiking an anxiety in Kelly. Something was about to happen, and she wanted it to.

"Do you have that aloe?" he asked as they approached the corner of the inn where their rooms were.

For a moment she floundered before she remembered that earlier in the day he had mentioned that he had sunburn on the back of his neck and she had said she had aloe gel. She nodded silently, unable to look at him as she unlocked the door to her room and rummaged through the array of toiletries on her dresser. She rubbed at her temples with her fingertips, closing her eyes. Obviously, they did not come in here for aloe.

"Can we just...talk about the elephant in the room?" She finally willed herself to look at him. He was leaning against the door frame looking at her, his hands shoved into the front pockets of his jeans. *If he does that thing, that James thing where he pretends we both don't know what I'm talking about, I'm going to scream.*

"Okay," he said quietly.

"I'm attracted to you," she said. Her stomach was twisting.

"Yes," he said, equally quiet.

"I think you're attracted to me."

"Yes." There was an intense, almost frantic look in his eyes.

"I'm engaged."

"I know."

"I can't, like—I can't."

"I know—"

"I just can't—"

"I understand—"

"I'm sorry."

"Don't be."

She bit back the tears that were starting to burn from her sinuses. "I think this has to be about how hard it was for us to stop being friends back then. It just dredges up all these emotions and it's overwhelming, and maybe that's what this is."

He leaned his temple against the door frame and nodded. He did not look like he agreed with her hypothesis, but he wasn't going to argue about it.

"You know I love you, right?" she said. *He'll do that thing—*

"I love you, too," he said. He bumped his head lightly against the door frame, once, twice, three times, as he thought. "Obviously, everything that's happening, that happened to Maddy, is terrible, but if the one good thing is that it brought you—all of you—back into my life, I can be happy about that."

She swallowed, finding the act almost impossible as her throat had swelled up. His gaze floated around the room before it settled on her, and he gave her a sad smile. "You can be the one that got away," he said.

She could feel the tears bubbling up, threatening almost violently to take over.

"Good night," James said. "I'm sure we'll have a lot to do tomorrow."

With that, he was gone, and Kelly sat on her bed for a long moment, turning her phone over and over in her hands. She unlocked it with shaking fingers and tapped on Ethan's name.

When he picked up, there was music in the background. "What's up?" Ethan said.

"I need to talk to you," she said.

"Hold on." Most of the background noise faded. "Is something wrong?"

"I'm sorry, I just needed to talk."

"About the funeral?"

"No. I… Since I got here, I've seen a bunch of old friends, including one who was close to my family. I haven't seen him in so long. Now that I'm here, it's just… There's a strong attraction between us."

Pause. "Why are you telling me this?"

"Because I don't think I would be attracted to him if I were happy."

"What?"

"I think it's a symptom of something we need to talk about."

"Wait, you told me you were going to a *funeral* for an entire week and actually you went there to fuck some guy?"

"I didn't say that!"

"Is it the guy you sent me a picture of?"

"Does it matter? I want to talk about whether or not we're happy together."

"Apparently, you aren't."

"Are you? Sometimes I feel like you despise me. You practically roll your eyes if I say the wrong thing around your friends. The last time we had dinner I asked you if you had to pick between Berkeley and MIT *as a joke*, because one is in Boston, where *I* live, you picked Berkeley."

"It was just a stupid question!"

"After I got hired, you even asked me if I'd consider moving to Illinois where you got a post-doc. On what planet does it make sense to give up a tenure track job that four hundred people applied to for *no* position in Illinois?"

"I only asked."

"I think you have the expectation that wherever you end up getting a job, I'm going to drop everything to be with you."

"I mean, definitely not if you're fucking some guy."

"Ethan," she said through her teeth. "I didn't sleep with anyone—that isn't the point. I told you I was attracted to him because I want to be honest."

There was a long pause. Then: "I thought you'd have the sense to not tell me something like this." Ethan hung up.

"No," she said quietly to the empty room, starting to cry. "I don't have the sense."

A knock came at her door. She stared at it, wiping her face with her hands. She blotted her face with her towel and thought about not opening the door. It would be James, wouldn't it?

But when she opened the door it was the entire crew, Jia and Casey in the front. She saw a split second of understanding on Jia's face—she could tell that Kelly had been crying—then Jia held up her cell phone. "Blub texted."

"Yeah?" Kelly said.

"They got the test results back of the material they found embedded at the base of Maddy's skull. It's pyrite."

Kelly closed her eyes. Not every kid in America grew up knowing what pyrite was, but every kid in Wesley Falls certainly did. Fool's gold. Commonly found in coal mines. "They killed her in the mine."

When she opened her eyes, Jia was looking at her sympathetically. "I think we've all known we have to go back down there at some point. It's time."

48

Padma

The following morning was spent with them purchasing various accoutrement for their expedition into the mine. When they were young it had been rope and glow sticks, now that they were older, they were more cognizant of the safety issues involved. They had headlamps, first-aid kits, and climbing accessories purchased from the closest REI.

They parked on the side of the road closest to the path leading up the mine, then began their ascent. At the top of the path they paused, Padma sipping from her bottle of water as she looked at the boarded-up entrance to the mine. "It's like all the graffiti's different but it still looks the same." Casey grunted an agreement and began to pull off some of the plywood so they could climb inside.

It was strange to place the memories side by side. Back then they hadn't known what they would find. Back then they had thought to bring granola bars and spare ponytail holders. Now Padma thought about the probability of slipping and breaking a tibia, of insurance premiums, and how she would explain it to Tamer that she had been traipsing around an abandoned mine. Because at least when you were a kid you could blame such reckless activities on being a kid.

The inside of the mine seemed ageless, though smaller than what Padma remembered. The path through to the Heart was uncomfortably tight, and she remembered that some of the paths would be even smaller. They stood for a moment at the precipice of the Heart, where the shearling men had been standing. A cool air rushed up through the center of the mine. "It still smells the same," she murmured.

"Like an animal," Jia whispered.

They began the descent down the Heart path, James leading with his map, Kelly assisting. Just as Padma stepped over some old machinery, Jia grabbed her abruptly by the back of her shirt, gasping. When she looked back at her friend, Jia gestured with her head to the rock wall to their right. "What?" Padma whispered, scared.

Jia edged toward the front of the group, and James stepped aside. She stood a foot away from the rock wall and turned on her cell phone flashlight, squinting against its painful brightness. They crowded around, but all Padma could see was mottled rock. "There's blood," Jia said. Casey reached forward, but Jia stayed his hand. "It's a crime scene." Jia fumbled, then withdrew a pen from her backpack. She held the cell phone unsteadily as she reached forward with the pen, then hooked it under something before she pulled it back slightly. Padma could see it now. A strand of light hair was stuck to the wall.

"Is this where it happened?" James said.

Jia was blinking rapidly. "She was heading into the mine, I think because she found out about the baby, and they followed." She looked at the ground, then back up the path. "They fought. One of them shoved her head against the wall and then she was dead."

James crouched and tried to examine the stone floor with his flashlight. "Jia," James said. It was clear what he was asking. What now?

Jia gestured to the Heart. "Let's keep going." She put her hand on Casey's backpack as she passed him. He was carrying the blowtorch that they had gotten at The Home Depot. They needed to get that ancient metal cabinet in the Elder room open, only now they had neither key. None of them fully understood what was in that cabinet, but if it was locked away, it held something important.

They continued to climb down mostly in silence, stepping

carefully. Padma told herself that this place was just a structure, nothing to be scared of. Something miners carved out to make money to support their families, but even that wasn't true. This mountain never should have been opened. She thought of what Jane Merrick had told Kelly. That she made him a quilt but he never used it because he didn't sleep.

What did he do, then? Urban legends about the mine sometimes included stories that it was haunted, that you could hear voices in the rumbling of rock. That something lived here. What if they weren't just legends but they were true? What if the pastor had roamed these paths at night and had for at least two hundred years? What if—

Padma gasped, freezing in her tracks, Casey running into her from behind. "What?" he said nervously.

"Guys, what if we're thinking about this all wrong?" she said. They gathered around her, their faces sweaty. "We've been assuming they made Taylor have that baby so they could sacrifice it to bring him back, but we actually don't have any evidence of that."

"Sure we do—" Casey started.

"It doesn't match up with the Circle Girl thing," she said, shaking her head. "Why are cultures obsessed with virginity?"

"I don't know, misogyny?" Kelly offered.

"Partly. But if some guy in the 1600s is selling off his daughter for marriage, promising that she's a virgin, why is that so important? Because it's a guarantee of paternity. No question that guy gets stuck raising someone else's child."

"What are you saying?" James said.

"If they were going to kill that baby, why would it have toys? Why did old lady Merrick talk about it like she *liked* the baby?" She looked around at her friends, and only Jia seemed like it was dawning on her. "They didn't sacrifice the baby to bring the pastor back. The pastor *is* the baby." Kelly choked on the water she was sipping. "It makes more sense," Padma said, excited. "Dave Lurie didn't appear till a couple years ago. He's what— twenty-something? Taylor had her baby twenty years ago."

"They…raised him down here?" James said, turning his head to stare down the Heart.

Jia played with her flashlight. "Dave Lurie looks like that Frenchman when the Wesleys first caught him. Young. He was maybe forty-something when we killed him. It's a cycle."

"But how does Taylor get knocked up if Jim Preiss was dead at the time?" Casey said.

"The blood," Jia said abruptly, and began to start down the path. "They were gathering it off the floor."

"Gathering blood off the floor?" Padma said as she followed, frustrated. "Who?"

"The Elders," Jia called back to her. "I saw it after we killed him."

"Saw what?" James said.

"I didn't understand it at the time, but I saw the Elders at the bottom of the mine. Where his body landed. They were hurrying, trying to gather his blood up off the ground."

"They used the blood to get Taylor pregnant somehow?" Padma asked.

"I'm guessing."

James nudged Padma and made a "what gives?" gesture.

"Jia, are you telling us everything you know?" Padma asked.

Jia paused, turning around with one hand on the stone wall. "Of course I am. Are you two going to navigate, or do you want me to?" she asked.

"You know the way?" James asked. Jia nodded and continued to lead, eventually coming to the turnoff and where the confusing labyrinth to the red door began. This time, instead of glow sticks and paper, James and Kelly left a trail of bright fluorescent tape stuck to the cave walls. Within twenty minutes they came to the door that led to the underground Golden Praise complex. It was smaller than Padma remembered, still bright red.

"I've been practicing my door-busting techniques," Casey said, approaching it. But then when he put his hand on the knob and turned, the door simply opened. The shock on his face made Padma want to laugh.

Jia led them directly to the Elder room with no hesitation. It smelled the same, Padma realized. Like incense and wet stone. There was the long oval table with the twelve chairs. There, at the far end, was the wooden cabinet with the metal urn with the key slits inside. Jia went to the cabinet and opened it. *She was terrified of it back then*, Padma remembered. Casey set down his backpack and knelt to open it as Kelly began to wander around the room. "Jia, why were you so scared of this cabinet back then? You backed out of the room, and he trapped you across the hall."

"It gave me a bad feeling," Jia said. If she had any such feeling now, she didn't show it. "There was blood in that chalice—"

"Guys?" Kelly called. "There's a door back here—we didn't notice it the first time. You need to see this." Her voice was flat.

Padma and the others went over and peered inside the small room that Kelly had revealed. Her eyes saw a giraffe, which her brain couldn't process. A giraffe and one of those wooden block puzzles with the little handles on each piece. A toddler bed with a mobile over it. Board books. "A nursery," she whispered. Jia was the only one who dared go inside, picking up the toy giraffe and running her fingers over it.

James began to laugh suddenly, sounding a little deranged. "This place is so fucked."

"Come on," Casey said, turning back to the Elder room. "Have any of you ever actually used a blowtorch?"

"Give it here," James said, holding a hand out. "Art school days."

James concentrated the flame of the blowtorch at the hinge of the ancient metal urn, alternating with Casey, who would then try to lever it open with the crowbar. The others watched helplessly, the bright flame of the torch burning an image into Padma's eyes as she blinked at the otherwise dark room. This went on for some time, and she realized that Jia was still standing at the doorway to the nursery, staring into it.

After a while Casey stepped back, wiping sweat off his brow with the back of his hand. "Anyone else have a go? The smell is getting to me."

"Let me," Kelly said, taking the crowbar.

"Want to do some exploring?" Padma said to Casey, gesturing for him to come along with her. When they exited the Elder room into the dark hallway, they each took a deep breath of moderately fresher air. Padma directed them down the hallway. "Do you think they took Maddy up out the mine entrance or through here?"

"Up out of the mine entrance would be faster because she didn't get down too far, but back through here is more private," he said.

"Maybe we could find evidence that they moved her body through here?" Padma said. "It directly implicates the church, while the crime scene itself might not. I mean, we won't know until we can get Blub out here with a real forensics team."

"There was that room with the hatch that goes to the church—which room was it?" Casey said.

They went down one hallway, then another, opening doors to look for the room with the trapdoor leading up to Golden Praise in it. Along the way, Padma swung her flashlight beam across the linoleum floor, hoping to find a smear of blood, anything that could be incriminating. Casey opened the door to an office and ran his flashlight along the ceiling. Excited, Padma pushed him into the room. It was the trapdoor room, except now there was no furniture in it.

"Do you think it's unlocked?" Padma said as Casey stood on his tiptoes, trying to reach for the string with the tips of his fingers.

"I always keep it unlocked."

They both spun around. The pastor was leaning against the wall, his arms folded across his chest. His teeth gleamed white in the darkness as he used one foot to swing the door closed. "I thought I felt someone down here."

"I've got a knife on me," Casey said, moving closer to Padma.

The pastor tilted his head to the side. "Don't be rude. I only came to talk." Padma directed her flashlight directly at his face and he cringed, bringing one hand up to his eyes.

"What do you want to talk about?" Casey asked stiffly.

"Wasn't it you who requested a chat?" the pastor said. Padma found his manner of speaking peculiar: it seemed old-fashioned and out of tune with the youth of his face.

"We know what you did to Maddy," Casey said, lowering both his voice and his head, reminding Padma of a bull about to charge. Though Casey was probably twice the size of the scrawny twenty-year-old in front of them, she would have felt better with James's gun, too, even though it was fake.

"Maddy?" he asked.

"You killed her," Casey said.

"No, I didn't," the pastor said, unfazed by either Casey's words or his threatening posture.

"We know what happened," Padma said. She did not want to speak because this would mean that the pastor's dark eyes would focus on her instead, which they did, but she kept going. "Maddy probably went into the mine, and Laurie sent some men after her. She said as much."

"Did she? It's a shame. I rather liked Maddy." He bumped off the wall and began to move slowly, putting his body directly between them and the door. "She was…spirited. She asked questions. Maybe one too many, but questions nonetheless."

"We were there," Casey said. "Back in 1995 when you killed those kids."

The pastor raised his eyebrows. "I killed those kids?"

Casey's brow furrowed. "No—not you specifically."

"How could I have done something I didn't do?"

"You asked them to," Casey snapped back.

"No, I didn't," the pastor said, his eyes sparkling.

"The Harvest," Padma said. He seemed interested in the fact that she knew the term. "We know all about it. That they kill for you."

"If you know about the Harvest, then you know that I gave them a choice," he said. He moved away from the door, as if he was taunting them by creating a free pathway to escape, daring them to use it. "The people that founded this town, they wanted all this." He made a grand gesture, which she supposed was to indicate everything about Wesley Falls—the church, the green lawns. "I asked them to name their price." He paused, putting an astonished look on his face. "They could have offered a bushel of wheat but instead they chose this."

"You would have taken a bushel of wheat?" Casey asked flatly.

"Certainly," he said, moving closer. "A bushel of wheat was quite valuable back then."

He's lying, Padma thought.

"They wanted a community. They wanted it created in their image. I did that for them. I get on a stage and say some words, and it makes them very happy."

"I remember once," Casey said, "I was sitting in church, and I had the Bible open. You quoted something on that same page. But you changed the words."

A grin spread over his face—he might have looked handsome if not for the horror Padma felt. "You'd be surprised how often I do that and no one notices."

"You don't care about the words," she realized.

"Why would I? They're just words." He reached into his pocket—Padma flinched—but what he brought out looked like a paper receipt, which he began to fold as he walked slowly around the room. "It is my nature to make deals with people, but I have not made a new deal for a very, very long time."

"Why not?" Padma interrupted.

He glanced at her, then focused on folding his little piece of paper. "I haven't needed to and it's rare that something interesting comes along. Your little coterie, for example. Let's say you wanted something badly," he said, his tone silky. "Say, a baby." He held his hand open, showing that he had folded the paper into the shape of a swaddled infant. Padma felt her blood run cold. "How badly do you want it? What would you be willing to give? What is it worth to you?"

Padma swatted the paper baby out of his hand. She didn't want to risk touching him, but the idea of it offended her too much. "We didn't come here for that," she finally managed to say.

"Didn't you?"

"We're going to open that cabinet," Casey said.

"What will we find in there?" Padma asked.

"A little piece of me," the pastor said, smiling faintly. "If I let you."

"Will you let us?"

"Do you want me to show you?"

49

James

James cringed, stepping back from the cabinet. They had gone through several rounds—him blowtorching then Kelly trying to force the urn open with the crowbar. They had made only modest progress, and now she had jammed the crowbar in and was throwing her whole weight on it—he worried about the crowbar snapping and hurting her. "This is going to take hours," he said.

Kelly looked at him but he could not see her face, the bright light of the blowtorch flame lingering over his vision. Something had happened, though, because her posture changed—she now held the crowbar as if it was a weapon and faced the doorway. James turned, blinking, unable to see what she was looking at for a few seconds. Casey... Padma... And someone else. "You called?" the pastor said, chuckling as he walked across the room, dragging his fingertips against the old wood of the massive table.

James's hands tightened on the blowtorch as the pastor approached him, unafraid. James looked at Kelly, and he wondered if they should kill him, set him on fire and Kelly could whack him with the crowbar. Kelly made a minute shake of her head. In his peripheral vision, he could see Jia emerging from the nursery. The pastor pulled something from his pocket. A key. It fit into the first lock with a satisfying click, then into the other. "Mine is the only one that will open both," he said, reaching in to take out the object that James had only seen for a few seconds twenty years ago. It resembled a tiny crystal vase, maybe six inches long, narrow at the bottom and wider at the top. "Lead crystal," the pastor said, taking it out and holding it like it was a can of Coke. "These people like their pomp and circumstance. But it is my means of regeneration."

"We're going to take that from you," James said.

The pastor smirked. "Do you think I would let you?"

"You might be willing to hand it over, yes," Jia said, emerging from the shadows. When the pastor saw her, his smile faded a little, but his eyes glittered with interest. "For the right price."

"What could you possibly have to offer me?"

"You've been waiting for us. For someone like me."

"What are you?" the pastor asked, dropping the sinister act. He asked this with the plain curiosity of a child asking about an insect he had never seen before.

"I am someone who would like to know what happened to our friend Maddy."

The pastor looked down at the crystal and bounced it in his hand. James's eyes had adjusted well enough to see that it wasn't clean: there was something staining the bottom of it. "She came down here. Maybe looking for this. Two men killed her, Albert Sullivan and Vance Sterling. She died instantly." He looked up at Jia. "Did you come here to make a deal with me?"

"Yes," Jia said.

What?! James thought.

"And what is it that you want?" he asked.

Jia pulled out one of the Elder chairs and sat in it calmly. She was putting on an act again, the same thing she had done at Taylor's house. The pastor took the seat across from her, placing the crystal in between them. *What is she doing?* James thought. Kelly had her mouth open, her hands frozen on the crowbar like she was a baseball player. Casey also looked confused. "We want your church. We want it dissolved. We want all the money to go away."

He laughed. "And why would I do that? Why would I give away my flock?"

"I'm not done," Jia continued. "No more Harvests. No more Elders."

"Please continue," he said, grinning. "I'm making a list."

"This," she said, pointing to the crystal. "We want that, too."

He laughed again, clapping his hands with delight. "You are very funny! And why, Jia Kwon, would I give you those things? What could possibly be worth all that?"

There was a long pause—James held his breath. Jia put her hands flat on the table. "I could set you free," she said. James had been staring closely at the pastor's face and the change when she said this was almost imperceptible. The smallest twitch of his eye.

"Set me free of what?"

"You know what," Jia said. She gestured around her with both hands. "You're trapped here, aren't you? Bound to the mountain and this little town. Because if you could leave you'd be long gone, off to bigger and brighter things. But if you made a deal with me instead, you would be free to go anywhere you pleased."

James's eyes shot to Padma, wondering if she knew what the hell was happening, but Padma looked just as stunned as he felt.

The pastor's smile had faded entirely. "That's not possible," he said.

"How do you know what I'm capable of?" Jia said. "A long time ago you said to me that you've never met anyone like me. That I'm like you. I am like you, but with one major difference. My friends here have all led blessed lives, all have successful careers. Note that not a single one of them lives here, and neither do I. I can do what you do, but I'm not tethered to any one place."

"How?" The pastor now had no pretense of trying to appear cool and sinister. "Where do you come from?"

"That's rather personal and we haven't reached that stage in our relationship, have we? If you gave me all that I ask for, I would break the ties that bind you here. You could walk outside this town and go wherever you pleased to find your next flock. But this would be mine," Jia said, cupping her hands around the crystal. "Do you understand what I'm saying? You would only live the rest of your natural life."

The pastor's eyes flicked from the crystal to Jia. He was making a calculation. "I'm not sure I believe you have the power to do this," the pastor said.

"If you give us time to prepare, I can show you my power."

"Even then. The force that binds me to this place is strong. It existed long before humans came to this land."

"I assure you, I can break it."

"And if you're wrong?"

"Then I'll take your place here and you'll be able to leave," Jia said, eliciting a gasp from Padma. "Do we have a deal?" Jia was standing up, holding her hand out.

"Jia, no—" James said.

The pastor stood up.

"Jia!" Casey shouted.

Jia shook the pastor's hand.

50

James

There was stony silence the entire drive back to the inn. James reflected on how drastically things had changed within the past few hours. Not too long ago Miss Laurie was using church goons to threaten them. Now they were being driven home by one of them in a luxury Town Car. After Jia and the pastor's handshake, the pastor had led them up through the church and offered them a ride home. The pastor's overly solicitous behavior was a dead giveaway: he wanted Jia's deal to be real. He wanted it badly. She had found his Achilles' heel.

Once they got into Jia's room, James checked to make sure the Town Car had driven away. "Jia, what the actual fuck was that?"

"What?" she said innocently. "Now we have a plan."

"What plan!" Padma shouted. "You just made a deal with a mountain demon!"

"It's not a real deal."

"But we don't know how this works," Casey said. "What if that handshake is binding? What if he takes your powers somehow or—"

"You get trapped inside this town like he is?" Padma finished.

Jia held up her hands. "Guys, calm down. *The deal doesn't matter.* We can't kill him without getting close to him. It's all so we can get him—alone—to a particular place, and then *blam!*" she said, hitting her palm with her fist.

"And what exactly is the *blam*?" James said.

"I was thinking," Jia said, sitting on the bed and crossing her legs. "We could set up a trap in the mine, then draw him to it for some magic ritual that would break his bond to this town. Padma could build a bomb—"

"I'm doing what now?"

"You're a chemist!"

"I'm an engineer!" Padma cried.

"It's like in Evansville," Kelly said, sounding excited as she flopped down on the bed next to Jia. "Except we do what they never did and kill him."

"Exactly," Jia said. "We need that chalice. And he's never going to trust us with it if we're antagonistic with him. If we destroy it along with him, no one can use it to regenerate him."

"But how does he use it to regenerate?" Padma asked.

"I don't know exactly, but it has to do with the blood at the bottom."

"Is it his blood?" Kelly asked.

Jia blinked. "It's Jim Preiss's blood. From when we killed him."

"I don't like this," Casey muttered.

"I thought we made decisions as a group," James said.

Jia looked at him, a sad smile curling her lips only a little. "I'm doing the best I can."

James closed the door to his room, then downed a bottle of water. Three hours of talking could make a headache. Padma lamented that in all the chemistry classes she had ever taken, not one included a section on bomb making. She had been put in charge of that aspect of their plan, Jia, the fake ritual to prove her power, and everyone would sort out the logistics. The one thing they had not finished deciding was exactly what to tell Blub.

James heard a knock on his door—it was Kelly. He stepped aside to let her in, figuring she would want to debrief what had just happened. "Isn't this nuts? Jia going rogue?" he said.

Kelly nodded distractedly, her gaze wandering around the room. "Yeah… That was strange." He waited for her to say something else, but she didn't.

"Are you okay?" he asked.

But then she was standing too close to him, wordless, looking directly at him. Oh, he thought. Maybe she hadn't come here to talk about Jia. Tentatively, she put a hand on his shoulder, her thumb coming to rest just under his collarbone. "What if... What if I just wanted to know?"

James turned to shut the door behind her then turned back, cupping her head in his hands and kissing her. He had tried to pretend that he could let go of the tension between them, but there was only so much he could pretend. He wanted to kiss her, wanted her to want him, wanted to forget about what was "right" and do what felt right. Her mouth felt right. The curve of her neck. He pulled her toward the bed and after falling upon it, slid his hands up under her shirt to feel the bare skin of her back.

Are you sure? he thought, and she was.

His desire to be close to her was tinged with an anxiety that she would change her mind, wake up from this dream. He thought that perhaps within the confines of this town, this room, there was a full awareness that this would be only one night. A thing she could label as a mistake and he would have to let it go and acknowledge that they would not get to have the world beyond this room.

It didn't truly occur to him until they were curled up after and nearly asleep, that the ease with which they had touched each other when they were younger had always been deeply important to him, though he hadn't understood it at the time. Whether it was squishing together on a hammock, or her resting her head on his legs as they read, or the times when she forcibly hugged him and he said "Ew, stop!" when he didn't really mean it and she knew. After his mother died, Kelly was the only person who consistently touched him in any sort of affectionate way. Her presence was steady and unshakable, something he in his youth both valued and took for granted.

He forced himself to not think about what would happen once they both left Wesley Falls. For now her back was pressed to his chest, her hair with a faint smell of lavender just under his nose, her hand over the arm he had looped under her waist and across her stomach.

This, he thought. *This, this, this.*

51

Kelly

When Kelly woke up, she could tell it was before sunrise because she could not yet see any sunlight pushing its cheerful way through the cheap curtains. James had one hand tucked under his head and was staring at the ceiling. "Hey," she said. He opened his mouth to respond—she was anxious as to what he would say but didn't want to show it—but instead, his stomach growled loudly. They both started laughing. "Tell me how you really feel," she said.

"Do you think anyone else is awake?" He reached for a package of Twinkies on the nightstand and downed one in three bites, leaving its twin resting on his chest. Kelly leaned down and bit the center of it, leaving a barbell shape behind. "What's wrong with you?" he said, laughing. "Who does that?" He attempted to grab her—she squirmed, they kissed, and she ate the remainder of the cake lying on her side and looking at him. He turned to face her, idly running his fingertips up her side. They stared at each other for a much longer time than she would have guessed him capable of, sometimes smiling, other times the smile fading away as their thoughts wandered to more serious things, but never breaking eye contact.

The alarm on her phone went off. James groaned and stuffed his face into a pillow as Kelly turned it off. "Time to go murder shopping," she said. "Do you think we can pull this off?"

"We have to," he said, his voice muffled.

"If my students could see me now! How I spent my summer vacation!"

"Priest hunting and a summer fling."

She bristled, glad that her back was to him. "Is that what this is to you?"

She could feel his alarm as he raised himself onto one elbow. "I mean… It's summer and you're wearing an engagement ring." Silently, she held up her hand, showing that she was no longer wearing her engagement ring. She had assumed he had seen this—if not before, then last night, when they had been touching each other everywhere.

"Wait—what?"

A knock came at the door. Kelly pulled a sheet around her like a toga and answered it. It was Casey. "Oh—you're fucking? Anyway, we're leaving in ten. Take a shower."

Kelly picked up her tank top and pulled it on as soon as the door was closed. "Can we—" James started.

"I promise we'll talk," she interrupted. "But we have a thousand things to do today."

She headed back to her room. She had assumed he had noticed the lack of ring—that this had factored into his calculus. Yesterday, while everyone else had been eating breakfast, she had been pacing in her room, having first a tearful phone call with Mimi, then a painful one with Ethan. Part of the reason the conversation could not wait till she was back home was that she did not want to enter the mine with loose ends haunting her. She was unhappy with Ethan; this was independent of anything she felt about James, but that did not mean that it wasn't confusing.

Today James and Casey were heading over to the mine to scout for locations while she, Jia, and Padma were then taking the minivan and driving an hour to a college library four towns over so Padma could do her research, then they would go shopping at various hardware stores until they had everything they needed. She was secretly glad for the separation by gender, so she could have some time to think.

"What if he doesn't come?" Kelly whispered. They were sitting in a private study room in a college library that was both blissfully well air-conditioned and nearly empty. No one had thought twice of the trio of women who entered to claim a study room and had then trickled in and out to get a variety of chemistry books. Padma was hunched over three of them, her pencil scratching across a sheet of paper.

"He'll come," Jia said, sipping her vending machine coffee. Her silver hair was once again tucked under a conservative black scarf. "He's been desperate to know the extent of my powers from the first time he saw me. He wants the deal."

"He'll know it's a trap."

"He'll wonder if it's a trap, but he's arrogant. Look at the difference of how he's responded to all of us." Jia stretched her hands out at opposite ends of the table. "We have the whole spectrum in the capstone group. At one end, you have Maddy, who he was actually nice to. Why? She's already part of the church. She's already a believer. That story she told us about when she ran to his house? I always wondered what would have happened if the Merricks hadn't interrupted."

"I always assumed he would bite her like a vampire. Or try to kiss her or something."

"But now we know. He gets this girl who is entirely broken, devastated because she's been taught the one thing she has of value is her virginity, and now she's lost it. I think he wanted to make a deal with her, or at least thought about it. But then he didn't."

"Because the Merricks interrupted."

"Maybe. I get the sense the Elders have boxed him in somewhat." Jia tapped her left hand against the table. "On the other end you have James, who he seems to hate. Why? Why him specifically, if we know it's the *town* that hates people who are different?"

"Because James doesn't believe in anything," Kelly realized. There were a million things James might have wished for back then, but he would have laughed in Preiss's face if he had offered him some magical deal. Even now, even when they knew that what they faced was supernatural, James had trouble accepting it. "A town full of people like James would be worthless to him. But where are you, then, on this spectrum?"

"I'm not on the spectrum. He's never seen anything like me. This is what we take advantage of. He's tired of serving the Elders. Remember, we never used to see him around town buying groceries or walking around or whatever. He has all these powers but they keep him caged like a pet."

"Guys, I can't do this," Padma said suddenly, setting her pencil down. "I don't know what I'm doing. What if it fails?" Kelly could see a hint of young Padma in her, the panicked "we are in over our heads and maybe we should just tell our parents" in her eyes. "What if you've made the deal and we don't kill him, then what happens to you? Does he get your soul or something?"

"It won't fail."

"Maybe we need a plan B," Kelly said. "We get the gun from Blub and we shoot him. Throw him down the shaft with the chalice."

"Would that be enough to destroy him?"

"Set it on fire, too?"

Padma sighed.

Soon, they left and went to three different home improvement stores to each buy a container of driveway cleaner. When they were back out on the road, Padma cried out suddenly, gesturing out her right-side window wildly. FIREWORKS FRENZY! the sign at the strip mall they were about to pass read. WE GOT EM YOU BLOW EM. Padma and Kelly hopped out while Jia took the minivan to get gas across the street.

"You think you can work with this?" Kelly whispered to Padma as they surveyed the garishly bright packages of small-scale explosives inside the store.

"Oh, yes." Padma crouched to examine the goods and Kelly glanced across the street at the gas station.

"Do you think Jia's acting strange?" Kelly asked.

"Jia's always strange," Padma said, distracted.

"She struck a deal with him without even talking to the rest of us."

Padma picked up an enormous firework and held it against her hip like it was a baby. "In high school, we got frustrated with her for not telling us what to do because she's psychic and we expected her to know everything. We can't be mad at her for doing what we wanted." Padma selected another firework, then frowned. "But yeah, sometimes I feel like she's hiding something."

Kelly dropped the plastic bag filled with half a dozen M80s onto the bed in Jia's room. When Casey peeled the plastic bag away, he paused and looked up at her, wearing a "we're really going to do this?" expression on his face.

"Can you guys take apart all the fireworks and put the powder into these bottles?" Padma said. She had dragged the driveway cleaner and a few other miscellaneous bottles to the bathroom to begin her mad scientist concoction.

Kelly used her house key to slice a flap of thick cardboard on a firework and began to unpeel it carefully. "Did you find a spot?" She directed the question at Casey, but she could feel James's presence next to her, as if he was burning ten degrees hotter than everyone else. *Summer fling.* He probably slept with a variety of beautiful women all the time. He was one of those guys whose youthful outcast identity had aged into effortless coolness.

"It was a long day," Casey said, "but we think we found the perfect place."

"We used the map some, but then went off grid," James said. He curled a piece of the *Wesley Falls Blotter* into a funnel, which he then stuffed into a glass bottle. "About midway down the Heart path, there's a big inlet off to the side, then a path that curves off there, toward Evansville, which is why we didn't include it on our map. If I had to guess, the place we found is under the halfway point of the path that goes to Evansville around the side of Devil's Peak."

"I like that," Jia said from inside the bathroom. She was measuring a cup of clear liquid onto a digital kitchen scale.

"We found a cave," Casey said. "It's big enough, and there's a small chamber next to it, like you asked."

"We're going to need to bring all this stuff down there during the day," Padma said. "And then you're going to summon him?"

"That's the plan," Jia said.

Once all the black powder had been removed from the fireworks and put into bottles, the project grew more complicated, as everything would depend on a timer. Someone would need to detonate it, but give them all enough time to get as far away as possible before it went off. They disassembled a few items purchased from the mall: a stopwatch, a radio-controlled car. Kelly felt increasingly useless as the job became more technical, and Padma shooed away anyone when it came to joining together wires or anything more complicated. Kelly stood aside, feeling useless. She looked across the room and realized that James was looking at her. A flush started in her chest, spreading across her body.

"I have to make a phone call," she said quietly, though no one noticed—they were too engrossed in their work. She left the room and passed Padma's room, then Casey's, before she heard James's footsteps behind her. She walked to his door rather than hers because his room was farther away. He opened the door for them silently, then locked it once they were inside the room. They kissed, wrapping their arms around each other.

Sex with James was different. Different than the men who had come before him, and certainly different than Ethan. He touched her face. There was more kissing—before, during, after. When they finished, the bur of anxiety reappeared in her stomach, and she had to hold him tightly because she was scared he would disappear again. Was this just a fling to him? Or worse—they were all putting themselves in danger, and James had always had such horrible luck. If the dice fell on a random number, it would be his and he would be taken from her. She could not protect him from all things, not what had happened back then, not the tragedy that had befallen him with Dominique, and not now. The fact that she loved him did not ward away any harm that could come to him.

"We should get back," she said, running her hands through her hair.

"They already know. Can we talk?" he said. He pulled on

his jeans and sat next to her. "That thing I said about a fling, I didn't mean it that way—"

"It's fine. I understand. You're single. You had condoms with you."

"What?" he said. The look on his face was genuinely confused, maybe a little annoyed.

"I mean… You had some with you."

"I'm single. I always have some. That doesn't mean I'm looking for sex everywhere I go."

"I didn't say that," she said meekly. "Just that… Just because of what happened, I don't want you to feel like obligated or something—"

"I hate when you do that," he interrupted. "You've made up this story in your head that I care less about you than you do about me. I don't normally do this, you know."

"Do what?"

"I've never slept with someone who was in a relationship with someone else. I don't want to be the thing that blows up your marriage but—"

"You didn't blow up my marriage." She felt at the empty place where her engagement ring used to be. He copied her body language, leaning forward, and she could feel his eyes on her. "I was unhappy with Ethan and good at telling myself that I wasn't. I don't know how much longer things would have lasted. But you forced the issue. I talked to him yesterday before we went into the mine."

"I don't want to be the thing that blows up your marriage but like… I'm not going to *not* do that." She looked up, surprised. "If there's one thing I know, it's that life is short. I already lost the three most important people to me. Dominique. My mom."

"Your dad," she finished.

"No, *you*, stupid," he said, pushing her shoulder so that she almost fell sideways on the bed. *"You,"* he said more seriously after she had laughed and righted herself. "I don't care if it's wrong. I want to be with you. Outside these walls."

She pressed her lips together, trying not to cry. There were the walls of this room, but there were also the spaces inside her, and James had occupied her heart long before anyone else had. She had imagined going home to her apartment and parsing the things of her relationship with Ethan. Who technically owned the DVD player or what would become of framed photographs. She had pictured working in her office alone, Mimi and her friends taking her out for drinks to cheer her up while she still felt hollow and guilty inside. Was he saying that this was not what her life would look like?

But James wasn't talking or smiling anymore. He was staring at his hands as he began to speak. "Casey and I were talking about what it's like to be here when we didn't have the best home lives. What it's like when you see other families having a nice Thanksgiving or Christmas. What being in this town again is like, all the bad feelings it brings up." His voice trailed off. Then he looked at her. "I was never safe here. It wasn't like a home," he said. "Home is supposed to be where you feel most yourself, where you can take off all the stresses of the day. This town was never that for me. For most people home is a place. But for me it's a person."

Then she felt herself break, a sob cracking her in two. She reached for him, clutching him around the neck, still not quite believing he was here.

52

Jia

It took longer than they had expected and the bomb wasn't ready and hidden until well into the night. This had been taxing, several trips up and down the mine, all of them carrying materials, Padma fretting that she didn't know what she was doing. The pastor's cave, as they were calling it, had been prepared, and Jia's cave beside it. They ate a meal together, their conversation steering clear of what was about to happen, then planning to reassemble in her room when Blub was coming over.

This is where the rubber meets the road, Jia thought, sitting on her bed in her robe. This was something her mother used to say that never made sense to her. Weren't tires always on the road? She laughed a little, having imagined this conversation between her and Su-Jin. *I'm scared they can read my face*, she thought to her mother, desperate for an answer back. Her friends loved her, but they would never fully understand her. She had to make the deal with the pastor because she knew that was the only way this could end. It had to end in the mine, because that was where it all started. These things were inevitable. Initially, she had thought the feelings she had since arriving here were from Maddy's murder and the discovery that the pastor was alive. That could be true, but there was more. Why did she feel as if she were careening toward darkness, that there was a *finality* to all this? A finality that would affect her and not her friends.

Jia glanced at the clock, then got dressed. Her friends arrived about ten minutes before Blub knocked on her door. "Hey there," he said, stooping as he came in. He was carrying a black bag. "What's the latest?" He took a seat in the desk chair that didn't seem built for someone his size.

"We found the crime scene," James said. He had unrolled the mine map on Jia's desk, the edges curling over. "It's in the mine, right about here." He placed a penny on the spot.

"Maddy had gone down there to do some investigating and Laurie Waterson sent some men after her," Jia said. "They slammed her head against the rock wall. I think you'll find some evidence there."

"It was Albert Sullivan and Vance Sterling," Padma added.

"How do you know this? She went down to the mine to investigate what exactly?" Blub asked.

"The pastor told us," Jia said. "There's a…" *There's a secret complex under Golden Praise that's attached to the mine and the pastor is a perpetually reincarnated being and we're not entirely sure how he keeps coming back.* "We're going to sound crazy if we try to explain it."

Blub put a paper cup into the dinky little coffee machine sitting on the desk and pressed the "on" button. "Try me," he said. By the time he had drunk most of his cup, they had related all they knew: the pastor and his deal, Miss Laurie, and Maddy asking too many questions. He kept a poker face the entire time, his gaze calmly focused on each person as they talked, not once interjecting. He squeezed the bridge of his nose with his thumb and forefinger. "So you are…"

"About to convince the pastor to go down into the mine so we can blow him up and stop this from happening again," Padma replied.

"Do you believe us?" Kelly asked.

"It's not that I don't believe you. I told you there was something weird going on in this town. I just didn't expect it to be *this* weird."

"Can you make an arrest based on what we've told you?" James asked.

"I can get a Pennsylvania State Trooper down to the crime scene to collect evidence. I can certainly start checking for the whereabouts of those two men on that day."

"Will it be enough?" Padma asked.

"I'll make it work."

"We mailed an anonymous package to the IRS and FBI," Padma added. "A tip-off about Golden Praise's tax evasion."

He started to laugh—the look on her face was so earnest. It was a little funny, Jia admitted, that they were talking about both killing a supernatural entity and mailing tax evidence. "Listen, we don't know what will actually happen," Padma said. "Even if we take him down, we want to make sure the church goes down, too. Since your deal isn't real, the pastor won't actually dismantle the church," she said to Jia.

"Right," Jia said. The reality was, she had no reason to believe the deal wasn't real, but she couldn't say this. There would be too much protest, too much arguing, when they had little time. She just needed to make sure her friends were not in the way.

"Well," Blub said, unzipping his black bag. "You didn't get this from me." He withdrew a pistol from his bag and placed it on the table, then followed this with a spare clip. "It's unregistered. Get rid of it when this is over." He stood up and went over to the door. Just before he left, he looked at them all and said, "Make me a promise? Only one person dies tonight."

"Who wants the gun?" Jia said. She was uncomfortable with its presence.

"I think James does," Casey said.

"I make tarts for a living!" James protested, but took the gun anyway.

Jia pulled out her phone and put it on the bed in front of her. "Are you guys ready?" They were. She put on speakerphone and dialed the direct number for Dave Lurie's office at Golden Praise.

There was a pause, then that silky voice. "Jia."

"I'm ready. Are you?"

"Ready for whatever smoke and mirrors you've prepared. Come to Central, and I'll take you down there the easy way."

"Thank you for that," she said, trying to force a smile into her voice.

"What should I expect?"

"You'll see."

They hung up. "I think you guys should wait outside the mine," Jia attempted. "I can detonate the bomb on my own."

They all stared at her. "What?" Padma said. "We're not leaving you alone with him."

"There's no point risking all of us when we don't have to," Jia said. "There's a chance the bomb could malfunction or something. Like the blast radius is bigger than we thought, and I don't have enough time to get away. Or it fails."

"We thought of that," Casey said. "If it fails, we overpower him. That's why we all need to be there."

Jia stared at the blank screen of her phone. She could feel Padma looking at her, her eyes burrowing into her. If she fought too hard on this point, it would draw questions. "Okay," she relented. "You're there for the first part. Once I actually sit him down for the ritual, you guys make for the landing closer to the Heart path. I'll meet you there once I've detonated the bomb. I won't be with him for more than two minutes. I need to act like I'm not afraid to be alone with him."

They talked a bit more about the plan, then decided they should have something decent to eat first. Casey, James, and Kelly left to pick up food, but Padma remained.

"You know what I keep wondering about?" Padma said, and Jia braced herself, busying herself with the coffee machine. "Taylor saying that it was supposed to be Maddy, but then they picked her because Maddy wasn't a virgin anymore. How do you suppose it works?"

"How they bring him back? I don't know. Just that it has to do with the blood."

Padma seemed reluctant to speak. "Do you remember what he said to you back then, the night he was in your bedroom? You told me he said something like, 'it will come out in the eyes.' We thought he was talking about taking your eyes out or something. I think he might have been talking about *genes*. That any child of yours would have eyes that look Asian."

Jia blanched. "He was thinking about making a kid with me?"

"I think he considered it. He was always fascinated with you— maybe he thought he could be even more powerful that way.

I'm guessing it was just a fanciful thought, because the church doesn't control you and he can't be reborn as a half-Asian baby in a town like this."

Jia hugged her knees into her chest. "Padma...that's super gross."

"I know," she said, patting her arm. "Are you scared?"

Jia blinked. Strangely, she was not. She was sad. Sad looking at Padma's earnest face because she wasn't being entirely honest with her. She couldn't be. Their priority had to be killing the pastor, making sure this cycle stopped. It had to happen no matter the cost. Some things could not be changed once they were foreseen. She had seen what would unfold. That was how it happened. It couldn't be stopped.

I love you guys so much, she thought, but didn't dare say, because Padma would question the sudden sentimentality. "Not when I'm with you," she said.

53

Jia

Casey put the minivan in Park, turned it off, and hesitated. He looked at James, then Padma and Kelly, and lastly Jia, who attempted to dry her sweaty hands on her thighs. She was wearing a silk kimono her mother would have loved, hoping it would give courage.

They got out and began to walk the path down to Central. The moon was fat in the sky, adding a pallor of pale blue-white light over Golden Praise's grounds. A series of landscaping lights lit the way, and through the windows it looked like only the lights in the main foyer were on. A man stood at the double doors, his arms folded across his chest. "He's waiting for you," he said, turning to unlock the doors and let them in. His eyes lingered on them for a moment as he frowned, then he headed down a dark hallway. Jia had to wonder what he was thinking, or maybe it was perfectly normal for there to be middle-of-the-night meetings at Golden Praise.

Then the foyer was dead silent. The moonlight filtered through the stained-glass windows cast strange colors across the dim room. Jia could hear footsteps before they could see anything. A figure emerged from the darkened hallway, the pastor with his hands clasped behind his back, wearing a well-fitted suit. "You came," he said.

"As promised," Jia said.

"Come along," the pastor said, making a gesture with his

head. He didn't seem bothered by the fact that she had brought an entourage, the same way he hadn't been frightened by them outnumbering him down in the Elder room.

The pastor led them down a few hallways, then into a nondescript office where he pushed aside a table, then opened the trapdoor. Someone had put a pile of crates into the room beneath so it wasn't an unreasonable jump. "After you," he said politely and they each climbed down.

She noticed, as James and Casey led the way to the cave they had set up, that the five of them moved with caution when navigating the mine, while the pastor could have been strolling down Main Street. Could he see in the dark? she wondered. Did he have no fear of falling? The climb down took more than an hour with no one speaking. A couple times Kelly turned back to look behind them, anxious that they were truly alone with the pastor. He hadn't even asked about bringing anyone else, Jia realized. Did any of them even know he was down here?

The cave that they had set up was maybe half the size of the modest rooms of the Wesley Falls Inn. It was lit by candles, the light flickering off the stone walls with their occasional glimmer of water. Jia sat cross-legged in front of a table that was actually a cardboard box from The Home Depot with a sheet from the inn thrown over it. She thought of the tableaus she used to set up at The Gem Shop and how much she had enjoyed creating a mood with various items. She had placed two candles on the table, one black, one white, both lit. In between them was her favorite stone: a hematite, which she had taken from the time capsule along with the other stones. Lastly, there was a deck of tarot cards wrapped in a silk scarf directly in front of her. Her friends arranged themselves around the room strategically. Kelly was behind her, standing next to a hidden crowbar resting in a shadowy nook. James had the gun, Casey a baseball bat, Padma a knife.

The pastor looked around with interest, taking in the candles, the little table, and even glanced to the left, to the dark inlet that led to an adjacent cave. "Why have the ritual all the way down here?" he asked.

"Because it's at the border between Evansville and Wesley Falls," Jia said. "It must happen here. Sit," she said to the pastor, trying to make her voice sound unafraid. *Just pretend he's a customer,* she imagined her mother telling her. Because everyone who walked into The Gem Shop for a reading had something in common, even the skeptics: some part of them wanted to believe that magic was real. If Jia had guessed correctly, the pastor also wanted to believe that she could do the things she was claiming she could do.

The pastor sat across from her at the table, cross-legged as well, not objecting to the hard stone. He paused to glance up at her friends, showing no concern for his vulnerable position on the floor, before he looked back at the table. "Did you bring it?" she asked.

He nodded, bringing out the small crystal container from an inside pocket in his jacket and placing it in front of her. "And now you're going to furnish some proof of your abilities?"

Jia freed the tarot cards from the scarf and shuffled them. "Pick seven," she said after she spread the cards out in front of him in an arc.

He picked the first few without breaking eye contact with her, a bemused smile on his face. *Isn't this cute?* that look said. After he had selected seven, he pushed the small pile across the table toward her. She took it, performing a quick sleight-of-hand to swap out the final card. The purpose of the reading was for him to walk away thinking that she had a lot to offer him. She had rigged the reading to end with a positive card, The Sun, something that said success, joy, and positivity: the happiest card, in her opinion, in the entire deck. But the other six cards were truly his selection. She needed the rest of the reading to be real, for both of them.

Beyond interpreting the symbols and placement of the cards, she needed to read *him.* But this was not like dipping into the minds of people she knew and loved: pushing gently with her mind in Philadelphia and seeing her mother washing dishes in Wesley Falls. Checking in on her business partner when she went through a depressed period a few years ago. The times she had dipped into Padma's head over the years. As far as she knew, she could only do that because of the bonds that she had with these people, the intimacy and trust allowing her access. She did not know the pastor. She did not even fully understand what kind of being he was. How could she push into a mind that was unfathomable?

She cleaned the spare cards off the table and looked at the dark material that stained the bottom of the crystal on the inside. An old layer of blood. His blood. *This is how I do it*, she realized. She reached down into the crystal, picking up a little of the crusted-over blood with the tip of her finger, then rubbed her thumb and forefinger together. This was a piece of him.

From the moment Jia had climbed down into the mine, she had felt that familiar discomfort in her stomach. Death happened here. There was a reverberating dark energy that bounced around, traveled down the labyrinth of tunnels and nooks. But when she touched his blood, the reverberating energy stopped being around her and went inside her. The sensation instantly made her want to panic, but she sat with the feeling, inviting it into her bones, and closed her eyes, letting it take her over. Who was this, this creature that sat across from her?

She put her fingertips on the first card on the left. "This card is you." She turned it over. The Two of Swords. A blindfolded figure holding a sword in each hand. "You stand at a crossroads, an important decision point, though you don't feel you have enough information to make the decision." He gave her a minute nod. "This next card is your obstacle." She turned over the Eight of Cups. "A relationship that once brought you a sense of joy is now stagnant and disappointing. You have no choice but to walk away."

"Your abilities are astounding," he said with soft sarcasm— more teasing than rude.

Jia ignored him and put her fingertips on the next card. "This is where you came from." The card she turned over was The Devil. He rested his head in one of his hands, the expression on his face indicating he thought she was entirely silly. She glanced at his eyes, which in the dark made her think of onyxes, then quickly averted her gaze—she feared that if she looked too long she would see that other version of him, the black vortices of his eyes. "It means imprisonment. A deep, terrible, uncontrollable hunger. A hunger so bad that it makes the passage of time immaterial for centuries. It drives people away from the mountain when all you want is for them to come closer." His smile faded ever so slightly.

Jia tapped the next card. "This card is you being born. The Seven of Swords. You were a man once. You hunted and trapped and loved the feeling of snow beneath your feet. You ventured far from your provincial town and had a talent for languages. The world felt open and vast to you." The pastor narrowed his eyes. "You're a thief. Your secret is that you wear a face but it isn't yours." He stared at her now, expressionless. Jia's pulse pounded in her ears. He didn't know, she realized, that they knew some of this from Evansville. Some but not all.

"This card is your death." She turned over the fifth card, which was, ironically, Death. "The end of one phase comes to a close. You have made two towns prosper in exchange for the Harvest. Wheat is sown. Apples planted. Children are born. They sing to you and it slakes your hunger. The churches grow." He was hypnotized, unblinking. "But you wear the body of a man. You are growing old, and it amuses you they didn't predict this. 'But what will become of us when you die?' they ask. 'The foundation I have built will die with me,' you say. But," she said, leaning forward, "there was a way, wasn't there?" Jia picked up the chalice and held it in both hands. "A way for you to carry on. You needed a vessel. A girl. A few drops of your blood into her mouth, and she becomes pregnant with your shadow self." His expression was flat now. *How can you know this?* that look said. "When you have grown too old and the shadow self is old enough, they slit your throat and anoint your shadow. You become him. They save some of your blood each time," she said, turning the crystal on its side to display the ancient material at the bottom, a mixture of every incarnation of the pastor that had ever existed.

It was perfectly silent in the cave except for the distant rumbling of rock. "This card is the past." Jia turned over the Four of Pentacles. "Greed. You agree to be bound to them in perpetuity as long as they continue to provide you with vessels. But they ask for even more. They ask you to serve no other but them. They have built another prison around you. They built their towns on the Harvest and the selection of a vessel once a generation."

"They killed some of the vessels after," he said suddenly, almost in a dreamy voice, throwing Jia off. "They disposed of them. It changed over time, became a thing of honor. They would marry off the girl to someone well connected after she carried to term. I always thought it strange, the symbolism they attached to everything."

Do I have him? Jia wondered, trying to contain her excitement. "This is your future," she said, tapping the last card. She turned it over, expecting The Sun as she had rigged it, but had to stifle her surprise when the card turned out to be The Tower. Had she failed in her sleight of hand? Her brain sputtered with how she could spin the card positively. It was, unfortunately, a card with an overtly dark and negative image on it: a flaming tower being struck by lightning while two people jumped to escape. "The Tower. Massive change and upheaval." *Also chaos and destruction*, she added silently. "Everything you once believed is now questioned." She sat back, folding her hands together in her lap. "Have I proved myself? Are you willing to enter into an agreement with me?"

His eyes were focused on the cards. "I am ready to break with the Elders. If I give you my church and this," he said, indicating the crystal, "I am a free man?"

"Yes."

"You have an agreement," he said without hesitation.

"Leave us," she said to her friends. "The ritual should take about an hour."

Casey gave her a wary look and her friends left the cave. They would be staggered on the way out, ready for her to run out so they could all be led out of the mine by James.

Once they had left, she picked up the black candle and gestured for him to follow her. The adjacent cave was smaller, pitch-black except for the flicker of flame. She set the candle down and gestured for him to sit, kneeling beside him. She withdrew a pouch from where she had left it earlier. There was old rusty machinery to the right, half-covered by an ancient tarp that smelled faintly of mildew. That side of the room, though, was barely visible.

Jia opened the pouch and slowly poured a circle of salt around the pastor. "This is a rare, pure form of sea salt," she said. It was actually Morton's kosher salt, purchased from the nearest grocery store. "It will protect you. For the duration of the ritual, you must remain within this circle. Do not leave it for any reason."

"How will I know when it's over?"

She gave him what she hoped was her own bemused look, like *she* thought *he* was being silly this time. "You'll know because you'll be free. You'll feel it." She withdrew two bundles from her pouch, one of which she set in front of him. Hers was a bundle of dried herbs tightly bound together with twine. She lit hers, then blew it out, leaving a smoldering end, which made fragrant smoke begin to float outward. "Light yours," she said, distractedly handing him her lighter.

He clicked the lighter and held the flame to his bundle but it didn't catch. Click. Click. Frustrated, he held the flame to the herbs for a more sustained period of time. Nothing. He paused, looking at Jia for guidance. She frowned, trying to put a look on her face that said, *Hmm, why can't you do that?* His bundle of "herbs" was a purely decorative item purchased from a local craft store. It was made of flame-retardant cloth. This was solely to throw him off, to again make him think that she could do things that he could not.

"Here, take this instead," she said, handing over her bundle. "I'll take this one," she said, getting to her feet. "Are you prepared?" He nodded. "Give me a minute to get set up. Then you'll hear me chanting."

"Very well."

54

Pastor

The pastor sat impatiently, his gaze wandering between the smoldering bundle of herbs and the black candle until he heard the sound of Jia speaking. He did not recognize the sounds she was making—it wasn't English. He pricked his ears, concentrating. Japanese? Was she speaking Japanese?

Humans were so peculiar. The robes they wore and the words they spoke were meaningless to him, but he had learned over the years that attaching secrecy and formality to the process that rebirthed him imparted the seriousness of his needs to his followers.

The extent of the girl's powers wasn't clear to him. But the evidence of her sight was apparent from her reading. The body he had claimed, the agreement he had made. It had been Jeremiah Wesley's own idea to create the Elders, to request the health and wealth they "needed" to assure his continuation. And in exchange he had agreed to serve only them. But what other choice did he have at the time? His mortal body had been dying. But he hadn't considered what this arrangement would feel like hundreds of years later. It's true that they released him from the mine and had given him form with the fur trapper. But he had never been able to cross over the town borders leading away from Evansville or Wesley Falls. He was bound to the mountain. And confines, he had discovered over the years, were tiresome.

He rubbed at his nose—the smoke from the herbal bundle bothered his sinuses. He blew on it to push it away from his immediate vicinity. There was some danger to an agreement with this girl, this Jia—he was not naive, he understood this, but the element of danger was in and of itself attractive. If he broke with the Elders and dissolved the church, he would lose his flock. This would take away his ready supply of sustenance, and if left in that state indefinitely, his hunger would begin to come back, rendering him more erratic and less human-seeming. But he would be free. He could roam the earth as he pleased. He could find others who would supply him with sustenance. He would build new flocks, maybe *several* flocks in multiple locations.

She had thought that the taking of the crystal vessel was a clever play, but had been wrong. Yes, she had taken away his ability to regenerate this body in the way he had since the founding of these towns, but he was wily. He had found a way to get a body when he had no body. He had found a way to continue when that body came to its natural end. If he had done it before, he could do it again, perhaps in a way that was less reliant on humans. There was *always* another way. She had been foolish to assume there wouldn't be.

There was a sound—a faint hissing. He perked his ears but it was hard to hear such a subtle sound over Jia chanting in the other room. He coughed, rubbing at his eyes. The herbs really had irritated them, but at least the bundle was almost done smoldering.

There—that sound again. Was it coming from inside the cave? He picked up the candle and held it aloft, looking around for the source of the noise. He could see very well in the dark, but the thing about the mine is that the perpetual darkness sometimes played tricks on the eyes. He paused with the candle in the air as he moved it to his right. Something shiny had glinted in the darkness. He tried to angle his body without leaving the salt circle so he could better see. There was an amorphous pile of machinery to his right, the tarp mostly covering it, but closer to the ground there was something shiny. Glass?

His eyes were stinging worse, and now his sinuses burned, and the inside of his chest hurt. That could not be from the herb bundle. He stretched, attempting to reach the tarp from his sitting position, but his arm was not long enough. He stood, careful to not touch the line of salt with his shoes, and though this extended his reach it wasn't far enough. Annoyed, he looked down, and quickly made a decision. He kept one foot firmly inside the salt circle and stepped out, reaching to pull back the tarp and see what was beneath.

The pastor stared, confused at the series of items in front of him. There was an upside-down plastic bottle, the kind soda came in. Something electronic was duct-taped to it, wires running out, and inside was a cloudy liquid. Another bottle, this one right side up, was glass and taped so the bottles were mouth to mouth. There must have been a mechanism to make the contents of the first bottle drip inside slowly, because the clear liquid came down drop by drop, and the second bottle was filled with a nasty-looking smoke. There was something else duct-taped to the second bottle at its base; he crouched and saw that it was a battery, then some other electronic device. From the device ran three wires of different colors. Those wires ran into another item, also inappropriately shiny, a household kitchen item that he struggled to remember the name of because he had never used one. *Pressure cooker.* He touched the top of it, felt something gritty, and brought his fingers closer to smell them. Despite the burning in his sinuses, he could smell a hint of sulfur.

He ignored his physical pain and considered the contraption in front of him with wonder. He had seen a lot of things. Towns in tumult. Shouting matches at community meetings. Mothers tearfully pushing aside their daughters. He had seen it over and over and over. He saw the apple orchard transform from an empty field to rows of seedlings to young trees to old ones that bore fruit. Fruit and flowers and wheat could be expected every year, like clockwork. So, too, were the petty concerns of humans. They wanted this but also wanted to make sure no one else had it. They wanted it at any cost. If he thought about it, wasn't when he was freed from the mountain the last time something really interesting happened?

He had to admit, that beneath all the ceremony, he had been for quite some time more than a little *bored.*

This was why, considering the bomb, a small smile appeared on his face, unseen by anyone else in the darkness. The last thought he had before the bomb went off was, *Oh, I've been had.*

55

Jia

Jia ran as fast as she dared with only two flashlights to guide her. It was too easy to make one bad step, to twist an ankle and trip. Once she had activated the detonator, she only had a few minutes to get as far away as possible. Hit the detonator in its hiding place in her cave, press Play on the long recording of her reading Japanese on her phone and leave it behind, and quietly go down the tunnel, not running until she felt she was far enough away from the pastor so that he couldn't hear her.

Padma had said she thought the explosion would be fairly contained, but Jia knew better than to risk it. The mine was old, and at any given time she could hear rock falling somewhere— it wasn't improbable that an explosion would cause a collapse. God, they were so stubborn, insisting that they all had to go up together. That just invited risk. But she hadn't been able to talk them out of it. She had also been unable to tell them about the dark, nagging feeling she had had for the past few days.

She was almost back to the Heart when she heard and felt the massive reverberation of the bomb going off. It had worked. She was still alive! Another turn and there was the Heart path, four different lanterns glowing in the darkness. The large silhouette of Casey standing the closest at the landing, then up a few yards past him was another one of her friends. Casey was yelling something—hurry, hurry. It was safer to run on the Heart path, it was more flatly hewn on the bottom than the tunnels, and fairly safe, as long as she stayed away from the precipice.

She ran a few steps, then saw something in her peripheral vision. Her body moved with inertia and could not respond fast enough to change her direction. A light was approaching from a side tunnel. She had barely turned her head, barely been able to comprehend that what she was looking at was the overly bright light of someone's cell phone flashlight, that a man was holding it, not one of her friends, and that he was heading straight for her.

It was too late to dodge—he was about to hit her. His body crashed into hers and she thrashed desperately, her immediate fear was both of them falling off the path and into the Heart. A big hand clasped around her throat, squeezing. For a moment she panicked, unable to think straight, then she remembered that they were all armed to varying degrees. She had a small hunting knife in her pouch. She freed it, stabbing upward into his gut.

There was a scream; she wasn't sure whose. The man, his face grimacing in pain and twisted into hate, grabbed for the knife. She shoved him but his fingers had grasped onto the belt of her kimono, giving it one violent tug with his full weight before he went over the edge. She lost her balance.

The weightlessness of being in the air seemed to stop time. She felt strangely at peace, as if she no longer had a body. In her mind she saw whiteness and she felt warm. They were there. Both her parents were there. They had been waiting all this time. *Mom—*

An intense pain ripped across her head, so stark that the whiteness and comfort it brought was ripped away. Was this what death felt like? Was this her hitting the bottom of the mine? She heard a sound and realized it was her own mouth moaning. Her head hurt. A sharp, fiery pain. Her legs kicked uselessly. She looked upward, confused. Casey hung over the edge, his arm muscles popping. He was holding her up by her hair. Someone was screaming. She heard Kelly's panicked voice. Casey was then reaching his other arm down and digging his hand into her shoulder painfully. With a grunt, her body was moving upward, and James's hands were there, too, now, grabbing her by her arm, nearly pulling it out of its socket.

They wrenched her up and over the edge, Jia landing on top

of James, James deliberately rolling his body away from the precipice and toward the wall. Casey had collapsed onto his back and was panting, chanting "what the fuck" under his breath over and over. Jia was crying. Kelly was also crying. James touched her scalp, cringing. "Are you okay? Are you okay?"

She could not explain that the tears were happiness, relief. "Let's get out of here," she said.

They stumbled out of the main entrance of the mine, exhausted and breathless. They had barely talked on the near-run up the Heart path in their eagerness to resurface as soon as possible.

Jia plopped down on a rock, unable to thwart the wave of fresh tears that erupted. "Jia, you were *this* close!" Padma exclaimed. She crouched down in front of her and dabbed at her scalp with a folded bandanna.

"I fell," Jia cried helplessly. "I fell."

Casey leaned over, hands on knees, and cringed as he saw Padma's bandanna, now stained with red. "You're bleeding. Honestly, Jia, I don't think I would have been able to see you if your hair was black," he said.

Jia stared at him, awed. "That... You just grabbed me? But I was supposed..."

"Supposed to what?" Padma said sharply.

"I didn't think I was going to make it out of there," she admitted. "I thought the mine was going to take me. Even if we killed him."

"I knew it! You saw something!" Padma exclaimed.

"You had a flash?" Casey said. Jia nodded. Casey shrugged. "I don't care." He stood up straight, squinting in the sun as he wiped sweat off his brow and she could easily see sixteen-year-old Casey. Casey did not believe there was a tide he couldn't turn.

"But I thought I would die...or the deal I made—"

"It was no match for my catlike reflexes!" he said, striking a pose. Jia started to laugh and cry at the same time, and Casey stooped down to hug her, picking her up in the process and holding her tightly. "It's okay. We're okay, right?"

"Did it work?" Kelly asked, still looking worried. "Is it over?"

Jia sniffed, wiping her face with the clean side of the bandanna. "He's dead."

"Let's head down," Padma said. "I never want to see this place again."

As they walked, Jia waited until she had drunk enough water to not feel light-headed to ask to borrow someone's phone. She called Blub on speakerphone and he picked up immediately. "It's done," she said.

"For real?"

"For real. I can feel it."

"What does it feel like?"

What *did* it feel like? It felt like a layer that had been there previously was gone. It felt like a nice summer day with puffy clouds in the sky and birds chirping. "It just feels like he's gone."

"Well," Blub said. "That's great to hear. I've got two friends from the Pennsylvania State Troopers with me. We're hoping to make an arrest for Maddy."

"Will it stick?" James asked.

"I hope so, based on what we found. Looks like there was a struggle so there's hair and clothing fibers, and we swabbed for DNA," Blub said.

"Um," James said uncertainly. "There's going to be another body. At the bottom of the mine."

"Who *was* that?" Jia couldn't help exclaiming.

"That was one of the church guys," James explained. "The guy who opened the doors for us at Golden Praise. He must have followed us when we went into the mine with the pastor."

"He attacked Jia," Casey said quickly. "Practically threw her into the Heart. It was self-defense."

"Did you shoot—never mind. Just get rid of that gun. I'm sure the Elders will make a ruckus, but I'm not sure how much influence they'll have now. I can arrest a few more of them if I can get either of the suspects to talk. I don't see how the church can survive this, if everything you said about the supernatural stuff is true."

"What is this town without the church?" James wondered.

"I hear it's got a great football program," Blub joked, deadpan. "I don't think it would be the worst idea for you to get out of town sooner rather than later, but stop by my office on your way out," he added.

"Roger that," Casey said.

They said goodbye and hung up. Every town had at least a few Blubs, Jia thought. Men who were good in some very basic way and couldn't help trying to make things better. Like the mine foreman at Evansville. Not everyone is willing to make a stand, but some people were.

"What am I supposed to do with this gun?" James wondered.

"Let's throw it in the lake," Casey said.

"Why don't we make a pit stop there?" Jia said. "I think it would be nice."

"Let's pour one out for Maddy," Casey said. "She never got a proper memorial."

It felt like the opposite of the last time they had killed the pastor in the mine. Instead of frantically dealing with the consequences and deciding to split from each other, they had finally set things right and there was a youthful, relieved energy in the air. They sat leisurely on the beach, making slow, happy conversation about Maddy. Padma pulled off her socks and shoes to dig her feet into the sand. "This one time in class the teacher announced that I broke the curve and Maddy did this—" Here she turned around in her seated position, narrowing her eyes in a perfect imitation of mean-girl Maddy. They laughed.

"The day after I first met her, I asked her something about her horse," Kelly said, "and she said, '*Which* horse?'"

Casey pulled off his shirt. "One time in seventh grade, I had a boner in homeroom—look, it happens—and she sends me a note, and it just says '*Ew.*'" James bent over, laughing silently, but Jia frowned. They had been so focused on trying to figure out what happened to Maddy that she hadn't had the chance to think about what Maddy—adult Maddy—had left behind.

James removed the gun from his bag and handed it to Casey gingerly. "You wanna test out your throwing arm?"

Casey nodded, taking it. "I'll go to the raft and throw it from there."

In various stages of undress, the rest of them entered the water, James and Kelly skipping stones and arguing about whose had gone farther. Padma nudged Jia once they had gotten in waist-deep. "You're going to be my friend now, right?" Padma said.

"Of course I am!"

"Come see me in New York!" Padma said, hugging her from the side. "I want you to meet my husband. And see my house. Oh, there's a little store in my town that reminds me of The Gem Shop!"

"You're taking the train back?" Padma nodded. "Maybe I'll go with you part of the way," Jia said. "There's a loose end I don't like. I want to go to upstate New York and find Maddy's people. They were denied a proper funeral. They probably don't even know she's dead," she said, flinching at the thought of having to be the one to tell them. "They deserve to know. And I want to know who she became."

"I like that," Padma said. She sighed. "Oh, Maddy. At least she went down fighting."

"No private conversations without me," Casey said, arriving with a splash of water. He dunked Padma's head under the water, eliciting a screech of protest when she resurfaced. "Do you think we'll go back today? Or tomorrow?"

"Whatever you feel like," Jia said.

"I miss Aaron. Oh, God, what am I going to tell him?" he sighed.

"I want to meet your hubby," Padma said.

"You have a standing invitation to Columbus, both of you. I can get you Buckeyes tickets."

Jia left them to football talk and dog paddled just past the raft, where Kelly and James had climbed up and were dangling their legs into the water. "I remember this one day at the lake," James said. "It must have been July. Someone swam a little radio out to the raft and all you guys were dancing while I was trying to light a cigarette. Maddy made fun of me and said I thought I was too cool to dance—this isn't true, I like to head bang with the best of them. So I was standing behind her and I started copying how she was dancing."

Kelly laughed. "I remember that. She was dancing all sexy." The memory seemed sharp suddenly. Maddy in her green bikini, swiveling her body, not caring what she looked like because no one was judging her. James behind her, cigarette pursed between his lips, a look of concentration on his face as he copied her movements with strange accuracy. Him freezing when she turned around abruptly, catching him—he was being just a little mean—but instead of getting angry she laughed and they kept dancing.

"She was happy that day," Jia said.

"We all were," James said, squinting at the water. "If you forgot everything else."

They were silent for a moment, and Jia sensed that perhaps her friends needed a moment alone and began to swim slowly away from them, trying to make it look like she wasn't listening.

"What are you doing?" James asked Kelly.

"Sitting?" she said, bewildered.

"I meant more like, what are you doing this summer?"

"I'm not teaching this summer. I work on my research and do some writing."

"Do you want to maybe... Maybe we can return the minivan and rent something nicer and drive up to Boston?" She turned to look at him. "I meant what I said before."

"But my job is in Boston and your business is in Denver," Kelly said, hesitant. She sounded like she wanted to be convinced.

James pretended to think it over with an exaggerated expression of concern on his face. "Is weed legal in Boston?"

"Not exactly," Kelly said, looking even more concerned.

He laughed, grabbing her hand. "I don't care about that. I can find a job any place where people eat food."

"I would never want you to give up your business for me. I'm so proud of you."

"Who says I have to give it up? I don't have to physically be there, not all the time. It's not wrong for you to ask what you want from people," he said.

"And what is it you want?"

"I want to drive up the coast with you and catch up on everything we missed in twenty years and eat some lobsters."

She hugged him, pressing her face into his shoulder.

Jia turned in the water so she could see them all. *They look so happy.* The only thing in the world she wanted was for them to all be happy. She tried to relax her mind, push gently against them. Sometimes she had difficulty telling the difference between her flashes of the future and the brightness of her own imagination. With her eyes still on Kelly and James, she could see them somewhere else. Kelly looking tan, a surfboard perched behind her. James with a hint of sunburn across his cheeks and nose, trying unsuccessfully to open a coconut while Kelly laughed at him. A different place, a different time. And there was Padma at the airport, a baby lashed to her body in a sling, a handsome man behind her carrying the car seat. Casey approached them, bellowing joyfully, his husband behind him wrangling two toddlers. Here, somewhere else, a darkened restaurant, she was sitting across from Padma, who was holding chopsticks, the tip of one smeared with wasabi. She was wagging her head in that way she did when she was dishing some juicy piece of gossip. Then, somewhere else, Jia saw herself folding a silk kimono, feeling its softness against her fingers as she handled it gently.

She tried to see Wesley Falls but couldn't. She ran up against a block like a white wall, but she realized that the wall didn't feel bad. It just felt flat, like a fact. She assured herself that this was because there was no more badness here, that they had succeeded. That they would head off to the train station, to the airport, and go their separate ways, except not really be separate anymore, and Wesley Falls would just be another town, the same as any other.

What she did not see, and what they could not anticipate, was the random probability of events that worked in their favor. Four days after the arrests were made for Maddy's murder, the story would be picked up by a true crime YouTuber, and Maddy's old essay about growing up in Golden Praise would resurface, making rounds as it now had a more sinister read to it. A number of Evangelical women came out with stories about what similar churches had done to them, about the long-term damage they continued to face after being shamed about their sexuality for so long.

In the weeks that followed, the Golden Praise community was grappling with the mysterious disappearance of Pastor Dave Lurie, the very public murder investigation of Maddy, and Blub enlisting the help of a small army of officers from the Pennsylvania State Police, including one in a gray suit rumored to actually be from the FBI.

The Capstone Five could not have predicted or known that the first person to consider their evidence of payroll tax fraud at the Criminal Investigation Division of the IRS was a special agent named Henry Slater, the best possible person to have this particular case cross his desk at this particular time. Slater was a recent hire who was detail oriented and eager to prove himself.

But what they got the most wrong—despite her many and correct protestations that she didn't know what she was doing—was the notion that Padma knew how to build a bomb. True, she did know a lot about chemistry, but she knew almost nothing about the chemistry of bomb making. She knew enough to make a bomb, but not enough to have any idea about its blast radius.

They had no way of knowing that in 1922, Mike Arnett, an employee of the Bureau of Mines, had attempted to fill a hollowed-out area of the mine with a mixture of gravel and wet sand to contain the Evansville fire. Mike was tired from long hours of working in grueling conditions, and it was difficult to breathe with the rudimentary cloth mask he was wearing. He filled the area reasonably well, well enough so that it did contain the fire, at least until a small explosion in the mine, exactly between Wesley Falls and Evansville, freed the fire.

It did not move fast, but it did move steadily. It took years before anyone actually realized that the underground fire had spread to Wesley Falls. Kids who snuck into the first few chambers of the mine complained that it smelled, and people stopped going there after someone passed out. People on the west side of town noticed in the winter of 2018 that snow melted when it hit their lawns and gardens, and residents started to complain that the tap water tasted funny.

By then, the financial troubles had hit Golden Praise so hard and the litigation was so tangled that the church complex remained abandoned. While the Sanctuary gathered dust, the abandoned Rec Building was seized by burnouts, who chased away the squirrels and turned it into an indoor skate park, at least until the air around Golden Praise began to smell bad.

At first, the cascade of people selling their homes was slow— these were people who sensed that something was off about this town, though there was no way they could have known that it was on fire. The true cascade happened after the subsidences started, random sinkholes appearing because beneath them, coal had burned away leaving a void, and what was on top collapsed to fill it in. Cars were consumed. A hole appeared in Main Street plaza, eating up the space where the Foto kiosk used to be. People began to sell their homes frantically, causing a panic. Those who were hit the hardest were the ones who already had tied their finances to the church. Toward the end, homes were abandoned and mortgages defaulted on because no one wanted to move to Wesley Falls.

The fire, as it crossed to the east side of Devil's Peak, also had an unexpected turn of luck. The red door burned, and beyond it the fire encountered hallways that had been dug out of the ground, which provided ventilation, which all fires need. The fire spread rapidly under the Golden Praise complex, burning from below, then up. The town was empty by then, so no one was there to see Golden Praise burn to the ground.

★ ★ ★ ★ ★

ACKNOWLEDGEMENTS

The town of Wesley Falls—and its ghost sister city of Evansville—are entirely fiction, located (vaguely) somewhere in northeastern Pennsylvania. The element of a perpetually burning underground mine fire was inspired by Centralia, Pennsylvania, which at the time of writing has been burning since the 1960s and continues to do so. My apologies for any eccentricities surrounding the Wesley mine—I did not design it to be a realistic portrayal of a coal mine because it is not a normal mine, but something more sinister. Its eerie presence was inspired by Héctor Tobar's excellent book *Deep Down Dark*, which tells the harrowing story of Chilean miners who were trapped underground for more than two months after a collapse.

Golden Praise is also fiction, but the negative effects of purity culture on Evangelical Christians and the dissemination of prosperity gospel through American megachurches, sadly, are not. And if it isn't clear, this book is an homage to Stephen King's *It*—I have always been taken with its focus on friendship, kids being in over their heads, and the return to a place that both is and isn't home.

Deep thanks to the team at Park Row and HarperCollins that has brought this book into the world: my editor Laura Brown for being willing to swing for the fences on a book this ambitious (not to mention wrangling the sprawling tome I handed in), and everyone from PR to marketing to cover design.

To my agent Rebecca Scherer and the team at JRA, for your guidance, feedback, and championing of my career.

To all the people that made my first book a success, from librarians to booksellers, bookstagrammers and podcasters, avid readers and reviewers, and the wonderful community of mystery writers that I have met.

To my DC writerly hive, especially Melissa Silverman and Gabrielle Lucille Fuentes, for listening to me spin ideas and panic about unreasonable things.

To my friends—this book is dedicated to you. When my first book came out, you bought it, but I did not expect you to end up proselytizing it to your dentists, hairdressers, moms, local bookstores, coworkers, cab drivers, and pretty much anyone who would listen.